GET EVEN

DETROIT THORN BIRDS DEFY MAFIA

MAFIA WORKS # 3

BY

LES COCHRAN

www.bookstandpublishing.com

Published by
Bookstand Publishing
Morgan Hill, CA 95037
4673_4

ISBN 978-1-63498-768-4

First Edition

Printed in the United States of America

ACKNOWLEDGEMENTS

In researching and writing the Detroit Thorn Birds series, I became acquainted with two men — Oscar Westerfield and Scott Burnstein — who made a significant difference in my ability to bring authenticity to the novels. Each brought their own expertise to the series that allowed me to narrow the line between fact and fiction.

The interviews with Oscar Westerfield, who was the Supervisory Special Agent of the FBI Detroit Division during the time of the series, were particularly rewarding. He provided countless experiences and insights that helped bring a sense of reality to *GET EVEN*.

Scott M. Burnstein's two books — *Motor City Mafia* and *Detroit True Crime Chronicles* — were of immense value in providing the context for my fictionalized characters. His in-depth research on and knowledge of the Detroit mafia brought a powerful perspective to *GET EVEN*.

A special thanks to Oscar and Scott for their willingness to share their experiences and expertise; they are the finest professional colleagues an author could have.

And guess what? I have Lin and LinDee on my side. I appreciate their meaningful assistance and ongoing support.

My wife Lin, spent countless hours reading each word, giving me feedback and providing "constructive criticism." She devoted hundreds of hours reacting to the storyline, raising questions to clarify and amend, and editing each chapter one more time, even after I thought it was completed.

The precise work of my editor LinDee Rochelle, Penchant for Penning, whose attention to detail and questions, complemented her tedious task of editing and critiquing. Going beyond the norm, she made insightful observations and provided meaningful suggestions. I appreciate, too, the levity she inserted into this painstaking process.

And thanks, to my readers — I listen — I hear what you say; I'm encouraged. I take your advice seriously.

Keep sending notes to LesCochranBlog.com, making comments on Facebook (Les-Cochran-Fiction-Author), and tweeting me @AffairsByLes. You're helping make my novels better!

The Celtic Legend of the Thorn Birds

There is a legend about a bird which sings only once in its life, more beautifully than any other creature on the face of the earth. From the moment it leaves its nest, it searches for a thorn tree, and does not rest until it has found one. Then, it impales its breast on the longest, sharpest thorn. But as it is dying, it rises above its own agony to out sing the lark and the nightingale. The thorn bird pays its life for that one song, and the whole world stills to listen, and God in his heaven smiles, as its best is brought only at the cost of great pain.

Colleen McCullough,
"The Thorn Birds," 1977.

In each of us there is something that cannot be denied. Maybe it's a desire to be the best we can be — the best mother, teacher, or banker — it doesn't matter what, as we strive to climb the highest pinnacle, solve a complex problem, or live one more day.

Like the thorn bird who sings its own song, some individuals strive to play the most beautiful music of all. They are the doers; the leaders — the people who make a difference. They are thorn birds. They work their hearts out without fear of failure, reprisal, or dying. They're driven, sometimes blindly, to accomplish a goal; they're on a mission. And so it is with the Detroit Thorn Birds; they're driven against all odds to take back their city.

Clark Phillips grew up on the Southwest side of Detroit. As a kid, he walked the Scotten/Vernor Highway beat with his dad, Lewis, a long-time-police officer. Following a summer job with his uncle at the Cadillac Plant on Scotten, he knew he'd become a Detroit cop.

CHAPTER ONE

Sitting beneath a large lime-green umbrella, Clark Phillips flipped through the sports section of the *Detroit Free Press*. His head snapped up at the sound of machine-gun fire clanging against metal. Lunging out of his chair, he pushed the table aside and hit the pavers with full force.

Pandemonium struck the eatery's courtyard. A screaming woman fell against the wrought-iron fence as her flowery straw hat sailed across the small patio. A tray of ice-filled glasses of water fell from the hands of a young waitress. Customers scrambled to the ground… chairs flew helter-skelter, as overturned tables blocked escape paths, glassware shattered, and particles of food showered the courtyard.

Silence filled the air inside the crowded Side Street Diner.

Questions of wonderment ran through the minds of the patrons.

No one moved, patron's expressions registered disbelief and fear.

An old man stared, frozen in place, looking from a window inside the restaurant, toward St. Clair Street.

Tires squealed, causing Clark to raise his head slightly.

He cautiously peered over the table's edge in time to catch a late model black Buick peeling around the corner onto Kercheval. Pulling his weapon, he jumped up and ran into the street in hopes of catching a glimpse of the license plate number, to no avail.

Looking *across the street,* he stared at the bullet holes riveted along the driver's side of the blue Chevy parked in front of his Mustang. One bullet hole had centered his windshield, shattering it, into a thousand pieces. Seeing the disparity between the two cars, left no doubt in his mind the incident was meant to send a message. *How in the hell could they know I'd be here? It was a private call. I didn't tell anyone.*

Turning slowly toward the café's garden area, he holstered his Beretta, and walked back into the courtyard. "It's all clear," Clark shouted. "I'm a Detroit police detective."

Not a head appeared.

The door to the restaurant cracked open and a bearded man peeked out.

"It's okay." Clark waved to him. "A random drive-by shooting," he lied, for the benefit of the customers.

"Are you positive?" the bearded man asked, hesitantly.

"Absolutely." Clark turned to the side and extended a hand to the lady lying by the fence. "Are you alright?"

"Yes, I think so." Her body shaking, she grabbed his hand to stand and threw her arms around his waist. "I'm so glad you were here. Anything could have happened."

Clark looked around the garden area. "Is everyone okay?"

Hands and heads slowly peered out from behind overturned tables and chairs.

"We're alright," came from a man huddled with his wife behind a table.

"We're good," an older man called out.

A timid chorus of "We're okay," filled the air.

Sirens blasted in the distance.

Clark motioned to the bearded man in the doorway, his starched white toque sat cockeyed on his head. "Your staff can straighten up. The police are on the way. I'll take care of the situation."

***

By the time Clark finished with his law enforcement colleagues huddled around the two cars, the glassware had been swept up, the tables and new water glasses had been restored to their original locations. Still, patrons sat nervously, talking about the gunfire, questioning each other as to whether they should stay.

The chef burst through the doorway with a tray of Bloody Marys. "Breakfast is on the house," he declared in a jovial manner, trying to calm everyone's nerves.

Hands gladly grabbed a glass; one customer took two.

Patrons buzzed about the shooting, leery of the situation. They talked about pent-up anxieties concerning public safety and the dope gangs who were raping the city. When would the problem be on their doorsteps in Grosse Pointe? Or had it just arrived?

Swinging open the front gate, Clark stepped into the café garden again. His appearance generated a sense of security.

Spontaneous applause erupted.

He gave the group a half-salute, walked thoughtfully to his table, and sank into the wire chair.

A sigh of relief spread across the courtyard.

The scare tactic for the young police detective, one of the few symbols of law and order in Detroit, had become a way of life. Five years ago, Police Chief Hart had named Clark to head up a joint team of Detroit's finest, along with a group of FBI agents. Since then, off and on, he'd obviously been *under surveillance by the mafia,* and some of his closest friends had been roughed up.

At the time, such joint efforts were unheard of — FBI officials always dragged their feet, and for good reason — police officers *talked too much; often spilling the beans.* FBI agents couldn't trust them; besides, the Detroit police department had a national reputation as the most corrupt force in the nation.

Earlier in the week, Clark had received a mysterious call from a woman asking him to meet her for breakfast at the restaurant around 9 o'clock. Initially, he'd been inclined to say no... yet, there was something compelling in her words — her voice stern and somber — and she seemed far more serious than most crank calls. *Hell, why not see what it's about?* he'd thought to himself.

Picking up the water-spotted sports page of the September 5, 1982, Sunday Edition, Clark glanced at the headlines — "A's Ease Pass Tigers." He'd watched with his dad as the Tigers lost yesterday's game. Being at home on Saturday or Sunday every weekend had become a family tradition. Best of all, his mother Fran always offered something hot and yummy from the oven. Huh, he thought, some things never change. *Dad was there, sitting in the screened porch on that old wicker chair, puffing that damn Corona, and releasing smoke-rings like an old-time steam locomotive. It's been like that since I was a kid.*

A petite blonde refilled Clark's white porcelain coffee mug and gave him a flirtatious wink, before darting away. Acknowledging the come-on sign, he smiled to himself and instinctively brushed back his thick, sandy brown hair. Things were different now; his love for Abby had become greater than he ever thought possible.

Hearing the creak from the courtyard gate, Clark laid the paper aside and glanced that way. A shapely woman stepped in; his glance turned into an appreciative stare. She had the look — stylish and well put together — wearing large-framed sunglasses, a black crystal Gucci handbag hung from her shoulder.

Dressed in a bright red, purple, and yellow floral print, she pushed her large, floppy straw hat slightly back on her forehead and slipped off her sunglasses. Standing just inside the gate, she searched the customers at each table before her blue eyes settled knowingly on Clark.

With a flick of the wrist, she sent him a subtle wave.

He gave her a thumbs-up and shifted his eyes away from her trim body, trying not to gawk.

The woman sashayed toward him in an ostentatious yet casual way. Appearing like a model out of *Vogue*, the exaggerated movement of her hips and shoulders demanded attention — her red heels clicked the brick pavers.

Heads turned her way as she passed each table.

Clark couldn't take his eyes off the diamond-studded red broach nestled in her décolletage. Exactly as she had described herself — long blonde hair, Swedish descent, 5' 8," — except she hadn't mentioned she could have passed for the younger sister of *Anita Ekberg*. How could he forget those *sexy eyes*? He'd just seen Ekberg play the role of Dr. Elsa Biebling in *S*H*E: Security Hazards Expert*.

Nearing the table, her lips parted in a soft, pleasant smile. "Are you Clark Phillips?"

He stood and responded, instinctively, "Detective Clark Phillips, Detroit PD." *Damn, why did I say that? She knew my rank when she called last week.*

"A friend." She extended her right hand.

"A friend." Figuring she wasn't going to give him her name, he held her hand in a firm handshake.

"May I?" She gestured toward the wire-back chair next to him.

"Yes, of course," he voiced in an apologetic tone. "Would you like a cup of coffee?"

"That would be nice, black please."

Clark motioned to the waitress.

The blonde hustled their way, made a note, and flitted away.

Zeroing in on his clean-cut shave and lightly starched, pressed shirt, the woman asked, "Are you always so prim and proper?"

"Usually." He shrugged. "Guess it's a result of growing up in a household with two hard working parents."

"Yeah, so I've learned. And both highly successful, I might add."

Turning his head to the side, Clark's inquisitive stare revealed his thoughts. *So I've learned? Where? How would she know?* He considered pursuing the point, then elected to let it slide.

The waitress appeared with a mug of coffee and left without a sound.

"Thank you for taking time to meet with me," she expressed sincerely. "I hope being late didn't inconvenience you."

He chuckled. "As a matter of fact, you missed the excitement."

Her face turned into a questioning glare. "Excitement?"

"There was a drive-by shooting across the street. The Chevy parked in front of my car got riddled with fourteen bullet holes."

Sliding to the edge of her chair, a pensive frown revealed tense anxiety. "It was the mafia, wasn't it? How did they know we were meeting? Are they here, now? Maybe they're watching. I have to leave."

Clark placed his hand on her wrist. "Hold on."

"I can't take any chances. I've worked too hard to prepare for this moment," her voice had an edgy tone. "I must leave."

Clark tightened his grip on her wrist and pointed out reassuringly. "There's no way they could know about our meeting."

"They had to know." She pulled her hand away and stood.

Clark eased up next to her. "It was probably a random drive-by shooting," he fibbed, trying to settle her nerves.

"Fourteen bullet holes, I don't think so."

"Well…" he spoke honestly, "They probably tailed me. It has nothing to do with you." He inched closer and spoke softly. "Trust me. I didn't tell anyone. At most it was a couple of thugs ordered to send me a message. They're long gone."

She released a heavy sigh. "You're positive?"

"Yes." He winked, reassuringly. "Relax… have some coffee."

Studying the individuals at the other tables, all deep in conversation, she gracefully slid back into the chair. "Thanks." She took a short sip. "The coffee here is as good as ever."

"Would you like something to eat?"

Shaking her head, side-to-side, she motioned to him. "No, but feel free to do so. The stuffed French toast used to be wonderful."

"No, I'm fine."

The *Vogue*-worthy beauty brushed wispy strands of blonde hair away from her face. "I'll get right to the point. My schedule is really tight; I have to be back in L.A. tonight."

He tried to come up with an appropriate remark. "How'd you find this place?" he asked as a last resort.

Hesitating for a moment, she responded guardedly. "I used to come here, a long time ago."

"Did you grow up in Detroit?"

"Ahh…" Pausing, she rubbed her fingertips slowly over her lips, as if evaluating his question. "Sort of…" She hesitated again for the longest moment before opening up. "I was raised in a very nice part of the city and had a wonderful family… I went to boarding school out east and spent the summers here, boating on the river."

"I enjoy that too…" Clark hesitated, and shifted the conversation. "Have you lived in California long?"

"Almost ten years. I spent my college years there and fell in love with the place."

Figuring he might as well move into the agenda, he asked, "You mentioned on the phone we had some things in common. So why are you back in Detroit?"

"Unfinished business."

Feeling she might say more, Clark waited.

She changed the topic. "Your father had a distinguished career as a patrolman on the southwest side. How's he doing?"

Question marks plastered Clark's brain; his face remained placid. *That was a strange thing to say. How did she know about dad? Has she been investigating me? Why would she do that?* His mind wandered before he decided to play it her way. "Thank you, so much." A special feeling of admiration for his father came over him. "He retired seven years ago and is doing quite well."

"Good for him." The woman watched a black car cruise by.

"Do you know my father?" Clark asked, trying to decipher how her words connected.

"Not really. A family acquaintance from long ago."

A family acquaintance… how does that relate? Rephrasing his question, Clark asked, "Why are you here?"

"Some unfinished business."

Crap, that's the same as before. Hiding his frustration, he paused with a chuckle. "There's a lot of unfinished business around here."

She gave him a casual glance and spoke deliberately. "You've established a remarkable record in a short period. I've been impressed with the thoroughness of your investigative work, particularly sorting out the issues in the Huston Nash case, and connecting his wife to the mob — that was really something."

Clark's mind twirled. *Nash case? That was five years ago. How does that relate?*

Swirling the dregs of her coffee, she idly tipped her mug side-to-side.

"Would you like a refill and Danish?" he asked, hoping she'd agree. "They have apple, cherry, and cream ones."

"Yes, a cherry one would be fine, thank you."

Clark motioned to the waitress standing by the gate.

She hustled over and took their order for two cherry Danishes.

Sliding her chair closer to him, the woman returned to the subject. "I was captivated by the way you determined the mobster was hiding in Miami. And putting away those scumbags at the DRC was quite an accomplishment." She flashed a subtle grin. "And all in one swoop — that was spectacular!"

"Thanks, that's nice of you to say," he replied, impressed by her knowledge and insights, yet wondering where this was headed. "Those were team efforts. Without the hard work and commitment of numerous individuals, none of it would have happened."

"Somehow, I figured you'd say that." She gave him an unconscious nod. "Fact is, every successful team as a strong leader."

Unable to hold back any longer, Clark waved his hand. "I appreciate your most gracious comments, but I assume our meeting is about more than my career."

Her penetrating stare revealed a sign of relief. "Yes, it is."

The waitress slid two plates in front of them — a large cherry Danish on each — and refilled their mugs.

Clark sliced into his and took a bite.

Clearly uncomfortable, she gazed off. "I've reflected on this moment countless times. Last night, my thoughts were clear... now, somehow, it's difficult to say."

"Things happen that way." Clark grinned, trying to reassure her.

She shook her head. "Maybe for some; but for me, expressing myself is usually easy."

Leaning back in his chair, Clark flicked his hand. "Why not start at the beginning and we'll go from there. No big deal."

"That's part of the problem." She looked him in the eye. "I can't share all of the details. I don't want to compromise your work."

"Compromise?" Confused, Clark pushed forward. "Okay, pick a point, any point, and, we'll go from *there*."

"Fair enough." She shifted uneasily in her chair. "I'm sure it's obvious... I hired a private detective to check you out."

Clark's lips moved slightly.

She raised a hand before he could say a word. "Wait, I want you to hear me out."

"Okay." He gobbled the last piece of Danish and rocked back on the wire-back chair.

"My research was well intended," she declared in all honesty. "I simply couldn't afford a slip-up or a false step. I had to be absolutely positive you were the right person and I could trust you. With that accomplished, I'm ready to share with you my sole mission in life."

A mystified expression crossed Clark's face. *At twenty-nine/thirty, she has a sole mission in life. It must be a real cause.*

Her voice stayed calm as the words rushed out. "I was going to say this in a pleasant manner, but there's nothing nice I can say about the two of them. They are the most despicable... ruthless... callous men on the planet. They're conniving. They have no concern for human dignity. They play the role of Mr. Nicey-Nicey; goody-two-shoes — you name it — the two bastards atop the mafia must be stopped."

Hearing the shocking description, Clark's face took on a perplexed look as he spoke slow and deliberately. "Are you talking about the top guys in the mafia — Boss Jake Nicolette and Underboss Angelo Travaglini?"

Her sharpened eyes revealed her thoughts. "You're damn right, I am," she whispered with a quiet snap; a sneer reddened her face. "I can't even say their names."

Clark edged his chair against hers. "Why them?" he asked in a comforting voice. "If you have an issue with the mafia, it's likely one of their lackeys who did the job — there're layers of soldiers below the two of them. The mafia is a large, complex organization. You just can't walk up to one of them and say…"

She touched his wrist, cutting him off. "I have a score to settle with each one of them and I won't stop 'til I've accomplished my goal."

"That's insane. The top dogs in the mob are virtually untouchable. We've tried to nail them for years." Collecting his thoughts, Clark inquired, "Maybe if you tell me why you're so insistent, I can help."

"I can't." she replied sharply. "It's personal."

"So you've asked me here to share your goal, but you're not going to tell me anything more. Why?"

"Clark, I have extreme confidence in you, but I can't… I can't disclose the specifics. At least not yet… and maybe never." She slid her fork into the last piece of Danish, eased it into her mouth and chewed gently. "I realize it's hard for you to understand, but I know exactly how I'm going to do it." She rose, took a few steps toward the gate, stopped, and turned halfway around. "Our paths will cross again."

"Wait," he called. "Where? When?"

She took a step back toward him. "I'll tell you more when the time is right." Her smile broadened. "I'll let you know when the time comes."

Closing the gate, she headed for a dark blue Porsche, and elegantly slipped in. Sitting there for at least a minute or so, she turned on the ignition, and squealed around the corner, down Kercheval.

Clark sat dumbfounded. *I don't understand. Unfinished business? She can't say anything. Our paths will cross. What's that about?*

The waitress refilled his coffee.

He picked up the hot simmering mug, stared at the steam, and placed it back on the table. "Damn, that's hot," he mumbled, his mind a blur. *I've had countless experiences… this takes the cake. I'll let you know. Shit, I can't grasp the meaning of any of this.*

He motioned to the waitress, ordered stuffed French toast, and picked up his mug.

In seemingly no time, a plate heaping with the restaurant's specialty was in front of him. He automatically covered the double-thick bread with a heavy dose of maple syrup and dug in. *Compromise me… how in the hell would she do that? Unfinished business; like what? An acquaintance of the family; how's that fit? Our paths will cross; when, where? I'll let you know when the time comes.*

Shaking his head, he shoveled the last piece of French toast in his mouth, his mind still unwilling to stop.

CHAPTER TWO

THE DETROIT NEWS
January 22, 1983

ADOLPH POWELL KILLED AT JOY ROAD LOUNGE

Payback comes in strange ways. Three years ago, Adolph "Doc Holiday" Powell was acquitted of three execution-style murders — the individuals were shot in the back of the head and beheaded.

Yesterday he paid the price. Having an afternoon drink at La Player's Lounge on Joy Road, with a $50 bill in hand to pay his tab, he was downing a cognac when he was blown away by a shotgun blast.

Rumors have it that Powell had become a government informant. If true, it would be a total turn around for him. Not long ago, he was reported to be the head of Detroit's most feared drug conglomerate; his group of henchmen, known as Murders Row, had supplied the finest European heroin to the Italian Mafia.

In his checkered past, Powell had benefited from several fortunate circumstances. With Murder Row's top enforcer, Chester Campbell imprisoned, he assumed those duties and quickly forced himself to the top of the organization. From a grizzled felon in New Orleans, to the top of one of Detroit's biggest drug cartels, Adolph Powell is at the end of the line.

BUTCH JONES PLEADS GUILTY TO HEADING CITYWIDE DRUG ENTERPRISE

Butch Jones, one of the City's most menacing drug lords, pleaded guilty to heading a criminal drug enterprise in exchange for a twelve-year sentence in prison. Officials estimate the gang was taking-in close to $8 million a week in heroin sales.

Most of his lieutenants followed suit and pleaded guilty to lesser charges. His two "Wrecking Crew" enforcers, Karl "Fat Pratt" Gatlin and Kevin "Lughead" Wilson agreed to become government witnesses.

***

Clifford McGill gazed down the Detroit River from his office on the twenty-sixth floor of the McNamara Building. The fortress-like skyscraper served as the headquarters for the Detroit Division of the FBI where he'd been the Special Agent-in-Charge for the past three years.

Hearing a rap on the door, Clifford turned. "Come in; it's unlocked."

Wearing a blue blazer and tan slacks, Clark stepped in and gave him a casual salute. "Phillips reporting for duty," he jested.

Clifford flicked his hand nonchalantly. "Glad you could stop by on such a short notice." He pointed to the chair in front of the large steel-frame desk. "Have a seat."

The no-nonsense, raw-boned Texan slid into his executive chair and propped his Lucchese Sand Shark cowboy boots atop the desk. "This place is shit-city. Has it always been this way?"

"Not really." Clark simpered, his lips tightened into a partial grin. "We had our problems like most big cities, but we were golden in the fifties and sixties — Motown was cranking out hits, the auto industry was booming — it couldn't have been better."

"Did the '67 riots do in the city?"

"Hmm, yes and no." Clark paused, collecting his thoughts, making sure he couched his words to accurately portray the city's demise.

"Yes and no. C'mon, Clark, give it to me straight."

Clearing his throat, Clark paused. "It's complex… I'll give you my take."

"Fair enough." Clifford grabbed the bill of his Stetson hat, flipped it on the desk and rocked back. "Let's hear it."

Trying to sort out how and where to begin, Clark talked slowly. "It goes way back… you have to remember, for years housing in Detroit was highly segregated; and worse yet, the predominately white police force disparaged blacks — degraded, scorned, and brutalized them. It was nothing for a couple of officers to line up a half dozen blacks and billy club each one until he fell to the ground."

"How was that possible?"

"It's hard to believe." Straightening his shirt collar, Clark shook his head. "My dad was on the police force for forty years — he heard it all the time — cops bragging about how they had beaten up, kicked, and pistol-whipped black men for no reason at all. It was common for them to smack women around. During the riots, two officers shot three black men at the Algiers Motel and covered it up. Not one policeman was convicted of a crime."

"I don't understand." Clifford rubbed his jaw. "How could that be? It was 1967 not 1867."

"That's the way it was." Clark shrugged his shoulders. "No one seemed to care."

"This place was not Selma; it was Detroit, Michigan."

"Yes, I know… I pointed out the same thing to my mother." Clark pursed his lips; his face reflected personal dismay. "My mother taught history and reminded me that social change takes a long time to evolve. She used the 1954 Supreme Court ruling of Brown vs. Board of Education of Topeka to make the point. 'After the conclusion of the Civil War, it took the courts nearly ninety years to rule separate but equal schools were not equal.' And that decision, she reminded me, occurred just thirty years ago. 'It takes a long time for people's attitudes to change,' she said."

Clifford rocked his head in rhythm with his chair, suggesting Clark's point was a thought he'd never considered.

"Anyway, the '67 riots should more appropriately be called a rebellion."

"A rebellion?" Clifford snapped his head back. "Why do you say that?"

"Race was a key factor… in real terms it was an uprising against police brutality, unfit housing, and the unfair treatment of blacks. It was a revolt of the economically deprived — poor blacks *and* whites — people whose voices had not been heard for decades," Clark verbalized insights he'd learned from his mother. "People hit the streets, with no regard for law and order, and ripped the city apart."

"Interesting." Clark's assessment peaked Clifford's curiosity. "Was that the end of it?"

"Nope… that was the beginning." Clark's mouth turned down. "The freeways were packed with families fleeing the city. Over two hundred thousand people left the city in the next three years. Two thousand stores that closed during the riots never reopened — there was no place for kids to work. The auto industry tanked — dads were out of a job. The economic downturn spread — moms couldn't find work. Neighborhoods collapsed — the city's social fabric frayed."

Catching his breath, Clark paused. "Sorry, I didn't mean for all of that to sound like a lecture."

"No, no." Clifford flipped a hand in Clark's direction. "You were brief and to the point. I got it."

"And…" Clark pushed on. "If that wasn't enough, heroin hit the streets big-time in the '70s."

"That was kind of late, wasn't it?" Clifford wrinkled his brow. "It was a problem in New York City in '66."

Clark's demeanor turned even more serious; he talked slowly. "Still, the timing couldn't have been worse. Most cops were on the take. Corruption ruled downtown. Dealing drugs meant jobs — in many cases, high paying jobs. Morals and the social structure disintegrated. Gangs controlled the neighborhoods and the mafia ruled the city."

Clifford eased his boots to the floor and rolled his chair to the desk. "Guess that's a good introduction into why I asked you to stop over this morning."

Knowing the purpose of the meeting was near, Clark leaned forward.

"DEA is sending fifty more agents to Detroit. Chief Hart and I have agreed to assign two of them to your joint FBI-DPD team. That way you'll have a direct line to the DEA, like you had with us for the last several years.

"Sounds good. I like that."

"They should be in the waiting room." He stood. "But, before I bring them in, I have a request of you."

"Of course," Clark emitted, without thought. "How can I help?"

"Don't be so quick on the draw," Clifford jested. "The fifty agents are coming from all over the country. They've all been briefed and have a study packet of material developed in Washington…" Clifford's face revealed disdain for the higher-ups. "Which means they don't have a clue about ground-level activity in Detroit. We can't afford a six-month learning period. We need them ready to hit the road when they arrive. Long story short, I'd like for you and your team to put on a short dog-and-pony show for them."

"Dog-and-pony?" Clark raised a brow, question marks scored his forehead.

Clifford laughed. "I sense your reaction. No need to worry, I've talked with our training folks. They'll help you work up two or three briefing sessions. They'll provide the format with all of the how's and why's. All you have to do is fill in the blanks."

***

Clark sank into the old wicker chair and waved his dad's cigar smoke away as he had done his whole life — from rehashing basketball games, to the lecture about not smoking marijuana — it didn't matter the issue, the routine was always the same.

Sitting across from him in the frayed wicker, his dad, Lewis, pointed to the TV. "Wait a minute, Petry is about to close the door on the Twins in the seventh."

Knowing better, Clark didn't say a word; instead, he raised a bottle of Stroh's to his dad.

A smoke ring floated to the ceiling of the screened porch, where not a breath of fresh air had penetrated all day.

"He got him out," Lewis exclaimed. "The Tigers scored five in the sixth and are ahead, 7 to 4."

"The Tigers might start off the season with a two-game winning streak."

"Maybe a sweep," his dad gleefully prognosticated. "Chet Lemon has four hits and Dan Petry has shut them out since the first. We have this one salted away."

Clark knew a game was never salted away until the final out was recorded, so he cheered with his dad until the Tigers had won 9 to 5.

Lewis snuffed out his Corona in the ashtray filled with butts, flipped off the television, and turned to Clark. "It's the middle of the week, why are you here?"

Clark didn't beat around the bush. "Dad, I need your assistance."

Lewis raised his eyebrows. "That's an interesting twist. How can I help?"

"The feds are sending in fifty more agents next week. McGill wants me to set up some briefing sessions for the new DEA agents."

"It's about time." Lewis gave Clark a disparaging glance. "Got a plan on how you're going to do that?"

Clark smiled delightedly with his dad's question. "That's part of why I need your help. I'm planning a series of presentations… fifteen to twenty minutes for each of my team members to bring the agents up to speed on drug activity in the city."

"Well… at least that makes sense."

"I told the team I'd work up a session on drug activity in the last ten to fifteen years."

"Humph," Lewis grunted. "You'd need fifteen days, full-time to do the job."

Clark ignored the reality of his dad's comment. "So could you give me three or four, maybe five points I need to make?"

Lewis stared up at the smoke-filled ceiling — his thoughts drifted — he released a nod, followed by a second and a third one. "Okay, grab yourself a pencil and yellow pad."

"Right now?"

"Why not?" Dad sucked in a deep breath. "You asked, we might as well do it now."

Clark jumped up and jerked open the sliders. "Okay," he replied on his way inside.

***

Settling back in the old wicker, Clark nodded. "I'm ready when you are."

Lewis rubbed his jaw a couple of times. "Hmm, keep it to twenty minutes… that's a tall order." He hesitated. "I'd start by giving them a brief historical overview, so they understand Detroit and how things evolved. They need to understand the white flight — how we lost people and economic power — that the city's social and economic infrastructure was fractured. Why the neighborhoods were destroyed… why jobs were hard to find… and that we lost most of the middle class." He downed the last of his Stroh's. "Many of the public housing projects, like Herman Gardens, shifted from racially diverse communities to homogeneous black residences. Extortion, robbery and drug activity grew rapidly. And, when the distribution of heroin became widespread at the end of the '70s, all hell broke loose."

Taking in a deep breath, Lewis sighed. "Let me tell you something that has been lodged in my mind for years. Use these homicide numbers; it'll be a good way to illustrate the point:

- In 1965 there were 138 murders

- In 1970 that had more than tripled to 488 murders

- The number peaked in 1974 at 714 murders in one year."

"Wow." Clark scribbled without a glance up. "Are you positive about these numbers?"

"Absolutely, I have the *Free Press* story with the numbers in my desk, center drawer. When we're finished, you can take it with you to make copies for the group."

"Good." Clark rose. "I'm having another beer, want one?"

Lewis peeked into the kitchen. "Is your mother here?"

"No, she's grocery shopping."

Dad's face lit up. "Yes… here take my empty bottle and throw it in the trash can in the garage."

Clark grabbed the bottle and returned in no time with two Stroh's, and asked, "Okay, where to now?"

"You need to give the agents an understanding of gang activity ten years ago, so when these names pop up they have a point of reference. If I was you I'd start with the Errol Flynns… you remember them."

"Yeah, they named themselves after the famous movie star and dressed like flamboyant gangsters. And…" Clark mimicked a hand-jive motion. "They used hand gestures to identify themselves in public."

"Gangsta jits." His dad added.

"Yeah, I remember doing those hand gestures." Clark cracked a small grin. "Guess I was too young to think much of its meaning or where it came from."

"It wasn't long before their semiotic use of hand gestures was incorporated into the 'Errol Flynn' dance. Party goers in the city copied them. At their peak in the '70s, over four hundred Errol Flynn gang members operated in broad daylight. Their impact was so great, the dance craze spread to territorial street gangs across the city. The Schoolcraft Boys, Fenkell Boys, 7 Mile Dogs, Linwood Boys bought in, and eventually it became part of the music culture nationwide."

"I had no idea it became that big."

Lewis rubbed his fingers through the remains of his thinning hair. "I'd mention Henry "Blaze" Marzette to illustrate another aspect of the heroin epidemic. As the Motor City's first true urban black Godfather, Henry developed a plan to create a citywide conglomerate of black bosses who would shut the Italian Mafia out of the inner-city drug industry."

"Really?" Clark's eyes opened wide. "He must have had balls."

"He was a high-risk, high-reward kind of guy, and was not one to shy away from a gamble. Anyway, he invited nearly thirty of the city's most powerful wholesale dealers to the Twenty Grand Motel on Warren, to pitch the idea."

"The place up on 14th Street and Warren Avenue?"

"Yeah, you got it."

From his chair, Clark shuffled his feet. "There was a dance hall next door."

Clark caught dad's wink.

"Using his power base as the leader of the West Side Seven, Henry proposed his contingent team up with the East Side 12. Playing the role of the ultimate politician, he stood in front of the group, as if holding court." Lewis paused with a chuckle. "I'll go slowly with the names of his buddies, so you can write them down. The cutesy nicknames of his buddies were another symbol of the times."

Lewis slowed, making sure Clark was ready. "Sitting in folding chairs to his sides was his inner-circle, Eddie 'Gentleman John' Claxton, Arnold 'Pretty Ricky' Wright, and James 'Jimmy the Killer' Moody. In front of him were more supporters with nicknames like 'Cincinnati Black', 'Mr. Clean', 'Texas Slim', and 'Big Son'."

Clark's eyes opened wide. "I got them all; that'll put a little levity into the talk."

"I thought you'd like them," Lewis leaned back in his chair. "Henry proposed all of the drug dealers in attendance come under his umbrella and collectively turn their backs on the Italian suppliers. Because of a recent deal he'd struck in Malaysia, he offered the other bosses enticing bottom-line prices and protection, should the mafia declare war."

"He must have had a big ego."

"Like I pointed out, he was a real Godfather."

"I guess so."

"After that you could have heard a pin drop. Knowing most of the men were ready to acquiesce, if only out of fear, Henry strutted around like a peacock… All of a sudden Nual Steele, a ruthless drug lord, stood up and charged Marzette. Henry's bodyguard interceded and there was a short scuffle before Steele left the room in a huff."

"Did that end it?" an eager Clark asked.

"No." Lewis slid forward. "All hell broke loose. In the next year and a half, over seventy-five murders were attributed to the war between the two groups." Lewis glanced at Clark, still writing on the pad. "Think you have enough for a start?"

"Oh my Gosh yes, you've given me more than enough. Thanks."

***

"In brief that's how I intend to start with the DEA agents," Clark indicated to the members of the joint FBI-DPD team. He turned to new DEA member Veronica Chavez, "What's your reaction to that kind of a kickoff?"

"I like it; it's perfect and to the point. In no time my mindset shifted from my Miami home-base, to Detroit.

"Good." Clark paused, then spoke in a more casual manner. "Earlier I gave the standard career introduction. Before we move on, I'd like to take a moment so all of us might know a little more about Veronica Chavez."

"Okay, I'll make it brief." She smiled, a pleasant smile. "I was born in Miami. My parents are from Caracas, Venezuela, and my husband Jose and I have two lovely girls and a rowdy boy — Alejandia is twelve and Maria Isabel is nine, and Jose Rafael is five. I love to read and recently finished Jackie Collins' *Hollywood Wives* and have started *The Name of the Rose* by Umberto Eco."

"Is that about a murder in a monastery in the 1300s?" Clark asked.

"Yes…" She curled an eyebrow in a questioning manner.

"I thought so. My mother is an avid reader; she's reading it too."

"Interesting… well, I guess that's enough for now."

Clark turned to the other new agent, Bennett, sitting across from Veronica. "Frank, tell us a little more about yourself."

"My pleasure," the square shouldered Brooklyn native expressed. "First though I want to say I particularly liked the early part of your planned presentation — setting of the stage was outstanding — it moved me right into Detroit." He rubbed his early stubble. "I'm thirty-three, a graduate of NYU, single, and a huge Dodger and Tommy Lasorda fan."

Clark jutted his jaw. "Well, maybe we'll meet you in the World Series."

"Wouldn't that be something?"

With a more serious expression, Clark nodded to Kimberly, posed at the end of the table. "How's your session coming along?"

She shook her head. "I've been inundated. I've gone through hundreds of juvenile court records and found several research studies. A lot of my findings came from the early explorations of Carl Taylor, a professor at Michigan State University. He's done some fascinating research on gangs in Detroit and is drafting a book titled *DANGEROUS SOCIETY*. It'll be published in another year.

"Sounds like it'll be an excellent resource."

"Yes… there's so much information. I'm trying to summarize everything in a series of one-liners, so the DEA agents will have a point of reference. So far I've developed three pages."

"Are you ready to share them?"

"Yes." Kimberly passed a set of paperclipped sheets around the table, waited until everyone had a packet, then pointed to the first sheet. "As you can see, there's a blank bullet point at the end of each sheet… there's more to come."

Glancing down the conference table at Clark, she paused. "It'd be good if the team members could read these before our next meeting. That way the old-timers would be ready to suggest additional points and Veronica and Frank could provide their feedback."

CHAPTER THREE

Clark spread Kimberly's three summaries across the table and waited for the team members to refill their coffee mugs. *She did a great job capturing the essence of gang activity. I'd always thought the city's problems would level off after the riots and start to improve. Black gangs selling heroin made sure that didn't happen... and then came the final blows. The US Supreme Court ruled against the city's plan to merge the fifty-three school districts in the Metro area into one comprehensive unit. With busing out, younger families fled the city to have their kids schooled in suburbia. Political corruption and unrealistic large employee contracts sent the budget reeling. With fewer students and decaying facilities, the quality of the schools fell off the table. And... being on the verge of bankruptcy the city was unable to respond.*

Noting the expanded team had assembled, Clark pointed to the sheets. "Kimberly is anxious to hear your thoughts so she can make revisions and have copies made." Nodding to her, he picked up his coffee mug. "The ball is in your court."

"Thanks." The chunky, large-breasted blonde moved closer to the conference table. "I'd like to start with the sheet titled 'How Drug Rings Work.'" Pausing, she glanced around the table. "Does anyone need an extra copy?"

Her biggest antagonist, Joseph "Pag" Pagnozzi, a Detroit police officer who graduated from Denby High, raised his hand. "I'll take anything you have."

Biting her lip, she tossed him a sheet. "And that's all you're getting."

Snickers filled the room.

Newcomers Chavez and Bennett glanced at each other. Veronica lifted an eyebrow with a questioning look. Bennett shrugged his shoulders.

Sitting between the two of them, Woodson whispered something in each one's ear.

Small grins spread across their faces.

How Drug Rings Work

- Runners sell an envelope to an addict for $13 — the organization receives $10 — and the runner gets $3. It's estimated that there are 50,000 addicts in the city.

- It's a matter of economics. If you're twelve years old, living in a Detroit housing project — your parents are out of work — and some guy in a fancy car comes by and tells you he can help you make $300 a day, you're going to listen.

- Fourteen- and fifteen-year-old gang supervisors recruit the twelve- and thirteen-year old "runners" to deliver the heroin. They can make as much as $2,000 to $5,000 a week.

- It isn't uncommon to find a twelve-year-old carrying two grand in their pockets. In the Jeffries Housing Project on the east side, teenagers are driving new Corvettes — their Christmas bonus for a job well done.

- There is a documented case of a fifteen-year-old boy walking into a Mercedes-Benz dealership with $62,000 in a paper bag and paying cash for a new car.

- And there are indications the situation is expanding — growing numbers of middle- and upper-class clientele are showing up on the drug lists of dealers.

Veronica held her copy up. "This is a wonderful start. The amount of money taken in by these bums blows my mind."

Kimberly smiled, her pride showing. "How can I make it better?"

Pag raised his hand.

Hesitating for a moment, Kimberly's eyes rolled. "Okay, go ahead.

"I think it'd be good to add how these kids are recruited and, other than cash, the benefits they receive."

She begrudgingly nodded approval of his suggestions and pulled a sheet from her stack of notes from Taylor's research. "How about adding these?

- Gang members are recruited from playgrounds, recreation centers, video arcades, and by friends.

- In addition to the cash they earn, they receive big bonuses, like trips to Las Vegas and New York, and expensive cars — Corvettes and Mercedes.

- They receive other materialistic rewards — gold chains, fur coats, sports attire — and, of course, all the girls they want."

"Yes, that would be good for the DEA agents to hear," added FBI agent Dick Woodson from Valparaiso, Indiana.

"Okay." She held up the second sheet. "Let's move on to 'How Kids View Selling Drugs.'"

Veronica's face revealed her despair. "You don't have to tell me more. I saw it in Caracas, too. Girls were begging drug dealers to take them to bed in the '70s."

"These guys are seen as kings of the subculture — they have it all."

"I guess…" Kimberly paused to scan the group. "Take a look at this next sheet… the kids have a distorted view of life. They take little pieces of information to rationalize their own behavior."

"Yeah," Pat chimed in. "But… in a way, part of their thinking is right. No one is stopping the sale of guns."

"You got that right," Woodson agreed. "And how about Philip Morris? Anyone stopping the sale of cigarettes?"

"Whiskey, too," someone added.

Kimberly held up the sheet, "How Kids View Selling Drugs," and asked once more. "Anyone have another thought?"

How Kids View Selling Drugs

- Selling drugs is the way to make it today. I don't give a damn about legal. What's legal anyway? Selling dope isn't any different than selling cars or a house. Anyway, I don't care about nobody. Me and my crew are important. We sell drugs to make a living — that's the way it is.

- It's like this, if I don't sell the shit, somebody else will. I get paid big bucks, slinging dope hard every day. So why should I take a minimum wage job at McDonalds?

- Everything is legal. Pork is deadly, bacon can kill you, whiskey, cigarettes, and guns are bad for you. Nobody is stopping those companies from selling their shit.

- I'm giving people a product they want. Anything wrong with that? I am not using shit; I'm just selling suckers something they want. People get high all over the country.

- I don't screw around with no dope. I save my money. If I wasn't selling dope, I'd be poor. Now, I'm set — got plenty of clothes, cash, and bitches — anything wrong with that?

Bennett raised his hand. "How was this allowed to continue?"

"Oh, I forgot to add that point." Kimberly's face flushed. "Since these kids were juveniles, the court system was overloaded, cases were backlogged for months. And, drug dealers were seen by the kids as role models. Imagine yourself being thirteen and seeing these dudes wearing gold chains, driving fancy cars…"

"Those are excellent points," Earl Walker, Clark's assistant interjected. "You might add a point on how gang members act."

"Good suggestion." Kimberly picked up another piece of paper. "How about this: Gangs work twenty-four hours a day, dealing drugs as if they have nothing to hide. And most important, they have professional legal advice on call whenever they need it."

"What kind of sleaze-bags are these lawyers?"

Earl's mouth curled with distaste. "They're like everyone else, the whole system is corrupt."

Kimberly motioned to the last sheet. "These kids have a totally distorted view of life; yet, you have to remember… *their views* are based upon *their experiences*. They haven't had any of the experiences we've had." She paused, making sure everyone had gotten the point. "Anyone have another suggestion?"

How Perceptions of Inner-city Kids Differ

- My cousin is high up with the crew. He gave his momma a new Riviera and lots of money. The preacher wouldn't look her way when she was poor; now he's hitting on her.

- This role model shit is phony. Teachers, preachers, policemen, lawyers, dentists — it doesn't matter — they're all fraudulent. They're all screwing around with dope.

- Marriage is for suckers. You don't have to marry someone just because she's pregnant. She can have the kid or not. The kid doesn't give a shit.

- Having babies is no big thing. I got four kids by different women. I don't do nothing for them. I figure it this way — didn't nobody give a damn about me and I made it okay.

- Marriage is for fools. You can shack-up all you want. Who needs to marry the bitch? Bang her; when you're tired of the bitch kick her ass to the curb… My old man did that to my momma.

Bennett shook his head. "This is a totally new sub-culture. They have a distorted view of everything… there is no concern for others… it's all about me. The new team members need to hear this… it'll be totally foreign to them."

"This is hard to believe," said Pat Fitzpatrick, the FBI agent from New Jersey. "But you're right on. I'd say, let it fly."

Agrees filled the room.

Clark looked around at everyone, no hands appeared. "Anyone else?"

Heads shook around the table.

"This is really good stuff." Pag winked.

"Great job!" Clark smiled at Kimberly. "Let's take a quick break."

***

"We have a new agenda."

Team members picked up their pens.

Clark waited, letting the silence gain everyone's attention. "In addition to the fifty new DEA agents, the FBI is upping their numbers, pushing the level of FBI agents here, to over two hundred. Clifford and I have agreed to give most of our attention to the escalating problem of drug-gang activity. The sale of heroin is spreading like wildfire."

"And that's only part of the story," Earl exclaimed. "With the auto industry laying off people by the thousands, the drug gangs are the city's primary employer. Nicole tells me people are afraid to walk down the street to pick up a loaf of bread. Neighborhoods that once held the city together are crumbling — physically and socially. It's like an epidemic sweeping the city."

Woodson spoke slowly and deliberately. "How are these gangs able to orchestrate such activity?"

"It blows my mind." Clark's head cocked to one side, sending a look of frustration. "Gangs seem to develop out of nowhere. Earl and I grew up in the southwest part of the city. Our school district ran from Livernois toward downtown to Tiger Stadium. There were the Bagley Boys, all white guys, and the Stilettos made up of Latinos whose dads worked at the Rouge. They were involved in penny-ante activity; mostly they had little turf battles between themselves. It was a way of life."

Earl nodded his agreement. "Violence was limited to an occasional minor knife wound."

Clark paused, reflecting about the good ol' days; he pulled out a recent *Free Press* story from his notebook, and turned to Woodson. "Here's an example of today's gangs. When Butch Jones pleaded guilty last March, the YBI — Young Boys, Inc. — was organized like a Fortune 500 corporation. It was highly decentralized — had divisions, units, and neighborhood districts. They had *three hundred people* coordinating thousands of kids, ten-, eleven-, and twelve-year-olds, who were making two grand a week."

"That's unbelievable," Veronica interjected. "How did they come up with that kind of know-how?"

Clark gave her an agreeable look. "Remember, these kids grew up in households where all the men worked in the auto plants. People talked about the unions and the SOB's at the top. These guys are no dummies; they picked up on things they heard and made good use of it. Imagine the type of organization you'd need to pull this off." Clark laughed outright. "Last year the YBI grossed $7.5 million a week, totaling over $400 million for the year."

New Yorker Frank Bennett's face went blank. "I can't imagine that kind of take... I doubt if any of the Five Families in New York City are raking in those kinds of dollars."

"The money is only part of the equation." Clark turned to Earl "The Pearl" Walker, his high school basketball teammate. "Earl, would you bring the team up to speed on current black gang activity?"

Earl winked and took charge. "With Butch Jones in jail, YBI is in flux — people are taking sides — there's internal house cleaning, and other gangs are seizing the opportunity. Recently, the Pony Down Gang took over a pair of YBI drug houses. In response, last week a group of YBI lieutenants staged an assault on three teenage Pony Down dealers on an east side street corner."

Trying to get Clark's attention, Fitzpatrick cleared his throat.

Dick Woodson interceded. "Earl, could you fill us in on the details?"

"No problem." Happy to do so, Earl's smile broadened across his face. "Okay, but first listen to these guys' names, it'll blow your mind... the YBI guys were George 'Scandalous Butch' Young, Vincent 'Sharkie' Reed, Kevin 'Bibbie' Terrell, and John 'Potsie' Piner."

"It sounds like the old days." Woodson verbalized on behalf of the group. "You gotta be shittin' me."

"No, I'm not. Anyway… in the middle of the day, this trio exited their car and opened fire on the kids with automatic weapons, killing one and wounding the other two."

"You're positive you're not reading a line out of an Al Capone book?" Kimberly questioned. "Was anyone caught?"

"Hah, that's another problem." Earl shook his head disgustedly. "The YBI is ruthless; they take no prisoners; they're more dangerous than the Purple Gang back in the '20s and '30s. If you ask me, I'd say we're in for two or three years of turf battles."

Pag raised his dark eyebrows. "That would be messy."

Earl chuckled. "That's a very good likelihood."

"YBI is intimidating, too," Pag reminded the group. "I've heard of times when as many as fifty members appeared at an event. Dressed in unison, wearing trendy clothes — one day they'd be sporting red Adidas track suits and Adidas Top 10 running shoes; the next, brown and green military fatigues and steel-toe boots. In the winter, they've been seen wearing brown fur-lined Max Julian hooded jackets."

"Hey, that's nothing," Earl pointed out. "I've seen them pull up in front of Cobo Hall for a sporting event in two dozen or more Mercedes or Corvettes."

Veronica's eyes gleamed with amazement. "No wonder they're the hottest thing in town."

"Hot! Every black man in the inner-city wants to be a part of them. Add in the black girls hanging on them. How could a poor kid ask for more?"

"I think we've had enough of that." Clark flicked his hand. "Let's move on to current happenings with Butch Jones and Ray Peoples in prison."

"That's easy," Earl announced. "The internal strife is unbelievable. No one is safe. There are so many deaths… some are not even reported in the press — it's a zoo." Earl paused, catching his breath. "And that's not the half of it. Remember the article Clark shared on the killing of William "Chilly Willie" Hunter outside a west side apartment?"

"Yeah," the group sounded.

"That was Pony Down action."

"Pony who?" Fitzgerald questioned, finally getting an opportunity to ask.

"The Pony Down Gang is up and coming." Earl's eyes narrowed in an unmerciful glare. "They're making inroads throughout the city; they've gained so much power they had the gall to stake out territory in the middle of YBI's west side home base. You can't believe the police reports I'm reading — baseball bat killings, carving people up in pieces, knifing individuals thirty or forty times — nothing is off limits."

Clark waved his hand — side to side. "Maybe we ought to save some of this for another day."

"Keep going." Kimberly voiced, a sense of interested enthusiasm in her tone. "I'd like to hear more about these gangs."

"We could go on all day."

Kimberly wrinkled her brow. "Why, how many are there?"

"In addition to Pony Down, the Davis Family and the Curry Brothers Gang are the other big ones. And, there's a slew of lower-tier black street gangs, like the Black Killers, Coney Oneys, and parts of the old Errol Flynns are still around."

Kimberly raised her hand. "Okay, I got the message. Clark's right, another day."

Clark motioned to Pag who was a boyhood teammate of Blackie Giardini. "Well Pag, anything new about your number three man in the mafia?"

"For the benefit of you new folks, Blackie Giardini, the current Street Boss in the mafia and I used to play on the same little league team." Fond memories fleeted through Pag's mind. "For clarification, Blackie is a close acquaintance not a friend."

"A fine line," Kimberly jabbed.

"Truce." Pag raised a hand. "Busting the blind pigs hit them hard — it was a real shocker."

"That was eighteen months ago," Clark interjected.

"Doesn't matter. Boss Jake Nicolette is pissed; he won't let it go... wants to know who leaked the information." Pag hesitated. "Hmm, guess that's it for now. I have a two-pager that summarizes the points."

Clark didn't move; his face expressionless, recalling his best friends — Carlos, Renzo, Ted, Nicole, and Caroline — had facilitated the operation. "Fine." Catching Pag's eye, he asked, "Anything you can tell us about the fallout in the police department resulting from the bust of the blind pigs?"

"Yeah, we finally have the attention of the police department. The numbers are adding up. There have been almost eighty resignations or retirements, forty-one are on unpaid administrative leave; Internal Affairs still has at least fifty ongoing investigations, and almost two hundred have taken jobs elsewhere."

"Nothing wrong with that," came from someone.

"You're right about that." Pag glanced around the table meaningfully. "It'll help the Chief clean up the department. I only wish we could tell which ones are the dirty cops."

"It's really hard." Clark declared with an expression of dismay. "There are plenty of files with not one shred of information on a police officer's performance."

"Many supervisors don't even conduct pro forma meetings with officers," Earl interjected

"Anything else, Pag?"

Clark caught the sideward movement of his head. "Moving right along. Kimberly, anything happening with the gypsies?"

She smiled wryly. "The gypsy community is finally easing back to a normal state. Since the blind pig raids there hasn't been a peep out of them — not a story or article in the paper — it's like nothing ever happened."

"Have you heard anything about the national scene?" Woodson asked.

"Yes." Clark expressed his mood with an excited little laugh. "I've been in contact with Jack Grimes in Seattle… the feds in Washington have hired him to head up the investigations across the nation. He indicated the killings have slowed considerably, except in New York City and Chicago. There have been several, maybe six, look-a-like killings there."

"Mutilations?" Woodson wondered aloud.

"We don't know. The police there haven't released the details; yet, they're positive the same persons were involved in the killings." Clark nodded to his left at the two FBI agents. "I guess that brings us to the national scene — The Commission and FBI headquarters in Washington. Who wants to handle it?"

"I'll do The Commission," Woodson offered.

"Guess, I'm left with headquarters," Fitzpatrick faked dejected disappointment.

"Okay." Woodson jested. "I'll let you go first."

Picking up the ball, Fitzpatrick opened up. "The Washington office is on high alert. The murders Kimberly mentioned has everyone in a tizzy. I haven't seen so much activity there since the Kennedy assassination." His mouth twisted into a quirky grin. "Guess that's it."

Taken by surprise, Woodson cocked his head, sending Pat a curious look, and turned toward the rest of the group. "I've been keeping tabs on The Commission. Our New York office reports that "Big" Paul Castellano, the boss of mafia bosses, has been calling in the Dons from all of the cities on a quarterly basis. Anxiety is high, particularly with the Five Families of New York and the Chicago Outfit. Rather than hosting one annual meeting, Castellano has scheduled another meeting in late June — it'll be their third meeting in nine months."

"Is that it?" Kimberly asked impatiently. "I want to hear about our new assignments."

"Fine with me." Clark smiled to himself. "First, do our rookies have anything to say?"

"It's a good thing you all will be briefing the new DEA agents." Veronica's voice hesitated slightly with disbelief. "There's no way they'd ever come up to speed — the place is out of control."

"I agree." Frank took a long pause. "Washington ought to send five hundred more DEA agents."

"Probably so," Clark admitted, that number was more in line with his own thinking. "Instead, they're getting us." Eyes zeroed in on him. "I'm assigning Kimberly, Frank, and Pag to head up our effort on the Davis Family. You'll be joining a DEA team who has been following them for four years. They're close to nailing down the entire family."

Clark glanced toward Pat, Veronica, and Woodson, and jested. "You'll have the opportunity to deal with Pony Down."

Kimberly poked fun at Earl, "Aren't the two of you doing anything?"

Knowing his upcoming assignment, Earl shifted uneasily in his chair.

"Figured you'd ask that." A large grin crossed Clark's face. "Earl will be chasing Rick Maserati."

"Maserati?" Kimberly covered her mouth and, after spouting off, asked softly. "Who the hell is he?"

"His real name is Richard Carter. He's a twenty-four-year-old who's running wild in town. Earl will be telling us more about him in a couple of weeks." Clark sucked in a deep breath. "That leaves the easy ones for me. Since we've cleaned out several of the mafia's mid-level guys, I'm giving my attention to the mafia's leadership core — Jake Nicolette, Angelo Travaglini, and Blackie Giardini."

"Wow!" Pag shouted in amazement. "Do you really think we can nail them?"

Clark flipped his hands in a questioning manner. "If we don't try we'll never know."

***

𝔇𝔢𝔱𝔯𝔬𝔦𝔱 𝔉𝔯𝔢𝔢 𝔓𝔯𝔢𝔰𝔰
May 13, 1983

YOUNG BOYS, INC.
OPERATIVES AMBUSHED

The power struggle within the Young Boys, Inc. continued yesterday afternoon as two of "Baby Ray" Peoples' top henchmen were ambushed. Eyewitnesses say Moe Henry Gibbs and Kurt McGurk shot Joseph "Wamp" Brown on the corner of Concord and Benson. Gregory "Special K" Kendricks survived the attack on the corners of Beaubian and Erskine.

While Butch Jones is in custody, informants say his followers continue to "tidy up" the organization, which means the elimination of Peoples' followers.

Police had not released additional information at press time.

CHAPTER FOUR

Staten Island, New York

The "boss of the bosses" stood on the portico of his seventeen-room replica of the White House. An eighth-grade dropout and butcher by trade, Paul Castellano had muscled his way to the top of the Gambino crime family — the nation's largest mafia family. A "made man" (a person certified by the mafia who'd killed another person), he'd been in and out of prison. Each time, he'd refused to cooperate with authorities and his stature in mob loyalty was enhanced.

Because of his reclusive nature, "Big Paul" as he preferred to be called, was known as the "Howard Hughes of the Mob." Often dressed in a floor-length red satin robe with gold embroidering, at six-foot-two, two-hundred-and-seventy pounds, he towered over the granite half-wall.

Reaching the top of the steps, he embraced each member of The Commission, kissed him on the cheek, and pointed down the glossy blue-gray marble hallway to the English gardens and Olympic-sized swimming pool, hidden behind his mansion. Following each Boss was his *consigliere* (chief advisor), and his bodyguards.

Meeting for the third time in less than a year, it was the first time in the organization's fifty-two-year history that the nation's top twenty-four mafia bosses had met multiple times, within a year's span. Having called the meeting for the last week in June to avoid the upcoming Fourth of July weekend, Castellano had used a patriotic theme to decorate the grounds.

Full-sized ice sculptures of Presidents Washington, Jefferson, Roosevelt and Kennedy, stood behind each of four elongated tables loaded with holiday cuisine. Positioned between the glistening turquoise-filled pool to the right and the perfectly manicured hedges and flower beds to the left, Castellano's chef had layered the tables with flamboyant Italian fare, representing the holiday seasons —

Thanksgiving, Christmas, Easter, and the Fourth of July. An added attraction at the Fourth's station was a grouping of Playboy Bunnies serving hot dogs and hamburgers with finger-licking condiments.

Continuing into the early evening, the bosses and *consiglieres* renewed old acquaintances and refilled their platter-sized plates. Precisely at nine thirty, Big Paul made his appearance at the marble railing — a story and a half above the entertainment center — a six-piece band on his left struck *La Luna Mezz' 'o mare* (popular *Godfather* movie tune).

Towering over the railing, Castellano raised his arms like a Pope might, and swayed to several verses.

Standing at attention, his underlings waited for his message.

The music stopped.

Big Paul lowered his arms in a stately manner, placed his meaty hands on the rail and gave a subtle nod. "Men…" he started in a slow and drawn manner. "I want to thank you for breaking away from your families and busy schedules. As you know we are confronted with a grave condition… a situation we've never faced before. But…" He looked up with a half chuckle. "That's the agenda for tomorrow morning. Tonight's a time to visit with old friends and celebrate our nation's great heritage.

***

Arriving early the next morning, Big Paul surveyed the lavish, original Italian oil paintings and Roman statues that lined the walls. A twelve-foot walnut table centered under a French Empire Crystal Chandelier waited for the power-position bosses and their *consiglieres*, from the other heads of the Five Families of New York — Anthony "Tony Ducks" Cotrallo, Carmine "Junior" Persico, Anthony "Fat Tony" Salerno, and Philip "Rusty" Rastelli — and Tony Accardo of the Chicago Outfit.

At the head of the table, a leather-armed, throne-like chair waited for Castellano.

Before taking his position, Big Paul made the rounds, embraced each of the voting members at the table, then turned toward the far corner of the room, and shouted, in his deep, boisterous voice, "John La Rocca, my good friend from Pittsburgh, good to see you."

LaRocca waved and broke away from a conversation with his Midwestern colleagues — James Licavoli from Cleveland, Peter Balistrieri from Milwaukee, and Missourians Anthony Giordano from St. Louis and Nicholas Civella from Kansas City — and headed Paul's way.

The two men walked briskly toward each other. LaRocca extended his arm around Big Paul, pulled him close, and whispered, "I hear the feds are on your case, hot and heavy."

"Huh." Castellano's mouth turned down. "They got nothing on me… a bunch of hoopla." Big Paul turned away and pointed. "My good friend, Santo Trafficante, Jr. looks like you've been spending plenty of time on the Tampa beach."

He waved and headed for the big table.

Buffalo's Joseph Todaro stepped in his pathway. Castellano slowed as the two came together. Todaro pulled him close. "You need to cool it, Big Paul, the feds are all over you."

Castellano pushed him away. "No need to worry. I've got my bases covered," he declared. Turning quickly away, he strolled to the head table.

Standing in front of his colleagues, Big Paul straightened his gold-lined satin robe and cleared his throat. "Men, we are facing the most dire conditions ever." He glanced around the room at his comrades of the other urban centers and paused to acknowledge the presence of some of his closest friends.

Pointing to the right, he nodded at L.A.'s Peter Milano. "Peter, stand up so your friends can acknowledge the Godfather of the West Coast."

Soft applause followed.

Turning his attention to the power structure seated before him — the boss from Chicago and the other bosses from New York City — Big Paul placed his hands on the table. "Men… at our meeting last fall, we discussed an FBI report uncovered by one of our members that detailed the killing of thirty-eight of our soldiers… at least one died in each of our own cities. At our spring meeting in Miami, each of you provided important details about these murders."

Castellano picked up a goblet of water and took a long drink. "Today, I'm saddened to announce six more men have fallen, brutalized and maimed in the most horrible fashion possible." He pounded the table with his fist. "We can no longer stand by; we must eradicate these sons-of-a-bitches!"

The men in the U-shaped configuration around *the table*, stood and with sustained applause, shouted, "Here… here."

Turning toward Angelo Mario, the San Jose boss, Big Paul slicked back his hair. "Please share with the group, your findings of the Seattle investigation."

The frail, gray-haired man from the Bay area rose slowly and spoke in a soft raspy voice, "We're dealing with a cold-blooded killer. These were innocent men who didn't deserve to die." He wiped his brow. "It's clear to me these murders were the result of a coordinated effort, likely the result of some kind of vendetta."

"Why do you say that?" Philadelphia's Nicodemo Scarfo asked.

The old man rocked back on his heels. "The killings in each city follow the same pattern. Though in some places the men were tortured and mutilated, in other cases they weren't, either way, most died a painful death. They were not random killings; in the weeks prior to their murders each man was reported in the media as being connected to organized crime."

Carlos Marcello of New Orleans raised his hand. "How could one person be aware of that many incidents scattered across the country?"

Angelo gave him a sour look, "Like Big Paul mentioned last fall, there is a definite connection… I don't know how or why… maybe it's the gypsy clan… maybe not… someway these bastards are spreading the word."

"Are you positive about that?" Joseph Campisi from Dallas asked.

The West Coast guru loosened his tie. "It all goes back to Seattle… where the killings started in the 1940s with the gypsies." He stood erect and sharpened his tone. "Gypsies are a strange lot. There's no way we can apply any of our logic to them."

Men around the room listened intently with their full attention.

"They are not like us. They're like the nomads of the past; they don't go to church or have a family dinner on Sunday. Their kids don't go to school like ours nor do they participate in governmental programs, like social security, welfare, and state and federal hospital care."

Raymond Patriarca of Providence/Boston shifted in his chair. "Where did they come from? How many are here?"

The old man flipped his hands in the air. "Most experts think they migrated from northwestern India to Europe over 1,500 years ago. Again, no one knows for sure; it's estimated there are over a million in the US."

"Wow, that's a lot of unknowns," Russel Bufalino of Scranton noted.

Philip Rastelli of the New York Bonanno Family raised his hand to Big Paul's nod. "I thought the gypsies were scam artists. I never heard of them killing people."

"You're right, for the most part, but there's a small sect from Romania that are knife fighters and killers."

Turning back to the West Coast guru, Big Paul asked, "Can you tell us anything else about gypsies?"

Marino picked up a scrap of paper and read forcefully, "Most gypsy families share the same birthday and the same or similar first names."

"Why do they do that?" Carmine Persico of the New York Colombo Family asked.

"They believe that everyone is equal in his own right and that one's birthday or name shouldn't elevate him or her above another person. As a result, most family members share the same birthday… usually January 1st."

"Huh, pretty dumb if you ask me."

"I'm not sure about that." New York's Victor Amuse of the Lucchese Family pointed out, "There's something to be liked about that… I suppose they all have the same last name too."

Marino's grin grew into a smile. "For the most part, yes. Andersons and Marks are quite common."

Big Paul slid back into his chair. "Will you tell us more about your findings?"

"It gets pretty gruesome." Angelo Marino shook his head. "Our digging went back to the early '40s in Seattle. Ned Moomau, who we think may be the father of Ted Moomau, mentioned by Detroit's Jake Nicollete in his report at our last meeting, refused to pay his monthly protection fee. After a series of incidents, the Seattle Mafia kidnapped his daughter, a beauty pageant queen, and sold her to one of the Chinese gangs on the shipyards."

Someone shouted from the gallery. "Those bastards have no regard for human life."

Raising his fist, Carlos Marcello from New Orleans shouted, "You're right about that."

"Wait." Marino waved his hands. "Next thing you know the old man received pictures of her dancing naked and men performing lewd acts with her. The old man went nuts."

"Who wouldn't?" Joseph Campisi of Dallas asked. "How did he handle it?"

"He went to Chinatown after the bastards... it was sad... he got beaten so badly, he crawled home."

"That's awful," someone mourned.

"Huh," Marino grunted, almost in tears. "By the time he could open his eyes, he received a picture of his daughter with a butcher knife plunged in her gut."

"Gross!" came from the gallery.

"I know," Big Paul sympathized. "Can you imagine someone taking such action?"

"Even so..." Carmine Persico removed his dark-rimmed glasses and placed them on the table. "It is hard to believe one person carried out such a vendetta for forty years."

"I agree," Anthony Salerno stroked his forehead in disbelief.

Big Paul stood. "That's the point... that's why we're here today. This is not a passing crime spree. This person... these persons... are highly organized and out to decimate our organization. Who the hell knows. Any one of us could be the next target."

A somber look spread over the faces of those in the room.

New York Lucchese Boss Anthony Corallos slammed his fist on the table. "Gypsy involvement is a theory; we don't yet know enough. Do we not have a shred of evidence on who these assassins are? No names? Nothing? We can't focus our energy solely on the gypsies."

"Anthony is right." Big Paul's eyes pierced those of the bosses around the power table — no one blinked. He scanned the faces of the other Bosses — no one moved. Taking in the line of discussion, he straightened his robe and measured his words. "Angelo Marino has done an excellent job of analyzing the killings in Seattle. While his conclusions don't necessarily apply equally across our cities, he's demonstrated the type of vengeance that must be forthcoming."

Silence fell across the room; heads turned to Big Paul.

A smirk crossed his face. "Each of you." He pointed to the bosses around the table and then to those seated on the perimeter. "Each of you must undertake the same kind of analysis we just heard from Angelo. He turned over every stone for the last forty years..." Big Paul paused, for effect. "I expect nothing less from everyone in this room. There's a son-of-a-bitch out there somewhere... maybe more than one. Comb your cities, search the neighborhoods, walk the streets, talk to your informants — someone knows something. Share any shred of information you find with me. We must not stop until we piece this puzzle together."

Big Paul sucked in a deep breath and snarled, "Dig deeper... make people weep... find the creeps!"

***

Clark grabbed a handful of chocolate chip cookies, stuffed one in his mouth, and opened the sliding door. Waving his free hand profusely, he searched for a breath of fresh air.

Without looking up, his dad released a perfectly-shaped smoke ring.

Waiting for his dad to announce the score, if the Tigers were ahead, Clark eased into his familiar place — a matching wicker chair across the room, with half the wear.

The inning ended.

"Trillo, Vukovich, Franco, and Bannister have all doubled against Petry. The Indians scored five in the seventh to lead 7 to 2. Turn the damn thing off." His dad snuffed the butt of his Corona into the ashtray. "Anything new with you?"

Chewing on his third cookie, Clark's mind filled with questions. "How did gang activity change so much from when I was in high school? I lived here while I was going to U of D — four years — I couldn't have lost track of things that fast."

The old man lowered his head, deep in thought for a moment, then looked his son in the eye. "It's hard to pinpoint a specific date or event when it all changed." Lewis let out a deep sigh. "Up until the mid-seventies, the numbers racket was the primary criminal activity in the black communities. A black racketeer named Eddie Wingate had a relationship with Mafia Boss Anthony Zerilli; they provided protection and he paid a tribute to them."

"How did that work?"

"The daily numbers were determined by a formula run by Rip Kourey, a Jewish mobster. He used the finish of the horse races at either Hazel Park or the DRC. If there was a big hit, he'd change the number, so it didn't cost the mafia too much of a payout. People around town knew the numbers were fixed..." He shrugged his shoulders. "They played anyway."

"How could people be so dumb?"

"I don't know... that's just the way it was."

"How about the level of crime in the neighborhoods?"

"There was some small-time local gang activity... penny-ante kind of stuff."

"Huh... how about all of the killings and murders? How did they fit in?"

"Most of that didn't happen in the local neighborhoods." Lewis leaned back and skewered his lips, as if trying to come up with the right words. "Real crime was at a different level — turf wars and power struggles."

"I guess that's where the story comes in that FBI agent Oscar Westerfield told me about. It was really funny."

Lewis cocked his head with an odd little grin. "I don't recall you telling me about that one. Can you give me a hint?

"The one about the dashboard..."

"Nope." Lewis cut him off. "Let's hear it."

"The FBI had been trying to nail one of the top guys in the mafia for a long time. Through an informant, they'd found out Vito Giacalone, the Underboss at the time, had a secret compartment built into the dashboard of his Cadillac, where he kept a loaded thirty-eight caliber revolver. Knowing it was against the law for a convicted felon, like him, to have a firearm, they knew they had him dead-to-rights."

"Why is that so funny?"

"It's the events that occurred afterward," Clark said briskly. "They got a search warrant and sure enough, it was there. All Oscar had to do was to hit a button under the dashboard and a flap would open up."

"Okay." Lewis sighed, setting up the punch line.

"Here's the deal..." Clark paused. "He knew one of the mafia's high-paid lawyers would tear him apart on the witness stand, so he had the dashboard removed from the car and placed on a stand, so it could be rolled into the courtroom. When he raised the issue, the mouthpiece for the mafia ranted and raved. Building suspense and intrigue, Oscar waited for the right time… the lawyer fell into the trap and asked, 'How would the jury ever be able to comprehend something like that? It isn't possible.'

The trap snapped.

Oscar motioned to one of his colleagues to roll the huge display in front of the jury box. He pushed the button and pulled out a toy gun. Jury members gasped.

The attorney for Vito went bananas and shouted, 'We don't need any kind of theatrical performances in the courtroom.' It didn't matter. Westerfield had made his point."

"Ha, I guess Oscar turned the tables on him."

"Yes, he did."

Lewis straightened noticeably. "Here's' another big name, Chester Wheeler Campbell — a black freelance hitman — did a lot of work for Murder's Row, probably had murdered a hundred people at the time. In fact…" Lewis hesitated and curled his brow. "I think he's scheduled to be released from prison next year."

"Really, guess I better put that on my list of things to check out." Clark stuffed down the last chocolate chip cookie. "Murder's Row… run by 'Big Frank Nitti' Usher and Harold Morton."

"You got it." Lewis nodded. "They were in power from around 1975 'til '79… and were the largest and most feared drug conglomerate in the city. They had a lethal crew of about fifty lieutenants and street workers that delivered the finest European heroin."

"Anything else?"

"No, you've helped me a lot. I want to ask mom something." He stood and cracked open the sliders. "Thanks, dad, should I turn the TV back on?"

"Yeah." Lewis sounded sarcastic. "Might as well get the bad news."

Clark hit the power button and headed for the living room.

As usual, his mother, Fran, was sitting in her favorite Chippendale chair reading a book.

Clark tiptoed in and eased onto the Chippendale on the other side of the end table.

"Just a minute." Keeping her eyes on the book, she didn't move. "I have two pages to go."

Clark felt like hustling to the kitchen and grabbing a couple more cookies, but knew better. Instead, he picked up a copy of *The Color Purple* by Alice Walker and read the summary on the back page.

By the time he'd finished, Fran was staring at him. "Does that peak your interest?"

"Hum… yes, in a way… the status of African-American women in rural Georgia in the 1930s — filled with violence, sexism, and racism — I wonder how much different it is from Detroit today?"

"Interesting you mentioned that point… it's the reason I'm reading it." She knew him well. "What did your dad say you should ask me?"

"Nothing this time." He gave her a sheepish look. "But based on dad's comments, I do have a question for you."

She flipped her hand, dishing out a go-ahead motion. "Dad and I were talking about the emergence of the drug culture in the '70s. It seemed like it happened almost overnight; did you see it coming in the schools?"

"Hmm, not really… drugs had always been around, but they never seemed to have had much impact on the schools. One day, a friend and I were having coffee; she was an elementary school teacher. She went into great detail about the changes she was seeing and mentioned, 'you won't believe this… young kids, seven and eight, are wearing expensive Nike and Reebok clothing.' It wasn't long before the high school parking lot was filled with new, fancy cars." Fran shook her head. "It was like a series of dominos — neighborhood stores closed, jobs for kids were gone, houses were abandoned, crime set in, people were afraid to be on the streets, drug people became role models — drugs and violence became a way of life."

"Now, I understand why you retired early."

"I didn't want to." She settled her reading glasses back on her nose. "Before, I used to look forward to teaching every day; it was a real joy. Next thing I know, I talked to your father every night about negative things that had happened in the school. Parents stopped coming to parent-teacher conferences. I couldn't reach them on the phone. I could see it coming… without parental support, you can't expect successful results. Finally, your dad convinced me to retire."

CHAPTER FIVE

Sitting on an elevated corner booth in the rear of the dimly lit neighborhood bar, Blackie Giardini hummed the melody of "Folsom Prison Blues." Born the same month in 1932 as Johnny Cash, Blackie had dressed in black since graduating from Notre Dame.

Slowly, twirling his large black-rimmed sunglasses, he reflected on the past six months. *First, Vicky left... I should have stopped her... no, she has her own life to live... to spread her wings. After three years she's gone forever — back to Oklahoma to work with the Cherokee Nation — I should have told her she was more than a mistress... damn... I miss her... worse yet, I can't talk to anyone about my Cher look-a-like. Joey is gone... goddamn bastards... if I ever get my hands on the guys who killed him, I'll tear them apart.*

Carmen Rizzuto, Joey's replacement, cracked the front door, shooting a light beam across the empty bar up to *the booth.* Reaching for the door handle, Carmen quickly closed it — a black pitch filled his senses — he rubbed his eyes, trying to adjust to the dim light.

Weaving his way between the empty tables, his mind fired up. *As Joey's best friend I had a leg up in the interview with Blackie, the Mafia's Street Boss. Shit... it's been four months since I started; I need to pull off something to earn my stripes. I know this is it.*

Waving a manila folder over his head, the six-foot-one, black-haired, one-hundred-and-sixty pounder, placed it on the edge of the table. "Boss, wait till you see the women I have for you to pick from."

Deep in thought, Blackie didn't look up. Instead, the mafia's number three-ranking man took a slug of his lukewarm coffee and shoved the empty mug toward the end of the table.

Unable to read Blackie's bland response, Carmen played it straight. "I'll get you a fresh mug of coffee, okay?"

Glancing up, he gave Carmen a partial grin. "Yes, thank you."

Hustling into the kitchen, Carmen gave himself a double pump. *It wasn't much. A good start for the day.* He filled their mugs and in no time was placing one in front of Blackie, the other one on the table across from him.

Blackie pointed to the end of the table. "Where's the folder?"

"Oh… sorry, Boss. I must have left it in the kitchen." He turned and hurried back into the kitchen. *Damn… how could I have done that?* Grabbing the folder, he shot through the café doors, nearly knocking them off their hinges. "Want to see them now?" he said excitedly, nearly shouting.

Blackie's mood hadn't changed. "Hmm, maybe later," he grunted. Rather downtrodden and bedraggled, not his normal self, Blackie lifted his head. "I can't get over the killing of Joey. He was my right hand; he would do anything for a person, and him being murdered in such a gruesome, painful way… why would anyone do that?"

Shaking his head, Carmen flipped his hands, palms up, as if questioning. "I can't figure it out. He was a great guy and you need to know, he idolized you; he admired how you were always one step ahead of the game."

"That's nice of you to say." Blackie gave him an unconscious shrug.

"I'm not saying it to be nice; it's the truth."

Blackie sat stiff as a stone statue. "All of those murders, three months apart on the 22nd of the month. Why? I don't get the connection."

"It's weird, Boss, and after Joey's death the killing stopped. Think someone was trying to send us a message?"

"Trying to send a message… maybe…" Blackie rubbed his jaw.

"Maybe the killing of Joey wasn't about him; maybe the murders were about sending a message to those of you at the top."

Blackie took a sip of his hot coffee. "If they were using Joey to send a message that means they must know his role here, and maybe… have met him." A puzzled look crossed Blackie's face, as he considered the concept. "Hmm… Carmen, I want you to analyze Joey's calendar for the entire year before he was killed. Find out who he met with — when, where, and why. Check the margins in his calendar to see if he wrote down a note or two. Who did he talked to on the phone? Did he make any notes? Got it?"

"Yes, sir, I'm on my way." Carmen slid toward the end of the booth.

"Wait a minute." Blackie's mind shifted into high gear; he sent a small pad of paper flying Carmen's way. "Take this and make some notes."

"I'm going through my calendar so you'll have a list of everyone Joey met in my meetings, okay?"

"Got it."

Blackie pulled a small black book from his sport coat pocket, turned the pages through the calendar, and stopped. "Red."

"I'm sorry, I don't think…"

Blackie cut him off. "She has red hair, hot as hell… a call-girl from Philly. We brought her in a few times to obtain information from Clark Phillips."

"Was she successful?"

"Successful… she banged the hell out of him; sucked out every tidbit of information he knew." He paused for a reflective moment. "Put her on your list. Abby Thompson."

Leafing through the next two months, Blackie stopped. "I have several here. I'll give you more details when you come back with your findings. For now, put these names on your list:

- Carlos Montes… he's a used car dealer

- Renzo Ricciuti is a small-time contractor

- Caroline Schaffer, sharp as hell, has legs like Tina Turner

- Ted Moomau, asshole

Carmen's eyes bugged up. *I'd like to ask for more, but maybe I should wait.* Blackie picked up on the questions that flickered across his face.

"I'll tell you more later." Blackie turned the page. "Add this one, too, Nicole Weatherspoon — a do-gooder — got beat up by the YBI." Glancing toward the front of the rundown bar, he thought for a long moment. "Yeah, add Clark Phillips. I don't know if Joey ever met Clark, but we sure in hell talked about him a lot."

***

Scanning the dimly lit nightclub, Kimberly's enthusiasm rose. From the bandstand to the stately backbar, to the table with white cloths — it had character. "How'd you find this place?"

Pag belly laughed. "I thought it'd peak your interest."

"Peak my interest… it's delightful; and did you see the marquee by the front door? They have live jazz at nine o'clock."

"I told you you'd love Cliff Bells."

"It looks like it has been here forever — I love the ambiance."

"You're close," Pag boasted, with growing pride. "It's a holdover from the past — originally it was a speakeasy — it was hot back in the '30s, '40s, and '50s. And… you can't beat their food."

"Table for two?" The hostess asked and following Pag's nod, guided them to a table in the center of the club.

Kimberly pulled out a chair facing the backbar from the '20s. "Seriously, how'd you find out about this place?"

Pag pushed his beer-belly up to the table. "I heard about it at the barber shop on Mack just east of Connor… I used to go there when I was a kid. I… go back once in a while."

"Why do you do that?"

"No specific reason." Not lying well, a muscle ticked in his jaw.

"I know that look… what's the deal?"

"I go back to keep the lines of communication open." He laughed. "There's a blind pig in the basement."

"And it's never gotten busted?"

"Some of our informants work out of there too, so they kind of look the other way."

"A blind pig, all right — *everyone looks the other way.*"

"It's local guys — playing cards that's all — there are no connections with any gangs or the mafia. It's just a friendly place to have a few beers and hang out."

"A few beers, in the barber shop?"

"Nah." He chuckled. "The tables are in the basement; they've fixed it up pretty nice… knocked out the wall between the pet store next door, so there's lots of room." He stopped, leaned across the table, and spoke in a low tone. "After I get my haircut, I go down to play a little poker. Wouldn't you know, a guy at the next table was spouting off about Ricky Davis."

"Ricky… the one in the Davis Family?"

"Yeah, he was loud enough for everyone to hear. My antennae went up. Next thing I know, he's saying Ricky likes jazz and comes here every Wednesday night."

"So that's why we're here; I was wondering why you picked a place like this to discuss the plan you had for me."

Trying to soften her up, Pag asked, "Want to start with some calamari?"

"I'm game as long as you're buying."

"Hah, it's actually on Clark's tab.

"Well then, I'll have a Manhattan — Crown Royal with two maraschino cherries to go with it."

"Okay, now we're getting somewhere," he jested.

Kimberly straightened her shoulders, extending her bust over the edge of the table. "You're not getting anywhere."

"Oh, no… I didn't mean it that way." Pag's voice remained calm. "If you're going undercover, you have to look and act the part."

She cast him a questioning eye. "So… what's that mean?"

"You have to have a drink in your hand… Manhattans are fine."

"And?"

"A blouse buttoned to the top won't cut it."

"I don't understand." Kimberly covered her cleavage with her hand. "I thought this was a practice run."

"It is. You have to play the role; he could come in anytime."

"Now I know… you're putting me on?"

"No, I'm not putting you on," he said matter-of-factly.

Glancing around, she paused for a moment. "Okay, then." She loosened the top button.

Pag rolled his hand for another one and a second.

She glanced down at her décolletage, partly exposed. "Okay, are you happy now?"

"Fine." Pag mumbled, "It's a start."

"A start?"

"Nothing, it's fine."

The drinks arrived and she took a sip. "You told me you'd fill me in once we got here, so let's hear the game plan."

"Okay, for some time the DEA has considered Ricky Davis, the younger brother of Reggie, the weak link in the Davis Family Gang. While Ricky had a well-known big mouth, the DEA bigwigs have not been able to capitalize on the weakness." He paused.

"Okay." Kimberly flipped her hands with a move-on gesture. "Get with it."

"Oh… well, I had to give you a little background." Pag gave her a disconcerted look. "After Veronica and Frank met you, they told their higher ups they thought you'd be a perfect undercover agent to infiltrate the Davis gang."

"Undercover… infiltrate, hold on." The thought shot a little tremor in her voice. "I'm a Lieutenant in the Child Abuse and Prostitution Section of the Detroit Police Department; I've never done anything like that."

"All the better…"

"All the better." She cut him off. "You gotta be kidding. I know… these drug leaders would just as soon kill you as look at you. No way, not me."

"No, Ricky's not that way — he's in his mid-twenties — a nice kid at heart."

"Yeah… sure… and he has a big one he'd love to stick in me… you're crazy, count me out."

"Kimberly, you haven't even heard the plan."

Taking a long sip of her Manhattan, she realized Pag was right. "Okay, but I'm not sleeping with any drug dealer."

"You don't have to *do anything like that.* You'll be here at Cliff Bells all the time and there'll be two undercover DEA agents watching every move."

"Hmm… all right," a tone of reluctance in her voice, "let's hear the rest."

"He'll likely come in tonight in an hour or so, eight or eight-thirty, and have a drink before the jazz starts. I've checked it out. He sits at the bar corner and swivels around to check out the women in the place."

"Oh boy, that's exciting. I'll be fresh meat."

Pag ignored the comment, knowing she was right. "Anyway, he tries to maneuver them to the corner table back to your right. If you turn slightly, you can see it."

Kimberly followed his directions and casually glanced that way. "The one with the art lamp hanging behind it with no picture."

"Yeah, that's *the table.* He's paid off the manager so no one else will sit there. When you sit down, you'll be sitting under the small beam of light."

Kimberly jerked around for a better look and turned back to Pag. "He'll have a bird's eye view of my…"

Knowing her thought, Pag interrupted. "That's the point. He likes to see who he's talking to."

"I don't think so."

"C'mon Kimberly, don't be a prude. Every guy you've ever met has looked at them."

"Maybe so, but they didn't see anything."

"Who cares, I bet you've worn a sexy half-moon dress to a special dance once or twice."

"Of course…"

Pag interrupted, and got serious, "Kimberly, this entire operation depends on you. Nothing is going to happen — you'll be safe — all you have to do is show off a little more each night." Kimberly started to react. Pag placed his finger over her lips. "We'll put a wire under your breast, so he can talk directly into the mike."

"Oh, how cute."

"Well, will you do it?"

"Is that all?"

"Yes, we'll make sure he sees you and set up a plan to get him to invite you to the table."

She took in a deep breath and grinned uncertainly.

***

Mafia Boss Jake Nicolette downed his second double chocolate donut and walked toward the center of the room. Standing at the head of the fifteen-foot conference table in the lower level of his plush Grosse Point Park mansion, he welcomed an expanded leadership team — the matter at hand required the best and most able men he had.

Tony Minelli settled into the black leather swivel rocker, nearest to his chair, on his right. The aging *consigliere* sipped on a cup of coffee. Tony had been a longtime friend of his father and had advised Jake since he'd become the Boss.

Jake nodded to his hand-picked *consigliere*-to-be, Michael Santo "Big Mike" Polizzi, seated to his right and to the right of Tony. To his left the Underboss — number two man — the handsome Angelo Travaglini and his backup, Anthony "Tony Z." Zerilli. Next to him Street Boss Blackie Giardini, dressed in black, his sunglasses folded in his sport coat pocket. The youngest of the group, Carmen Rizzuto eased uncomfortably, into the rocker next to his boss.

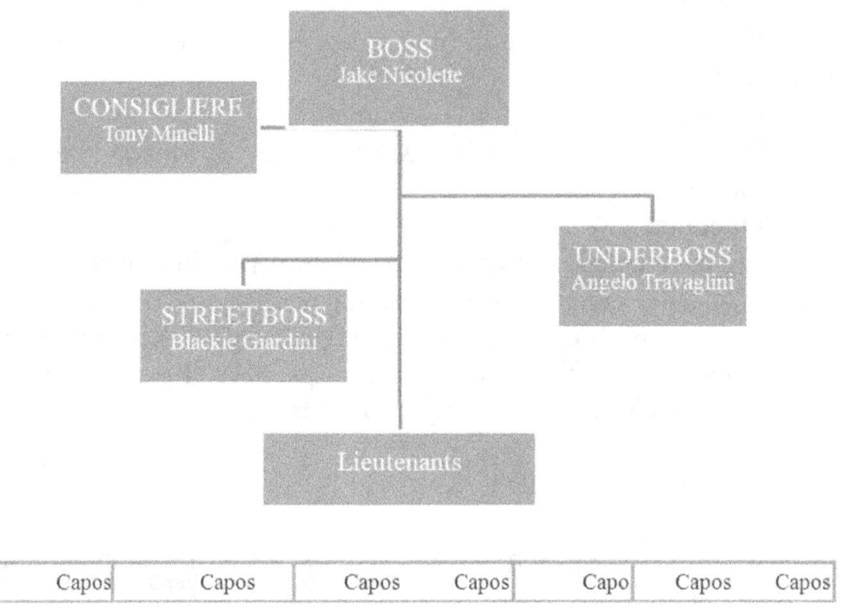

At the foot of the table, among others, several strong lieutenants — Pete Cavataio, Jack "Jackie the Kid" Giacalone, Vito "Billy Jack" Giacalone, Harry Maciarz, Vincent Meli, Joseph "Joe Hooks" Mirabile, James Stabile, and Anthony "Tony T." Tocco.

Jake stood, refilled his cup, and turned back toward the table. "If you want any more coffee you better fill up now, this is going to be a long meeting."

Everyone, except the *consigliere* rose and lined up at the table. Jake took advantage of the opportunity to chat briefly with "Jackie the Kid" Giacalone, then eased back into his swivel rocker and whispered to Tony Minelli. "He's going to be sitting in my chair one of these days."

Tony did something he always did. Nodding slowly, he ran his fingers through the curled fringe around the back of his head. "You got that right. And, it won't be long before "Big Mike" Polizzi is in my chair."

Jake smiled at him, a friendly smile, rolled his chair to the head of the table, and patiently waited as long as he could. Unable to delay any longer, he started before Angelo had taken his seat. "As you all know, last week I attended a meeting with the other bosses in Castellino's place on Staten Island." He slowed and fired up fiercely, "We have a crisis!"

Rolling tight against the table, his underlings came to attention.

"'Big Paul' has directed the bosses across the country to analyze each of the recent murders to see if there's been any similar ones that have occurred in the past, in our individual territories. Tony and I have gone through the years one by one, and have not come up with anything like the four recent murders... does anyone recall anything like these cases?"

Jake took his time, his piercing eyes penetrating those of each man, securing a shake of the head as he worked his way around the table. Coming back to Tony, he stopped. "Huh, four brutal killings... I guess that's it." Jake shook his head; his frustration showed in the curl of his brow.

"After the murders ended here, there were five of our guys killed in New York City — one from each family — and another one murdered in Chicago."

"Jesus Christ," Angelo blurted. "What the hell is going on?"

"Wait, there's more." Jake raised his hand. "An informant got us an FBI list that indicates there have been over forty murders perpetrated against us in the nation."

"Forty... are they positive they're all connected?" came from the other end of the table.

Jake's eyes narrowed. "It looks like it."

"Holy shit..." Angelo paused, wondering why no one had examined the issue before now. "How in the hell could anyone pull off that many murders without one of our guys making a connection?"

"We talked about that at the meeting." Jake inhaled a deep, calming breath. "One happened in St. Louis, later there was one in Providence, then another one in New Orleans... no one made the connection. The FBI believes someone out there wants to *get even*!"

"*Get even!*" Angelo stroked his long black hair. "With who?"

"That's the $64,000 question. Until it's answered, all of us are at risk."

Somber faces looked at him from around the table.

Jake turned to his adviser. "Tony, you were at the meeting, any idea on how we might move forward?"

Tony nodded; picking his words slowly — his voice quivered; his anxiety noticeable. "We need to form teams that focus solely on one murder and one murder only. Team members must dig beyond the obvious; they must find out the personal stuff — who didn't like them, who had an argument with them, who hated them — who they slept with and who else slept with her."

"Yes, that makes sense. Somewhere out there, there's a connection." Jake stood and pointed, in an authoritarian way. "Blackie, I want you to pursue the bastards who killed Joey."

"Absolutely. Carmen and I are already making a list of his contacts over the past year."

"Excellent… and don't forget his earlier years. You know… some people hold a grudge forever."

"No question." Tony's forehead wrinkled. "Some nuts never let go."

Jake turned to Angelo. "Do you have a preference?"

"Not really… well, I take that back, Sam Narduzzi, the owner of Last Call. I was there the night his dad opened the place… must have been twenty years ago."

"Makes sense." Jake turned to the *consigliere*. "Tony, looks like you get Lonnie Williams and Billy Fletcher, the two YBI hoodlums."

"It'll be a pleasure. The bastards sold drugs to seven-year-olds, can you believe that?"

CHAPTER SIX

Earl cracked open the front door of the Sax Club and stepped back — vibrations of Dolly Parton's recent hit — "Nine to Five" ricocheted off a passing car. He sucked in a breath of fresh air and headed across the smoke-filled room for *the booth*; the place where the guys had congregated since Clark's college classmate bought the place seven years ago. *Back in the 1960s, the Sax Club had been one of the hottest topless bars in town. Like most establishments in the city it had fallen on hard times and closed. When his friends bought the rundown building in '76, he'd started coming on Friday nights to help them out. As a matter of fact, he'd helped himself to more than burgers and fries, but... that was long ago when he was young and fancy-free.*

Earl made his way through the standing throng cheering for an encore. The DJ accommodated them and dropped the needle — "Nine to Five" — blasted louder than before.

Cheers and catcalls filled the bar. The topless dancers at the three silver poles did more to please the patrons. Following the lead of the sexy blonde on the center pole, the other two ripped off almost every stitch of clothing, and teased the guys seated around the stage.

Cheers bounced off the walls. Strobe lights flashed — red, green, and yellow — fives, ten, and twenty-dollar bills flew onto the stage floor.

As the commotion died down, Earl slid in next to Renzo Ricciuti and nudged him in the side. "You doing okay?"

His longtime contractor friend winked. "Couldn't be any better... want a beer?"

Earl nodded, and the curly black-haired Italian grabbed a pitcher of Stroh's and poured him a full mug.

"About time you got here," Carlos Montes, an assertive Mexican-American, shouted from the other end of the table. He, too, had grown up in the same neighborhood as Clark, Earl, and Renzo. Clark and Earl had attended Western High School and Renzo and he had graduated from Detroit Holy Redeemer, just a few blocks down Vernor Highway. "Figured you'd be nabbing another one of those mafia guys," Carlos called to Clark.

"Not tonight." Clark gave him a short, excited laugh. "Poker is on my mind; plan to take some of that used car money you've been raking in."

"Hah, you sound like Rosa Maria." Carlos twisted the corner of his mouth into a sour grimace. "Time I'm finished with the wholesale — minus cars to the mafia and paying dues to the teamsters — there's not much left."

"Teamsters," Earl spit out. "Why do you have to pay *them*?"

"They've added a tax for each car they deliver."

Clark lifted his head; gave him a disturbing look. "When did this start?"

"Two or three weeks ago." Carlos thought for a moment. "At first I thought it was another one of the mafia tactics. Come to find out it was a new rule by some guy called Proctor."

"Ralph Proctor?"

"Yeah, he's the one. They made him sound like someone important."

"Important!" Earl's voice elevated. "Hell, he's one of the most powerful men in the Teamsters; he's the president of Local 124 — Hoffa's old local — they control most of the union activity around here."

"Holy shit, why didn't someone tell me?"

"Tell you…? We just found out about it. What did they do?"

Carlos sucked in a deep breath. "I have contracts with the biggest automobile dealers in suburbia to buy their trade-ins — it's good for both of us. I receive a truckload or two from each of them every week. Ten days ago, two burly assholes came by and declared they were adding a twenty-five-dollar tariff for each car delivered. That might not sound like much… but it's a hundred and fifty dollars a load, and that adds up."

"Why do you pay?" Ted queried.

"Hah… no pay, no cars. I pay the driver cash on-the-barrelhead before he unloads a car."

Ted tensed. "I wouldn't pay the bastards a cent. I'd hire my own drivers and tell them to… buzz off."

"I can't do that either. All of the truck drivers are members of the Teamsters. If any non-union person moves a truck ten feet, he'll be in the hospital with a couple of broken arms." Carlos threw his hands in the air. "Enough of that. I'm ready for some poker. Let's go upstairs."

***

Father Dom stood in his regular location in the door frame, greeting the crew as they filed into the room — two curtainless windows along the back wall facing the alley and a broken fan hanging over the poker table.

Father Dom had known Carlos and Renzo since they were students, when he was the principal at Detroit Holy Redeemer. After graduation from the University of Detroit, the two had returned to the southwestern neighborhood and worked with him on various fundraising activities for the school.

Being his turn to provide snacks, Father Dom had loaded the table beneath the windows with his favorite treats — peanut M&M's, chocolate-covered pretzels, chips and dip, and two heaping plates of subs. On the floor to the right, he'd filled Clark's old Tiger cooler with ice and bottles of Stroh's.

Within minutes the guys had filled their plates, grabbed a beer, and settled in.

Calling "Dealer's Choice," Renzo flipped the cards face-up in front of each one.

Receiving the first ace, Carlos picked up the made deck, turned to his right, and plopped it down in front of Clark. "Your cut."

The poker marathon was on. And, other than poker lingo, nothing was said until Father Dom stood at nine o'clock, on the dot, and announced, "Break Time."

One by one, the guys hit the head.

Lingering longer than usual, they caught up on the things they'd missed during the two months they hadn't met, Earl talked nonstop about Nicole and the things he'd done with her two boys.

Renzo butted in. "Anything else you want to tell us about the two of you?"

Realizing he'd monopolized the conversation, Earl hung his head. "Guess that's all."

Ted announced plans for Laverne and him to be married next Valentine's Day — no surprise. Carlos shared that Rosa Maria had accepted her third term as PTA president at Detroit Holy Redeemer.

After everyone had returned to their poker positions, Father Dom turned to Clark. "You've been particularly quiet tonight. Anything happening with you?"

"Don't ask him anything," Ted spouted. "He can't say a word; things with him are hush-hush… like always."

Catching Earl's eye, Clark winked. "Not so!"

Jaws dropped around the table at the thought of Clark sharing department information.

Not sure what may lay ahead, Father Dom ventured, "Well… let's hear it."

"It isn't a pretty picture." Clark took his time, nodded to Earl. "Give them an overview of the magnitude of our city's drug problem."

Unconsciously, Earl ran his hand over his shiny head. "As you know, the drug problem hit our city like a tidal wave — it's been like night and day. Our information indicates there are over fifty thousand heroin junkies in the city."

"Fifty thousand!" Ted exclaimed. "How many were there three years ago?"

"We're not positive." Earl wiped his brow. "Somewhere in the range of five thousand."

Renzo didn't move; he stared blankly. "That's unbelievable — ten times more junkies in three years."

"That's only half of the story." Earl reflected briefly; he'd seen the evolution unfold himself. "The inner-city streets are a living hell. We couldn't treat all the drug addicts if we wanted to. Social agencies are backed up for months; the courts are way behind. We've become a city of drug fiefdoms."

His words drew silence; there was nothing more to say. Like many citizens, the guys had read the daily news stories, but somehow the magnitude of the situation hadn't sunk in.

Ted spoke up. "And all these years I thought the mafia was the bad guys… at least they had rules and showed concern for the average person. These gangs have no respect for anyone."

Father Dom hung his head. "We've failed; those of us in the Church have given Sunday masses, but have forgotten the masses."

"It's not only the Church, Father," Clark pointed out. "My mother told me three-fourths of the city's eleventh graders were reading at or below the fourth-grade level, and the city's dropout rate is over 50 percent. The future really looks bleak!"

"The public schools are not alone." Carlos didn't blink an eye; he wasn't stunned. "Rosa Maria told me the parochial schools are facing the same problems." He shrugged his shoulders. "Maybe not to that magnitude, but similar issues are not far away for the Catholic schools."

Clark nodded, his expression grim. "Not to brush this aside, but someone asked about our agenda… to put it mildly — its drug organizations and drug dealers — the DEA is inundated. We have been asked to lend them a helping hand."

"That won't make a difference," Ted voiced in a low, harsh tone. "If you shut down a gang today, there'll be two more tomorrow."

"You're probably right." Clark's jaw jutted out in defiance. "But… if we don't take the first step we'll never make progress." He paused, draining the last of his beer. "We're making no secrets about it… we're going all-out after two of the most brutal gangs in town."

All eyes shifted to Clark, knowing it was a rare moment when he divulged anything job-related. "We're doubling-down with the DEA on the Davis Family Gang in the short-term and going full force after the Pony Down Crew. In the weeks ahead, Earl and I will have plenty to tell you about these drug lords and some of their associates."

***

Kimberly leaned over and slid into the booth, giving Pag an eyeful.

His eyes bugged. "I guess I made the point."

She smiled, noting his interest.

He turned away, so as not to stare down the gapping, unbuttoned top.

"So… what do you think?" she asked enthusiastically, a sense of unabashed pride in her voice.

"You'll capture more than his attention." Pag glanced at his watch, "It's almost 8:30. Ricky should be coming in shortly. Once he orders a drink, you can stomp off to the restroom like you're in a snit.

When you come back we'll argue some more and you can tell me to get out of here. The rest is up to you."

"Thanks," she said, still slightly unsure of herself.

Out of the corner of his eye, Pag caught the front door opening and nodded. "He just walked in."

Kimberly sat anxiously, waiting with anticipation. She raised her glass and downed the Manhattan.

"Okay, he's easing up to the bar, ordering, and now — he's swiveling the other way — don't look now his eyes are coming our way."

Kimberly pushed her empty glass across the table; it hit Pag on the chest, flew to the floor, and shattered into a hundred pieces.

"What are you doing?" Pag asked, not realizing she was already playing her role.

"I'm telling you," she shouted, loud enough for all the patrons to hear. "Tell that bitch of yours that you're getting a divorce or I'm out of here." She sobbed, pulled a tissue from her purse, dabbed her cheeks, slid out of the booth, and ran into the bathroom.

Taking it all in, Ricky leaned over to the bartender, mumbled something, and angled his stool facing the restroom.

A waitress hurriedly swept up the mess.

Acting as if nothing had happened, Pag ordered calamari and another round.

Ten minutes later, Kimberly stepped out of the bathroom, sniffled, and walked straight to the booth where Pag waited.

Pag lowered his glass, covered his mouth and whispered softly, "Sorry, I didn't know you were performing."

"The hell you're not going to tell her." She swung her hand across the table, knocking over the drinks and sending the calamari flying.

Pag threw his napkin at her and jumped up. "That's it, I'm not taking any more of your shit."

He bolted for the door and marched out.

"Don't let the door hit you on the ass!" she shouted to his back. Kimberly picked up her own napkin and tried to clean up the table debris.

Two waitresses came to her rescue, cleaned and reset the table. "I'll bring you an order of calamari — it's on the house — would you like another Manhattan, too?"

"Ah… not right now, maybe later."

"Of course, just let me know."

Watching from the bar, Ricky waited for his opportunity, then eased off his stool, and walked slowly her way.

Kimberly picked up her purse, took her time sorting through the pockets, as if looking for something, and glanced up. "Something you want?" she asked curtly.

"I'm sorry, I couldn't help overhearing you… I thought you might like a drink to unwind."

"I don't think so." She buried her head back in her purse.

"It must be awfully important."

"Important… what?" Slowly she raised her head, letting her eyes lead the way from his crouch to his dark face.

"Whatever is in your purse. It must be awfully important."

"I'm sorry." She giggled, "I'm a little discombobulated."

"Little wonder, the way that guy treated you." He flashed an infectious smile. "I'll buy you a drink if you'd like to unwind a bit."

"That's very kind, considering the crap I've gone through with…"

"Hey," he cut her off. "No strings… there's no reason an attractive lady like you should sit here alone; besides, you deserve a break."

Rolling her eyes down his slender frame, she locked in on his large gold belt buckle with a diamond studded "R," moved up, past his gold chain, and landed with a smile on his face. "Sure, why not?"

"Great." He extended his large black hand. "I'm Ricky Davis."

Ignoring his gesture, she shrugged. "Fine with me… have a seat, I'm Kimberly."

"May I buy you a drink?"

"Ah… sure, a Manhattan — Crown Royal with two maraschino cherries."

"First class, I like that." He signaled to the waitress across the crowded room.

Making her way through the throng, she wasted no time hustling his way.

"The lady will have a Crown Royal Manhattan with two maraschino cherries and… I'll have one too, without the cherries."

She gazed at him with open interest. "Do you always drink Manhattans?" Kimberly asked softly.

"Only when a beautiful lady is having one."

"I've heard that line before." She leaned back and pulled her shirt-button tight, covering her exposed décolletage. "You're not hitting on me?"

"No, no." He waved his hands, gesturing for emphasis. "Just speaking the fact."

"Pretty smooth, aren't you?" She released the button, returning *his birds-eye view*. "Where do you work?"

He paused momentarily. "I'm an international distributor."

"Wow… that sounds impressive. What kind of products do you distribute?"

Laughing hard, he covered his mouth, trying not to make a scene. "You really don't know who I am, do you?"

A scowl flickered across her forehead. "Of course, I do… you're Ricky Davis."

He let out a hoot, an uncontrolled howl. "Wait till Reggie hears about this!"

The waitress placed the drinks on the table, gave him a strange look, and slipped away.

Holding back a fake smile, Kimberly covered her mouth. "I don't see what's so funny."

He choked, trying to talk, and sucked in a deep breath. "My brothers and I head up the Davis Family Gang — we distribute heroin, cocaine, and marijuana nationwide."

"Sure." Kimberly chuckled. "And I'm an undercover agent."

Laughing out of control, his eyes trolled her cleavage. "That's a good one."

Looking at him seriously, Kimberly cocked her head. "Are you really a drug dealer?"

"Yeah, we're one of the biggest in the city."

She gave him a mysterious look. "Ricky, you can't say that, I could be an…"

Laughing heartily, he winked. "With equipment like yours, I don't think so… you could make a lot more money on your own."

Kimberly bristled. "Are you suggesting I'm a…"

"No, no… ma'am."

Her eyes pierced him. "I'm not your ma'am." She grabbed her purse, as if to leave.

"Wait… wait, I'm sorry, I…" He held back what might be another offensive word. "No offense, ma'am… sorry… it's something we say all the time where I'm from." He covered his mouth again. "I am truly sorry. I didn't mean to offend you. Sometimes my language is not exactly proper."

Kimberly took her time assessing him. "Fair enough, I like a man who's willing to admit a mistake."

Raising his glass, Ricky waited for Kimberly to pick up hers. "Here's to the woman who could give *the princess* a run for her money." They clinked.

"The Princess?" Twisting her head toward him, Kimberly squinted. "Who is the princess?"

"No offense… I was comparing you with Mayor Young's niece — she's known as the *"ghetto princess"* — if something is happening, Cathy Volsan is there. Most often she is with the top dog."

Kimberly raised her hands in a questioning fashion. "Top dog?"

"Oh, my jargon for big drug dealers. She's been seen at parties with most every major dealer in town. She's beautiful, well educated, and carries herself in a dignified manner — just like you."

"Well, it sounds like I just got a point."

"Point…!" He chuckled. "You could score all you want to… Whoops!" He covered his mouth. "Did I say that in the wrong way?"

"No, it's quite alright." She slid her arm across the table and gently rubbed his hand. "It was really nice of you to ask."

"Guess I got a point." He chuckled.

She smiled affectionately. "Yes, you did."

"Rumor has it that Johnny Curry is her latest catch."

"Curry?" Kimberly questioned and pushed deeper. "Is he a top dog, too?"

"Yeah, you might say that." He snickered, then downed his Manhattan. Ricky motioned to the waitress for another. "Make it a double," he said, turning back to Kimberly. "The Curry brothers are a long story… sounds like the jazz group is cranking up." He pointed to the small stage. "How about we meet here next Wednesday night, say eight-thirty and I'll tell you about the Currys?"

Kimberly leaned across the table and circled her index finger over the top of his hand. "I'd like that."

CHAPTER SEVEN

Squeezing into the standing-room only crowd at Cliff Bells a little later than planned, Kimberly surveyed the room, looking for Ricky.

He leaped to his feet from a small secluded table and made his way through the throng. "Good to see you," he shouted above the din. Being shoved against her, he peered down her half-moon red sweater and swallowed hard, quelling his rising feelings.

Regaining his focus, he motioned to *the table*. "Would you like to join me?"

"Yes, I'd like that," she responded as intended.

Guiding her to *the table,* he positioned her under *the light beam*, and eased into the chair across from her. He smiled broadly, pleased with the unobstructed view. "Miles Davis is playing tonight."

"Yes, I saw that on the marquee. I thought he retired in 1975, because of health reasons."

"He did… a couple years ago… he started making a comeback and now at fifty-five he's flying high."

"His electric fusion style back in the early seventies was really great."

"I thought so too; now he's returned to the trumpet and is on tour playing songs out of his new album, 'The Man with a Horn.'" Ricky pushed a Manhattan toward her and raised his glass. "We can talk after the first set." Raising his glass to hers, "Here's to a wonderful evening."

"I'll drink to that."

Following the performance of "Fat Time," "Back Seat Betty," and "Shout," the two stood to applause and collapsed in their chairs after the rousing set.

"I've never heard better."

"I agree… he's the best."

Hustling over with his pre-ordered drinks, the waitress placed her Manhattan and his double on the table.

Kimberly gave him a thumbs up. "Huh, pretty smart… how'd you think of that?"

"An old trick I learned long ago." The twenty-five-year-old winked. "Did you have an enjoyable fourth of July?"

"Yes, thanks for asking. I went on a picnic with my parents, saw a parade with them in my home town of Dowagiac, and drove home early so I could watch the fireworks on TV. How about you?"

"I worked straight through the weekend — Saturday, Sunday, and Monday — didn't even know it was the fourth until I saw the fireworks on the way home."

"What were you doing?"

"Answering the phone. Reggie was working out of his mansion in Beverly Hills and several of my kinfolks were busy operating our Miami office. That meant I had to call around the world to ensure the connections between our drug suppliers and our delivery network went smoothly."

"Ricky, I told you before, I don't think you should be talking about that."

"No big deal." He picked up his Manhattan, drained it in one long gulp, and waved to the waitress for another round.

"Ricky, I haven't finished half of mine."

"Don't worry, the night is young." He scratched his head. "Now, where was I… oh yes, my phone calls. I talked to our contacts in Jamaica, Ghana, Nigeria, Holland, Haiti, Thailand, and Great Britain."

"How'd you do that? Do they all speak English?"

"Yes." He laughed. "English is the international language of drug suppliers. The only problem is I have to set my alarm, so I call them at the correct time."

She shook her head. "I'd never be able to do that. I barely get to the office at 8:00."

"Hey, when your livelihood depends upon it, you do what it takes. We've cut out the mafia and are delivering high grade heroin, cocaine, and marijuana to all of the cities in Michigan and most of the urban centers in the Midwest."

"That's mind-boggling. How long has your family been doing this?"

"Reggie started it ten years ago. We're supplying most of the non-YBI areas of Detroit."

"You're way out of my league." Kimberly finished her drink. "Non-YBI… I need another Manhattan."

He flashed the waitress for another round. "YBI is a major drug ring that's in big-time trouble. Their leaders are in prison — the organization is in disarray — the insiders in one group are killing their counterparts on the other side. There's way too much publicity; the feds are all over them."

"Guess I read about some of those killings, but it didn't make much sense to me."

"Doesn't make much sense to anyone. Reggie's going to call a high-level meeting of the other kingpins. We have to do something about those bastards."

"Interesting." Kimberly took a long sip, then glanced up with her dreamy eyes. "Last time you mentioned the Curry brothers. How do they fit in?"

"Oh yeah, I'll fill you in when the next set is over."

He motioned to the waitress. "Another double." He winked at Kimberly. "Make it two doubles."

She started to say something, decided it best not to break her momentum.

The set ended with a rousing round of applause, and Ricky wasted no time following *the beam.* Staring with a broad smile, he glanced at her half full glass, downed his and ordered himself another double.

"The Curry brothers are really cool; they stay in the shadows — no big headline or bloodshed for them — yet, on the street they're feared across town. They've been around for five or six years and control the entire eastside."

"I thought YBI and Pony Down were the top dogs."

"The feds and the general public believe that. They're killing themselves off on the westside. The twin brother Currys — 'Big Man' Leo and 'Little Man' Johnny — must be laughing to themselves." He leaned across the table and whispered. "They have two dozen heroin dens across town. I heard they plan to cut and sell an estimated $200 million of powder over the next three years."

"Wow, I can't believe that."

"Yeah." Ricky shook his head. "And the feds act like they're not even around."

Kimberly leaned back, making sure *the beam* lit his fire, reached across the table, caressed his forearm, and slurred, "Wanta slide your chair over on my side of the table for the second half?"

***

With mugs of coffee steaming in front of the other team members, the group stood when the door opened and Kimberly slipped in.

Cheers drowned out her words.

After a few moments, Veronica raised her hand to quiet the ongoing applause. "We've all listened to last week's tapes. Our Director in Washington, D.C., asked me to extend his personal congratulations to you, Kimberly, for an outstanding performance. He thinks the upcoming meeting with Ricky might be the break we need."

"I picked up on that too. That's why I asked him to move over and sit by me."

"The Director thought so." Veronica gave her a questioning look. "I'm not positive how I might ask this question… the Director thought he could detect heavy breathing just before the last melody. Can you clarify this?"

Kimberly's face reddened. "I… hum… I wanted to make sure he'd be there next week."

"So if I may ask, who was the source of the heavy breathing?"

"Not me," she responded instantly. "I put my hand on his leg."

"His leg?"

"Well… kind of…"

"I think we've heard enough," Clark interjected. "You've made the point."

Kimberly sighed with relief. "Thank you."

Veronica glanced at her notes. "Next week, we'll have an audio and video setup on that table. Kimberly, you need to make sure he's on your side of the table. With the light there we'll get a good image of him while he's spilling the beans."

"That won't be hard… I mean…"

Laughter erupted around the table.

Kimberly put her hands over her rosy cheeks. "Sometimes things don't come out right, hmm…"

"Yes, the Director understands, but he wants to make sure the event goes properly. This will be the big one; we can't afford any impression that his comments may have been unduly influenced by your actions. Do you understand… Kimberly?"

"Yes, of course."

"That means under no circumstances may you take your hands off the top of the table."

The room dissolved into heehees.

***

After refilling his coffee cup, Jake continued to pace back and forth, the length of his conference table. *Four gangland mutilations by gypsies — who knows — maybe they were copycats. Some of the killings on the East and West coasts were not mutilations; still, they were brutal. How could anyone coordinate such activity, all of them occurring on the twenty-second of the month? Who could mastermind something like that? Why?*

He turned toward the end of the table for the umpteenth time, heard a voice from the doorway behind him, and turned.

"Boss, how you doing this morning?"

Jake grinned at his old adviser. "Tony, why are you here so early?"

"I don't know… couldn't sleep, I guess, I kept thinking about the meeting at Castellino's, and all of those murders… forty years and no one picked up on it."

"Yeah, and all of them on the twenty-second of the month… how could that be?"

"How could they go undetected for that long?"

"It escapes me." Jake stepped toward the coffee pot and the array of donuts and sweet rolls. "Help yourself, Tony, we might be in for another long morning."

"Thanks, the double-chocolates really look good."

Jake refilled his cup and paused, hearing footsteps on the marble floor down the hallway. "We'll have to talk later. Sounds like the boys are coming now."

Appearing in the doorway, Angelo's powerful voice boomed, "Morning Boss… Tony."

The two nodded.

Blackie acknowledged Jake more cordially. "Nice to see you. Looks like it's going to be a beautiful day, maybe get up to eighty-five." He turned to Tony. "You're looking good; didn't see your name in the obituaries this morning."

The old man smiled. "I checked them out before I left."

"Tony, did you watch the Tigers game yesterday against California?" Angelo asked with a trace of his Italian accent in his raspy voice.

"Only the first three innings; Jack Morris gave up three runs, so I turned it off."

"You should have watched the rest. He was great! Pitched ten innings and didn't give up another run."

"Did the Tigers win?"

"Yeah, Lance Parrish hit a home run in the top of the twelfth… they won 4 to 3."

"Wow, that must have been some game."

Jake stepped aside, his mind not on the ball game, and waited for his lieutenants to appear.

Right on time, "Jackie the Kid" Giacalone and Vito Giacalone led the way.

Jake embraced each one and motioned to the table with coffee and pastries. "Better load up over there. Looks like we're in for a real session."

Getting the message, the underlings filled their cups, grabbed a couple of sweets apiece and eased up to the walnut table.

Jake gave them a moment to be seated, then moved swiftly into the agenda. "We have two items to discuss today. First, I'm anxious to hear your findings on the assigned murders, and secondly, we need to give special attention to how our findings relate to the national scene. There are forty other killings out there… we have to find the connection."

Jake scrutinized the men around the table, in his normal calm manner, landing on his number two man. "Angelo, want to start it off?"

Swallowing a bite of donut, Angelo spoke slowly. "The Narduzzi murder caught everyone off guard. His wife is still in shock — she cried most of the time I was there — no one in the family has heard anything out of the ordinary.”

Blackie slid his chair closer to the table. “How about his girlfriend?”

“Huh,” a surprised Angelo grunted. “How’d you know about her?”

“Jake asked us to contact all of the informants, pimps we knew.”

“Doesn’t matter.” Jake interceded between the established veteran and the rising star. “How much do we know about her, Angelo?”

“She has plenty of equipment; hangs around with Cathy Volsan.”

That name got Jake’s attention. “Mayor Young’s niece?”

“That’s the one. She’s in with all of the big-name drug dealers.”

“Hum.” Jake rubbed his jaw. “Drugs connect Lonnie Williams and Billy Fletcher, and maybe… Narduzzi. Where’s the drug tie to Naples?”

Blackie came to the defense of his former assistant. “Joey was clean as a whistle; he never had any dealing with druggies.”

“Right,” Jake agreed. “Someone could be making a point with us.”

“Holy shit.” A ruthless sneer crossed Angelo’s face. “That opens up another can of worms. It could be the Davis Family Gang, the Curry Brothers, YBI, Pony Down, or…”

Jake cut him off. “Okay, enough on those assholes for now. Let’s finish up with Narduzzi. Anything else new on him?”

“Hell, with his temper, it could have been anyone, the beerman, the iceman… who knows?” Jackie the Kid interjected.

“You’re right,” Angelo acknowledged. “He had a shouting match, almost a fist fight with Renzo Ricciuti.”

“The contractor?” Blackie asked rhetorically. “We had some dealings with him, too.”

“Was Joey there?” Jake asked with a pencil in hand.

“Yeah, it was some of the stuff we were doing on Clark Phillips.”

“Interesting.” Jake jotted down Clark’s name. “We’ll come back to Ricciuti later; anyone else have something on Phillips?”

Tony raised his hand. “Kind of… indirectly… Phillips is a good friend of the Weatherspoon woman who was beaten up by some of the YBI boys.”

"Nicole Weatherspoon, I know her," Blackie admitted, half in admiration. "She's one strong woman, has several convenience stores in the inner-city."

"You think she's connected with the druggies?" Jake asked.

Blackie belly laughed. "She's probably pissed them all off. She's a no-nonsense woman. She's the one who created those *drug free zones* around her places."

Jake looked thoughtfully for a moment. "Yes, I recall reading about her. She had her picture in the paper with Mayor Young."

"Right, he committed one hundred thousand dollars to her project."

"Hmm," Jake mused in a reflective tone and turned to Blackie. "Tell us about your connections with Clark Phillips."

"Like Joey, I haven't had any direct contacts with him… we've had several dealings with his cohorts."

Blackie piqued Jake's interest. "In addition to the ones you already mention… who else?

"Well… there's Carlos Montes, the used car dealer where we get our cars."

"Yeah, I remember him," Jake spouted. "He's the one with the big Buy American signs all over town."

"Right." Blackie sneered. "The other dude is Ted Moomau. He's a gypsy and a hothead — I had to separate Joey and him at one of our meetings."

"Damn," spilled out of Tony.

"Anyone else?" Jake asked.

"Maybe a few other non-players… and of course, all of these guys are connected to Clark Phillips."

Jake rocked back in his chair. "Well guys, what do you think?" His dark, piercing eyes zeroed in on each man, one by one.

No one uttered a word.

Turning to his top adviser, he asked, "Tony, where to from here?"

Curling the gray fringe hairs around the back of his bald head, the old man eased his chair closer to the table. "It seems like we should take two actions."

"Two," Jake was startled, but in a controlled manner, motioned for his *consigliere* to continue.

"Like you indicated at the onset, we need to separate our 'who did it' question and 'how does it connect' with the national scene…"

Angelo tossed in a ringer. "Maybe there's no connection to what's going on nationally?"

"In most cases, I'd agree, but in this situation, there's one telling fact." Tony paused, letting his point settle in. "Fact is, the killings here and all the other murders across the country occurred on the twenty-second of the month — it's impossible for that to be a coincidence."

Heads nodded around the table.

"Any thoughts on how we might proceed?" Jake asked the group.

Continuing to curl the strands on his fringe, the old man double-nodded. "We've got a lot of digging to do on all of the names mentioned here this morning. We have to be careful not to tip our hand; yet, we have to let them know we're on to them."

"So, what's on your mind?" Jake asked, anxiously.

"All of the names are connected to Clark Phillips in one way or another. Obviously, we can't take him out without having every federal agent in the country on our ass. But… maybe a little scare, you know — a bump and run — nothing serious, just enough to let the assholes know we're not going to stand around and do nothing."

"I like that." Jake turned to his Underboss, "Angelo, have one of the boys take care of it; nothing major just a little fender bender to bruise him up."

"Got it."

"It's getting close to lunch. Let's hold the second part of our agenda until our next meeting. In the meantime, analyze each point we've discussed. Somewhere there's a connection."

CHAPTER EIGHT

Kimberly made her way through the maze of tables packed with jazz enthusiasts at Cliff Bells. She spotted a hand waving from the table in the back.

Ricky squeezed through the crowd from the other way and reached out with a light embrace, then turned and pointed to the chair directly under *the beam.*

Grinning to herself, Kimberly leaned forward and eased onto the chair, stimulating his senses. Giving him one more treat, she bent down slowly and placed her purse under the chair.

The bug-eyed Ricky bumped into the table, nearly knocking over the two Manhattans he'd pre-ordered.

Grabbing her glass, she smiled broadly. "Guess you're using that same old Manhattan gimmick." She giggled and picked up her glass. "Here's to a most enjoyable evening."

"With good food and great jazz."

"And good company," she agreed.

Ricky tipped his glass. "I've ordered some calamari and barbequed spare ribs, I hope that's okay?"

"Perfect." She pulled up her sweater top, so as not to be too obvious. "You're a thoughtful gentleman."

"I try."

"You do very well."

The waitress placed the tableware and hors d'oeuvres in front of them. He ordered another round; making sure his drink was a double.

The jazz quartet struck a beat; the volume increased.

Sitting across the table, the two inched closer — Ricky took advantage of the opportunity to gaze down once more. Twisting and turning throughout the set, she made sure he continued to loosen his tongue.

The set ended with a rousing approval from the standing crowd.

Kimberly leaned closer, nudging her right breast closer to him, and looked up at Ricky with dreamy eyes. "It's getting noisy in here. Why don't you move your chair over to my side so it'll be easier to talk?"

Moving in without hesitation, she knew his thoughts. She had her own; following marching orders, she clasped her hands on top of the table so they'd be in full view of the camera.

"Anything new in your life?" she asked casually.

"You won't believe it," he announced, sounding like he'd waited all week to tell her.

Kimberly played dumb. "The Tigers made a big trade."

"No… no." He took another sip. "The meeting…"

Playing it cool, she twisted her head, cocking it to the side.

"The meeting my brother was planning…"

"Oh yes, about those guys in the…"

"YBI," Ricky interrupted. "It's going to happen next Wednesday at Seal Murray's penthouse apartment in the Jeffersonian Hotel."

"Seal Murray? Is he another bigwig in your company?"

"Company!" Ricky double-nodded. "I like that."

She gave him an inquisitive look. "Do you call your group something else?"

"No, it's not that. It's just how you say things. I like your personality, your levity… it so different from the assholes I deal with all day." He covered his mouth. "Sorry."

"That's okay." Her grin turned into a smile. "You're doing quite well."

He ordered another double, nudged closer, and placed his hand on her thigh.

Whoops, I didn't mean that well.

"Could you help me understand better…? I'm really a good listener," she imparted, hoping to divert his attention from her under-the-table-parts.

"That's another thing I like about you, your genuine interest in our conversations." Ricky paused for a short moment, as if collecting his thoughts. "Seal Murray has been an integral part of the YBI's leadership core. Butch Jones…" He stopped. "Before you ask, Butch is one of the YBI bosses. Seal and him have been good friends, since grade school."

"Got it; Jones was recently indicted," Kimberly interjected. "I read that in the paper."

"Right… anyway, several years ago, my brother Duane was driving Seal's yellow Fleetwood Cadillac around town. Someone tipped off the police. Long story short, it was reported in the local press. Butch Jones was furious; he wanted to know who Seal supported."

"Seems like a reasonable question."

"Yeah, I guess." Ricky leaned back in the chair. "There had been two or three smaller issues over the years, before it erupted, again, in August."

"Last year?"

"Yeah in '82." Ricky kissed her on the cheek; his fingertips neared the promised land.

Nonchalantly she pushed her butt as far back into the chair as possible to give herself a little breathing room.

His hand regained the lost territory.

She sat stoic. *Crap, I can't put my hands under the table… if I don't he'll think he has full range.*

Ricky continued to spill the beans. "One of our female couriers, working on behalf of Duane and his wife, Alicia, got busted when she departed an Amsterdam flight at Chicago's O'Hare International with 1.5 kilos of pure heroin hidden in coffee cans."

"In coffee cans?" She sighed, her mind on other parts of her body, and eked out, "Why did they do that?"

"She tried to save her ass, ended up giving the feds a bunch of shit about our organization." His shoulders sagged. "It ripped a hole in our international supply chain."

Take a deep breath. The wire will pick up everything. Kimberly's mind whirled; she tried to remain focused. "How so?"

"For years, we had been sending drugs untouched through customs — from the Asian Triangle, Great Britain, and Africa — in hand-carved religious statues carried by men and women traveling as Christian missionaries."

"Wow, that's really ingenious. Who came up with that idea?"

"Reggie, he's the brains behind our entire organization." Ricky continued to blab. "He has a longtime grudge against the YBI, and now they're acting like assholes, killing soldiers like flies. Everyone is upset; and the feds are all over us."

"Why is the meeting being held at Murray's apartment?"

"It's really a cool place. He'll have babes and booze. Besides…" Ricky whispered in her ear, "Seal keeps all of the records there; it's a safe place."

Knowing she'd gotten more information than expected, Kimberly focused on the performers, hoping that would help maintain her control.

The set ended.

Everyone stood… *Thank God…* and gave the group a robust round of applause.

***

Waiting at the front door of the Roman Village in Dearborn, Antionio Rugiero's wife, Mama Rita, hugged three of the women — Wendy Ricciuti, Rosa Maria Montes, and Laverne Belk — who'd made the restaurant their monthly luncheon place for the past three years.

Next in line was Abby Thompson, Clark's special friend who'd joined the group six months ago. Mama Rita gave her a brief hug, stepped back and looked at her, up and down. "My, my, Antionio, was right, I can see why you're the apple of Clark's eye."

Taken back, the red-faced woman was at a loss for a reply. "Than… Thank you, your words are most generous."

"I'm coming," a shout, came from the parking lot. Nicole Weatherspoon slammed the car door and jogged to the front door. "Sorry, I'm a bit late."

"Not at all." Mama Rita gave her a lingering embrace and kissed Nicole on the cheek. Having developed a special affinity for each other, the two dynamos chatted briefly before going, hand-in-hand, inside.

The women sat at the corner table surrounded on two sides by an Italian countryside mural. Mama Rita had already filled their glasses with her favorite Chianti and placed a second bottle in the center of the table.

Laverne, Ted's attractive blonde fiancée, raised her glass and toasted, "Here's to an exciting fall and a successful end of the year."

Taking a flyer, Wendy ventured, "Does that mean Ted and you have set a date?"

"Sneaky, aren't you," the MD from Wayne State University Hospital quipped. "The answer is… yes, St. Valentine's Day!"

"Oh my gosh, I can't believe it," Wendy shouted.

Everyone around the table jumped up and congratulated her.

"Sounds like another bottle of Chianti, if you ask me," Abby stated.

"It isn't too late to practice your pediatric specialty," the normally quiet Rosa Maria popped in.

"I don't think so. Abby is a more appropriate age for that."

Heads turned toward her.

Caught off guard, Abby broke a partial smile. "It'd be okay with me. But Clark doesn't have time to even shop for an engagement ring. He's snowed under with black gang activities; drugs are a citywide epidemic."

"She's right about drugs." Nicole swirled the wine in her glass. "Things have changed dramatically in the past three years. It's like night and day; neighborhoods are crumbling like sand castles in a hurricane. Pretty soon there'll be nothing left."

Wendy found a positive note. "Still, Nicole, you have to be proud of the crime-free zones you've created around your stores."

"Yes, I am." She gave the group a faint grin. "But…, they're becoming islands in a sea of despair. In some neighborhoods, there's nothing left — a liquor store, pawn shop, and a couple of Arab convenience stores."

"None of them have any roots in the community; they're only there for the money."

"Crime is creeping closer to our restaurant too," Rosa Maria added in despair. "Carlos had Renzo install a chain-link fence around our parking lot with barbwire on top."

"It's a shame," Nicole lamented. "Sometimes I think no one cares about anything other than drug money."

"Why do you say that?" Abby asked. "I lived my entire life in Philadelphia… we had drugs and mafia killings, probably the most violent mob in the country; still, no one talked about the level of civil disobedience you're talking about here."

"Detroit was like that too… the heroin blitz hit at the worst possible time. We had massive job losses in the auto industry and there was a middle-class flight to suburbia. Shops closed and crime increased — it was a vicious circle. Neighborhoods were left barren and hopeless. And worse of all, the domino effect eroded the family structure."

"How so?"

"In just a few years, youngsters were involved in crime, twelve-year-olds were selling drugs… and in some cases, these kids were the only breadwinner in the family."

"The town went drug crazy." Wendy stood, out of frustration. "I used to sit on our front porch with my boys and talk to passing neighbors. Now, no one stops by. The dope peddlers put an end to all of that. If you're on the porch, they'll try to sell you drugs."

Rosa Maria squeezed her eyes closed with an expression of pain. "I heard the same thing from a friend. Everyone in their neighborhood stays inside. If they go anywhere, drug pushers break in and steal anything they can carry. Sometimes, drug addicts even break in when they are home and watching TV. It's terrible!"

"Wow." Abby was stunned. "No wonder the only thing Clark can talk about is black gangs."

Laverne grabbed the bottle in the center of the table and refilled their wine glasses. "I've heard enough about drugs and gangs, let's talk about something else."

"Yes, I agree." Nicole raised her glass. "My grandmother always stressed, you can't complain about something unless you've tried to do something about it."

***

Lewis slammed the porch slider door and marched into the kitchen.

"Did the Tigers lose again?" Fran asked.

"Yeah, I can't believe it. We got seven hits and five runs off of Vida Blue in four innings, and lost 7 to 5," he groused. "Trammel is the only decent player we have."

"Now, now, Lewis, I'm sure the Tigers have several fine young men."

"Maybe so, but they can't hit their weight."

"There'll be another game tomorrow." Fran pointed to the dining room. "You can set the table now; Abby and Clark will be arriving any time."

"I'm on my way." He stopped and turned back toward the kitchen. "Has he mentioned anything about the two of them getting married?"

Fran gave him a disgusted look. "He always says he's too busy and fluffs me off."

"I think you ought to push him a little… she has a real pair."

"Lewis! I can't believe you said that."

"Well, she…"

"Lewis, you hush now… set the table and hurry up. I just heard a car door slam."

Clark walked in, in an uncharacteristically quiet manner, put his arms around his mother from her backside, and pecked her on the side of the cheek.

"What's going on?" She pulled away before he could answer and turned toward him.

Clark handed her a dozen red roses.

"Roses…"

He cut her off in a joking manner, "To celebrate the last day of July."

Fran cocked her head to the side in a questioning manner.

"It's a special day for us. Four years ago we were on Mackinac Island…"

"Yes, I recall," Fran interrupted.

"Abby and I had several dates before that, but we both agree… something happened that weekend." Trying to act coy, Clark's voice slowed, drawing out the words. "Rather … than … having…"

Abby waved her hand, motioning for him to get on with it.

"So, we decided not to have another date to remember."

An overly anxious Fran gave him an inquisitive look. "Does that mean…?"

Abby proudly held her left hand out, showing off her glistening diamond ring.

"Oh my gosh." Fran covered her mouth with both hands, then flung her arms around Abby and held her for the longest moment. "I'm so happy." A tear ran down her cheek; she pulled one arm away, grabbed Clark, and hugged the two of them. "Lewis, Lewis!" She jumped up and down. "Come in here, Lewis."

He poked his head into the kitchen. "What is it, dear?"

"Come over here and look at Abby's *ring* finger."

He walked briskly toward her. "Wow, that's something else." He gave her a gentle embrace and stepped back. "We're so pleased to welcome you, but… are you positive you want *him*?"

"Oh yes, I've never known anyone like him." Abby extended her arms and pulled them close. "He told me he's a lot like the two of you."

"Oh no." Lewis shook his head. "You can't butter me up that easily… to tell the truth, he's more like Fran.

"What smells so good?" Abby asked.

"That's the chuck roast, redskin potatoes, and carrots in the pressure cooker." Fran paused. "Oh my, I need to take the rolls out of the oven."

"Hmm, sounds wonderful." Abby grabbed an apron. "Can I help?

***

Dishes were passed and plates filled.

Fran waited patiently, with a hundred and one questions any future mother-in-law might have, until everyone else had sliced into the tender chuck roast. She looked fondly at Abby. "Tell us about growing up in Philadelphia. Where did you go to college?"

"Mom!" Clark exclaimed. "She just sat down, it isn't like she hasn't been here before."

"It's different now." Fran sent a smile his way. "I'm so excited, she's going to be part of the…"

"It's alright," Abby interrupted. "My mother would have the same questions."

"So there, Clark, you'll be on the firing line when the two of you go to Philadelphia."

"I'm excited, too." Abby took a sip of Lambrusco. "I was an honor student in high school and ran track."

"Track," Lewis announced, with a level of surprise and interest.

"Tell him about your track career," Clark garbled, his mouth half full.

Fran frowned across the table and bit her tongue.

"I was an All-Stater and set the state record in the four-hundred-yard dash."

Lewis weighed in. "You must be pretty fast on your feet."

She winked at him. "Not as fast as your wit."

His face glowed, like he'd been given an award.

"I turned down a track scholarship and accepted an academic scholarship at the University of Pennsylvania. I majored in computer science and after graduation took a computer job at Bloomingdales, where I did a little modeling, too."

Lewis eased closer to the table as if ready to say something, and then catching Fran's eye, took a second helping of mashed potatoes. "How did you get to Detroit?"

"It was one of those whimsical kind of things," she fibbed, with Clark's knowledge. "I saw a job offer in a professional journal with a big salary increase at GM, and said to myself, 'why not?'"

Fran jumped back in. "Where did you meet Clark?"

Abby flashed a *dreamy smile.* "I saw an upcoming ad for a Kenny G. performance in the *Free Press*, so I asked my girlfriend to go with me. Wouldn't you know, two days before the performance she came down with the flu, so I went to the Sax Club alone."

"I'll pick it up from there," Clark offered. "I saw the same ad, but… time I got around to buying a ticket they were sold out. Knowing the bouncer, I went anyway, gave him ten bucks and slipped into the packed place. I was about ready to leave when I saw a hand waving and pointing at a vacant chair — that hand belonged to the most beautiful woman in the world."

***

Following dessert and dishes, the two women joined the men, deep in conversation, in the living room. Fran led the way for the two through the archway, both of them with cups of coffee in each hand.

Lewis looked up with a smile. "Enough of that. We can finish up later."

"Don't let us interrupt you." Abby flashed *the smile.* "No need to stop on account of us."

Lewis waved her off. "Shop talk about gangs and how they've changed everything."

Fran tried a little smile. "That and the Tigers are the only two things they've talked about lately."

"If you don't mind, I'd like to hear more. We had the same problems in Philly… nothing like the massive devastation that occurred here, though."

"It'll be fine." Fran laughed, knowing the odds were against her. "Better than replaying the Tigers' season."

Clark motioned for Abby to join him on the sofa. "Where would you like us to start?"

"Hmm, I don't know… Clark keeps talking about the corporate-like structure of the big gangs. I don't understand how these gangs are able to control hundreds of kids — twelve, thirteen-year-olds — they're barely teenagers."

"Here's my take." Lewis stroked his jaw a couple of times. "The gangs or crews, whichever they prefer to be called, have a strict honor code."

"Honor…" Abby hesitated at the sound, "there's no honor among thieves; these guys are crooks."

"It sounds like an oxymoron, but they literally control the kids. It's *all about the money*. The drug lords have it all — big cars, girls, prestige — they're role models. Without selling drugs, these kids have nothing."

"Selling drugs…?"

"It's that or nothing." Lewis pleaded the case. "You may be surprised to know, these kingpins require complete loyalty; they strictly prohibit the *use* of drugs among their cadre. Any deviation results in a beating, some of which are fatal."

"Gang life has become the new mainstream of thinking for these kids." Clark tossed his thick hair back. "There are no Robin Hoods for them; they take from the poor and leave them poorer."

"They know drugs are bad… still, they sell them to others."

"It doesn't matter to them." Lewis scrunched his shoulders. "It's like you have something that others want; it may be bad, but it's survival for you — money — a chance for the good life."

Abby gulped, recalling a portion of her own life.

Clark jumped in. "These kids have a distorted view of the good life. They have nothing; they are *driven by money, and with it, they can achieve everything they want.*"

Fran chimed in. "In many cases, these young kids are the breadwinners of the family. The family structure is strained by divorce, family deaths, members in jail, and fatherless families. I read a recent report that indicated 80 percent of the families in the inner city have an income under $4,000 and are headed by a single mom."

"I get it… still, I wonder how." Abby's mind swirled with a jumbled question. "How, did all of this come about in such a short period of time?"

"I'll start." Lewis announced. "Before the riots, neighborhoods across the city were composed of a hard-working class, middle class, professionals, and lower class, all integrated into one. People were making big money — Detroit was on a roll. Then, it started to slide. The auto industry went into the dumps and heroin hit — it was the worst possible combination. In a large part of the city we now have a one-dimensional society composed almost totally of the socially and economically poor."

"That's a good way of saying it," Fran assured him. "It hit the schools hard too. Rather than education being the way out of the inner city, it's now viewed as worthless. Kids are dropping out like flies; we have a 50 percent dropout rate."

CHAPTER NINE

Glancing around the upscale bar, Earl slipped into the black leather club chair and slid it up to the shiny-top mahogany table for two. "Every time we come to The Ghostbar I feel like I'm some bigwig."

Clark gave him a half grin. "You are… the all-time basketball leading scorer in Detroit high school history."

Earl smiled and said, "Nah, it's the ambiance. Look at the dark paneling, the high-gloss mahogany bar, and the mural on the ceiling. No wonder it's your favorite place to slip away."

"The Whitney is one of Detroit's iconic Gilded Age mansions. The food in the restaurant downstairs is something else, too."

"I'm going to bring Nicole here for our next special occasion."

Clark eased closer to the table, his interest piqued. "Are you trying to tell me something?"

"Don't I wish?"

"You never know, sometime you might get lucky."

The barmaid appeared, placed a couple of napkins in front of them, centered a bowl of mixed nuts, and leaned down conveniently for Clark to see her belly button. "What would you like, sweetie?"

"The usual." Clark glanced at Earl's bugged eyes. "Vodka and tonic for you?"

A nod was the best Earl could muster before her departure. "What the hell was that about?"

"Ah… nothing, we had a fling long ago." Clark laughed hardily.

"Whatever… I'd advise you not to bring Abby here."

"Good point." Clark pulled a small black notebook from his pocket. "I want to have a little uninterrupted time for us to think about the plans the mafia might have."

"Hah… that's impossible. They're always five steps ahead of everyone."

Clark nodded slowly, as if contemplating. "Well… guess that means we'll have to think five steps ahead too."

Glancing at the backbar, Earl lifted an eyebrow. "You better think five steps ahead to stay cool, here she comes with our drinks."

Clark grabbed a handful of nuts and pushed the bowl across the table, trying to avoid the obvious.

The waitress showed off her equipment.

Earl missed his own message; his eyes slid down her cleavage.

Clark knew his thoughts. "I was five steps ahead, where was your mind?"

"Ha, ha." Earl seemed embarrassed, just a little, before getting back to business. "Okay, wise guy, how in the hell are we going to think like them?"

"To start, we're going to roleplay. You're going to think like Blackie and I'll be Jake."

"Why are you the Boss?" Earl jested.

"Because I am." Clark winked. "Let's think in terms of priorities… out of everyone involved in our blind pig scam, who's the one most likely to be singled out by the mafia?"

"No question, Ted Moomau," he replied without hesitation. "That pissing contest he got into with Joey Naples is the first thing on my… Blackie's mind."

"Right, and even more important…" Clark paused for a moment. "He's a gypsy. And, the mafia has Grimes' report pointing to possible gypsy involvement in all of those mob killings."

"Gosh, you're right. How are we going to stop them?"

"That's the question. How do we move five steps ahead of them before they decide to do something to Ted?"

Running his hand over his black shiny head, Earl wrinkled his brow. "Geez, I don't know. Set up a diversionary action?"

"Huh, like what?"

"Hell, I just took two steps forward coming up with that. It's your turn."

"Hmm… we think of a way to point the finger at someone else."

"Yeah, but then we'd have the same problem with them."

"Or… we find a way to demonstrate Ted is not the one."

A question mark flashed on Earl's forehead. "And just how are we going to prove he is innocent?"

"That's it." Clark stared at him for the longest moment, lengthening the time of silence.

"What's it, Clark? What is *it*?"

"DNA." Clark's smirk slid into a grin. "The project Sharon Wilson is working on in England."

"Yeah… I remember, she's working with a professor to see if they can make the connection between a person's hair and the hair follicles found on a comb."

"Right, last time I heard from her they were really close. She thought it might even be used in court in another year or so." Clark took a reflective moment. "If you can use DNA to prove someone is guilty, the reverse is true."

"Yes, of course, so we use DNA to prove Ted is innocent."

"Right, I'm calling Sharon tomorrow." Clark glanced at the barmaid and motioned for another round. "Hopefully she'll be able to get some kind of test kit to compare Ted's DNA with that found at the Narduzzi and Naples crime scenes. Assuming there's no match, where do we go from there?"

Earl looked a little surprised. "We'll have to make sure the mafia receives the information."

Without looking up, Clark gave him a slight thumbs up.

"Here she comes… it's your turn to step up." Clark grabbed a few nuts and glanced up at the painting hanging on the end wall.

Earl turned in time to catch a full view of her décolletage.

Placing the drinks on the table, she leaned toward him, picked up the empty bowl, and winked at Earl. "I'll refill your bowl."

"Thanks," he said, trying to refocus his thoughts. "Where… were we?" he stammered in relief.

"Ha, I told you." Clark smiled, broadly. "How do we make sure the information on Ted gets to the mafia in a credible manner?"

"That's an easy one." Earl's face lit up. "Tell anyone at 1300 Beaubien. The place leaks like a sieve."

"Perfect." Clark stopped, deep in thought. "Hmm…"

"Now what?"

Clark nodded to himself. "We need a second kit for Ted's dad."

"Right, and how about his uncle?"

"I-I don't think so. I assume we won't have to test him because he's Ned's brother."

"Okay, let's work our way through the rest of our team."

Earl shook his head. "I don't see how they could connect Renzo or Carlos to anything."

"I don't either." Clark thought further. "Let's think ahead. If they tried, what is the way they might connect the two of them?"

"Hmm… I don't know," Earl muttered.

"What evidence might they find?" Clark hesitated. "I got it. They could find a bug. We have to make sure both of them have removed the bugs they planted." In a reassuring tone, Clark directed Earl, "Ask Renzo if he has taken all of the bugs out of the blind pigs we hit… and have Carlos do the same with all the cars. Call them right away. If there are any left, have them removed ASAP."

"Got it."

"Let's talk about ways they might connect the women."

"The women? There's no way… Oh my gosh, Nicole helped them plan the entire bust."

"Yeah, and Abby was a double agent." He downed the last of his Tanqueray and picked up the toothpick and olive. "Caroline was in the mix, big time, too."

"How do we deal with them?"

"We need to think about that…" Clark glanced at his watch. "I gotta meet Abby in a half hour. Next time, we have to talk about a strategy for each of the women."

***

Chairs around the small conference table on the 26th floor of the McNamara Building filled quickly, as new DEA representatives Frank Bennett and Veronica Chavez slipped into the last two places. More introverted than you might expect, for a lawyer from New York City, Frank took out his pad and waited. Veronica more than made up for his quiet nature; she was already poking fun at Pag.

Appearing at the door, deep in conversation with his sidekick, Earl Walker, Clark strode toward the head of the table, dumped a handful of papers, and continued onto the coffee pot. Earl plopped down in the vacant chair next to his.

Carrying his mug of coffee back to the table, Clark nodded to the pile. "I'd say we're in for a long morning."

Pag and Veronica acted like a pair in the catbird seat, barely able to wait to share the facts they'd uncovered. Sitting next to them, FBI agent Dick Woodson seemed non-committal, as you might expect.

Clark glanced their way. "Well… who wants to lead off the discussion on Pony Down?"

"I will." Dick raised his hand. "We've agreed for me to start with a little background on the Pony Down Crew."

Clark motioned for him to go ahead.

The flattop from Indiana gave Clark a half grin, started to open his file, and then closed it. "Before I move into the history of the Pony Down Crew, I want to answer the question all of you have asked — Pony Down comes from Pony shoes." He chuckled, the biggest laugh he could muster. "For years, Adidas has been the standard bearer in upscale shoes. In 1972 Pony shoes were founded as a freewheeling-company with the slogan 'do whatever it takes'… in effect to challenge Adidas. They signed a bunch of big name athletic stars who, I'd say were mavericks — soccer star Pele, baseball all-star Reggie Jackson, and the entire Oakland Raiders football team."

"Yeah, I wore Pony shoes in college," Earl popped in.

"In 1980, LeRoy "Gus" Buttrom, the brain trust of the Pony Down Crew embraced the same philosophy and decided to challenge the YBI."

"Wow." Pag shook his head. "That was a big nut to crack."

"You have to understand; the Buttrom brothers are fearless… maybe it's better to say — ruthless. LeRoy works behind the scenes. Tony "The Snake" Buttrom heads up enforcement, and Walter is the front man."

"No wonder I've heard more about Walter," Pag offered, echoing the local street perspective.

"No doubt." Woodson continued down his script. "Having grown up near West Seven Mile Road and Murray Hill in northwest Detroit, the Buttrom's were boyhood friends with several YBI members. Leroy mobilized some of them and unleashed an assault on YBI drug dealers in that area. He had a simple plan — offer them a better deal, if the dealer refused, kill him — it didn't take long for the message to surface."

"How did YBI react?"

"All hell broke loose from the enforcement arms of both groups… and it's still going on. Remember the Buttrom brothers started as juvenile delinquents; they don't give a shit about anything."

Frank Bennett wore a curious look of introspection. "I don't understand how they recruited these kids to work for them?"

"The Buttrom boys were more aggressive than other gangs; they preached to the kids in the school yards, parks, and recreation centers, and gave the kids better deals — more money, jewelry, and clothes — it didn't take long for the twelve- and thirteen-year-olds to buy-in."

"It's hard to blame them," Kimberly squeezed into the chatter, with sincere empathy.

"Point made," Woodson acknowledged. "It wasn't long before the kids gained a grossly distorted version of *the good life*. Their values changed; family values changed. They were willing to kill to gain the status they desired. Their mothers became accustomed to wearing furs and driving big cars — they were proud of their boys."

"Were girls involved in gang activity?" Kimberly asked.

"At first, they were hangers-on — they loved riding around in a new convertible — being treated like a queen." Woodson paused. "As they grew older, many of these girls became actively involved in gangs; some formed female gangs. In the research mentioned earlier Professor Taylor found some startling facts." He stopped, picked up a handful of 3x5 cards, and passed them out. "The points were so overwhelming, I had them printed up on cards. Take a moment to read them."

Current Female Gang Activity

- 32 percent of inner-city girls are involved in a female gang.

- 73 percent of them have been involved in a violent crime.

- 78 percent of them are in school.

- 34 percent of them sell drugs.

- 87 percent of them have a gun or other weapon.

Woodson continued, "And yes, I'll answer the question on all of your minds — female gangs are *no different* than their male counterparts. It isn't unusual for these girls to be *carrying an Uzi and firing rounds at will.*"

Surprised by the facts, blank faces stared back at him from around the table.

Dick nodded to Pag. "Your turn to bring the group up to date."

"Sure, over the past two years, Pony Down has hit their stride. They've recruited dozens of adolescent street dealers — many of them fifteen by now — into supervisory positions, having had three years of experience with the YBI. Pony Down has destroyed YBI drug houses and started selling their own brands of heroin. Flashy names, like 'GQ,' 'Shotgun Special,' 'Papa Smurf,' and 'Devil's Dust' dominate the streets of Northwest Detroit. YBI dealers have been told to join *Pony Down or pack up and leave town.* Most of them have signed up."

"Just like that?" Kimberly asked.

"Not quite. YBI kept fighting even though the war was over when *they lost the streets.*"

Bennett frowned, with a puzzled looked. "Where were the police?"

Pag answered, "The tactic of using juveniles to peddle their product had confounded law enforcement groups — juvenile courts are swamped; the police are virtually powerless against the legions of preteen dealers and runners. By the end of last year, it was estimated that Pony Down had over three hundred dealers who had raked in over $100 million in profit."

"Profit!" Earl shuttered. "That's roughly two million a week."

"I know, it's hard to believe that they mounted that kind of an organization in three years of operation," Veronica picked up the ball. "With Butch Jones and Ray Peoples in jail and the internal fighting going on in the troubled YBI, the Crew has not only usurped YBI territory, they've successfully recruited the best and brightest Young Boys enforcers, runners, and salesmen."

Kimberly wrinkled her nose. "Salesmen… I've not heard anyone use that title when referring to any of the gangs. Have I missed something or…?"

"It's interesting you picked up on that point. Pony Down, like YBI, is organized like a major corporation. They have salesmen, directors, distributors…"

"I got it," Kimberly cut him off. "Guess salesmen… made the point. I never followed the chain of command down to the streets."

"It sounds like a corporate takeover," Earl nodded.

"Right…" Pag agreed. "Billboards with graffiti were like corporate memos — 'I Pony Down' was all over town. Blue and White Pony sweat suits replaced YBI fur-lined Max Julian jackets as the hottest clothing in Herman Gardens, Brewster Douglas, and the other projects."

"I don't understand it." Kimberly blurted out in frustration. "How…? Where do people come up with the money to buy drugs and all of this stuff?"

"Like Clark mentioned, heroin has produced a new subculture — it's okay to rob, steal, and kill — *it's all about the money*."

Registering his shock, Earl shook his head. "I never realized how much things had changed since I graduated from Western."

Pag threw his arms wide. "It doesn't stop there. The Pony Down Crew is now using the same strategies to infiltrate suburbia. It's like an epidemic; there are no boundaries."

"Sounds like a good stopping point." Clark glimpsed at his watch. "It's almost noon. Anyone have something else to add?" He made a quick scan around the table. "Great job. Put your thinking caps on for next time, we have plenty of work ahead if we're going to crack the Pony Down Crew."

Feeling good about the Pony Down report, Clark took the elevator to the first floor, waved to the security guard, and walked into a pleasant late summer breeze. Turning east on Michigan Avenue, he waited at the stoplight at Washington Boulevard. Thoughts of Abby filled his mind. *I can hardly wait to see her flashing that diamond in public.* He waited patiently with his thoughts. They'd made the first Monday of each month a luncheon date at a restaurant in Greektown.

Seeing the light change, he stepped around a large puddle of water left from a morning shower and walked across Washington Boulevard.

Out of nowhere, a black sedan squealed around the corner, hitting Clark full-force. His body went airborne, creamed off the windshield of a parked car, and fell onto the sidewalk.

Brakes shrieked; a woman screamed — people scrambled — two cars crashed.

Clark's broken body lay limp on the sidewalk.

The sedan sped away.

THE DETROIT NEWS
August 1, 1983

HEAD OF FBI-POLICE TEAM INJURED

Detective Clark Phillips, the lead man in the FBI-Detroit Police probe into mafia activities was seriously injured today in a hit and run accident, around noon at the intersection of Michigan Avenue and Washington Boulevard.

The crosswalk was loaded with pedestrians.

A bystander said it looked like the late model black sedan hit a wet spot and swerved directly into his pathway. A woman on the other side of the street pointed out, "It looked like the car plucked him out of the crowd. His body catapulted into the windshield of a parked car and landed on the sidewalk."

An unidentified medic referred to Phillips's injuries as being life-threatening.

At press time, a representative of Ford Hospital indicated the extent of his injuries were unknown.

CHAPTER TEN

At the foot of the hospital bed, Father Dom led a prayer for Clark — his body wrapped in mummy-like fashion, head to toe with a plethora of wires and life-support tubes overhead — then stepped back and mumbled a personal prayer. He'd had the same feelings when Clark's friend, Alyse was killed. He'd prayed for Nicole and her boys after his death in a horrible fire induced by the mob. *I hope my prayers are heard. So many people are depending on Clark.*

Standing on the left side with her head bowed, Fran clutched Clark's hand, her eyes swollen. Draped across the bed, Abby wiped the tears from her cheeks. Lewis stood, shaking on the other side, one hand gripping Clark's hand, the other clenching the side rail for support.

Clark's extensive surgery for multiple fractures and internal injuries had lasted over eight hours. Doctors at Ford Hospital did all they could; the chief of staff indicated the only thing they could do now was pray and wait, "It's up to God and Clark."

Nicole and Earl, Wendy and Renzo, and Rosa Maria and Carlos sat in the waiting room, hoping, and whispering their own prayers.

Time passed sluggishly; the clock hands moved in slow motion.

The guys took turns making coffee runs to the cafeteria and the women worked their ways through tattered magazines.

Wendy turned to Rosa Maria. "Anything new with you?"

She bit her lip, obviously not wanting to share the thought in her mind. "I-I-I don't know what to do… about Miguel."

"What is it? Is there something wrong?"

Rosa Maria shifted in her chair, uncomfortably. "When I washed his jeans, I found a Stiletto switchblade knife in his pocket."

"What did you do?"

"Carlos and I talked. We're going to have a sit-down tonight… We're really worried; the Stilettos are the biggest gang in our neighborhood."

"Do you think he's a member?"

"We're not sure. We haven't seen anything unusual in his behavior… I did notice some bruises on his arm last week."

"We went through the same thing last year with Lorenzo. The pressure on boys to join a gang — it's macho — the girls think it's really cool."

"What did you say to him?"

"We told him gangs are selfish — they only think about the gang. We used some thorn bird examples on how Nicole, Clark and Earl had helped others."

"Did it work out okay?"

"Yes, we pointed out several nice girls at church. That was the big winner. He's going steady with one of them now and has no interest in being in a gang."

"That's a good idea." Rosa Maria stood and moved the chair next to Carlos.

Upstairs, the clock neared midnight, Fran whispered something to Lewis and went down to the elevator.

Seeing her coming down the hallway, Earl jumped up and rushed to her side. "Have you heard anything?" he asked frantically.

The rest of the group hurried over and huddled around her.

"I don't have anything more to report other than the comment, that wasn't supposed to be mentioned by a young intern, 'Mr. Phillips has less that a 20 percent chance.'"

"Oh my," one of the women uttered softly.

"Guess it could be worse… we're waiting and praying. All of you might as well go home. We'll call if anything changes."

"Are you positive?" Renzo asked.

"Absolutely, Clark will need you when…" Fran broke down in tears.

"He's going to make it." Earl squeezed her tight. "I remember his last-second shot against Holy Redeemer; he didn't have a chance to make it, but he did.

"Yeah." Carlos shook his head. "I couldn't believe it."

"I'm staying here," Earl announced. "Come down if you have any news and I'll call everyone."

Upstairs, Abby remained steadfast at Clark's bedside. The morning shift arrived; Renzo replaced Earl at Clark's bedside.

At four o'clock, Carlos traded places with Renzo, and at eleven, Earl switched with him.

The pattern continued over the next several days.

***

"You wouldn't believe it, Carmen; I've never seen Jake so mad. He stomped around Angelo like he was going to kill him, and kept shouting, 'How many times did I tell you…? How many times did I tell you?' He put a real scare into him. And then, heading for his chair, Jake stopped for a moment, turned, and started again. 'If Clark dies, every goddamn federal agent in the country will be down our throat. Jesus Christ…' He kicked the table leg; I thought he'd broken it. Finally, Tony grabbed him by the arm and pulled him aside to calm him down."

"How did Angelo react?"

"He just sat there and took it. There was nothing he could say; anything would have made it worse. If he'd stood up, I'm sure Jake would have decked him."

"I'd liked to have been a mouse in the corner to see all of that."

Sipping on a small glass of Drambuie, Blackie leaned back in the worn booth. "Any thoughts or impressions from your probe of Clark's buddies?"

"Hmm… two or three… Renzo Ruccitti and Carlos Montes are local guys. They went to Holy Redeemer and U of D. There's nothing special about them; they work hard and are regular church goers. Our bankers say they pay their bills on a timely basis and their debt levels are normal. There's nothing in their backgrounds to suggest they would be involved in anything devious… they're not that type."

"How about Ted Moomau?"

"Now, there's a different animal — a hothead. Hearsay has him as a gypsy from Seattle. I've not been able…"

Blackie cut him off. "I know you've not been able to verify that."

Carmen stared anxiously. "How'd you know?"

"No one can verify anything about them. Gypsies have their own closed culture."

"Huh, no wonder I received the same blank look whenever I asked about him."

"Anything else you learned about Moomau?"

"He's engaged to an MD at Wayne State… but that's it."

"That's a strange combination, but… who knows nowadays."

"Should I keep checking on them?"

"Give your full attention to Ted… someone knows something," Blackie told Carmen with an air of a man in command. "I know Jake will ask about him; he's our only potential national connection."

"Okay… how about the women we talked about earlier?"

"I'm not positive, yet. All three are strong women, so they're still suspects." He stroked his five o'clock shadow. "Maybe I should say, *very* strong women; each with her own agenda — Caroline Schaffer is concerned about the welfare of young women, Nicole Weatherspoon is into community stuff in general, and Abby Thompson… shit, she's hot as hell. I don't see her getting into anything like closing our blind pigs. Besides, she's gone back to Philly."

Pausing like he'd struck another thought, Blackie's lips parted. "Now there's a challenge." He imagined being alone with any one of them and laughed. "Find me a mistress who has the looks of any of those women and a brain to match."

"Oh, that reminds me, Boss." A sheepish look spread over Carmen's face. "When I was going over Joey's calendar, I saw a note that Vicky called. I checked the area code. It was from Oklahoma."

"Jesus Christ!" Blackie nearly jumped out of the booth. "When? Was there a message?"

"It looked like 'come back' or something like that, I'm not positive."

"When was that?"

"Ah… maybe three months ago."

"Shit. Get me his calendar."

"Right now?"

"Hell yes." Blackie took a sip of his drink. *Geez, I miss her. I should have let her know she was more than a mistress.*

***

Seeing Carmen step back into the room, Blackie shouted, "Hurry up… give me the calendar. What month is the note on?"

Rushing past the empty chairs, Carmen held out the calendar. "Here it is, May."

Blackie grabbed it, read the note, picked up the extension phone, and called the number. Tapping the table with his index finger, he waited patiently for someone to answer, and then left a message. "It's the number for the Cherokee Nation where she works. I'll keep calling her."

Blackie downed the last of his Drambuie and slid the empty glass across the table. Carmen grabbed it, went to the bar, refilled it, and sat it in front of Blackie. "Where to now, Boss?"

"I guess we're back to Ted." He paused, his brain whirling, deep in thought. "I keep thinking about Jake's comment, 'dig deep, dig some more, turn over every stone, and dig some more.' There has to be something more… something obvious, what are we missing?"

Carmen shrugged, not having a clue how to respond to Blackie's thoughts.

"Okay, let's go back to that early morning when they hit our places. Carmen, get out a pad."

His new lackey quickly had a pad and pen in hand.

"Listen for a minute." Blackie's mind slipped into high gear. "They hit our ten most profitable blind pigs at the same time. Not one of our police officers knew about the bust until it happened. Each of the ten blind pigs had just been newly remodeled." He took a long sip and drew his brows together in puzzlement. "Arrest warrants included seventy-five or so capos." Looking up at Carmen, he paused. "What am I missing?"

"I-I can't think of a thing."

"There has to be something else."

Carmen's mind wandered aimlessly, hoping he might come up with an intellectual gem. "They didn't indict any lieutenant or anyone in the upper circles."

"Right." Blackie felt the answer was near. "And, why was that?" he asked rhetorically. "Because they didn't have the goods on us," Blackie answered. "Okay Carmen, write these points down:

- How'd they know these were our most profitable blind pigs?

- How'd they know the addresses?

- How'd they know which ones were open?

- Why did they hit only the newly remodeled ones?

- How'd they get the goods on that many capos?

- And, why weren't they able to come up with enough evidence to indict anyone in the top tier?"

"Wow boss, how'd you come up with all that?"

Blackie smiled, not wanting to embarrass his new assistant. "Have these typed up on a page and make five copies for my next meeting with Jake."

***

Trying to stay awake after a week in the hospital rotation, Renzo paced gingerly around the hospital room. Stubbing his toe on the bedpost, he staggered forward, then caught himself on the handrail, just a foot away from Clark's chest. He gathered himself, leaned over the wires and tubes, and spoke in an elevated tone, "Goddamn it Clark, I'm tired of pussyfooting around. I remember when you pulled that shot out of your ass; I'm not going to remember you as someone dying in bed." He grabbed Clark's hand and squeezed hard. "Goddamn it, open your eyes."

Clark lay motionless.

Renzo shouted, "Goddamn, pull one out of your ass — open your eyes!"

Clark's body twitched, catching Renzo's attention. He gently shook Clark's arm. "Clark, listen to me, do it, pull another one out... you can do it."

An eyelid shuttered, opened, and closed.

"Clark," he shouted, louder than before. "Open your eyes!"

Clark cracked an eye open, then the other one slowly, as if he was prying it apart.

"Blink if you can hear me, Clark."

Gradually his right eye opened and closed.

"You're going to make it... you're going to make it," Renzo shouted. Hustling to the door, he flung it open and hollered down the hallway. "Nurse... nurse, hurry, he snapped out of it."

***

Ten days later, Clark lay half asleep thinking how lucky he'd been — a dislocated right arm, two breaks in the left arm, a broken right hip, and a broken femur and tibia in his left leg — his internal injuries were on the mend.

Opening his eyes, he glanced at Abby. She looked far worse than him, exhausted from worry and hours on end at his bedside. She nodded, trying not to fall asleep.

"Abby," Clark whispered softly.

She jumped up, as if on high alert.

Clark's lips formed a partial grin and he motioned her closer.

She rushed to his bedside and bent close. "Yes, dear," she said, with affectionate anxiety.

He smiled affectionately and winked. "Want to have sex?"

She pulled back. "Clark… I can't believe you said that."

He laughed.

"You rat fink."

"Well then, pack your bag and go home. You need your rest… probably more than me."

"I want to stay a little longer…"

He cut her off. "Abby, please…"

She pushed her oily hair aside. "Guess you're right. I haven't done my hair in a week."

"Go on… get out of here."

"Okay." She grabbed her toothbrush, stuffed her clothes in an overnight bag, walked over and gave him a passionate kiss. "There, that's all the sex you're getting."

"Better than nothing," he quipped, as he watched her sashay out.

Feeling better, Clark thought about the strange way in which their relationship had evolved. *I fell for her the first time we met; it was like a fairytale come true. We did everything together — we were a perfect fit — then she told me she was working for the mob. Damn! She'd been pumping me for every piece of information I had. How could I have been so dumb? Before her, I'd never uttered a word out of line. Huh, now she's back from Philadelphia and we're in love. Geez, I love her.* He dozed off.

"Mr. Phillips… Mr. Phillips," a nurse said. "You have a telephone call. Do you want to take it?"

"Yeah… I guess." He looked at the cast on his broken arm and the sling holding his right arm. "I can hold the phone if you can plug it into the jack for me."

"Sure, no problem."

She plugged in the telephone, dialed, and hung up. The phone rang almost instantaneously. She picked it up. "Are you calling for Clark Phillips?" Following an unconscious nod, she tucked the phone between his sling and cheek. "Go ahead."

"Hello," he responded automatically. "This is Clark Phillips."

"Are you going to be okay?" a soft, sweet voice asked.

"Ah… yes," he replied, hesitating with a sense of apprehension.

"That's good."

He didn't respond.

"You don't remember me, do you?"

"Your voice sounds familiar… things are still a little foggy."

"That's only natural from the ordeal you've gone through."

"I'm sorry…" He curled his brow. "Who are you…? How'd you know what I went through?"

"We met some time ago for breakfast at the Side Street Café in Grosse Pointe."

"Oh yes, you had checked me out for a future assignment…" His mind whirled. "You were going to call me when you need me... I hope that doesn't mean now?"

"No, no. I won't need you for some time. Things are falling in place… it won't be until…" She stopped short. "I'm making sure you'll be back on the job by… the beginning of next year."

"January 1 is my goal."

"Good, that's all I need to know."

"Could you tell me anything about…?"

She cut him off. "I've got to go now. I'll call when I need you."

"Wait." Hearing a dial tone, he called to the nurse waiting in the hallway. "I'm finished."

***

"I like your questions, Blackie." Jake glanced at the others. "Finally, someone has gotten us off dead center." He leaned back in his swivel rocker and turned. "Well… Tony?"

"Excellent framework." As usual the old man's fingers curled the fringe on the back of his head. "It moves us to think beyond the obvious."

After his chewing-out at the last meeting, Angelo was slow to respond. "I'll apply them to the Narduzzi killing, too."

"Yes," Tony agreed. "I'll do the same on my own for the YBI murders."

Jake gazed off into space, his mind spinning with new thoughts. "I want to walk through every possibility." He looked around the table. "Okay, who knew these blind pigs were our moneymakers?" he asked; his eyes piercing those of his underlings positioned around the table. "Angelo, what do you think?"

The suave, debonair man rubbed his five o'clock stubble. "None of the lackeys knew; someone in mid-management knew… they could have spilled the beans."

"Why?" Jake straightened his back. "Is there a stoolie out there?"

Tony's frown rolled off his face. "I don't think so. These guys have been in the organization for years. We've never had a problem with any of them… not one."

"Huh, let's go on to the addresses. Other than the guys we've mentioned, who else knew?" Jake studied each man.

Blank faces looked back at him.

Jake's finger circled around the group.

"Tony."

"Angelo."

"Blackie."

Hum… maybe Ricciuti?"

Heads snapped Blackie's way.

"Renzo Ricciuti… the contractor on all the projects, and one of Clark Phillips' buddies.

Jake's face reddened. "So he knew… that means Phillips knew and all of his buddies… who knows where the list ends?"

"Phillips runs a pretty tight ship," Tony interjected. "I'd doubt if the word went beyond his immediate team."

"Agree." Blackie nodded.

"Let's move on to the next point, how would they know which ones were open?" Jake's eyes roamed the table. "Blackie."

The newcomer to the *power group* eased off his large horn-rim, black sunglasses, and laid them on the table. "Ted Moomau and Caroline Schaffer ran the apartment building where the whores live. They had to know who's working where and when."

Jake twisted his head. "And, they are Clark Phillips' friends."

"You got it." A smile grew on Blackie's face then faded away. "Caroline Schaffer is a stripper at the Sax Club; Phillips banged her for a couple of years."

"Jesus Christ!" Jake exclaimed, his frustration showing for the first time. "And they hit the newly remodeled blind pigs, because…"

"That's the ones they knew about," the group interrupted in unison.

"Thanks," Jake responded, sounding jovial in an effort to hide his anxiety. "Since all of you are so smart, how did they obtain direct testimony, as cited in the indictments, from so many capos?"

No one raised a hand.

"And, how is it that not one lieutenant got indicted?"

Blackie picked up his sunglasses and twirled them once, twice, and again. "They bugged a place where all of the capos are!" he spouted.

"And, where might that be?" Jake asked, his tone sharp.

"Tony."

"Angelo."

"Blackie."

He stared at Blackie, looked away, and glanced back. "Blackie."

Blackie folded his sunglasses and laid them on the table. "We talked about all of Clark's buddies, except Carlos Montes."

"Yeah," Angelo interjected. "Buy American."

Blackie's smiled broadened, like he'd caught a big fish. "The used car dealer where we buy our cars for the capos… they talk in the cars…" Blackie's eyes glittered with a suppressed sense of accomplishment. "Maybe he bugged our cars… the bastard could have double-crossed us. It's a scam… Phillips screwed us… his cronies were part of it — Ricciuti, Moomau, Montes — they set us up!"

Jake sneered. "Bastards!"

"How could they have pulled off such a scam?" Tony asked.

Nodding to himself, Blackie smirked. "Nicole Weatherspoon… she has the smarts and the knowhow!"

CHAPTER ELEVEN

THE DETROIT NEWS
August 4, 1983

DAVIS FAMILY GANG INDICTED

The fate of the Davis Family Gang (DFG) was sealed today when the federal government unveiled a 57-count indictment for drug trafficking and tax evasion. Through the efforts of an undercover agent, the DEA used audio and video surveillance equipment to record a high-level meeting of city drug kingpins, and seize documents and telephone records regarding the group's internal operations.

Regarded as one of the top ten heroin operations in North America, the DFG's drug network stretched across four continents, and provided high-grade heroin, cocaine, and marijuana to multiple cities in the United States.

All members of the leadership team, except Reggie Davis, were placed in the Wayne County Jail this morning. The whereabouts of Reggie Davis, the gang leader is unknown.

***

Local officials of the DEA and FBI crowded around the walls of the small conference room atop the McNamara Building. Clark's team filed in and took their regular positions around the table.

Hearing Kimberly's high heels pounding down the hallway, the entire group stood. FBI Agent-in-Charge, Clifford McGill raised a hand, silencing the group.

Kimberly stepped into the doorway.

Hoots and hollers accompanied loud rhythmic applause.

Caught off guard, Kimberly's cheeks glowed rosy red. She placed her hands over her face and wiped away a tear.

"Here's to our heroine." Pag raised his coffee mug. "A new Detroit thorn bird!"

"No… no." She shook her head forcefully. "It's not about me… it was the team."

McGill smiled broadly. "A team yes, but as we all know a team's success is measured by the leader's ability. You're the one… you made it happen!" He stepped in front of her and extended his hand. "And to you young lady, our sincere congratulations for a job well done."

Cheers filled the room as he finished and exited, "Here… here!"

The visitors mingled around her for a while, shaking Kimberly's hand and extending their personal regard, then gradually left the room.

Earl rolled his chair to the vacant space at the head of the table. "Well… I guess you're stuck with me for the time being."

"I hope that's not long," Pag joked and rotated toward Kimberly. "I never heard an explanation for the heavy breathing on the one tape."

"And you're not going to."

Hearing her tone, Pag laughed, knowing he'd pushed the issue as far as he could go.

"Kimberly." Her head swiveled to Dick Woodson's waving hand. "Being a new undercover agent, I'm wondering when your stress level was the highest?"

"All the time," she jested and paused for a moment, collecting her thoughts. "Hmm… I think there were two times… the night before I was to meet Ricky for the first time was awful, I didn't sleep a wink… and then sitting there with that beam of light shooting down… maybe it wasn't stress, but I was really embarrassed."

"How about when you were talking with him?" Bennett asked.

"No… he's a kid with lots of money and little experience. I was in control all the time."

Veronica eased up to the table. "Kimberly, I want you to know that the entire DEA team thought you were terrific, and they wanted me to extend their personal congratulations!"

"Thank you, that's nice of them." She sucked in a deep breath and turned to Earl. "Well, Mr. Chairman, what's next on our agenda?"

"Cutting off the mafia's next move," he responded, without hesitation.

***

Detroit Free Press

September 3, 1983

Section F

NORTHSIDE STRIP CLUB FIREBOMBED

Overnight the upper floor of the Sax Club was totally destroyed by a firebomb. Arriving at 11:35 pm Friday night, firemen found the rear portion of the second floor engulfed in flames.

Firefighters were able to limit the fire to the upper floor, but the owner indicated water damage on the first floor would force the club to close for some time.

***

Earl sat patiently, in the head chair — beads of moisture covered his shiny head. Waiting for the team to assemble, he pulled a handkerchief from his back pocket and swiped at the dampness. *I met with the guys in the poker club about the firebombing. To a man, they knew it was a warning; fortunately, poker on the first Friday had been cancelled because of Clark's injuries. Thank God, Carlos had already debugged the cars and the Chief had gotten a new search warrant, so Renzo could clean up Narduzzi's place. First, it was Clark and now the rest of us — they've figured it out — there's certainly no way they could connect Nicole to the bust of the blind pigs… or was there?*

"Good morning, Boss."

Earl looked up; his thoughts shifted to the task ahead. "Get out of here, Pag," objecting to the Boss reference. "I'm just chairing the meetings for another month or so."

"Sitting at the head spot, you look like the boss to me," Pag jested.

"Good morning, Boss," Kimberly announced, as she walked in and filled her mug.

Before Earl could say a word, "Good morning, Boss," echoed, as each team member walked in.

Realizing it was a setup; Earl waited until everyone had their coffee and gathered around the table. "Okay, who started this nonsense?"

Figures pointed to the next person around the table.

"I got it, and thanks… I guess." Earl smiled broadly. "Before we hear the update on Pony Down today, I have a question for Pag."

The graduate of Denby High eased closer to the table.

"After Clark was hit, did you receive a call from your old little league shortstop, Blackie Giardini, saying it was a big mistake?"

"Yes, Blackie called and wanted to know how he was." Pag spoke matter-of-factly. "It was supposed to be a minor incident… a scare tactic. Someone screwed up!"

"Did you get a call after the firebombing of the Sax Club?"

"No, why?"

"Just double-checking to see if it was intentional. Any thoughts from the rest of you?"

"Clearly, it was a message for all of us," Bennett announced.

Heads nodded, "Absolutely," the others agreed.

"I think I ought to submit a request to Clifford to provide FBI protection for the Riccuti's, Montes's, and Moomau. Anyone have a problem with that?"

Again, he received affirmative nods.

"I'll talk with him as soon as we're finished." Earl looked at DEA agent Bennett. "Frank, are you on tap to share the latest on Pony Down?"

"Guess, you noticed I had my folder open."

Earl nodded.

"The turf war has gone bananas. Last week, rivals of the Curry Family, got Buttrom involved in an act of supreme contempt and disrespect. LeRoy's two-year-old nephew was kidnapped and held for a $100,000 ransom. The Currys were incensed and our office got a personal call from Buttrom *telling us to stay out* of the investigation."

"I don't think so," Pag interjected.

"You're right." Bennett reiterated. "Our director said that wasn't possible. Buttrom was hot, and said, 'Striking a blow at the organization was one thing, but attacking a family member was a different matter.' As you know from the story in the paper, Walter and one of his henchmen opened fire on one of the kidnappers at a police-monitored drop-off, botching the ransom drop."

"Anything new?" Kimberly asked, anxiously.

"Buttrom placed a $250,000 bounty on the heads of the kidnappers." Bennett paused, holding the group in suspense. "The kid was dropped off, unharmed, at a McDonald's last night."

***

"What are we talking about today?" Lewis asked, as he cranked up the rented hospital bed they'd placed in their living room.

Clark pursed his lips and looked his dad squarely in the eye. "Alex Karras."

"Alex Karras… is he in the news again?"

"No, I'm interested in knowing how the department handled his case."

"Why?" Lewis pull a Chippendale closer. "That was back in '63… twenty years ago."

"I know." Clark brushed back his unusually long, uncut sandy hair with his right hand — the arm finally out of the sling. "I'd like to know the extent of department involvement?"

"Are you just interested?" Lewis anticipated the answer. "Or, is it a job-related question?"

Clark gave him a smirky smile. "Job related."

"Wanta talk about it, now?" Lewis asked, hoping the answer would be yes.

"Hmm… no, maybe later. Do you need to do a little digging?"

"No, I lived it… I can give you the facts right now."

"Okay." Clark grabbed a pencil and picked up the yellow pad from his lap. "Fire away."

"Alex Karras was a first-round pick of the Lions in… 1958, and played for them until 1970, except for '63 when he was suspended by the NFL for a year."

"He was a big guy, wasn't he?"

"Big and tough. He learned to play football in a parking lot near his home in Gary, Indiana — he didn't wear pads — became a four-time Indiana All-Stater. At the University of Iowa, he won the Outland Trophy as the outstanding lineman in the country."

"And with the Lions?"

"Big… 280, he was big everything — was a defensive tackle on the 1960s All-Decade NFL team.

"So how did he go astray?"

"Huh…" Lewis laughed. "He was always astray… he was in and out of the doghouse with coach Evashevski at Iowa. He fussed with the Lions' coaches. I don't know how many times it was rumored he'd quit."

"He must have been a real character."

"Hmm, yes and no…" Lewis flipped each hand in a different direction. "In some ways, I really liked him; he was a great player. But, too independent for things back then — his ego was bigger than he was — no one was going to tell Alex Karras how to do anything."

"Is that how he got sideways with the NFL?"

"Those are some of the reasons… you have to remember, these were the '60s, things were hot and rocking. The NFL was coming of age; in 1962 the NFL signed its first contract with CBS. Suddenly, TV was a new venue for gambling."

"A *new venue*, what's that mean?"

"People could analyze the upcoming game, check the point spread, determine who and how much they'd bet, call their bookie, and watch the game. Everyone in the city was betting on the games… baseball too. So it's only natural for a lot of big-name athletes to be involved — Pete Rose, Denny McLain, Paul Hornung. It was nothing for your mother and me to have dinner in the Grecian Gardens and see Alex Karras and Lions players Wayne Walker, and 'Night Train' Lane, each down a platter of lamb chops before heading to the back room…"

"Something happening back there?"

"There was a gambling table for high-rollers — top mafia guys, entertainment figures, politicians, and some of our cops — you name it, they all stopped by on a regular basis."

"Did police officials know about it?"

"Hah, everyone knew, from Police Commissioner George Edwards on down."

"So, how does this connect with the NFL?"

"Pete Rozelle, the new commissioner, knew gambling was a pervasive problem in the NFL. His predecessor had placed a cadre of ex-FBI agents in all of the league cities to, as he called it, keep tabs of 'misconduct.' In my opinion, it was all about gambling, and Rozelle needed a big name or two to make a point and establish himself."

"So he waited."

"Right, in early January 1963, Commissioner Edwards notified the Lions and ten days later NFL authorities noted the police had seen Lions players on numerous occasions in the company of Vito and Anthony Giacalone."

"Let me think." Clark raised his hand, for his dad to stop. "At the time, Vito was the Mafia Underboss and Anthony was the Street Boss."

"Yes, you get an 'A' in history today. Unfortunately for him, a few days later, Karras confessed on the 'Brinkley Journal' that he had bet on NFL games."

"Geez, how dumb can a guy be?

"Back to his ego… that's all Rozelle needed. He'd landed the best defensive player in the league. He fined the other guys caught at the gambling table $1,950 each — John Gordy, Gary Lowe, Joe Schmidt, Wayne Walker, and Sam Williams — and moved on to Paul Hornung. Now, he had the top defensive and offensive players in the fold. Both got suspended for a year."

"That's all there was to it?" he asked.

"How much time do you have?"

Pointing to the casts on his legs and other arm, Clark laughed. "Two months."

"Okay, here's as Paul Harvey would say, 'The rest of the story.'" Lewis paused, collecting his thoughts. "I'll give you two more pieces that came to light in the ensuing investigation. After that you need to get some rest."

"Fair enough."

"First, it was learned that Karras was co-owner of the Lindell A.C. Bar, with Jim and John Butsicaris." The old man slowed. "It so happens, the two brothers were under surveillance by the FBI because of their association with gamblers and bookmakers. It was the sports bar of the time, athletic mementoes covered the walls — baseball bats, helmets, gloves, photos of the Lions, Tigers, and Red Wings — opposing players in town most always ended up there. The Lions pressured Karras to sell his interests in the club known for its backroom gambling. He refused and announced he would not give up his $50,000 investment without a fight... of course, he lost."

"Sounds like his ego again."

Dad nodded his agreement. "They also learned about the party bus that had been under surveillance for some time. The Giacalone brothers — Tony, Jack, and Billy Jack — used it all over town. One time, the police followed Billy Jack, who was at the wheel, to the Sindbad strip club down by the River. He pulled the party bus up close, scooped up the barmen and all of the entertainers, and drove off into the night."

"And nobody did a thing?"

"No, that's the way it was. The bus was like a moving gambling hall. It had a loaded bar, card tables, loungers, plush carpeting, and bunk beds in the back."

"Sounds like a wide-open whorehouse, too."

"You got that right." Dad belly laughed. "Anyway, they returned on the bus from a pre-season football game in Cleveland. An FBI surveillance crew saw Karras and another Lions player climb into the bus for the three-hour ride back to Detroit. The Commissioner had all he needed."

"I guess so." Clark laid his pencil and pad down. "How about we talk about Denny McLain next time?"

"Next time." His dad chuckled. "And maybe, you can tell me where all of this is headed."

"Maybe." Clark pulled up the sheet and closed his eyes.

***

Clark waited in the hospital bed for his dad to finish his Corona out on the back porch. It'd been three weeks since the hit and run, and he was gaining strength. With casts still on both legs, he knew mobility was still six weeks off. That'd be the beginning of the basketball season for the Pistons and he'd have to follow up on the tip from his very reliable T-3 informant. *Should he tell his dad who he was going to investigate? Why not? Huh, he'll probably be pissed off and say, "no way."* He picked up a glass of water and sipped on the straw. *I can't believe all the things mom told me that Abby did during my hospital stay. I love her so much.*

Clark heard the slider door open and close.

"Can I bring you a couple of chocolate chips on my way in?"

"That'd be great, Dad."

Lewis carried in a small plate filled with cookies. "I brought a couple extras for me." He stuffed one in his mouth and glanced at Clark, posed like a little kid waiting to hear about his hero. "Looks like you're ready to hear about Denny McLain."

"Yes, I am." Clark lifted a pencil. "When I was a kid, I couldn't wait for his turn to come around in the rotation; he was a great pitcher."

"Well, he wasn't always great. Early in his career, you never knew which Denny McLain would show up. In his first game in the majors, at the age of nineteen, he held the White Sox to one run and hit a home run. Wow, I thought to myself, we really have something here. Next thing I know he's back in the minors."

"Did he have an attitude?"

"An *attitude*? He made Karras look like small potatoes.

"But he had talent…"

"Yeah, and lots of it." Dad cut Clark off. "He was a kid with a great fastball; unfortunately, he was a thrower, not a pitcher. The Tigers hired Johnny Sain as their pitching coach; he knew everything about pitching and the psychology of pitching, hoping he could teach Denny."

"I recall those years. He won thirty games in 1968. Dizzy Dean was there to congratulate him because he was the last one to win thirty games."

"Now there was a pair — two thirty-game winners — you never knew what they'd say or do." His dad chuckled, and grabbed the last cookie. "Enough of that."

"Wait, tell me about McLain's foot injury."

"Okay, this is the last one."

Clark winked. "Okay… I got it."

"In 1970, *Sports Illustrated* and *Penthouse* both published articles about McClain's involvement with bookmaking. That's when several sources alleged the foot injury he sustained during the '67 season was from a mobster stomping on his foot, because of McLain's failure to pay off on a bet. After that more and more came out about his gambling and bookmaking activities. In 1970, Commissioner Kuhn suspended him for three months. Then he was suspended by the Tigers and before that ended, the Commissioner suspended him for the rest of the season for carrying a gun on the team plane."

"Sounds like he wouldn't let things end." Clark moved back to his agenda. "How much involvement did the Detroit police department have?"

"I'm not sure… mostly it was the digging of the media. And Denny, himself."

"What do you mean?"

"It was his mouth; he was brash and outspoken. You never knew what he'd say… one time he was criticizing the fans, then he was on his teammates. I wait, even now, to read something new about him… he's a loose cannon."

"So the key in these cases was the league's involvement."

Lewis doubled-nodded. "Yeah, I never thought about it that way… but, without the Commissioner's support, you're a fish swimming upstream — you'd need a powerful criminal case." Lewis paused. "Remember, the bigger the name, the greater the public support."

"I thought it was, 'the bigger the name, the harder they fall.'"

"Only in storybooks." Lewis looked Clark in the eye. "Who are you considering?"

"Between the two of us?"

"Sure, of course."

Playing a game, Clark looked around as if someone might be listening. "Okay, I'll say his name; no comments, okay?"

"Okay, okay, who is it?"

"Isiah Thomas."

CHAPTER TWELVE

Jake took a sip of Jack Daniels and propped his tennis shoes on the rim of the metal table. *Life is good. I have a wonderful wife. The kids are either in college or have already graduated. I've been blessed in my career. Working for my dad set me on the right course. Who could have imagined that I would own numerous companies and have extensive real estate holdings?*

Smiling to himself, he thought about the day. *Guess my workouts in the weight room and extra practice on the court paid off. I had it all going today... beat the thirty-year-old in straight sets with my overpowering serves and precision baseline shots. Not bad for a guy in his early fifties.*

"Here's to the Hillcrest Country Club tennis champion." His advisor, Tony Minelli, sitting to his right, raised a glass of Crown Royal.

Jake clinked his glassed. "I'll drink to that."

"You made it look easy: it seemed like you barely broke a sweat."

"It may have appeared that way…" An expression of pleasure filled Jake's face. "I learned that from my old man when I was selling cars at his dealership." A reflective grin of his father's mentoring flickered across his face. "Never let the other guy know what's going on in your mind. If you're prepared and work hard, you don't have to worry about failure."

"Your father was a great man; I learned a lot from him, too."

"And, he from you." Jake downed his drink and glanced over his shoulder toward center court. "Who's in the women's finals?"

Tony raised his eyebrows; a partial grin grew into a smile.

Jake scowled, *what's with him? He never smiles like that.* "I asked a simple question, what's with the shit-eating smile?"

Tony motioned over Jake's shoulder. "See for yourself."

Jake moved slowly, as if reluctant to follow his adviser's suggestion, and eased his chair toward the court.

Tony held back his thoughts and watched Jake.

Jake shook his head, as if his vision had blurred, and turned back to Tony. "Who the hell is she?"

"Every guy at the club has been asking that."

"Tony, what the hell do you know about her?" Jake spun his chair back to center court, taking in her tan, slender legs, her white shorts shaped by a firm ass, and the half-button white top that provided a tempting peek. "Jesus Christ, Tony, tell me about her." He motioned to the waiter, stationed for him in the corner, and shouted, "Another round, make it a double."

The young man nodded and hustled to the bar.

Jake turned back to center court; his eyes glued to the well-trimmed, firm body.

A grinning Tony leaned closer. "So, what do you think?"

"Shit, you know what I think. I've never seen a woman with such perfect proportions, slender yet, so… shit, who is she?"

The young waiter placed a brimming glass in front of each of the men.

Without taking his eyes off her, Jake grabbed his glass of Jack Daniels. "Tell me, Tony, what do you know about her?"

"Well… let me… see," he started in a drawn-out fashion."

Jake motion for him to speed up. "Get on with it, Tony, get to the point."

"Okay… okay," he savored the moment to enjoy a rare time teasing Jake. She's Amanda Howard; she joined the club last spring and paid cash for the year."

"Cash… that's interesting." Jake flipped his hand, motioning for Tony to go on.

"She gave two addresses on the application; one in Palo Alto, California, and one in the Millender Center at 555 Brush Street."

"Down by the Renaissance Center… that's a high rent district."

"High rent is right, you can see the river and downtown from every apartment." Tony paused, making Jake squirm before putting out more information. "She's thirty-one… that's all that was on the application."

"I want to know more." Jake set his glass on the table and motioned to the waiter for another round. "Call Peter Milino in L.A.; remind him that he owes me one."

"For…"

Jake waved him off. "Just tell him that."

"Okay." His adviser pulled out a small black book and made a note.

Jake propped his tennis shoes on the edge of the table again, and leaned back, "I'm going to check out her backhand."

Tony held back a laugh. "Just her backhand?"

***

Pag parked and locked his car on a side street, walked with head lowered to the corner and turned right. Glancing at the old storefronts, a grin parted his lips. He passed the hardware store where his dad had sent him on weekends, the butcher shop where he'd picked up his mom's order on the way home from school, and the pharmacy with the soda fountain — *they made the best green rivers and chocolate malts!*

At the corner, he paused for the longest moment before opening the door of the neighborhood bar. Stepping inside, he glanced at the familiar digs — three pool tables and a dart board off to the right; on the left, tables scattered helter-skelter. As always, sitting in the elevated booth, beyond the dimly lit serving area, his high school buddy, Blackie Giardini.

Pag pushed the tables aside from the night before, clearing a walkway to the steps leading to the booth.

"Morning," his old friend greeted him. Pointing to the chair at the end of the booth, Blackie removed his sunglasses and placed them in his black sport coat pocket. "How's my old catcher doing?"

Pag's smiled, remembering the good ol' days. *Winning the eastside little league baseball championship was as vivid as ever. I hit two home runs and Blackie drove in the winning run.* "Those were the days, huh, Blackie."

"A lot of water over the dam." Blackie's piercing stare held him in check. "What can I do for you?"

Pag hung his head and spoke in a soft voice. "I need a personal loan."

Blackie stayed focused, didn't blink. "You know, they don't come cheap, even for a friend."

"I know… Dorothy's health has declined; she requires a kidney dialysis machine. It's going to cost us big time."

Having dated her most of the way through high school, Blackie smiled affectionately. "How much will it require?"

"I'm not positive… If I consolidate all of our funds, I'll be short, hmm… maybe… $20… $25,000."

"That much!" Blackie seemed a little surprised. "When would you need it?"

With his hopes on the rise, Pag released a sigh. "Maybe $10,000 now and the rest in the weeks ahead."

Reflecting on their friendship, Blackie gazed off into the darkness. "15 percent."

"15 percent!" Pag gasped, not expecting that amount. "After all these years… Blackie, I was hoping for something closer to 5 percent."

Blackie read him the script. "5 to 10 percent for family and friends, 20 to 25 percent for those with mafia debt, and 15 percent for those given special treatment."

Pag bristled; his face reddened. "Special treatment…?"

Slowly picking up the folder to his right, Blackie read the name on the label — Joseph "Pag" Pagnazzi, 4251 East Maple Street. That's you, right?"

"Shit." Pag's shoulder sagged; his hopes sunk with his heart.

Pulling a sheet from the folder, he looked Pag squarely in the eye. "Gambling debt at Kelly's, below the barber shop and pet store — $17,100, at Ralph's another $14,300, and at Ruby's $6,500."

"They're all independent gambling places," he declared; his blood pressure rising. "How did you obtain those?"

"We're the collection agency for anything over ten grand," Blackie stated, matter-of-factly. "I tossed in Ruby's for good measure… I'm positive you wouldn't want Dorothy to see these." He slid three pictures of Pag in bed banging prostitutes.

"How'd you…" He paused, knowing the mob regularly took pictures of clients.

"I like this one the best." He read the woman's first name on the back of the picture and tossed it to the end of the table. "Looks like Sherry gives great blow jobs!"

Pag collapsed against the back of the chair.

"So, let's see what we have." Blackie pulled out a pen and a sheet of paper and recorded the numbers. "$17,100 + $14,300 + $6,500 + $25,000 for treatment = $62,900… at 15 percent. Let's see, that's $9,435 in interest. Adding those two for this year, the total of $72,335… that's quite a tab."

Pag stared, his mind muddled; his anxiety grew, he was scared shitless.

"I'll round it off to $72,000 and… divided by twelve, you'll have payments of $1000 per month…" He paused, giving it more thought. "Hmm… so at the end of year one, you'll owe $60,000 plus 15 percent for the next year, that'll leave a balance of $69,000 for year two."

"That's adding interest on top of interest… I'll never be able to payoff the loan."

"15 percent on the unpaid balance," Blackie said casually.

"Jesus Christ, Blackie…"

"Hold on," he cut him off. "Or… I could waive the monthly fee, with the understanding that I'd reduce the $72,000 amount by $24,000 each time you help me out. Three little favors."

"Goddamn, Blackie, you know I can't do that."

"Hey, it sounds a lot better than explaining Sherry's picture to Dorothy."

Pag tried to come up with a rational argument, but… could only plead his case. "You wouldn't do that, after all these years."

"Shit man, you were the one sitting on the chair, stripped from the waist down." Blackie shot from the hip. "I didn't tell you to spread your legs."

"Jesus Blackie, we're friends."

Blackie turned the tables, playing on his words. "You're right… and friends help each other out."

***

Abby handed Clark a slice of hot apple pie. "Remember the time you asked, 'could I have a slice of hot apple pie?'" She giggled, revealing her *perfect smile.* "I didn't understand…"

"Yeah, I could tell." He eased forward in the rental bed and sliced into the pie. "I couldn't believe it when the waitress at Marcus

Hamburgers sat that freshly baked apple pie in front of me... that's when our reunion started."

"You never took me to the derivation of the phrase."

Clark ducked the point. "An old family secret," he gleeked.

"I'm sorry if it was such a struggle for you..."

"No reason to rehash all of that..." Clark interrupted. "Down deep I wanted to be with you; it just took some time to work through the things that had happened."

"Me too, I still can't explain it. One day I'm giving Blackie Giardini information and the next day, I'm falling in love with you." Abby cocked her head to the side in an uneasy manner. "The worst time for me was that night I told you I was working for the mob. I wanted to hug and kiss you all over... you looked like you'd lost your best friend. I felt so bad."

She sniffled holding back a tear of joy.

"Okay, no rehashing." She changed the subject. "The women are really concerned... after seeing what the mafia did to you. They're afraid it's only the first step in their effort to *get even!*"

"*Get even...* You shouldn't have used that term," Clark interrupted.

"Why?"

"It'll probably elevate even more the nervousness of the women. We have to strike that phrase from our usage."

"Okay... but I'm concerned."

"Why? You weren't involved in the blind pig bust that night."

"Hmm, I don't think Blackie would agree. Maybe not that night, but if he ever sees me with you, he'll think I double-crossed him."

Clark hadn't thought of that possibility; he leaned his head back against the pillow. "Hmm."

"I'm coloring my hair black, letting it grow out, putting my contacts away, and starting to wear a pair of horn-rim dark glasses."

"You don't need to do that; besides, it may raise the anxiety of the women even more."

"I've been thinking about doing it anyway, so I don't think it'll be a big deal."

Clark thought further. "Nicole could be in the same position. Guess, Earl and I need to have a session."

"How should I handle this with them? Any advice?"

"I'd try to reassure Rosa Maria and Wendy. Since Renzo was able to remove the bugs from the blind pigs and Carlos got them out of the automobiles, I think the heat is off of them."

"You may think the heat is off them, but the women are still nervous as hell. You may have to find a way to protect their families, so everyone has some peace of mind.

"Hadn't thought of doing that. Maybe you're right.

"How about Laverne?"

"I'm concerned for her. We're all trying to find a gypsy connection. They might not wait for a solid link; they could beat up Ted and kidnap her."

***

Archbishop Dooley opened the door and motioned in Father Dom. *It was like walking back in time. An ornate framed painting of Pope John Paul II hung behind a large walnut desk. Gold inlay furniture and heavy red drapery hung against the dark wood paneling gave a sense of overpowering opulence.*

"Would you like a cup of tea?" the robed Archbishop asked as he walked slowly toward a small table in the corner.

"Yes, that would be nice." Father Dom settled in his usual position on the small loveseat across from the large-backed chair, with a coffee table between.

The Archbishop placed a tray with two cups and a pot of tea on the table. "Do you need anything in it?"

"No, black will be fine."

"Good." He filled two cups, took his position in *the chair*, and moved directly into his agenda. "I'm concerned with the growing number of complaints I'm receiving. Some of them may be frivolous, but others may require attention and we have no way to process them."

Not knowing the agenda, Father Dom nodded and took a sip.

"I was intrigued the other day by the fact the Detroit Public Schools had established a position and the Office of the Ombudsman. Do you know much about the concept?"

"Little more than was in the article. It comes from Sweden, where ombudsmen were given considerable latitude to investigate citizen complaints about the government."

"Correct." The Archbishop restated his thoughts. "It sounds like the school district will follow the same model to address the growing number of parental issues regarding the schools."

"Yes, I think it's a good move."

Encouraged by his support, the Archbishop pushed forward. "I like the concept too, but it seems we need something more."

Father Dom took a sip, waiting for further definition.

"Our internal structure is significantly different…" He paused a moment, straightening his robe. "There's not a viable way for issues to be addressed without entering into one of our formal procedures which often become quite complicated. I fear much goes on that is unreported."

"Based upon my experience, I'm in total agreement," he stated in a strong tone. "I believe in delegated authority, but with no limits or controls, it can lead to devious action."

"I was afraid you'd say that." The Archbishop seemed relieved. "I'm going to create an ombudsman position with expanded authority to investigate internal issues as well as those from our parishioners. How do you react to that?"

"I think it'd be a terrific idea and… it'd make an important statement."

"Based on your experience with the Mexican incident, I'd like for you to become our first ombudsman. Would you do that?"

"Yes, of course."

CHAPTER THIRTEEN

Running the team meeting like an old pro, Earl turned to Kimberly. "Want to update us on the Curry Brothers?"

A hint of nervousness caused a slight tremor in her voice. "We've divided our presentation into three segments. Frank will start out with some background info on them, Pag will talk about Johnny, and I'll close with some insights about Kathy Volsan, Johnny's girlfriend."

"I've heard about her." Raising his eyebrows, Earl cracked a pretentious grin. "That should be interesting."

Frank opened his file and cleared his throat. "The Curry Brothers have been running under the radar since 1978. While westside organizations, YBI and Pony Down have collected the headlines, the Currys have been equally successful on the eastside. Working under the tutelage of their father, Sam 'Sammy Mack' Curry, who gave them startup cash, they've functioned more like the mob than the other two — no headlines, no reported violence, no gang wars — they're a close-knit family at the top."

"That's an interesting perspective," said Earl about the mob reference. "I've not heard that analogy before." He popped his infectious smile. "I like it."

"Thanks… it came to me as an outsider. Each one knows his role; 'Sammy Mack' acting like the Godfather, Leonard 'Big Man' Curry working out front, Johnny 'Little Man' working behind the scenes, and their younger brother Rudell 'Boo' being groomed as a lieutenant."

Hearing Johnny's name mentioned, Pag shifted into gear. "No one can hold a candle to him; he has street savvy and knows how to make things happen… no one messes with him. He's slick, too; you'd never see Leonard or him on the nightly news. They keep a low public profile. To the contrary, if you were in Belle Isle some Sunday, you'll likely see Johnny drive by in a new Caddy wearing the *hottest threads."*

"Speaking of hot," Johnny's biggest catch might be Cathy Volsan, the *ghetto princess.* She's a twenty-year-old, drug-addicted diva who can have anyone she wants. The two have been dating for some time. Since she's Mayor Young's favorite niece, it's made him virtually untouchable. And when she wants action, she brings in her drug-dealing father, Willie Clyde Volsan, who buys off the police."

Pag tossed out a thought for good measure. "Sounds like they're all connected."

"That's the point." Frank mentioned, in his quiet voice. "Just like the mafia."

"How did they manage to stay out of the newspaper?" Veronica asked.

"They stick to their business, selling marijuana and more recently heroin. On the streets, their name is as big as any of the gangs."

Veronica leaned forward. "I'll be interested to learn how much they're bringing in."

"From the information I've been collecting, we may have to use a calculator," Kimberly suggested, in a jovial manner. "Hopefully, we'll have that information for our next update."

"Speaking of numbers, maybe Kimberly ought to update our new members on her twenty-two theory," Pag said in his normal antisocial nature toward her.

She gave him an 'oh, here we go again' glance.

Earl picked up on the logical aspect of his comment. "That's not a bad idea…" Earl's serious tone got everyone's attention. "I'm not sure how twenty-two fits into the mafia killings scheme of things, but there's no doubt in my mind there's some kind of connection. Go ahead, Kimberly."

She wrinkled her nose at Pag, *so there!*

"I've done a lot of digging into numerology… the more I learn, the more I believe in the connection. If nothing else makes sense, the most telling aspect is the four mob-related killings here that all occurred on the twenty-second day of the month, and forty other mafia killings across the country happened on the *twenty-second day of the month."*

"I agree," Earl chimed in. "Four murders in Detroit could be a coincidence or maybe some kind of copycat series, but there's no way forty-four killings across the nation could be a coincidence — *they're connected*!"

"Good point." Frank Bennett stroked his jaw. "Any ideas on how they might connect?"

"That's the sixty-four-thousand-dollar question."

Veronica spoke spontaneously, "Maybe it's some means of communication."

Heads bounced from her to Kimberly.

"*Communications?*" Kimberly's hand covered her mouth. "Yes, of course… the killings occur on the twenty-second and that way you know someone in our group was responsible for it."

"Our group?" Pag pleaded his innocence. "*Who's in our group?*"

Appearing deep in thought, Fitzpatrick ventured, "People who believe in the same thing."

"A cult or maybe members of an organization," Bennett added.

Nodding, Veronica smiled with enthusiasm. "Individuals that don't like the mafia."

"Hell, there are lots of people like that," Pag stated, as if dismissing the line of discussion.

Earl continued to probe. "Who would have the wherewithal? Or, the ability to pull it off?"

"I have it… well, at least, the process," Kimberly admitted, easing closer to the table. "Anti-mafia people in St. Louis read *The New York Times* on the 23rd and learn about a mafia person being killed there on the 22nd. The *same* anti-mafia people read the *Los Angeles Times* and learned someone killed a mafia person on the West Coast on the 22nd."

Fitzpatrick's reflective tone continued. "Someone has to be keeping score and sharing the information with other anti-mafia people across the country."

"Okay." Pag flipped a hand. "Let's say this type of communication is possible. Who are they? How are they connected? Why are they killing off Mafiosos?"

***

Arriving a few minutes late for their four o'clock meeting, Jake pulled up a chair across from Tony at Hillcrest's Nineteenth Hole. With a sigh of appreciation, he picked up the waiting glass of Jack Daniels ordered by his adviser. "Here's to you." He clinked Tony's glass of Crown Royal.

Tony nodded. "I think you have a winner," knowing Amanda was on Jake's mind.

"Well…?" he asked anxiously.

"Geez… relax, have a drink."

Leaning on the back legs of the chair, Jake took a slug and exhaled a long sigh. "Okay, I'm relaxed."

He'd never seen Jake conduct himself with such eager enthusiasm. Tony chuckled. "You're acting like a teenager…"

Jake cut him off. "So, tell me… what'd you find out?"

"Three things." Knowing Jake's keen interest, Tony took his time, enjoying the moment. "I followed up on her employer's phone number in L.A." Tony paused and took a sip.

Jake waved his hand. "Tony, I know you're putting me on. Let's hear it."

"Jesus Jake, if you weren't talking I would have been finished by now."

Taking a sip, Jake rolled his head.

"She's one of the top two or three models in L.A.… receives big bucks for making an appearance. Her list of clients is a mile long."

"And the guys… how about the guys?"

"There's a long list of suiters…"

"Any serious ones?" Jake cut him off.

Watching Jake's impatience grow, Tony downed his Crown Royal and motioned to the waiter for another round. "There's no one special… movie star, Dodger player, or Laker… zero!

"Hmm." Jake's interest grew.

"I called the number off her club application for Stanford University, too." Tony smiled, "Here's part of the list." He pulled out a sheet and read: "Graduated cum laude, with a 3.52 GPA, majored in economics, four varsity awards in tennis, All-Pacific Coast Conference tennis singles champion, and Homecoming Queen." He paused, reveling in his findings. "Want anything more?"

"I want to meet her." Jake licked his lips. "How do I meet her?"

"I thought you'd never ask." Tony finger-curled his gray fringe. "There are four women who play tennis Saturday. Two of them are connected to us; I'll give them a little spending money. The other one we'll play by ear. Maybe she'll leave early or go to the bathroom. Whenever there's an opening, you can move in."

***

Deep in conversation, the group didn't notice Laverne picked up a second bottle of Chianti and refilled their glasses. Two weeks after the firebombing, the women were still hyper as hell.

Wendy grabbed her glass and sucked down a slug. "I'm going bananas."

"We have to play it cool," Abby suggested, trying to hide her own anxiety.

"Easy for you to say, you don't have any kids," Wendy replied, in an abnormally sharp tone. "Sorry."

"No problem." Abby smiled, a forgiving smile. "There's so much going on. We're all up tight."

"Earl is doing everything he can. He has a surveillance team watching our house twenty-four hours a day," Wendy stated, her voice cracking with emotion. "There's an agent following Renzo all day, and one behind me when I take the kids to school… still, I'm afraid to go to the hair salon."

"I feel the same way." Rosa Maria took an unusually long sip of wine. "I'm scared to open a closet door."

"We just have to plow forward," Nicole said, her confidence spilling out.

"I don't know if I should tell the kids or not." Rosa Maria expressed nervous apprehension. "Have you told your boys?"

"Yes." Nicole straightened her shoulders. "We didn't use the word mafia. They're so young we didn't think that would have any meaning. We simply told them there are some bad boys out there who may want to hurt us… so we all have to be extra careful."

Wendy almost smiled, relieved. "I like your use of the term *we*, it makes it sound like something we are all facing."

"People at the hospital don't have a clue about all of this. FBI agents stand out like a sore thumb. I'm playing dumb." Laverne turned to Nicole. "How are you doing?"

"Earl has taken care of everything. He told me to go ahead and be normal, do normal things, be careful, and go on my merry way."

"Merry way!" Wendy exclaimed. "How can you say that, Nicole," she asked in a voice, louder than before. "How can…"

Nicole raised her hand. "I know Earl and the agents are doing everything humanly possible." She paused, holding everyone's attention. "Whatever we're feeling, it's ten times worse for our men. They must have our support; we must stand tall."

***

Unable to wait, Jake arrived early at the club. He prowled, restlessly, checked the tennis court to see if the four were still playing — in the second set. *Geez, she's hot. I wonder if she'll shower before they have drinks. Damn, Tony didn't tell me which table they usually sit at. Maybe the bartender knows. I'm going to ask him.*

On the way to the Nineteenth Hole, he glanced at his watch — 3:20 — *I wonder when Tony will be here?* Sliding up to the high-gloss oak bar, he ordered a Jack Daniels and waited for a casual opening to question the barkeep. "The four women play… playing tennis," he stammered uncharacteristically, "do… do you recall where they usually sit?"

The handsome, dark, curly-haired dude pointed to the round table in the center of the room.

Jake sighed in relief, checked his watch — 3:28. He glanced out the window — *the match is still going on. Where's Tony?* He took a long sip and twisted the barstool toward *the table. Where will she sit? I don't want to face her back.* He glimpsed at his watch—3:33—*Damn, where's Tony?*

He casually strolled by the window — *they're still playing* — he continued on to the bathroom. *What's wrong with me? She's just another chick… no she isn't; she's something special.* Walking back into the bar, Jake glanced at his watch — 3:41 — and picked up his drink.

Tony waved from the far corner table, a Crown Royal in the other hand.

Jake rushed his way. "They're off the court. Do you know where she'll sit?"

"Geez, relax… wait here, in the corner; you'll be facing her. They always freshen up before coming in — it takes time — they'll probably be out around 4:00."

Jake glanced at his watch — 3:54.

Tony shook his head. "Haven't you ever asked a woman out on a date before?"

"Of course." He stopped, realizing Tony was putting him on. "Okay, I got it."

Glancing out the window, the old man smiled. "I can see their reflection in the glass, here they come… don't turn around."

Making eye contact with the two slightly older ones, Tony nodded as they took their regular seats. He leaned over the table and whispered, "Good view, huh?"

"Perfect."

"The ones on each side will leave after one drink. Whenever the other leaves, you can make your move… the rest is up to you," he described for the third time.

The two men ordered another round.

A half hour later, the two women at *the table* stood and gave their farewell.

Tony rose, followed them out with a hundred-dollar bill folded in his hand for each, and returned wearing a big smile.

Jake watched him strut across the room, like a peacock. "What's with you?"

Tony eased up close. "It sounds like you made a point… she asked one of them, 'who is the handsome man in the corner?'"

Jake's eyes sparkled. "Good."

The two men chit-chatted for another twenty-five minutes or so.

"The other woman is leaving… heading to the bathroom with her purse."

Tony glanced over his shoulder. "Take your time… wait two minutes." He laid his pocket watch on the table. "Don't move unless you catch her eye… then go for it."

Jake sat, looking cool — then it happened, he caught her eye. She gave him a partial smile.

***

Jake picked up his drink and ambled her way. "Mind if I join you?"

She eyed him, once over. "My friend will be back in a minute. She just went to the restroom."

"I watched you win the women's championship two weeks ago. I was wondering where you learned to play so well."

Giving him a doubtful glance, she pursed her lips. "I attended a prep school."

"I bet you played in college." He gestured to the chair. "Do you mind?"

Eyeing him again, she hesitated before pointing to the chair. "I played at Stanford."

"Brains and beauty."

She wrinkled her nose. "A man of your stature… should do better than that."

He laughed, relieved. "You checked me out?"

"Only to see who else was in the room. It's important to know who's in the room. It's part of my profession."

"Your profession…"

She interrupted. "I'm a professional model. You never know who may be watching… another contract may be in the offering."

His eyes automatically wandered over her tight white sweater.

Acting as if she didn't notice, she asked, "What kind of business are you in?"

"Real estate." Out of the corner of his eye, he saw Tony and the other woman walk down the hallway, toward the door.

"I bet you're quite successful."

"Why do you say that?"

"Hmm, I just have a sense about things like that… am I correct?"

His smirk grew into a grin. "May I buy you a drink?"

She took her time, as if choosing her words carefully. "That'd be nice, but I have another commitment." She picked up her purse.

"How about a raincheck for next Saturday?"

She cocked her head, considering his offer. "Hmm… maybe…"

***

Glancing out the window a week later, at the empty parking lot, Jake's hopes sunk. *Raincheck, huh* — lightning struck once, twice, and again — illuminating the golf course. The supposedly light morning rain had turned into a storm.

Picking up his second Jack Daniels, Jake downed it and crunched on the ice. *Guess I'll have to hope for a real raincheck.* He placed the glass on the table.

"Could I buy you another Jack Daniels?"

Jake twisted his head.

She stood there, more beautiful than ever. She repeated, with a tight smile, "Could I buy you another Jack Daniels?"

"Yes… yes, of course." He held his empty glass high.

She called to the bartender. "A Jack Daniels and a vodka gimlet… Grey Goose, please."

Placing her umbrella next to the chair across from him, Amanda wiped a few raindrops from her face. "Did you order this rain?" she jested.

"No way, I thought you might not show."

"I didn't have anything else to do." She paused before releasing a smile. "No, I was actually looking forward to meeting you."

Intrigued by her direct statement, he plowed forward. "Why's that?"

She spoke with confidence, matter-of-factly. "Jacob Nicolette prefers being called Jake." Sipping on her gimlet, she wet her lips in a sexy manner. "A highly successful businessman, a prominent Grosse Point Park family man, one of Detroit's top philanthropists, a real estate mogul, and…" Pausing to eye his well-trimmed upper body, she gave him a sexy grin. "And an interestingly handsome man."

"Bartender, we'll have another round, this one is on me," he jested, as he rocked back in his chair and took his time. Her insights were captivating — collecting his thoughts, he asked, "Do you always do that kind of research on a person?"

She measured his body language and smiled; a pleasant smile. "Only when it's a person of interest."

Jake's excitement grew. "The feeling is mutual."

She leaned back, making sure he sensed her *interest.*

Jake picked up on her move. "I didn't mean to come off sounding *too strong.*"

"Not a problem."

Pressing forward, he asked, "Have you ever seen an international tennis finals?"

"I've enjoyed several preliminary matches, but… no, I've never seen the finals."

"Good." He decided to go for it. "I have two tickets for the Virginia Slims ITF finals at Cobo Hall on Sunday, October 9th. Would you like to go?"

"Oh yes, I'd love to," she said without hesitation. "I've read about it. Chrissie Evert and all of the big names will be there."

CHAPTER FOURTEEN

"For he's a jolly good fellow, for he's a jolly good fellow
For he's a jolly good fellow... which nobody can deny
Which nobody can deny, which nobody can deny
For he's a jolly good fellow, for he's a jolly good fellow
For he's a jolly good fellow... which nobody can deny!"

"Good to have you back, Clark," someone shouted from the other side of the Sax Club.

"Over here, Clark, we've got hot pretzels and beer." Renzo pointed to the two pitchers of Stroh's centered on the table.

"Sounds great." Clark slid into the U-shaped booth. "I haven't had pretzels and beer in months."

Renzo, Carlos, Ted and Earl repeatedly asked questions about Clark's injuries. "How'd you deal with two broken legs...? Broken wrist...? Fractured hip...? Punctured lung...? And multiple concussions...?"

By the time they'd finished, their two traditional pitchers of beer were gone, and the group was ready for the business at hand — poker upstairs.

Leading the way, Clark inspected the newly remodeled digs. "Wow, look at this place — knotty-wood paneling, green shag carpeting, and a fan that works."

The guys eyed the place, each giving it their own kudos.

Father Dom greeted each one with a brief embrace and pointed to the snacks Renzo had brought, courtesy of Rosa Maria — Italian sausage, fried ravioli, veal croquettes, spaghetti fritters with ham, bacon-wrapped artichokes, a large ricotta and red pepper frittata, and garlic bread.

"That's quite a spread!" Carlos exclaimed.

Father Dom spoke softly with Clark, blessed him, and gave him an engaging hug.

Renzo filled a heaping plate, grabbed a beer, plopped down in a chair, and picked up the deck. "Dealer's choice," he shouted.

"Hold your horses," Earl called. "I haven't picked up half of the hors d'oeuvres, yet."

"Two-minute warning," he fired back.

The group loaded their plates and gathered around the table.

It was poker as usual.

Two hours passed.

Instead of calling his traditional "Break Time," Father Dom threw down the cards. "I've had enough with the mafia."

Hearing his sharp, uncharacteristic tone, all eyes turned his way.

"I've had enough." He stood up and declared. "First, it was Alyse… then they rough up Clark. How do we know one of us won't be next? I'm using the muscle of my ombudsman role to dig into their activity."

Glancing up at him, Ted frowned. "Om… buds… who?"

Father Dom chuckled. "I thought I'd catch someone with that. It's my new title; Archbishop Dooley will make the announcement next week…"

"Renzo interrupted, "What's an ombudsman?"

"It's a person empowered to conduct independent investigations within an organization. I have full power to dig into any complaint filed by a person in the community or an employee within the Archdioceses, or… to pursue any issue that comes to my attention."

"Wow… sounds pretty powerful to me," Ted stated. "Can you investigate anyone?"

"Yes, I have access to any file and report directly to the Archbishop."

Carlos squinted at him; his head cocked to the side. "Do you have an *issue* in mind?"

"As a matter of fact, I have a long list of questionable financial matters to start with, particularly donations handled at the parish level. As I've mentioned before, the system runs on *faith*. I believe *faith* works in personal instances, but when it comes to money — priests are human — there's just too much at stake to *run on faith*."

"I knew it." Throwing his hands high, Ted went bananas. "So the priests are crooks too."

"I can't say that positively," Father Dom responded diplomatically. "I'm just saying there is plenty of leeway for unethical activity."

"Unethical, shit… Father, call a spade a spade, some priests engage in criminal activity."

Father Dom twisted his lips in a quirky manner. "You can say that if you want."

"How are you going to approach this issue?" Clark inquired, his interest growing.

"I've already met with six priests from different parishes." He paused, making sure he had their attention.

Ted jumped in. "What'd you find out?"

"The same thing I had anticipated. Three of them had well-defined processes that incorporated a broad cross-section of their parishioners — meeting minutes, regular reports, and information shared parish wide — everything was open."

"How about the others?" Ted piped up, figuring the other shoe was ready to fall.

Father Dom responded in a casual, relaxed manner. "The differences were as stark as you might expect — no committees, no minutes, parishes run from the top, loosey-goosey — no accountability."

"Where to from here?" Clark asked.

"I'll meet with fathers from a half dozen more parishes and develop guidelines and procedures the Archbishop *might* share with his cabinet."

"Might?" Ted questioned, sarcastically.

"I can't speak for the Archbishop. There are over two hundred and fifty parishes in the Detroit Archdiocese. He has to decide how he'll handle it."

Ted bristled. "I can tell you how I'd handle it."

Clark's interest piqued. "If you find some kind of criminal activity, will the police be involved?"

"It depends on the magnitude and the circumstances…"

"That means…" Ted interrupted. "It'll be swept under the carpet."

***

Jake nodded at the Grecian Gardens waitress to fill their wine glasses. "I would have bet a grand they bugged the leased cars and newly renovated blind pigs."

"I figured that too." Glancing around one of the mob's favorite hangouts, Blackie set down his half-full glass of Chianti. "It made perfectly good sense."

Jake turned to Angelo. "Are you positive the cars weren't bugged?"

"I stood there and watched the boys rip off door panels, pull out the insulation, tear the trunk apart, and search around the engine. I'm telling you, Boss, there was nothing."

Pausing, with questions peppering his mind and disappointment on his face, Jake nodded to the waitress and tossed down the menu. "Let's order lunch. I'll have a cup of wedding soup and the meatball casserole."

Tony, Angelo, and Blackie ordered their standard pasta dishes.

Normal conversation over lunch was lacking, the minds of the group dwelled on their latest findings. The men raced through their entrées without making eye contact with each other.

Waiting for Blackie to finish, Jake stared at Angelo. "Nothing else… there has to be something."

"Nothing, I can think of… it took three extra days to complete the search of the last car."

Jake curled his brow. "Why's that?"

"It had a flat tire, so they had it picked up and towed into to Montes' shop. It was there for a day or so."

"Why was it towed? Why didn't they fix the tire where the car was?"

"Don't know."

"Shit." Jake slammed the table with his hand, showing a rare moment of frustration.

Blackie jumped up, making a screeching sound with his chair, as if it had scraped against the floor, then nodded his apology to the patrons seated nearby.

"Blackie, did you do the same thing at the blind pigs?" Jake asked softly.

"Absolutely, the guys ripped out drywall and stripped wires. I personally checked everything from the front door to the power box out back." He rolled his shoulders. "There was nothing."

Jake pressed further. "Nothing unusual?" He turned to Angelo. "How about you, did you uncover anything?"

"Ah… not really…"

Not really?" Jake cut him off. "What does that mean?"

"We had to wait to get into Narduzzi's place. The FBI had it taped off as a crime zone."

"Why? He was killed several months ago?" Jake asked directly, his tone sharp.

"Someone said they had a new tip."

"Tip… bullshit, something is going on."

"We didn't pick up any information or rumors."

"How long were they there? Who went inside?" Jake's face reddened, his anger close to erupting, had they not been in a restaurant.

"For a couple of days; they reported the crime was still unsolved. That's all."

"Did you check with our boys downtown?"

"Yeah, no one from the Detroit police force knew anything. Everyone was wearing FBI jackets."

"FBI… that's strange." Jake hesitated, then decided to move on. "Okay… let's turn to the apartment building where the whores lived. Ted Moomau and… what's her name?"

"Caroline Schaffer."

"Oh yeah." Jake broke a soft smile. "Nice legs. Blackie, did you find anything?"

"A little."

"And?" Motioning for him to move on, Jake eased up to the table.

"There was a scheduling board on the wall."

"A scheduling board? What the hell were they scheduling?"

"It had the girls' names and where they worked every night."

"So, that's how they knew which places to hit." Jake brooded for a moment. "Anything else?"

"Yeah, Caroline Schaffer worked in DPD legal before she took the job with us."

"How'd you find that out?" Blackie, who had hired her, asked.

"A couple of cops downtown told me. I had another one check out human resources and… sure enough, she's an employee there."

"An employee, damn… she was working undercover." Jake's voice remained calm. "Find anything on Ted Moomau?"

"Not much more than we've heard before." Tony admitted. "He's a gypsy, supposedly from Seattle. He moved to Detroit eight, ten years ago... bought several apartment buildings. He's the maintenance man in the one where he lives."

"He owns the building and is the maintenance man?"

"That's right... before he got engaged to a doctor that lived there, he serviced the single women in the building," Blackie said with a wink.

"Nah," Jake slurred in disbelief. "You have to be shittin' me."

"No, I'm not. Apparently, he has a *big one* and took care of eight or nine women a week."

"Jesus Christ, what kind of a guy is he?"

Tony smiled. "One with a lot of endurance."

The grouped laughed.

Jake sucked in a deep breath. "Is that it?"

"Oh, I almost forgot." Tony recalled, "Ted's dad and uncle visit three or four times a year and are always here for Thanksgiving."

Jake glanced around the table. "I want all of you to put your attention on Ted. He's the only national connection we have. We need to find out everything we can."

Tony shook his head. "Cracking anyone in the gypsy community won't be easy."

Jake turned to Blackie. "Figure out a way. Big Paul will want to know about him. Do you understand...? Make it happen."

"Yes sir," Blackie replied, knowing it was a rare moment when he'd received such a directive.

"Guess we're adjourned." Jake tossed his napkin on the table.

The group stood and headed for the door.

Jake motioned to Angelo. "Hang around, I have one more thing for you.

***

Weaving his way through the small café in the Cadillac Hotel, Clark walked briskly toward the booth hidden in the rear alcove. Halfway through the nearly empty coffee shop, he spotted the top of a familiar brown, bald head.

Stepping around the archway, he extended his hand to the slight-framed Puerto Rican. "Luis, how are you doing?"

The slim, aged man glanced up with his familiar smile. "Thirty-five pounds lighter since we did the Freddie Salem and Hazel Park cases."

"You look great."

"I guess…" He gave Clark an unhappy glance. "Momma said, it's back to my normal routine — toast and jelly — no more donuts or 'Farmer three-egg breakfasts.'"

Motioning to the waitress for a cup of coffee, Clark eased in across from the FBI's top informant. *Over the years, Luis has proven to be one of the most dependable sources of information, earning the FBI's highest classification, a T-3.*

The waitress placed a cup of steaming coffee in front of Clark and refilled Luis' cup.

Clark slurped a short sip and got to his agenda. "I'm following up on the gambling activities of some of the sports stars in town and came across the name of *Isiah Thomas.*"

Luis shifted uncomfortably; his eyes widened.

"Can you tell me anything about him?"

"He's the Piston's leading scorer," he voiced coyly.

"I heard he's in deep with the mob."

"In deep!" Luis laughed. "More like… over his head."

"How bad is it?"

Luis slid his left hand halfway across the table, his fingers motioning in a 'come-on, give it to me' fashion.

A partial grin crossed Clark's jaw. He reached into his shirt pocket, pulled out a half-folded white envelope, and tossed it toward him.

Luis opened it, counted out five one-hundred-dollar bills, and placed it in his sweater-vest pocket. "That's a good down payment. It'll be another five hundred next time we meet."

"What else can you tell me?"

"Isiah regularly hosts a gambling party at his place… hmm… Henry Allen Hilf and Edward 'Baldy' Sarkesian are always there."

Clark tightened his lips. "If they're there, it's really big."

"He mixes up the other invitees with big-time gamblers, and some of the top executives from around town. Have your friends at the FBI stake out the place, you'll see.

"How deep is over his head?"

Luis pursed his lips. "I'd suggest you watch a couple of the Pistons games and check the point spread."

"Point spread?" Bells rang, Clark spoke softly, "You mean he's shaving points?"

"Can't say, you'll have to check it out for yourself." Luis slid out of the booth. "I'll see what else I can find."

***

Strolling into The Ghostbar for the first time in several years, brought back old memories for Caroline. The place hadn't changed — the same high-gloss mahogany framed by the glass backbar, loaded with bottles of booze, the black leather club chairs, and the dimly lit, romantic ambiance. *Clark and I used to spend hour after hour here, doing nothing, just talking, and holding hands. Ha, I remember the time I seduced him — he was acting cool until I moved my hand up his leg, and then it was all over.*

Snapping back to reality, Caroline caught Clark's subtle half wave. She smiled and headed his way.

Approaching *the table*, she winked. "It's been a long time since we met here." She glanced down at his leg propped like it was that night.

Picking up on her glance, he grinned, more like a *shit-eating smile*, and eased his leg under the table. "A lot of water over the dam since then."

She laughed, easing into the leather club chair across the small, round mahogany table. "More like a flood."

"Want a drink?"

"Ah, I can't stay long," she replied, anxiously pensive. "There're a few things I want to say."

Knowing it was her nickel, Clark took a long sip of Tanqueray and nodded.

She opened up. "Clark, there are so many personal things I want to tell you. I hardly know where to start." Trying to catch a breath, she sighed, regaining her composure. "Guess I'm a little nervous…" She reached across the table and rubbed the top of his hand.

Not knowing where all of this was going, he gave her a pleasant smile.

"There are so many things..." She choked up, pulled a tissue from her purse, and dabbed her cheeks. "I just want to thank you for being the first man who... who loved me as a woman and not for my body. There were so many times... so many ways... thank you so much."

Clark placed his hand on top of hers; his heart recalling those days, long ago. *She was the one who changed my life. We talked about all kinds of things; I never felt so close to a woman. I can't believe I cheated on her, one afternoon with a twenty-one-year-old. Damn!*

She read his thoughts and reflected for a moment. "It was good," she said spontaneously then clamped her mouth. "I appreciate, too, the special efforts you made with Chief Hart to facilitate my employment. I really enjoyed working in the legal department, and helping the young women was a joy. And Ted Moomau, he was a hoot, helping set up the bust of the mafia's blind pigs... that's something I'll never forget."

She sniffled and wiped a remaining tear. "Yet... you know those memories of my grandmother picking me up off the street and giving me a real life are so strong... I can't turn my back on the young homeless girls on the streets of my home town, Gary, Indiana.

Recalling the times she'd talked about life on the streets, being used by men as a teenager, his emotions tugged at his heart. Clark tightened his grip on her hand.

Straightening her shoulders, her voice revealed her resolve. "I've taken a job in a social agency in Gary. I'm going back home... next Friday night will be my last dance at the Sax Club." She gazed into his eyes. "Will you be there?'

"Yes, of course."

"Good, I'll arrange a special seat for you."

Clark's old memories wanted him to say a hundred things he knew he couldn't. "I'm so happy for you." He swallowed hard. "I'm going to miss you; yet, I know it's the right thing to do. Good for you."

"Thank you." Caroline bit her lip, stood, and turned her head away. "I have to go." She rushed to the doorway, stopped and turned. "Thanks, Clark... thanks for being a real man."

***

A Tanqueray later, Clark had barely moved when Earl stuck his head around the doorway. Observing a strange look on Clark's face, he walked gingerly toward the table. "You okay?" he asked softly.

Doing a double-take, Clark shook his head. "Yeah… I'm fine."

Earl eased into the black leather chair across from him. "You don't seem to be fine."

"Yeah, I am." He turned his head side to side. "I just had an emotional chat with Caroline."

Earl cocked his head to the left. "Want me to order a drink?"

"Huh." A smirk crossed Clark's face. "Not unless you want to see that cleavage again."

"No thanks." Earl gave him a "no-no" hand gesture. "Nicole has more than enough and…"

"That's enough," Clark cut him off. "I got it."

The waitress bounced over and stopped short, giving Earl an eyeful. "Is there something you'd like?"

"Hum." Earl snuck a peek and glanced away.

She twisted to the side for his benefit. "Well?"

"A vodka and tonic," he said without looking up.

Clark laughed. "She's going to get in your pants one of these nights."

"No way!" Collecting his thoughts, Earl stared at Clark. "So, how was it with Caroline?"

"Ah…" Clark sucked in a deep breath. "We reminisced a bit…"

Earl threw up his hand as a stop sign. "No need to go any further."

"No, it wasn't like that." Clark shrugged. "It just made me think of the good ol' days."

"Yeah, and the two of you had plenty of them."

"It wasn't so much of that."

"Well man, what was it then?"

"Next Friday will be her last dance at the Sax Club. She's moving out of town."

"No, where's she going?"

"Back home to Gary, Indiana."

"Gary… that place is the pits."

Clark nodded. "That's why she's going there. She plans to work with underprivileged young girls."

"Yes, I recall. She mentioned that several times; she's always wanted to do the same thing for young girls her grandmother had done for her."

"You got it!"

Earl tried to shift Clark's thoughts away from Caroline. "Did you find out anything about the DNA testing?"

"Yes, Sharon Wilson is coming home for Thanksgiving. She will be bringing two trial kits to check the DNA of Ted and his dad."

"How does it work?"

"She can use about anything for test purposes; a person's hair follicle or their saliva."

"How accurate is it?"

"Right now its accuracy rate is about 90 percent. Its founder, Professor Alec Jefferys thinks it'll be virtually foolproof within the next couple of years. At that point, we'll be able to use it in court cases."

"Wow, that'll change the entire game."

"You can say that again." Clark held up his hand, then leaned over and picked up a large brown envelope. "Talking about games… here are two sets of season tickets for the Pistons. They are straight across from the Pistons' bench, so you'll have a great view of everything."

"O… okay." Earl gave him an inquisitive look.

"I want you to keep an eye on *Isiah Thomas* and the guys in the four seats, right behind the bench, three rows up.

"And what am I watching for?"

"Any sign, signal, or nod you may pick up. There's a chance *Isiah* is shaving points."

"Isiah Thomas… no way!"

"I hope not, too. It's rumored he's in over his head with the mob."

"Huh, does it matter who I take?"

"No, take Nicole — four eyes are better than two — just remember the primary purpose. Oh, that reminds me, how is she doing with the extra security around?"

Grinding his teeth, Earl gave him an example of her "if I have to" attitude. "You know Nicole, she'll push on regardless of the situation."

"I know, that's what bothers me sometimes."

CHAPTER FIFTEEN

"How'd you ever find these seats? Right behind the player's benches. They're perfect… I enjoy watching the players towel-off; you can learn a lot about how they think they're playing."

"Hmm, never thought about that. Guess I'll have to check around to see who's watching when I play at the Club."

"That's not necessary." Amanda tossed her long blonde hair aside. "I watched your championship win, there were plenty of women watching."

"Really." Jake acted surprised. Knowing many of them would spread their legs upon the snap of his finger, he changed the subject. "Do you know much about today's finalist?"

"A little," she said, knowing full well she'd talked to the two many times. "Virginia Ruzici has been around a little longer. She's from Romania and has a powerful forehand. When she's on, she dominates; won the French Open in 1978."

His mind swirled, digging deep in his memory banks. "Wasn't she the one who won all kinds of accolades for her sportsmanship a few years ago?"

"Yes, at Wimbledon in the same year. She played Evonne Goolagong Crowley, who had an injured ankle. Crowley collapsed during play. Her husband raced onto the court, technically defaulting the match. When Mrs. Crowley recovered, Ruzici agreed for her to continue the match. Ruzici ended up losing 7—5 and 6—3."

Amanda turned to Jake, sending him a curious glance. "Not many men would know that."

"I'm a tennis buff — men or women, it doesn't matter — I follow both sides of the court."

"*Both sides of the court.* I like the way you say that, like both are equal."

"They are; women are more skilled, men are stronger," he explained with conviction. "How about Ruzici's opponent Kathy Jordon?"

"I really like her — she's an up and comer — the first player to beat Chris Evert before the semifinals in a Grand Slam tournament; she defeated Chris earlier this year in the third round at Wimbledon, 6—1 and 7—6."

"It's too bad you won't be able to see Chris Evert play."

"I know… she's been nursing an ankle injury for some time. It's better to walk off the court than to risk further injury."

"Pretty smart," he replied, knowing how she felt; he spoke honestly. "A lot of guys would *gut it out.*"

"Are you speaking from experience?"

Jake lowered his head. "I'm afraid so."

"I'm rooting for Kathy Jordon, how about you?"

Sensing his opportunity to get closer, he took his time and spoke slowly, tossing out a fishing line. "I think Ruzici will win; so here's the deal… if Jordon loses, we'll have dinner tonight at Joe Muer's."

"Joe Muer's… I've heard so much about it — it's pretty expensive — the best seafood in town."

"It's close *to your* place."

"Yes, I know." She stared back without giving him a hint. *I have to make it clear, so he doesn't think he'll be getting anything after dinner.* "Guess you did your homework too."

"You can never do too much research."

"You got that right."

Waiting for a positive response, he fidgeted in his chair and asked, "So, what do you say?"

She thought about saying 'yes' — didn't want to sound too eager so she tried to buy some time. "What if Jordon wins?"

"The odds are against her."

"How can you say that?" Amanda asked, maintaining a pleasant expression. "Jordon is ranked seventh in the world and Ruzici is seeded eighth."

Not wanting to divulge the Vegas line, he walked a tightrope. "Ruzici has been in twenty-seven WTA finals and won twelve times. Jordon has been in fifteen WTA finals, winning only three times — I think it's Ruzici."

***

Following a 4—6, 6—4, 6—2, Ruzici win, Jake's driver drove the two from Cobo Hall to Joe Muer's, less than five minutes away. The driver jumped out and opened the rear door.

Jake slipped out and extended his hand to her. "May I?"

She stared him in the eye, giving his offer more than a passing thought. She considered saying no, thought maybe, and finally settled on, "Yes, that would be very considerate," she offered, with the extension of a soft touch of his hand.

He guided Amanda through the front door up to the receptionist — an attractive, thirtyish brunette gave him a pleasant smile. "Your window table is ready, Mr. Nicolette, right this way."

Picking up on the familiar greeting, Amanda leaned close to him and whispered, "Guess you come here often."

Jake squeezed her hand and winked. "Whenever I can."

Positioning Amanda on the black leather booth with a perfect view of the sunset, Jake's back slightly to the west, the hostess placed the menus in front of them. "Ernest will be along shortly to take your drink orders… Rubio will be your server for the evening."

"Wow, I can see straight down the Detroit River — it's as picturesque as could be."

"I thought you would like it."

Ernest appeared. "Would the lady like a drink this evening?"

"Yes," she voiced in a convincing manner. "I'll have a Vodka Gimlet."

"Perfect." He turned to Jake. "And for you, Mr. Nicolette?"

She glanced at him. "Sounds like everyone knows you."

"Standard protocol." He fluffed it off. "I'll have a Jack Daniels on the rocks."

Admiring the pressed white table cloth and precisely positioned glass with a knife angled on the butter plates, Amanda opened the menu and scanned down the list of starters — deviled crab balls, calamari, oysters Rockefeller, shrimp Ilene, lobster corn dogs, spicy tuna tartar, smoked Scottish Salmon… "With appetizers like these, who would ever order an entrée?"

Knowing the menu by heart, Jake gave her his full attention. "Wait till you see that list… you'll want to order each item."

Ernest returned with their drinks.

Jake picked up his Jack Daniels, clinked her glass, and toasted, "Here's to a wonderful evening." *I hope her apartment is in the offering.*

Making sure the evening *only included dinner*, she made her intentions clear. "I'm *positive* we'll have a terrific dinner."

One who's been around the block many times, he knew she was in a class above most women he'd taken to dinner. *Just as I expected... Amanda is not a push over!*

The two chit-chatted over another round, before Rubio asked, "Could I interest you in an appetizer tonight... you can't go wrong on any one you might pick."

Jake gave her a go ahead flick of the wrist. "You pick one and I'll pick one, so we can share."

"Perfect." Amanda surveyed the long list, then glanced over at him. "Which one are you picking?"

Smiling, Jake surprisingly announced, "I'd like to order oysters Rockefeller and the spicy tuna."

She stared at him, startled. "Where did the *one* go?"

Laughing, he pointed out. "Well... I left a couple for you."

After avoiding the hot dogs at the tennis match, her hunger took over. "We'll also have an order of the tempura asparagus and Scottish salmon."

A half hour later, Jake forked the last slice of spicy tuna into his mouth. "Have you made a choice for dinner?"

She shook her head; her stomach directed her toward a lighter entrée. "Each of the seafood features sound great — Georges Banks scallops, Rushing Waters Rainbow Trout, Atlantic Monkfish — I don't know. How about you?"

"Fruits of the Sea."

"Where is that?"

"Under the Classics Seafood section."

Her eyes wandered down the menu... stopped at his selection. "Shrimp, scallops, clams, and mussels in a rich bouillabaisse crème, tossed with linguine pasta... oh my, it sounds wonderful... too much for me."

Contrary to their earlier inclinations, the two had full entrees — Jake settling on the Classics selection and Amanda having monkfish. Their conversation ranged far and wide, from sports — tennis, football, and the Tigers' prospects for the '84 season — to personal items that added little to the knowledge they already had about each other. *More important than the words were how they were conveyed. There were no pauses — their conversation was seamless — the words between the two of them flowed smoothly.*

Jake fumbled with his linen napkin, and thought how he'd always meant to be faithful to his wife. His intentions were good; yet, there was a strong attraction for Amanda. His mind whirled, with hope and excitement; he only had to *be patient* and play the game — slow and easy. He put on a pleasant, almost innocent sort of an expression as he studied her. Waiting for the chance, he didn't want to blow this opportunity.

Amanda gripped the stem of her wine glass and stared downriver at the city's glow. Her face had reflected a little embarrassment on occasion. He understood her perfectly. Over the evening, she had cocked her head several times, in an easy manner, and studied him as he studied her. Her smile warmed over dinner and revealed more than a hint of interest.

Rubio stood quietly at the table while the two kibitzed.

Jake looked up.

"Could I interest you in dessert tonight? We have…"

"No, I need a doggie bag, please," Amanda cut him off. "I'll be walking to my apartment tonight."

***

"I'm going down for hotdogs and beer, anything else you want before the game starts?"

Fixated on the crowd and the size of the arena, Nicole's head barely moved. "No, I'm fine."

Earl turned and headed for the concession stand.

Her eyes wandered the Silverdome. *I can't imagine this place with 82,000 crazy Lions' fans. Tough duty for Earl, he has to watch the Pistons play all year. Who is Isiah? Why does Earl keep saying, 'he hopes the rumors aren't true?'* Opening the program, she searched for the name she'd heard about — his full-page picture appeared — Isiah Thomas. *Wow, he's really handsome; terrific smile.* She eagerly skimmed his bio:

- 1981   NCAA — All-American, 6'- 1" - Point Guard
- 1981   Led Indiana University to NCAA National Championship
- 1981   Drafted Second Overall by the Pistons
- 1982-3   Leading Scorer for the Pistons

Returning with two foaming beer containers, Earl asked, "Could you grab a beer?"

"Sure." She took one and sipped around the top of the container.

Earl took a gulp and wiped the foam from his lips. Noticing Isiah's picture lying on her lap, he winked. "So, whataya think about him?"

"He's… he's something else. I bet he had the women going crazy over him at Indiana."

Earl raised his eyebrow in a telling manner. "Rumor has it he thinks he's hotter than ever."

"I can see why." Not positive, confused by his strange expression, she asked, "Is that the reason Clark assigned you to his case?"

"Ah…" Earl hesitated. "I wish it was that easy."

Nicole's eyes turned cold. "What do you mean by that?"

The PA announcer blasted, "Ladies and gentlemen, please rise for the singing of our national anthem by Motown recording star, Diana Ross."

The arena erupted with cheers mixed with applause.

Placing their right hands over their hearts, Nicole and Earl sang every word.

At the conclusion, Earl pecked her on the cheek and whispered, "I'm so proud of you… I just love you."

"Get out of here." Pushing him away, she frowned, gave him a little shrug. "What was that all about?"

"Nothing… I just felt like saying it."

"You're so sweet." She smiled a pleasant smile. "Anyway, back to the point… you mentioned, it's not an easy assignment?"

Unwrapping the hotdog, Earl took a large bite off the end. A yellow blob of mustard squirted onto his pant leg. "Damn."

Nicole handed him a napkin.

Earl dabbed at it and made an even greater mess. He rubbed the stain, then stuffed the napkin in the bag.

Nicole bit her lip. "Well?"

"There were some grumblings about his play last year."

"Why? He was the leading scorer." She shook her head, in disagreement. "Sounds like sour grapes, if you ask me."

"Could be," Earl admitted. "There were some games… toward the end of the year, where it appeared he slacked off. Some of the media even thought he may have faked an injury."

"Faked an injury!" She frowned. *I don't think so.* "Why would he do that?"

"That's the question I'm supposed to figure out."

"I don't understand."

Earl ran his hand over his glistening bald head. "Do you know anything about point shaving?"

Nicole gave him a questioning look. "Not really."

"Okay, point shaving is when a player might purposely miss a shot, create a turnover or fake an injury to keep the score within a specific range."

"Why would he do that?"

"There is a betting line in Las Vegas that's used by local bookies across the nation for most every college and pro sporting event in the country — it's a big business. For example, in the sports section of *The Detroit News*, you'll see a basketball team may be favored to win by sixteen points. A gambler might wager thousands of dollars this will happen. When a player is bribed to intentionally keep the winning margin less than sixteen points, it's called point shaving."

"Why would a player of the stature of Isiah Thomas do something like that?"

"That's why we're trying to find out whether or not he's addicted to gambling. Word is that he is in debt, big-time, to the mafia."

The game buzzer sounded.

***

Clark followed the 6' 4" bouncer to the bar stools below the stage of the Sax Club's stainless steel center pole. Brushing a hand over his blonde flattop, the two hundred and sixty pounder pointed to the vacant stool, between Clark's high school musketeers — Carlos, Renzo, and Earl — Clark eased in between Renzo and Earl.

"What the hell is going on?" a surprised Renzo asked.

With a blank face, Clark rolled his shoulders. *The guys knew Caroline Shaffer had dumped him when she learned Clark had cheated on her. Ever since, he and his buddies had been relegated to the corner booth farthest from the dance floor.*

Carlos leaned around in front of Renzo. "I don't understand... is something going on between the two of you?"

His face still unreadable, Clark threw a hand in the air as if to say, "I'm innocent; I know nothing."

Knowing Clark's past, Earl stared back, not positive of Clark's virtue. "Are you sure something isn't...?"

"I'm positive," Clark stressed, remaining adamant. "We just had a brief conversation last week."

All heads turned Clark's way, waiting for the other shoe to fall.

The interlude music stopped; the DJ cleared his voice. "Tonight, I'm pleased to welcome Caroline Schaffer for the last time."

The guys glanced side-to-side and turned to Clark.

He pointed to the DJ's location, positioned high above the bar, just off the stairs leading to the second floor.

"After twelve years, the next dance will be Caroline's last performance. Appropriately, she has selected Donna Summer's 'Last Dance.'" He paused, waiting for Caroline to step onto the stage. "And here she is... Detroit's number one dancer and... I might add, the only one with a law degree."

Hoots and hollers bounced off the walls.

Caroline stole center stage, grabbed the silver pole, pulled her body close, and seductively glided up and down.

Cat calls... applause and cheers filled the space.

Following the initial slow, easy beat of "Last Dance," she slinked toward Clark. Bending low, her open blouse pushed her pasties within inches of his nose.

Earl's eyes popped.

Clark's memories stirred — the times she'd danced privately — in the shower, his bedroom, and on the dining room table. *She was a perfect ten — in every way — shapely, great legs, long flowing black hair, and smart as a whip.*

She moved lower and lower — her skimpy shorts rotating — his eyes following each move as she eased up, and broke into the up tempo beat of the "Last Dance."

Her body flew wildly, each move dramatically choreographed.

The aroused crowd rose, stomped and cheered to the rhythmic beat.

As she turned back toward Clark, the music slowed. Rubbing her stomach, she slipped off her shorts, and pointed to her G-string.

The guys squeezed closer to the stage.

"Do you have a hard on?" Earl whispered.

Clark didn't take his eyes off her. "No, I…"

"Shit man, I do." Earl adjusted himself.

Clark's smile broadened.

Shaking her head "no," Caroline pointed to her G-string.

The guys laughed.

A gleeful Clark pulled a twenty from his wallet and tucked it in with his finger.

Tens and twenties flew from all directions, covering the dance floor.

Caroline bowed and bowed again before slinking off to the slow, sexy beat.

Cheers for more came from the patrons.

Caroline stopped halfway up the stage stairs, blew a kiss to the audience, turned and walked into the darkness.

***

Upstairs at the Sax Club, Father Dom had slipped outside the doorway to catch a glimpse of his friends. Still bugged-eyed from the show, the guys filed upstairs, each catching his broad smile.

Bringing up the rear, Clark grabbed his arm to walk him in. "How about that performance, Father?"

Holding back his real thoughts, the old man winked. "The two of you must have been a real thing."

Clark could only nod. "You got that right."

"Come in," called Ted, who'd slipped in during the commotion. "I've opened the beer so you can cool off."

Clark grabbed the bottle and downed a slug.

Carlos made his way down the table loaded with snacks — M&M's, Italian subs, chips and dip, and peanuts — all provided by Father Dom as this week's host.

Renzo picked up the deck and shuffled. "Dealer's choice!"

Comments about Caroline's provocative dance substituted for the normal poker lingo.

Father Dom's traditional call, "Break Time," broke the pattern.

The guys hit the head and then loaded their plates. Popping the top on a beer bottle, Earl cocked his head. "Did you hear that?"

A not too concerned Father Dom fluffed it off. "Sounded like someone with a handful of firecrackers."

"No way." Clark shook his head. "It was an Uzi… maybe two."

CHAPTER SIXTEEN

Detroit Free Press

November 5, 1983

Section C

STRIPPER'S LAST DANCE ENDS IN TRAGEDY

At 7:17 last night Caroline Shaffer slid down the center pole at the Sax Club. Performing her perfectly choreographed dance to Donna Summer's "Last Dance," the popular stripper received an extended, standing ovation.

At 10:43, she was machine-gunned down in a gangland-style killing. Waiting at the stoplight at W. McNichols and Log Cabin Street, her car was pinned between two black late-model Buicks. A third Buick pulled alongside with machine guns aimed for the front and back windows, and unloaded a barrage of bullets, riddling her body and dark blue Camaro with forty-eight holes.

As prophetic as it may seem, Sax Club owner Mark Resnick indicated Ms. Shaffer had announced her performance would be her last dance. Having recently completed her law degree, she was excited about moving back to her Gary, Indiana hometown to work with underprivileged young girls. "Sad," Resnick

expressed, "Caroline was the nicest person and best performer we've ever had."

***

Ten days later, Clark sat alone in The Ghostbar, sipping on a second Tanqueray, and staring into space — oblivious to the back and forth parading of the waitress — his thoughts centered on Caroline. He couldn't get the lyrics of the "Last Dance" out of his mind:

Last dance
Last chance, for love
Yes, it's my last chance, for romance, tonight.

I need you, by me.
Beside me, to guide me.
To hold me, to scold me.
'Cause when I'm bad
I'm so bad.

So let's dance, the last dance
Let's dance, the last dance
Let's dance, this last dance tonight.

He downed his Tanqueray. *Why did they pick her? Of all people, she was the least deserving. Why?*

"You okay?"

"Shit... I don't know. I handled Caroline's funeral and all of that... guess reality is setting in. I can't get her off my mind. I love Abby; still, Caroline and I shared so much and had so many wonderful experiences, I just... I don't know how to explain it."

Earl sat silently, thoughts of his former wife raced through his mind. "If it helps any, I went through the same thing when my wife died from leukemia. I repeatedly asked, 'why...?' she was the most wonderful person in the world."

"I feel the same way. It doesn't make sense."

"I guess that's life, Clark." Earl rose above the immediate situation. "Consider the way it is now..." He paused, getting Clark's attention. "You have Abby and I have Nicole, how could it be better than that?"

"Yeah, I know you're right." Clark downed his drink. Earl reached over and patted him on the back.

Clark sucked in a deep breath. "Guess we ought to move on with today's agenda."

"Right."

Feeling like crap, Clark tried to clear his mind. "Shit man, I can't get her off my mind… a useless killing. I'll find the bastards and *get even.*"

Earl shook his head. "Clark, you know you can't do that."

"Don't tell me what I can do, I'm going to…"

"Hold it right there." Earl raised his hand as a stop sign. "You're going to find the culprits and pursue legal means to put them away."

Clark sucked in a deep breath, his mind twisting and twirling. "Okay, I'm setting up a meeting with Luis to have him dig into the situation."

"Now that makes sense." Having encouraged Clark to do the right thing, Earl shifted the conversation. "Let's hear about today's agenda."

Clark took his time trying to avoid the inevitable. "I read, again, the report from Kimberly, Frank, and Pag on the Curry Brothers… it's fine. But if we're ever gonna get the goods on them, more of the same won't cut it. We need firsthand evidence."

Sensing the forthcoming assignment, Earl leaned back in the chair and stared at the muraled ceiling.

Rubbing his hands together, nervously, Clark spoke slowly. "I hate to put it this way… since you're the only black person on our team…"

"I know," Earl cut him off, relieving the pressure from Clark. "I need to go undercover."

Clark nodded; his face paled. "I know you enjoy watching the Pistons, but I'll have to re-assign that too."

"I understand."

"I've set up a meeting with Fitzpatrick and Bennett to pick up the ball."

"Oh." Earl's face saddened. "Can I do one more? I planned to take J. J. tonight."

"No problem. That might be a nice way to start the transition."

"So, where to tomorrow?"

"There's an old brick house that's not in too bad a shape on a side street, just off Gratiot and McClellan… you put down $2,500 and bought it for $25,000."

"I know that area; it's by the Top Hat Hamburger joint."

"Right."

"I think the feds overpaid."

"Huh." Clark smiled, thought of the recent shooting on that street. "You're probably right."

"So, let's hear it?"

Clark tossed a large brown envelope on the table in front of Earl. "The FBI has created a totally new identity for you — driver's license, Cadillac Plant ID, credit cards, the whole shebang — for Clarence Tidwell, with your age and birth date."

"Well, at least I got something of mine out of it," he jested.

"There's five hundred bucks in there and address for the closest Goodwill and Salvation Army stores for your new duds — head to toe — don't miss a thing."

Earl laughed. "Guess you mean no Gucci shoes."

"Not unless you earn them. You have to get in tight with Maserati Rick. Once you've done that it'll be easier to slip in with the Curry Brothers."

Earl hesitantly asked, "How long do you think it'll take to get the goods on him?"

Clark rolled his shoulders. "The feds aren't positive… three or four months, maybe longer."

"I won't be able to see or communicate with Nicole?"

"Right, and she won't be able to tell anyone where you've gone." Clark tried to add a positive spin. "The FBI will arrange periodic weekend get-a-ways, so you can see Nicole… and so they can change the battery on your wire."

"Oh, thanks."

***

"Got some good stuff for you."

Startled, deep in thought, Clark glanced up from his cold coffee to see Luis' fingers moving in a "give it to me" fashion. "Cash up front."

Without question, Clark pulled out an envelope and tossed it on the table.

Luis slipped it in his pocket, motioned to the waitress for coffee, slid into the booth across from him, and stared. "You look like shit. You all right?"

"Lost a close friend… a very close friend. I'm getting better, but once in a while it hits me pretty hard."

"I understand that… seems like something happens to one of my buddies on a regular basis." Slurping on his coffee, Luis peeked up, under the bill of his ball cap. "Is that woman who was machine-gunned still on your mind?"

Clark's head jerked up. "How'd you know that?"

"Humph," Luis grunted. "A good friend once told me, 'it's amazing what you hear, when you listen…' that's my business."

Recalling the time he'd shared his dad's favorite saying with Luis, a congenial grin spread across Clark's face.

"Heard the two of you were hot and heavy."

"You got that right." Clark gave him a smile as he nodded. "Hope you have more information than that."

Staring into Clark's eyes, Luis paused. "Anything you want me to do?"

Wanting to kill the bastards who'd killed Caroline, Clark knew he couldn't ask the question the way he wanted to. Caught between a rock and a hard spot, he only stared.

Sensing Clark's deep, personal feelings, Luis picked up the ball. "Seems like you might want a personal favor."

Clark cocked his head to the side, unable to think clearly.

"Fine." Luis's eyes narrowed in a glare. "I'll find the names of the drivers and the shooters for you."

Clark opened his mouth.

Luis pushed his hand in the air toward Clark. "No charge… this one is on me." He drained his coffee cup. "Back to the reason we're here. Yes, I have lots of information." He pulled a piece of scrap paper from his shirt pocket. "Isiah Thomas hosts a high-stakes dice game at his suburban mansion twice a month and loses regularly."

"Right, you mentioned that last time."

"Well, here's the rest of the story," Luis said in Paul Harvey fashion. "Isiah's gambling habit is out of control. Have one of your guys talk to his teammate, Mark Aguirre. The two of them were boyhood pals; he's trying to help Isiah and is ready to spill the beans."

"That's a strange move."

"Hey, I'm telling you man, one of my friends talked to him; Aguirre will do anything to stop Isiah from going off the deep end."

"Are you positive he's in that deep?" Clark questioned, hoping it wasn't true.

"Jesus, Clark, when the mafia's head gambling guys are going into his mansion on a regular basis you know things are happening."

"You know their names?" Clark asked; still not wanting to hear the truth.

"Goddamn, Clark, like William 'Buffalo Bill' Gibera, Frank 'New York Frankie' Inglese, 'Baldy' Sarkesian, Henry Allen Hilf, and since he got out of jail, Freddie Salem. Other than having Nicolette in the room, it couldn't be any bigger."

"All at one time?"

"Nah, they mix and match, so guys will bring in other big-hitters and no one will get suspicious."

"Guess they know how to pull things off." Clark started to fold his notebook. "Is that it?"

"No, I have more." Luis waved to the waitress for a second order of toast and jelly. "Thomas' best friend owns a local grocery store and is cashing Isiah's checks to keep him supplied with cash. And hear this…" Luis paused for effect. "Eugene Baratta, the bagman, runs back and forth to keep the big mafia guys informed on the size of his debt."

"Okay…" Clark uttered, buying time, trying to sort out the importance of that piece of information.

Reading the question marks on Clark's face, Luis threw his hands in the air. "That means the mafia is ready to put the squeeze on him. You need to pay close attention to the point spreads from here to the end of the season."

***

"Sounds like the list of questions you typed up put Jake into high gear."

"Yeah, he liked them." Blackie reflected. *Give Jake a tidbit of information and his brain fires in ten different directions. I've never seen anyone with the ability to analyze an issue or tear apart a person's rational so quickly — he's amazing.*

"Where to now?" Carmen was curious to know what Jake came up with from the list.

"Jake is all over Ted Moomau and the gypsy connection. We have to find out more."

"Boss, I've tried every technique… every trick I know. Whenever I sit down to talk with a gypsy, he clams up and gives me a strange look."

"Want me to authorize some muscle?"

Carmen tilted his head to the side. "Hum, I'm afraid to take that step. From what I've heard, the entire community shuts down when they sense trouble from the outside."

Blackie pulled a wad of hundreds out of his pocket and tossed them on the table. "Here, see what you can buy."

"Will do." Carmen glimpsed at his watch in a manner so he wouldn't tip off Blackie — 9:58.

Blackie frowned, noticing Carmen's sneak peek at his watch. He gave him a deadpan stare. "You got a hot date?"

"Ah… no…" Carmen, stood, slid out of the booth and headed for the bar.

Hearing a door open and close, Blackie called, "What's going on?"

"More than you could imagine," Carmen shouted. "Look who's here."

Vicky Cromwell, his longtime mistress appeared in the doorway.

***

Gazing around the Caucus Club, Jake sipped on his second Jack Daniels on the rocks. *This is an amazing place. For over thirty years, it's been the place for the "power lunch," and a clandestine place where men can bring their girlfriends for a luncheon getaway. Ha… back in '61 an unknown Barbra Streisand launched her vocal career here.* His thoughts shifted to Amanda. *She's unreal; I can't stop thinking about her.*

Wearing a casual, low-cut, black dress, Amanda stepped in the place located in the Penobscot Building. Jake's description of Amanda was perfect; the hostess motioned to her. "Right this way, Mr. Nicolette is waiting for you."

Surprised by the reception, Amanda nodded and followed the slender brunette.

Approaching Jake's table, Amanda turned slightly to the side showing off her profile for his benefit.

Jake's eyes casually inspected her, then quickly glanced at the plush surroundings, trying not to give away his interest.

Knowing he'd received the message, Amanda grinned to herself while glancing at the restaurant's elegant, old-world atmosphere. "This place is charming." She stroked the white linen tablecloth and picked up the silver ring holding a black napkin. "First class, if I do say so myself."

"First class…" Jake smiled to himself; time for my *old line.* "First class, deserves first class."

She'd heard the line before, but still rewarded him with a grin. "Smooth aren't you?"

"Not as smooth as I am honest and forthright."

She gave him a pleasant look; her eyes searched him up and down, followed the lines of his gray turtleneck, over his pecs, and around his square shoulders. "Do you work out often?"

Pleased she'd noticed the results of his daily schedule, he spoke with pride, "An hour or so a day."

"Have you done that long?"

"Most of my life…"

"It shows… nice."

"Thanks," he said, unable to come up with a witty response. "How about you?"

"Like you, I guess." She admitted, "It's a constant challenge to keep slim and trim."

Eyeing the black brooch lodged in her décolletage, he suppressed his thought. "You've done extremely well; you should be proud of your many accomplishments, too. Being one of the top models in L.A. is no easy task."

Analyzing his words, Amanda took her time. *Ah hah, sounds like someone made a call or two.* "Guess you've done some research."

He measured his words. "In my business, it's important to know who you're talking to."

"So what else do you know?"

"Oh…" He paused and shifted the subject. "Would you like 'The Bullshot?'"

She pondered, trying to make the connection. "Is that a trick question?"

164

"No. Most women would say yes to be polite."

"Oh…" She looked him in the eye. "How many women have you asked to have 'The Bullshot?'"

Knowing he'd shot himself in the foot, he countered, "Guess you're a quick-thinker."

She responded immediately. "In my business, it's important to be alert to what is said."

"Touché." *God, she's smart.*

Her eyes connected with his. "Tell me about 'The Bullshot.'"

"Do you want the whole spiel or just the ingredients?"

She thought a moment; her look would have seduced him had it lasted longer. "Let's start with the ingredients."

"Okay, here goes." Feeling comfortable, Jake relaxed, leaned back and spoke freely, *like chatting with an old friend.* "The base is composed of three to five ounces of bouillon or beef broth, diluted with water, two parts broth to one part water."

"Hmm." She licked her lips, sensually. You tempted my taste buds already." She pushed herself forward, giving him her full attention and *getting his.*

"Pour in two ounces of Vodka and as much Tabasco and Worcestershire sauce as you want. I have them add a couple of queen olives and a stalk of celery."

"Wow, that's not your typical Bloody Mary. Yes, I'll have one, a Nicolette Bullshot."

"I like that." He gave her a pleasant expression. "Original… I'll ask the owners to put it on the menu." Jake motioned to the waitress then ordered his specialty; his mind more on Amanda than the drink. *An arousal feeling just came, a reaction.*

"I'd like to hear the *whole spiel.*"

He stared at her in a questioning manner, one of interest. "No one has ever asked for that."

She had rehearsed for the moment. "Guess you'll find out I'm not the typical L.A. model."

He smiled, knowing she was not your typical fly-by-night woman. *She has class, a professional sense about her. No, dummy, she knows what's going on.* He let out a soft, gentle sigh. "I've already concluded that."

CHAPTER SEVENTEEN

After a most relaxing luncheon with Amanda at the Caucus Club, Jake flipped a napkin over his empty plate and glanced up at the front door. He spotted his number two man — a playboy — with a young, attractive woman; he motioned for them to join them.

While they headed his way, Jake whispered to Amanda. "That's my good friend Angelo Travaglini and his friend, I hope you don't mind if they join us?"

She flashed him a glowing smile. "Not at all, I want to meet all of your friends."

Angelo walked briskly toward Jake and stopped next to the table. Jake stood and the two embraced. Angelo stepped back and turned to the woman. "Jake, I want you to meet Catarina Esposito."

Introductions followed and the four took their seats.

Glancing at Catarina, Jake thought Gina Lollobrigida had just joined the table. *Holy shit, look at those knockers.*

Reading his mind, she winked.

"Two Bullshots, extra spicy," Angelo called out. "Jake, how about you?"

Jake caught Amanda's nod. "Yes, I'll have a Grand Marnier, and you, Amanda?"

"Coffee with Baileys."

Angelo's eyes crisscrossed Amanda's perfectly shaped body, turned away, and winked at Jake. "How long have you been hiding her?"

"We met after the tennis championships at the Club. Amanda won the Women's Division, was All-Pacific Coast at Southern Cal."

"Wow, that's impressive." Angelo gave her a pleasant grin and turned to the right. "Catarina was a swimmer in college. Tell them about yourself, sweetie."

"I went to Lehigh University in Bethlehem, Pennsylvania. It's a well-recognized college with about five thousand students." She nodded to Amanda. "A little different than USC… I was a distance swimmer, still hold the school record in the thousand."

"Good for you." Jake thought that was interesting. "Where are you from?"

"Detroit… but I went to a girl's school in Charleston, South Carolina."

Jake hesitated, decided not to pursue it. "Guess we're in the presence of two smart women." *With great bodies, he wanted to say;* instead, he glanced at Angelo. "How long have the two of you been seeing each other?"

Angelo's face came alive. "We met at the Grand Prix boat race last June. We were on a luxury cruise, maybe thirty people, wouldn't you say, honey?"

"Thirty-two to be exact." Catarina blew him a kiss. "It was a day-long cruise with drinks, lunch, and dinner. There was dancing and… we had lots of fun."

"I heard the race from my place." Amanda smiled, just a little. "Was the race loud where you were?"

"Yes," Catarina covered her ears, demonstrating the volume. "The crew cranked up the music and made it much more comfortable. It was a beautiful, sunny day — perfect for the race — and perfect for me."

"Perfect for both of us." Angelo kissed her on the cheek. "There were over 70,000 people at the event."

"Maybe we ought to go on a yacht trip — that'd be a nice way to spend a Sunday. "How about that, Amanda?"

"Yes, I'd love to."

The drinks arrived and Jake toasted the women. "Here's to our most beautiful ladies."

"I'll drink to that," Angelo added.

Catarina took a short sip and stood. "Please excuse me for a moment; I have to make a pit stop."

"Yes, I'll join you." Amanda rose and followed her.

Jake leaned across the table and spoke in a soft tone. "What happened to Barbara Nash?"

"Oh, she's fine, a little stuffy sometimes. We go out for dinner most every week."

Laughing softly, Jake slapped his leg. "Double dipping, huh."

***

Sharon Wilson sat on Laverne and Ted's sofa waiting for Clark and Abby. Before Clark met Abby, Sharon and Clark had been a thing for several years, but somehow, it never seemed to click. They were both heavily involved in their careers and couldn't find time for each other. Petite and cute as hell, she was a farm girl from Stevensville, on the eastern shore of Lake Michigan, and he's an urban guy. At times, the differences were like oil and water.

Abby came on the scene about the same time Sharon received a three-year fellowship to the University of Leicester in England — a convenient separation for both — her and Clark. Back in the States for Thanksgiving, Sharon served as the primary assistant to Alec Jeffreys, who's developing a new technique referred to as DNA fingerprinting. He's close to a breakthrough. His DNA research is being used in numerous settings, although it has not yet been used in a criminal court case.

Following a casual knock, Clark opened the door for Abby and stepped in behind her. "We're here," he glanced at his watch, "right on time — 10:30."

Sharon stood and stepped toward him. "Guess things haven't changed."

Clark's extended hand was bypassed by her brief embrace. Leaning back, she asked, "How have you been?"

"Fine," he said, caught off guard.

"Good for you." She turned to Abby. "You look terrific, guess life has been treating you well too."

"Couldn't be better."

The two shook hands, each giving the other a pleasant look.

Sharon winked, looking at Abby's diamond ring, "Good for you."

"Thanks," Abby mouthed.

Not seeing Ted or his dad, Ned, Clark asked, "Where are the two 'Guinea' pigs?"

Sharon squinted at him, irritated. "Clark, you shouldn't say that."

"Story of my life," he jested. "I never did get it right."

Laverne interjected. "Ted's waking up his dad; he got in late last night."

"Checking out the blind pigs, again?"

"I guess, you'd think he'd get tired of carousing every night he's here."

Abby tossed out a positive spin. "Maybe that's better than bugging you all day."

"You got that right," Laverne said firmly with a grin, showing she was kidding. "Actually, he's a joy to have around, ends up taking us out for dinner most every night."

Sharon gave her an agreeable smile. "Can't complain about that."

Laverne changed the subject and asked the question on everyone's mind. "So how long will this procedure take?"

Sharon gave the group a broad smile. "For you guys, five minutes. For me… five or six hours in a lab at Wayne State."

Ted and Ned appeared.

Laverne grabbed Ted and planted a smacker on his lips. "Perfect timing."

He turned as if to walk away. "That was pretty good; I think I'll try it again."

"Ted!" He caught Laverne's eye.

Clark chuckled. "See there, Sharon, some things never change."

"No comment." Sharon picked up a small black kit, the size of a three-ring binder, and opened it on the dining room table. Taking a chair at the head of the table, she glanced up. "Okay 'Guinea' pigs, as Clark calls you, I need for one of you to set on each side of me."

Not sure of what they were in for, Ted and Ned walked slowly up to the table and pulled out a chair, as requested.

Acting as if he was in for a major ordeal, she solemnly asked, "Okay Ted, lean your head forward and open your mouth." Pausing for a moment, taking an extra few seconds to add to the drama, she held a plastic swab in front of him. "Open wide."

Scooping the swab under his tongue, she pulled it out. "Okay, that's it."

"That's it?" Startled, Ted questioned, "What did you do?"

Sharon paused, knowing he wasn't kidding. "I took a sample of what is called 'passive drool.' The rest is up to me in the lab," she explained and turned to Ned. "Think you can handle that much activity?"

"Absolutely. I thought it was going to be a big ordeal."

She repeated the procedure on Ned and turned to the group. "Anyone else?" Giggling, she closed her kit. "Hopefully, I'll be able to tell you the results before the end of the Lions and Steelers game."

170

***

"When will the turkey be ready?" Ted shouted from the La-Z-Boy in the living room.

"Halftime," Laverne shouted back. "Why don't you get off your butt and put the hors d'oeuvres on the table, so everyone can snack before the game starts."

"Great idea," Clark chimed in, giving Ted a jab.

"Okay… okay." Ted took his time, slowly unraveling himself from the chair.

"Can I help?" Abby offered.

"You can cut the veggies, if you want."

"I can handle that."

Clark raised his head off the sofa. "Is anyone else coming over?"

Laverne poked her head around the kitchen cabinets. "Father Dom will be here around game time; everyone else is enjoying a family dinner."

Ted placed a dish on the table and turned back toward the living room. "I haven't heard anything about DNA fingerprinting… can anyone fill me in?"

"I'll try." Clark propped himself up on the arm of the sofa. "Sharon's boss, Professor Jeffreys, has been studying X-ray film imaging for some time. He's found a way to determine if there's a connection between the molecules found in a person's saliva or hair follicles with substances found in a different location."

"Like in a crime scene," Ted ventured.

"Could be." Clark straightened up and flopped his legs on the floor. "So far, most of the applications have been in paternity cases. It's used extensively for paternity suits in England."

Ned put his plate on the TV tray. "How does it work?"

"Don't ask me anything more… I'm near the end of my pay grade." Clark confessed. "As I understand the various forms of DNA fingerprinting, it's almost foolproof — it makes a perfect, positive identification; it can also prove there's no possibility a person was connected with the situation."

Ned perked up. "So, she can prove that Ted and I were not involved in any of those killings."

"You can bet your ass she can," Clark voiced in a sharp tone, surprising the group, except for Ned who was used to such vernacular.

Ned stood and grabbed a beer. "Damn, that's good news. Thanks for helping me out."

"I thought that'd grab your attention." Clark chuckled. "I gave Sharon some evidence from the crime scene. If there's no match between the molecules on those surfaces and your saliva, there's no possible way either one of you could have been at the crime scene."

***

After rapping softly on the door during the commotion, Father Dom poked his head inside the door. "Anyone home?" he jested.

"Yes, you're just in time for the game," Clark called.

Ted stood and pointed to the dining room table. "Grab a plate, Father, and load up."

"Don't worry about me." Heading for the table, he filled his plate, grabbed a beer, and eased onto the sofa, next to Clark. "What are our chances today?"

Clark gave him a hopeless expression. "I'll give you a hint… we're 6 and 6 and the Steelers are 9 and 2."

"Sounds like a rout."

Ned, hesitated, "I'll bet five bucks on the Lions. Anyone want to bet?"

"I do." Ted raised his head from the La-Z-Boy.

"You never know."

"Sure." Ted dozed back off.

"Billy Sims scored. Did you see that?" Ned asked.

Ted didn't budge.

"Murray kicked a field goal. Did you see that?"

Ted barely stirred. "Wake me up at halftime."

His dad pooh-poohed him. "The Lions are going to win."

Ted fingered him.

"Ted, it's almost halftime, will you cut the turkey?"

"Yeah." He pushed the La-Z-Boy down. "What's the score?"

"The Lions are up 24 to 3," Father Dom pointed out.

Ted's eyes zeroed in on the TV's halftime score. "Shit, why didn't you wake me up before?"

"Ted, it's time to cut the turkey," blasted from the kitchen

He pulled himself out of the chair. "I'm on the way, darling."

Ted fulfilled his duties and the women loaded the table with standard Thanksgiving fanfare — glazed sweet potatoes, cranberry sauce, mashed potatoes and gravy, green beans — along with two big platters of sliced turkey.

The women moved to the small table in the kitchen and the men took over the living room — both groups happy in their own right.

By the time the men packed away two helpings, the Lions had salted away a 31 to 3 third quarter lead.

The women gave the men a choice between pumpkin and apple pie.

Ted took both.

"45 to 3, it's all over," Father Dom announced to the sleeping men. "Eric Hipple was 10 out of 16, Billy Sims rushed for a hundred and six yards, and the Lions intercepted the Steelers five times."

Glancing at the final score, Clark, Ted, and Ned rubbed their eyes.

Ted wadded up a five and threw it at his dad.

The phone rang.

All eyes turned appropriately to stare at it.

Laverne picked up the receiver. "Hello," she said, hesitantly.

"Laverne, it's Sharon, may I speak with Clark?"

She motioned to him.

Clark jumped up and grabbed the phone. Listening intently, he gave the group a thumbs up. "Thanks, Sharon, we really appreciate your extra effort." He nodded a couple of times. "Thanks again." Hanging up, he turned to the group. "The results were negative — there's no way Ted or Ned were at the crime scene — I have proof!"

"Hallelujah!" Laverne shouted.

The group cheered and congratulated the two men."

***

Gazing at the river from his conference room in the McNamara Building, Clark watched a mini ice flow make its way downriver. *Looks like the morning freeway, huh.* His attention shifted to the upcoming report from Fitzpatrick and Bennett on the Pistons' games on the 25th and 29th. *The informant has never been wrong... my gut says... geez, I hope this is a first.*

Hearing the door open, Clark turned. "How'd it go?" he asked anxiously, his heart in his mouth.

Fitzpatrick twisted his head and pressed his lips, like he was trying to hold back the words. "I don't know, boss. He either had two bad shooting nights or…"

"Get on with it," Clark interrupted. "Walk me through the game on the 25th."

"I can handle that." Bennett slid into the swivel rocker next to Clark and opened his notebook. "The Pistons were three-point favorites over the Washington Bullets and lost by nine. Isiah was up and down; on one series I thought he was a high-schooler; next time down the floor, I thought he was a world-beater, making a steal and doing a power slam-dunk."

"That doesn't sound too bad."

"Yeah, but his shooting was not good, particularly when the game was close — it could have gone either way — he missed three shots in a row, ended up shooting six for eighteen."

"Not good, for a guy like him." Clark held his breath. "Anything else?"

"Ah… yeah. Edward 'Baldy' Sarkesian and Henry Allen Hilf, gambling lieutenants for the mafia and a couple goons, were in the seats right behind the bench."

"Did you see anything?"

"Hmm… I couldn't tell. The two of them were up and down — bringing back hot dogs, popcorn, and nachos — the whole game."

"Up and down… Isiah was up and down, too. Could you make any connection with that?"

"We didn't realize it at first. Both of them must weigh two hundred and fifty pounds…"

"Why didn't they send their lackeys?"

"We talked about that… something had to be going on. Guess we missed it."

"Or there was nothing going on," Clark expressed, hoping against growing odds. "Hear anything from the street?"

"Yeah, supposedly, the mob made big money on the game."

Clark ground his teeth. "Let's move onto the 29th."

"This one was a little more obvious, at least, in terms of the point spread," Fitzpatrick pointed out. "They played the Cavaliers."

"Cavaliers don't have shit," Clark proclaimed.

"Right, the point spread had the Pistons' winning by fifteen."

"And?"

"They won by ten… Isiah was three out of twelve."

"Wow, somebody could have made big money."

"Yeah, Sarkesian and Hilf were the only two there and hear this… neither left his seat all night."

"Hmm, sounds fishy if you ask me."

CHAPTER EIGHTEEN

Following the midway poker break, the guys reassembled around the table. Father Dom passed out copies of the front page of the recent issue of *THE MICHIGAN CATHOLIC*. "Here, take a minute to read this."

THE MICHIGAN CATHOLIC

December 1983

Detroit Businessman Donates $500,000

GROSSE POINT PARK — Father Bernardo Cassidy of St. Monticello Church announced receipt of a $500,000 donation from prominent local businessman Jacob Nicolette. Father Cassidy indicated a significant portion of the funds will be used for the projects underway in the capital project's drive.

Father Cassidy also mentioned over the years, Mr. Nicolette has been one of the most generous donators in the Archdiocese of Detroit.

Glancing at the title of the newsletter, Ted asked, "What's this all about, Father."

Clark skimmed the story and responded quickly. "I didn't see that in the *Free Press* or *The Detroit News.*"

Father Dom wore a curious look. "I wondered about that too. I searched everywhere I could… didn't find anything." He glanced around the table. "Did any of you read a story about Nicolette's gift?"

Heads shook sideways — no.

"If it would have been in there, I'm sure I would have noticed Nicolette's name," Earl added.

Clark pondered; his mind considering the worst. "What do you think, Father?"

"I'm thinking Nicolette may be money laundering."

"Money laundering!" Earl interjected. "I wouldn't be surprised. Rumors have it the mafia is pushing all of the buttons."

"Buttons?" Ted questioned. "I don't understand."

"The feds are clamping down on the mob from every angle," Earl said. "The mafia is looking for every way possible to launder money. The big rumor out there is that they're trying to take over Motown."

"Motown… why?" Renzo frowned.

"They don't care about the record industry; they'd gain control, so they could use it as a source to launder cash." Earl pointed out. "Apparently, they're already into some of the performers."

"Performers?" Renzo tossed his hands widely apart. "Christ, where does it end?"

"Weird, uh?" Carlos' mind swirled with possibilities. "Like who?"

"Mary Wells has been seen at several of their parties. There are words swirling around Smokey Robinson, Barbara McNair, Sylvia… and some others."

Ted cut him off, "How about the guy at the top… Berry Gordy?"

"The man keeps saying he's clean, but that hasn't stopped the rumors from popping up."

"I want to go back to the church story." Carlos stepped up. "Do you really think there's laundering going on in the Catholic Church?"

"I'd like to say no, but the more I dig… the more likely it seems to be a reality." Father Dom gave him *a troubled look*. "I've double-checked the records at the Archdiocese level for the Nicoletti gift — fifty thousand dollars was recorded."

"Wow… that's all!" Ted exclaimed.

"Wait." Father Dom raised his hand. "I'm not finished. Next, I'll meet with the priest at the church to see what he has to say about the remaining dollars."

Carlos held up the article. "The news story says a large portion will be used for the capital project drive. Isn't that possible?"

"Yes, of course. If it shows up in the campaign fund, everything will be kosher."

Clark's interest peaked. "How will you be able to check that without people getting suspicious?"

"I've told the Archbishop, I'd like to make it a part of our regular reviews. Once he signs off on my template, it'll be applied to the financial aspects of all parishes… so, when I visit St. Monticello it'll be part of a diocese-wide process."

***

Pag gave the barber a dollar tip, glanced out the window at the traffic buzzing by on Mack, and turned, heading for the back stairwell. Reaching the basement tile floor, he picked up a beer from the open bar and walked over to the empty chair, next to Blackie. "Mind if I join you?" he asked as accepted protocol had it.

His old buddies nodded.

Blackie hand gestured. "Over here, I've been saving a seat for you… want some of that police department dough."

The guys laughed along with Blackie, and dealt Pag in.

He lost fifty or sixty bucks, before one of them said he had to take a leak.

The rest fell in line.

Pag motioned Blackie to the corner. "I have some important information to trade for twenty-four grand."

Blackie cast him a doubtful eye. "Let's hear the information first, and then I'll determine the amount."

Pag inched closer, speaking in a soft tone. "The FBI conducted DNA tests on Ted Moomau and his father, Ned… the evidence is clear, they are not associated — in any way — with the string of gangland mutilation-murders."

Blackie eased closer, the information peaking his interest. "DNA… I've heard a little about it, tell me more."

"It's a new procedure in which lab people analyze crime-scene evidence with anything connected with an individual — hair follicles, saliva, clothing — to see if there is any connection."

"How do they do that?"

"It's high-level research, using X-rays and microscopes, I guess."

Blackie nervously rubbed his hand across his mouth. "How accurate is it?"

"It's a slam dunk."

"You're positive."

"Absolutely."

"Huh." Blackie mulled over the implications of DNA. "Guess that'll change everything." He pulled off his sunglasses and twirled them once and again. "That'll bring your tab down to forty-eight grand."

***

"Damn, it's cold out there." Clark stomped his shoes on the foyer rug, trying to loosen the snow. "Dad, can you take this bushel basket of gifts? I'm going to slip off my shoes."

"Yeah, I got it." Lewis grabbed the basket and peaked at the tags. "Hey, I see a couple gifts for me."

"Lewis! You're always snooping." Fran waved her index finger at him. "Just put the gifts under the tree."

He hustled into the living room. "How cold is it?"

"It's the coldest Christmas Day ever," Fran announced. "Nine below."

Abby rubbed her hands together. "The wind is cutting... chilled me to the bone."

Lewis popped his head in the doorway. "The winds are twenty-five miles per hour with gusts up to forty."

"It feels like it's fifty below." Clark headed for his mom.

She backed away. "Don't put your cold hands on me. You can give me a hug after you slice the ham."

Abby pulled an apron from the pantry. "How can I help?"

"You can fill the glasses with water, dear. By then the biscuits will be ready."

***

Wearing his new sweater and slippers, Lewis leaned back in his favorite leather chair.

"Looks like another good Christmas."

"Mom, that was a wonderful dinner." Abby jumped up and hugged her. "And the apple slices... the icing on top was out of this world, where..."

Fran winked, sending her a message. "An old family recipe. I'll give it to you some day."

"Mom, there you go again, pushing things along," Clark piped in.

Abby raised a hand. "Be quiet, Clark, your mother can say whatever she wants."

"You better do as she says, Clark." Lewis laughed, and changed the subject. "That was good news about Ted and his dad. Are you going to pass that information on to the mafia?"

"I've taken care of that," Clark said, not wanting to say too much.

"How is Sharon doing?" Fran asked.

"We didn't talk much… she was very professional."

"She looked great." Abby mentioned, in all sincerity.

Dad rocked forward. "Anything you can say about Isiah?"

"Hmm…" Clark rubbed his jaw, not wanting to be overly pessimistic. "It's not going well for him. The FBI surveillance teams have the mafia's top lieutenants in his mansion. The same guys have seats right behind the bench. One of our informants said Thomas is in debt big-time."

"Big-time… what does that mean?"

"Half a million, maybe more."

"Jesus Christ, what's wrong with him?"

"An informant told us, 'He has such a big ego, he thinks he can win!'"

"Maybe on the court when he's playing his game, but when he's playing their game, there's no way he can win." Lewis waved his hands frantically. "That reminds me of the connections the mob has with other segments of our community."

"Funny you mention that. Clifford is pushing to see how far the mafia tentacles reach into our community. He even recalled Dick Woodson, who'd been on loan to our committee to help out."

Dad's frown covered his forehead. "Why did he do that and leave you shorthanded?"

"It'll only be for another month or two. Woodson did the same thing when he was in Chicago, so Clifford wanted to take advantage of his experience.

***

Sitting on the far end of a row of empty chrome-rimmed, red vinyl stools, Earl glanced at the bullet holes in the windows of the Top Hat Hamburger joint on the corner of Gratiot and McClellan. In the summer, the place was a haven for drug dealers from the eastside of Detroit. *Huh,* he grunted to himself. *It's so cold today, not even the druggies are out… must be ten days now of subfreezing temperatures.*

He wrapped his hands around the steaming mug of coffee, still trying to thaw them from the short walk to the place. *This seems like an unlikely hangout for dealers. The checkered black and white tile floors and white porcelain-enamel walls outside are supposed to symbolize old fashioned cleanliness and purity — no purity in the heroin delivered here. And here I am, waiting to be interviewed by "Maserati" Rick Carter, the emerging kingpin of drug trafficking on the eastside.*

Seeing a powder-blue Mercedes Benz pull up, Earl's eyes opened wide. *A Mercedes Benz… that can't be.* He watched the flashy dressed man, with gold chains and diamond medallions hanging from his neck, slide out from behind the steering wheel and head for the front door.

Richard "Maserati" Carter opened the door and stepped toward Earl, spinning every chrome stool as he passed by. He extended his gold ring-filled hand, "Clarence Tidwell, I presume."

Earl aka Clarence, stood and grabbed his hand firmly. "Yes, sir."

"Where in the hell did you find those clothes?"

Clarence gave him a sheepish grin. "Goodwill and…"

Maserati cut him off. "I'll tell you one thing, if you're going to work for me, I'll take you down to The Broadway so you can dress in proper attire."

"Yes, sir."

Glancing at him one more time, Maserati's mouth quivered. "Your shoes look like shit."

"I've been laid off for six months. It was either eat or be without a sheet."

"Huh, I like that… a sense of humor." Maserati continued quizzing him. "Where did you work?"

"Sixteen years at the Cadillac plant on Scotten."

"Down by Western High?"

"Yeah, I went to high school there."

Maserati stroked his small, manicured mustache. "Let me see your hands."

Clarence extended his hands, palms up, for inspection.

Maserati rubbed his callus-free hands.

Knowing his intent, Clarence quickly responded. "Before they eliminated the third shift, I was a line-supervisor at night for the last five years.

"My sources say you're a good guy. You do drugs?"

"No sir, never have."

"Good for you… I don't understand why so many dumb bastards do."

He leaned back. "So… why do you want to work for Maserati Rick?"

"I was proud to work at Cadillac. We made the best cars in the world. I've spent the past several months exploring my options, checking out you and the others… I've heard, several times, you'll be number one on the eastside in a couple of years. I'd be proud to work for you."

"Huh, smooth…" Staring at him, Maserati sucked in a deep breath. "What are you having for lunch?"

"A chili cheese dog, chili cheese fries, and a large Coke."

"Done your research too." Maserati winked, then motioned to the heavyset cook/waiter for the day at the far end of the bar. "Sam… orders of my standard for my new assistant Clarence and me." Spinning his stool back toward Clarence, he asked, "You know how to cut heroin?"

"No, sir."

Maserati curled his lip. "Don't give me any of that 'sir' shit… just call me Rick."

"Yes, s… Rick."

A partial grin from Rick emerged and quickly slipped away. "Okay, when we're finished, you can follow me to my crack house just down the street. I'll give you your first lesson."

"Sounds good to me."

***

Clarence fell into a daily routine. Starting out at Maserati's flat near East Jefferson Avenue and Alter Road, he unlocked the door and turned off the elaborate security system for the fortified, military style bunker. Picking up a wrapped kilo package of heroin, he double-checked the inventory, and headed for another crack house.

By the end of the week, he would have traveled up and down the streets of old, abandoned or burnt-out buildings on the eastside of the city, to over twenty crack houses. The abandoned buildings ravaged by arson or neglect were *perfect* locations for Carter's operation — they're obscure, secluded, and left no rent-receipt trail.

Taking the kilo in the back room of a crack house, Clarence locked the door and unwrapped the heroin on a table loaded with the needed cutting tools. Knowing he'd be an easy target for a small-time drug dealer, he placed his cocked Berretta on the table. After that, it was a simple process of following the procedures. Cut the heroin, mixing the white powder with the designated amount of a non-intoxicating substance — sucrose, starch, talcum powder, caffeine, or crushed over-the-counter painkillers — and placing the mixture in small plastic bags, labeling them with the street name for each brand.

Glancing around, Clarence shook his head, sadly understanding the sweet tasting sucrose package would hook another kid. *These guys are heartless. Robbing the poor, addicting kids, and coercing the kids to rob more victims; it's a vicious circle. And over there... a jug on the corner of the table... the same stuff already mixed in liquid form, ready for addicts to inject themselves.* He bit his lip. *The only good part of this was Maserati bought nothing but the best. If people only knew what heroin can do. The stuff from most dealers varies between 3 and 99 percent pure, making the impact of a batch highly unpredictable.*

***

THE DETROIT NEWS
January 11, 1984

END OF A DYING BREED—
LICAVOLI DEAD AT 81

Peter Licavoli Sr., the racketeer who headed Detroit's Purple Gang during the Prohibition era, died

yesterday. From the time he organized the gang, more than 50 years ago, he was charged with 38 crimes, including murder. Yet, he served a little more than five and a half years in prison.

Following the 1,200 car-procession to the grave of Salvatore Catalanotte in 1930, a gang war erupted in Detroit for control of the city's rackets. Licavoli aligned himself with the winning Nicolette faction, which became the precursor to today's Detroit Partnership.

Senator Estes Kefauver, who headed an extensive investigation into organized crime, called Mr. Licavoli "one of the most cold blooded and contemptuous characters to appear before his committee.

In 1963, Detroit Police Commissioner Edwards testified that Mr. Licavoli was one of five Mafia Dons who headed illegal enterprises that grossed a total of $150 million a year.

***

A black Buick sedan slowed and stopped in front of the Caucus Club. Popping out of the front door, the driver hurried around to the back of the car and opened the door for Jake.

With her hand on Jake's, Amanda eased out of the back seat, one long leg with a dark green spike heel slid onto the pavement, followed by the other, showing off a form-fitting, forest green knit dress. She adjusted her long sleeves, and pulled her white fur-collared, vest jacket snugly around her neck.

Walking inside, the receptionist motioned for the two to follow her to his special table — tucked away in the far corner. Trying not to stare at her perfect body, Jake motioned for her to join him on the same side of the table. He wanted to say something about her form-fitting dress, but couldn't think of the proper words. Instead, he eased his hand against hers.

She placed her hand on top of his and held gently.

Encouraged by her acceptance, Jake contemplated his next move. *I don't want to rush her. Watching a tennis match, having an early dinner at Joe Muer's, followed by several lunches here, she must know how I feel. Damn, I don't know how long it's been since I felt this way. I need to say something to her.*

The waitress interrupted his train of thought. "Would you like to order a drink before lunch, Mr. Nicolette?"

Nodding to Amanda, he motioned for her to go ahead. "Yes, of course… I'll have a Nicolette Bullshot." Her eyes shifted to him, with a coy smile.

"Yes, make it two," he agreed, squeezing her hand.

Holding hands under the table, the two chatted like newlyweds.

The drinks arrived.

Their conversation didn't skip a beat.

Jake continued to search for a way to *pop the question,* with no luck. "The Pistons won their sixth in a row Saturday; beat Cleveland in overtime."

Sipping on her Bullshot, Amanda nodded. "Yes, I read the box score… 132 to 131. Isiah Thomas really played well."

"Do you follow basketball?"

"Some… I watch the Pistons whenever they're on TV."

"I have season tickets; would you like to go sometime?"

"Yes, I'd love to."

Jake paused, hoping it was the right time; his adrenaline pumped like a major decision was ready to burst out of him. "The London Chop House is across the street. It has wonderful food; it's…"

"Yes, I'd like to," she interrupted, taking the pressure off.

"Oh… great… How about Wednesday night, about 8:00… I'll pick you up."

"Perfect."

CHAPTER NINETEEN

Maserati parked his Mercedes Benz in front of The Broadway clothing store located downtown at 1247 Broadway, just two blocks from police headquarters. He opened the door.

"Mind if I ask you a question before we go in?"

Maserati turned to him. "Of course, go ahead."

"There's one thing I don't understand," Clarence said. "You're called 'Maserati Rick'; yet, you drive a Mercedes Benz?"

"Hah." Maserati chuckled. "You're not the first one to ask. "It goes back to when I was a kid." He briefly reminisced about the good ol' days. "I grew up on the same street as Thomas Hearns…"

Clarence interrupted, "Hitman Hearns?"

"The one and only." Maserati broke into a partial grin. "We all wanted to be the top dog; we competed with each other on everything and tried to outdo each other — *every hour of the day.* Two years ago, I was his bodyguard and started hanging around Kronk's Gym. I got to know Sugar Ray Leonard and Don King. Well, I couldn't be seen driving a Ford. So I got my first Mercedes." He sucked in a deep breath. "Turns out, about the same time, Demetrius Holloway and I formed our own enterprise. Now I'm in competition with him — he's a big dude — he buys a bigger, newer model Mercedes. Not, to be outdone, I buy a better model. He ups me again."

"Where does this end?"

"Hey, you're a good straight man." Rick smiled, building up to the punch-line. "So I said to myself, I'm going to up him once and for all… I go to Ohio and buy the latest model Maserati."

"What happened?"

"As soon as I pulled into the driveway of a downtown nightclub, the guys shouted, 'Maserati Rick, Maserati Rick…' and it stuck."

"That's crazy."

Looking Clarence squarely in the eye, Maserati paused for a moment. "I like you… you're more mature than most of the guys. You ask good questions... you understand... I don't have to explain the details. We're going to dress you up with some new duds — the latest European designer pants, jeans, shirts, shoes, belts — the whole shebang. I'm promoting you."

"Wow." Taken aback, Clarence was speechless for a moment. "Geez, thanks... what am I going to do?"

"You're going to be my assistant. You'll start by going to Miami twice a month and delivering heroin — a kilo at a time — to the big dealers."

"A kilo?" Clarence sounded shocked.

"These are the top-of-the-line dealers. They know when they buy a kilo from me, it's the best they can buy. I'm phasing them out of heroin and moving them into cocaine."

"Do you have many buyers like that?"

"Probably... forty-five or fifty, most of them in upscale sections of Detroit and suburbia."

"What's next?" Clarence probed.

Maserati spoke with pride. "We'll do the same in all of the crack houses."

***

A drumming sound, like a marching band, thumped in Clarence's ear. He glanced at the clock radio — 5:20 — and reached for the telephone. *Who the hell is calling me at this time in the morning?*

"Morning, this is Clarence," he squeaked out.

"This is Rick. Pack your overnight bag; we're leaving for Miami at seven o'clock. Come over to my condo in the Millender Center — 555 Brush Street."

Clarence shook the cobwebs out of his head. "Okay, I'll grab a bite and be right over."

"No need to grab a bite; Tracy will have bacon and eggs on the table... oh, and bring one of those snappy outfits on a hanger, I bought for you at The Broadway. When we return there'll be a big party going on up here."

"Got it, will do.

"Oh yeah... leave your car at the front entrance. I've made arrangements..."

"Anything else."

"No, just hustle your butt over here."

***

An hour later, Clarence hit the elevator button for the top floor apartment. He'd been there once before. *The place is spectacular... lots of open space, brightly colored paints — reds, yellows, and blues — modern furniture, and expensive abstract art. It's like nothing I've ever seen.*

Stepping out of the elevator, he came face to face with Tracy Cowen, Maserati Rick's devoted girlfriend. *She's as attractive as Rick described; and in that light blue pantsuit, she's worth a million dollars. And that rock on her hand; it must be four or five carats.*

"Clarence Tidwell, I've heard so much about you. It's so nice to meet you." Her eyes worked over his firm frame; a half grin emerged. "I can see why Rick thinks so highly of you."

"The feeling is mutual... I didn't realize you were so attractive."

She tossed him one more glance, then turned for the door. "Breakfast is ready. Do you want orange juice or V-8?"

"V-8, please."

"Rick mentioned you'd say that. The two of you are very much alike."

"Thank you, but I know who the boss is."

"Smooth aren't you." She smiled broadly and glanced at the bedroom. She called, "I can't believe it, Rick... Clarence is here and having V-8 just like you."

Rick bounced through the doorway, appearing dapper as usual—burnt orange pants with matching shirt half buttoned, showing off his hairy chest and making room for the oversized gold chain hanging halfway down to his belt. "Clarence, you made good time."

"You announced we had to leave at seven." He glimpsed his watch. "Twenty minutes for breakfast."

Rick punctuated his light mood with an excited laugh. "Didn't I tell you Tracy, this guy is okay?"

"He's a real catch." Eyeing him once more, she winked at Clarence. "Breakfast is served."

The two men joined her at the small round kitchen table, their plates loaded with bacon, eggs, biscuits, and gravy, along with a steaming mug of coffee on the right.

"Toast anyone?" Tracy asked as she passed a plate of lightly toasted bread with a dish of peach jam on it.

"Everything tastes wonderful," Clarence said, looking at Tracy. "Do you fix breakfast like this every morning?"

"You gotta be kidding." She cocked her head, sending Rick a curious smile. "This is a rarity; only when Rick is on a tight schedule."

"I really appreciate it, Babe," he mumbled, his mouth half full.

The two men shovelled in the grub and at precisely seven o'clock, Rick stood. "Gotta go, sweetie." He bent over and gave her a smacker on the cheek.

"Just a minute, hon." She jumped up. "I get more than that before you go on a trip." And laid a deep French kiss on him.

"Wow." He lifted an eyebrow. "Next time you're going along."

***

Two days after driving for twenty hours, Maserati pulled his black BMW into a deserted warehouse district in Miami and flicked off the car lights.

"Open the glove compartment, Clarence." He twisted one knee to the side. "There are two ski masks in there for us."

Following directions, Clarence pulled them out, handed one to Rick, and followed his lead in slipping the other ski mask over his head.

"Okay, here's the deal, I'll drive up to the overhead door of the third building on the left. "Over there." He pointed. "I'll turn the lights off and on twice and wait for them turn on the light above the office door. As soon as they flick the light two times again, I'll turn our lights off and on. The overhead door will open, I'll drive in and they'll close it."

"Is that it?"

"Yep, don't say a word, just watch!"

Clarence paid close attention to every detail of the building — inside and out.

"I'll release the trunk lid and two or three short men — I assume they're Mexicans or Puerto Ricans — wearing ski masks will fill up the trunk with a hundred kilo packages of heroin and fifty packages of cocaine."

"A hundred and fifty packages of narcotics?"

Maserati nodded. "As soon as the trunk lid slams, the overhead door will open, and I'll back up and drive away."

"No one says a word?" Clarence quizzed, without an opportunity for him to respond. "You don't pay them?"

"Right, no one says anything — there are no traceable actions, no money changing hands."

"Just like that."

"Yeah, I know these guys." He laughed, shaking his head. "Besides, they know where to find me. I've already made a down payment and they know I'll transfer the rest of the funds as soon as I double-check the goods when we return."

"It must cost a mint."

"Yeah… I receive a real volume discount." His voice revealed an assured confidence. "They don't have another customer in the country that purchases a hundred and fifty kilos at a time."

"How long will that last us?"

"Two weeks; and it'll be your turn to make a trip."

"Me?"

"You saw what happened. You're a fast learner, so from now on, you're on your own."

***

Rick and Clarence unloaded the haul at Maserati's fortress, near Alter and East Jefferson, then headed back to his downtown condo. Stopping under the canopy, Rick turned off the ignition. "Now comes your payback."

Giving him a meaningful glance, Clarence smiled, just a little. "Payback? I don't understand."

"Tracy has already announced I will be arriving late with my number one assistant…"

Clarence cut him off. "Did I receive a promotion?"

Maserati laughed, meaningfully. "You will if you make it through the night."

"Make it through the night?" A questioning frown crossed Clarence's brow. "Why do you say that?"

Lifting his head to meet Clarence's eyes, Rick broke into a smile. "The clothes you brought over are in an apartment on the first floor. After we clean up, we'll put on the Ritz and go up the elevator; you're going to enter a room like you've never experienced before."

Glancing at Clarence's befuddled face, Maserati broke into laughter.

"Do I get a hint?"

"Sure, there'll be fifteen or twenty of the most beautiful women in the city — black and white — pick whichever one you want. I'll give you the key to the first-floor apartment and you can bang her all night."

"Ah…"

Rick cut Clarence off before he could say a word. "There'll also be several councilmen, our state reps, three or four execs from the auto industry, our biggest dealers, and four white boys from the burbs."

"Do we have a goal to accomplish with them?"

Rick leaned back. "Have a good time…"

"That's a given." Clarence cleared his throat. "Beyond that, there must be a reason why you invited them."

"Guess I hadn't thought much beyond giving them a little reward."

Clarence gave him a double nod. "I'm sure they'll appreciate your generosity."

"So?"

"So, it's an opportunity for us to gain the upper hand."

Maserati rubbed his upper lip with the tips of his forefinger, in thought. "You're serious about accomplishing something, aren't you?" Rick asked rhetorically to Clarence's nod. "Well then… next month, I'm increasing the costs by 25 percent for the four guys from the suburbs. Set that up."

"I can do anything I want?"

"Hell, yes, I don't give a shit about them — they've got all kinds of money." Rick opened his door. "C'mon, momma's waiting."

***

Dressed in red — Italian shirt and pants — wearing white bucks, and a white tie, Rick opened the door and stepped into his condo.

A siren went off, drowning-out conversation. Cheers erupted. "Maserati Rick… Maserati Rick… Maserati Rick."

Raising his hands over his head, he quieted the crowd of nearly seventy. "I don't want to interrupt the party. I just want to introduce my new number one man, Clarence Tidwell," he announced, loud enough for all to hear. He nudged Clarence forward.

Applause filled the room.

A voluminous broad standing next to them, rubbed her hand over Clarence's bald head. "I'm *ready*, Baby!

Clarence laid a smacker on her cheek to the crowd's reverberating roar.

"Let the party begin," Maserati shouted.

The five-man combo in the corner of the living room struck up Bruce Springsteen's "Dancing in the Dark."

Clarence glad-handed those around him, grabbed a beer at the bar, and gazed across the lavish condo to the balcony overlooking the city. *Rick was right. I've never seen so much carefree opulence in my life... talk about letting it all hang out. Jesus, these broads are unbelievable.* He took a slug. *There's Thomas Hearns, the city's budget director, a couple city council members, and gobs of people whose pictures have been in the paper. Where are the suburban drug dealers?*

His eyes landed on the four guys huddled on the balcony. Stepping over to the bar, he whispered something in the bartender's ear, picked up a bottle of beer, and made his way to the balcony.

After going through ceremonial welcoming and chit-chatting briefly, Clarence nodded to the vacant table behind them. "Mind if we talk a little business?"

The guys' eyes opened wide; their heads automatically nodded in agreement. Clarence motioned to the bartender and before the four had settled in at the patio table, a round of doubles was set before them.

Clarence eased his chair up to the table and spoke in a low, firm voice. "Our costs are being jacked up by our supplier and Maserati has to pass part of it on to you..." He paused setting them up for the punchline. Each of them leaned further over the table toward him. "Starting next month, the price per kilo will increase 40 percent."

"Forty percent, Jesus Christ, we can't afford that kind of increase," a guy proclaimed.

"Yeah, yeah... that's too much," the others chimed in.

Clarence slid up tight to the table and leaned forward. "Hey, Maserati doesn't like it either. Miami is jacking up the prices. Maserati is eating the costs for the first month."

"Eating the costs?" one of them repeated.

Clarence shot him a look. "So, here's the deal… next month I will deliver two kilos to each of you for the price of one."

"Two for one, you gotta be shittin' me," the tall guy echoed on behalf of the group.

"No shit," Clarence savored the moment, knowing he had them in the palm of his hand. "After that, the price will be increased 40 percent. That's a real deal, don't you think?" Catching the group off guard, Clarence continued. "Before the night is over, I want each of you to thank Rick for helping you out…" He paused, letting it sink in. "Will all of you do that for me?"

Catching the nod from each of the four, Clarence hit them with the closer. "Good." The bartender sat a bottle of the booze they'd been drinking in front of the four dealers. "So, here's the rest of the deal." He tossed the key to the first-floor apartment on the table. "Here's the key to room 104, it's a four-bedroom apartment and it's yours for the night. Pick any woman in the place, it's on the house."

The eyes of the four bulged in unison. "You mean…"

Clarence interrupted, "No strings… other than thanking Maserati for taking care of the increase." He scrutinized them, securing a nod from each.

***

A tall, attractive black woman made her way to the table where Clarence had just plopped down. "Mind if I join you?"

Feeling good about pulling off his little coupe, Clarence casually flipped his hand toward the chair across the table from him.

Taking advantage of the opportunity, she winked and eased into the chair next to him. Before he could lift his beer, she had her hand in his crotch.

Clarence smiled politely, gently lifted her hand, and placed it on the table. "That's taken for the night."

Her sensual eyes slid down his muscular frame and back up. "How about a raincheck?"

Maserati burst onto the balcony. "Okay, let's hear about the deal."

Gloating like he'd grabbed the panties of the hottest chick, Clarence cooled it with the lovely woman. With a look from Rick she left them alone.

"You told me to take care of it, so I did."

"I know that." Rick grabbed a chair, spun it around, sat down, and hung his arms over the back of the chair. "They're all happy. What the hell did you do?"

"It was simple. I told them next month, I'd give them two kilos for the price of one…"

About to interrupt, Rick's face reddened.

"Hold it." Clarence pushed his hand forward, as if signaling like a stop sign. "After that the increase will be 40 percent."

"40 percent, Jesus… how'd you pull that off?"

"A bottle of booze, a babe, and a bed."

"The hell you say."

"I had the staff clean our stuff out room 104. The four of them are getting laid while your closed-circuit cameras are taping it all."

Maserati slapped Clarence on the back. "Oh my God, that's a real coup!

CHAPTER TWENTY

Jake slipped a waist-length Maximilian white mink around Amanda's shoulders. "How does that feel, sweetie?"

"Oh, I just love it." She ran her fingers up and down the fur and around her neck. "It's wonderful, thank you."

"It's nothing… most important, it looks wonderful on you."

Amanda pecked him on the cheek. "It's so cuddly, maybe I'll sleep with it tonight."

"With just that on?" He jested, in hopes he might be there too.

She gave him a soft, sexy smile, and winked. "Maybe."

Feeling like a teenage boy, he wanted to jump in bed with her right now. Instead, he gently took her hand and strolled into the restaurant.

Seated in his favorite place, a small half-moon booth, each of them ordered their drinks — Jack Daniels for him and Vodka Gimlet for her.

Jake raised his Old Fashioned glass and tilted it slightly, touching her cone-shaped martini glass. "Here's to a wonderful dinner."

"And to many more." She looked over the top of her glass, her eyes glued sensually on him.

Interpreting *many more* to mean more than might have been meant, he swallowed discretely, trying not to reveal his inner feelings. "How about this place? Do you like it?"

"Since moving from L.A., I'd heard lots about the London Chop House, but I never realized it was so elegant." Amanda glanced at the décor. "The dimly lit ambiance is romantic and the small lamp on the table is so cute." She rubbed her hand over the seat of the dark leather booth and inched closer to him. "Smooth… nice."

"It's been named one of the top restaurants in the nation for the past several years. Lester and Sam Gruber started it back in '38. One of them is here each night… I'll introduce you when whichever one comes around."

"Oh, you don't have to do that," she said, somewhat embarrassed.

"It's not a problem, I want him to meet you."

Amanda glanced at the number of couples in the place. "Are you sure we should be here? There are several men here with…"

"Don't worry." Jake interrupted. "Most of the guys are long-term friends or colleagues. No one talks about who is here; it's been like that for years."

"Well." She made a face, frowning. "You're positive."

"Absolutely… there's no way I'd ever embarrass you or put you in a difficult position."

She tipped the last of her gimlet and asked, "Tell me what you really do?"

Startled by her directness, Jake leaned back in the booth and studied her; his piercing eyes softened. He tried a little smile, collecting the words.

Tense inside, she tried not to show it.

He responded slowly, "I'm not sure what you mean," he paused. Jake picked up his glass and took a sip — his eyes still focused on her. "I'm a businessman with a large portfolio of real estate holdings."

She pressed forward. "I heard you were the Boss of the Detroit Mafia, but never acknowledged it."

He facepalmed a moment, then slowly lowered his hands. "Rumors like that have been around since I was out of college. My old man was a big shot in the mafia, so everyone said I was being groomed for the top spot." He hesitated, uncharacteristically, before continuing. "After I was out of college there was a rumor that I was a *made man* and ready to take over.

"A *made man?*" She sputtered, not having a clue of its meaning.

"Yeah… It means you've killed a person." He didn't want to appear nervous giving her so much personal information. "Some people believe killing someone is a prerequisite to moving up in the ranks of the mafia."

"Have… you?" she asked, a lump in her throat.

"Absolutely not," he lied.

Amanda's body language suggested she was ready to stand up. "Look, I've been entirely truthful about my background and have answered numerous questions." She stared him down. "If you expect more of me, I expect you to be open and truthful in every respect, as well, fair enough?"

"Oh, yes," he responded quickly, surprised by her candor.

She waited, gave him a slight hand gesture. "Well?"

Having never admitted to being the Boss, Jake felt a stream of perspiration run under his arm. "Are you ready to order?" he asked, deflecting the question.

"Yes." Amanda glanced up at the waiter. "I'll have the oysters Rockefeller and soup… oh my, they all sound so good — crab bisque, French onion, and clam & corn chowder — which would you order?"

The older waiter glanced around and answered in a soft tone. "I think the lady would like the chowder, with bacon and roasted garlic."

"Perfect." She winked at him and turned the menu to the entrees. "And… double-cut lamb chops."

"Excellent, that would have been my choice." He turned to Jake. "And for you, Mr. Nicolette?"

"I'll have the calamari, a Caesar salad, and New York strip…"

"Rare, as usual, sir?"

"Yes, that'll be fine." He picked up the leather-bound wine list and turned to Amanda. "Would a red be fine with you?"

"Yes, of course."

"We'll have a bottle of… Antinori Tignanello." He turned to Amanda. "It's my favorite blend from Tuscany. It has the personality of a Sangiovese; it'll be perfect with your lamb chops."

"Sounds wonderful." She whispered to Jake. "Has he been here a long time?"

Jake's mouth turned down. "I can't remember when he wasn't here."

"I thought so."

Letting him think her probing was over, Amanda waited for the right moment, hanging on like a terrier.

The soups and salads were served.

The waiter nodded. "Bon Appétit."

"The chowder is wonderful."

"One of my favorites, too."

Taking her time, she sipped on a spoonful of chowder and laid her spoon aside. "Let's try it this way. What are the rumors you've heard about the organizational structure of the mafia?"

Catching onto her strategy, Jake smirked, knowing she was far savvier than most men. The way her question was phrased allowed him to speak truthfully.

"Well, if you put it that way…" Taking his time, Jake finished his second Jack Daniels and motioned for another. "I hear that Angelo Travaglini is the Underboss."

"Angelo… the same Angelo we met with Catarina at the Caucus Club?"

"Yes."

"Underboss? You need to help me out on that," she fibbed.

Enjoying her game, Jake gave her a half grin. "It means he's the number two man in the mafia."

"Oh… according to rumor," she continued to probe. "Blackie Giardini is number three in the pecking order and is called the Street Boss."

Jake shook his head, realizing *she had done her homework*. "You must have spent a lot of time listening to rumors."

Amanda gave him a sly grin, both of them knowing the *words were the truth*.

The entrees arrived, and the conversation slowed to periodic moments of chit-chat about items of no meaning. Pushing the remaining bite of his strip steak away, Jake clasped her hand. "So, where to now?" he asked, his hopes high, unable to say more.

Knowing full well his interest, she proposed. "I thought next Friday we might start with dinner at Joe Muer's and then… we could walk over to my place for an after-dinner drink."

"Are you propositioning me?"

In a slow, sensual way her eyes rose and joined his. "Isn't that what you want?"

***

"Dad, you won't believe it, One of our team members has uncovered a scheme where mobsters drive police cars to Detroit Metro."

"Nah, I can't believe that."

"It's true, dad." Clark let go with an expressive grin. "We've double-checked it."

Knowing anything was possible with the corrupt force, his dad leaned back. "Okay, let's hear it."

"A police car pulls up next to a black sedan at one of the airport motels. A mafia lackey jumps out wearing a fake uniform, hands the policeman a couple hundred bucks and the key to a room where a prostitute awaits."

"I got it," his dad jumped in. "The lackey drives the police car to Metro airport, picks up the drugs and returns the car."

Clark smiled. "You're smarter than you look," he jested.

"Have you ever heard of such a thing?"

His dad mulled over the question. "Well, maybe not like that, but it reminds me of how the airport was used in the past."

Clark gave him a quizzical look. "I don't recall you ever saying anything about that."

"Humph." Lewis laughed. "Every spring when the snow melted, we'd get one call after another."

"A call?" Clark wondered anew. "From where?"

"Wherever a pile of snow at the end of a parking lot had melted — there was a body."

"No… you gotta be kidding me."

His dad shook his head. "One spring we found six bodies in the snow bank at the end of the long-term parking lot."

"That's *crazy!*"

"Talk about crazy, anything new happening with your Isiah Thomas investigation?"

"Huh." Clark sat stiff as a stone statue. "I don't know how to figure it out. The Pistons have been on the upswing for the past two or three weeks. They've won seven out of their last nine games, and the next four games coming up they'll be the favorite."

Lewis twisted his mouth into a quirky grin. "Maybe that's part of the strategy."

"Strategy?" Clark tilted his head. "What do you mean by that?"

"The oddsmakers give extra weight to how the team has played lately, particularly the last few games, so win, win, win, increases the likelihood of winning; thereby, increasing the point spread."

"I got it!" Clark exclaimed, his intellect finally clicking. "So if you know they will not beat the point spread, you can bet big money and win a lot."

"And," his dad paused, "if you bet they'll lose — against the odds — you can haul in big bucks."

"The Pistons will be big favorites when they play the Nets this Wednesday… want to bet?"

***

Dressed in winter attire, Clark's team, including a new face sitting next to him, gathered around the conference table.

Across from him with a steaming cup of coffee in front of her, Veronica, transferred from Miami, shivered one more time. "Do you think the temperature will ever go above zero?

A sneer slid across Clark's face, adding a sense of hopelessness. "I heard this is the coldest January ever. Forty would seem like a heat wave."

"Yeah, people would be out washing their cars." Pag joked.

Clark turned to the short black man sitting next to him. "Before we start on today's agenda, I want to introduce the newest member of our team." He paused for effect. "Please welcome Willie Ross."

His nod followed their applause.

"The floor is yours." Clark swept a flourishing hand to him. "Want to give them a brief glimpse of your background?"

"Okay, I'm married, have two kids, and a wonderful wife, Sharia, who somehow has tolerated me for twelve years. I'm thirty-one, grew up in the Point Breeze area of Philadelphia."

Pat Fitzpatrick, the agent from New Jersey, came to attention. "You know where the Southphilly Seafood Market is?"

"Yeah, on South 18th street and Dickinson. My home is on Wilder, the next street over."

"One of those brick row houses?"

"Right; the only way you can tell them apart is by the color of the brick or if they've been painted."

"Excuse me." Clark cut off the conversation between the two. "You can rehash neighborhoods over coffee. Anything else we ought to know?"

"Yeah… probably…" He paused, as if counting. "For eight years I was a member of the Black Mafia."

"You're connected to Clyde 'Apples' Ross, one of the fourteen founders of the group, aren't you? I read about him in the Jersey papers. They controlled most of the black areas in the city — drug trafficking, prostitution, and extortion — most organized crime activities just like the mafia here.”

“Pat.” Clark raised his hand. “How about we let Willie have a word.”

“Sorry.” Fitzpatrick eased back into his chair.

“‘Apples’ Ross was one tough guy — my kinfolk. Five assholes from the Black Mafia gang-raped my sister.” Willie glanced around the table. “My apologies for my French to the ladies.” He paused, collecting his composure. “Things were tough. I didn’t have a dad around, so it was up to me to keep the family afloat. I sold drugs to feed our family. When I was fifteen, the FBI gave me a choice; essentially it was, ‘Kid you’re going to prison for fifteen to twenty years or you can become an undercover informant’ — that was a no-brainer.”

“You’re the guy.” Pat covered his mouth.

“Yes, I testified against the Black Mafia in the fall of 1974 court case by the Justice Department that led to the imprisonment of their top twenty-one leaders.” He rolled his shoulders. “Obviously, that blew my cover so, almost ten years later here I am.”

***

“Agenda item number one,” Clark started. “Earlier, I mentioned, the magnitude of Earl’s work on Maserati Rick would require more time than I had anticipated. The FBI has assigned Willie to do undercover work on the Curry Brothers; they’ll be a hard nut to crack. Any questions?”

Seeing no hands, Clark moved on. “Item number two. In regard to Earl’s activity, I’m pleased to report he’s made significant inroads and is working directly with Maserati Rick.”

“I’m not surprised,” Pag stated.

“Neither am I.” Clark spoke with pride about his lifelong friend. “In a nutshell, he’s moved up from cutting heroin for the crack houses to picking up a hundred or more kilos of heroin and cocaine from Miami.”

“Miami, I could handle that.” Kimberly flashed an unusually sexy smile.

“I’m afraid it’s not too exciting — in and out the same night — a stop overnight and deliver the goods the next day.” Clark slid up to the table. “Half of the kilos are being sold to dealers in the upscale sections of Detroit and suburbia. And, they're increasing the proportion of cocaine with every shipment."

"God… damn," Pag voiced, his tone strong. "I knew cocaine was on the way and expanding into the burbs; it opens the door to unlimited potential."

Heads nodded around the table.

"Item number three." Clark gazed toward the end of the table. "This one is for Kimberly…"

She perked up, pulling her collar tight around her neck against the cold. "The year-end report from Jack Grimes, the FBI guru on nationwide killings of mobsters, cited three more killings in the last quarter. And, each one was on the…" She paused, to orchestrate the response. "And, each one was on the…?" she prompted them.

"Twenty-second," the group shouted in unison.

"I may be a terrier, but I haven't accomplished anything yet." Her reddened face still aglow.

Where did they occur?" Pag asked.

Kimberly read from the sheet, "One in Chicago and Kansas City on October 22nd and one in Dallas on December 22nd. According to Grimes that brings the total to fifty-one since 1942.

***

Triggered by the morning's disclosure, Kimberly sat somberly at her dinette table slushing the remains of her second glass of Galo Chablis. *Three more mafia capos killed in the last three months, in different cities, all on the 22nd of the month. Fifty-one mobsters murdered in forty years, all on the 22nd. And, those are the ones the FBI knows about. For all we know, the number could be a hundred and fifty.*

She downed the remainder of the bottle and opened another. *Veronica's thought that 22nd might be some form of communication; makes sense. Who's communicating with whom? What are they communicating? And why?*

Kimberly's frustration was nothing new — it'd been going on for four years — Pag had been her chief antagonist ever since. Even when she went to the bathroom, he shouted 'twenty-two skidoo.'" *Darn, I'll show him.*

Recently, her torment had become a nightly experience.

Tonight was no different.

She had already scribbled 22 on her yellow pad, tore off eight or ten sheets, wadded them up, and tossed them in the wastebasket.

Filling her glass, she took a sip and scribbled, again, 22…

Trying to come up with another approach, she wrote 22 then added 22. Forty-four didn't go anywhere.

She jotted 22 sideways, upside down, and on an angle… nothing, again.

Kimberly tried different impressions — dark and bold, different fonts — Old English — still nothing. *Damn, I know the answer is here.*

Finishing off the Chablis, her eyes drooped and her head slumped onto her folded arms.

Waking up out of a dead sleep, her head snapped up, like a lightning bolt — totally alert—she picked up her pencil and slowly drew a block-form 2, backward—on a 45-degree angle—making it appear like a tilted Z. She drew another Z, perpendicular to the first one, crossing at right angles in the center.

Humm…

Having a notion of the symbol she was creating, she drew a Nazi swastika, and stared.

Grabbing a pad of paper, she hurriedly jotted down her thoughts:

What the hell! Could it be?
This is 1984 not 1944.
Why would Nazis be communicating this way?
About what?
Why?

CHAPTER TWENTY-ONE

Arriving early at Joe Muer's, Jake straightened the yellow turtleneck under his blue blazer, slid onto a red padded stool at the piano bar, and ordered a Jack Daniels. Glancing at the checkered tile floor and then up at the elaborate French chandelier centered above, his mind flashed back to the first day he'd seen her. *There was something about her; classy, yet, fresh and natural. It was more than her moves on the tennis court.*

A tap on the shoulder interrupted his thoughts. "May I join you?"

Twisting his head, he faced her décolletage revealed by a low-cut V-neck and form-fitting purple dress.

Sliding his eyes up to hers, she winked. "Do you like it?"

Caught without a word in mind, he stammered. "Why… yes."

Knowing his thoughts were centered on her cleavage, she joked, "I'm talking about the dress."

"Yes… of course, it's beautiful. Where did you buy it?"

"One of my favorite boutiques in Santa Monica."

"Maybe we could go there some time."

"I'd like that."

Jake's fantasy shifted dreamily to watching her in a personal style show. *The hell with that, I want her right now.* Pushing the fantasy aside, he stood, took her by the hand, and guided her to the receptionist.

"Good evening, Mr. Nicolette. Right this way." The tall, slender hostess led them to the last table with a water view.

"Do you like this spot?"

"It's perfect." Amanda gazed down river — lights twinkled on both sides — the downtown aglow. "It's so relaxing here. I just love this place."

Jake reached across the table, placed his hand on top of hers, and ran his index finger between each of her fingers.

Rubio approached the table and waited, as if oblivious to their tenderness.

Casting a smile upward, Amanda glanced his way.

"Would you like to start with a drink this evening?"

"Oh yes..." Jake stumbled, engulfed in his fantasy. "We'll have a Jack Daniels on the rocks and... a Vodka Gimlet," he added catching her nod.

The two chatted over a round of drinks and orders of fried calamari, steamed mussels, and an extra order of French bread. Their closeness was a picture, as if they'd been lovers who'd been in bed with each other countless times. Amanda rubbed his other hand; their eyes and body language saying more than words could convey.

Rubio appeared at the table and waited, watching the two lovebirds deep in conversation. He cleared his throat.

Jake's wink followed Amanda's smile.

"Before you place your orders for tonight, I'm pleased to announce a special treat to top off your evening's delight."

Jake thought nothing could top off being with Amanda all night.

The waiter tempted both of them. "The nationally renowned Chef Thomas Harte, founder of 'My Daddy's Cheesecake' is with us tonight. Based on your choice, he will personalize a mini-cheesecake for you."

"Our choice!" Jake exclaimed.

"Yes, you can pick the flavor of a candy bar. He's made them in our kitchen with the finest ingredients — Guittard chocolate — and he'll personally deliver your choice."

"Oh my," Amanda gasped. "That makes me think about not having an entrée."

"That would be a first for me. Why not?"

She gave him a sly, sensual smile. "I was thinking about a different first."

Jake swallowed hard. "Let's do it... two firsts in one night."

Unable to avoid hearing the conversation, Rubio's eyes bugged. "Would you like for me to invite Chef Harte out now?"

"Yes!" Amanda said emphatically.

Within minutes, a surprisingly trim, mustached man whose youthful appearance belied his age, entered the room wearing a white toque positioned squarely on his head. He walked briskly toward their table. Chef Harte announced himself and went into his spiel about making the cakes, ending with, "For tonight I suggest a selection from one of my favorites — Almond Joy, Butterfinger, or a Clark bar."

Jake gestured for Amanda to go first. "Hmm… Butterfinger to go."

"Excellent choice." The chef turned and nodded. "And you, Mr. Nicolette."

"I'll have an… Almond Joy… oh yes, to go."

***

"Which one would you like first?"

A Cheshire grin filled Jake's face; his thoughts not on cheesecake.

"Butterfinger or Almond Joy?" Amanda brushed him away. "First." She pointed to the two boxes resting on the small table in the living room, overlooking the Detroit River.

"You pick."

She studied the boxes, then slid the one on the right toward him. "Open this one, I'll get forks and plates."

She hurried to the kitchen and was back in no time — an Almond Joy cheesecake positioned in front of Jake. "Did you cheat?"

"No, why would I do that?"

She cast him a questioning eye, eased onto the chair across from him, and cut two slices from the Almond Joy. Pushing the larger portion toward him, she sliced a small piece off the other one. "Hmm, that's delicious… but I can't eat another bite." She rose and headed for the other end of her apartment. "You can finish yours while I slip into something more comfortable."

Watching her disappear into the dark, Jake took a bite, then another, and another, before he realized only one morsel remained. *Geez, maybe I should save that until she returns, maybe… hell with it, I can't wait — his desire pressed his pants — I wonder what she'll be wearing?* He nervously glanced at his watch — time seemed to stop — he stood and looked out the window at the twinkling lights framing the river.

He felt her arms wrap around his waist. "Enjoying the view?" she asked in a soft, sensual whisper.

His heart jumped into his mouth, he choked out, "It's very nice."

"I think so too." Her hands slowly unbuckled his belt, unzipped his pants, and let them slide to the floor.

Jake started to turn.

She pulled herself tight against his back. "Relax, sweetie…"

He twitterpated — his hormones raced through his boxer shorts.

Her hands inched upward, loosening his shirt, one button at a time, then unbuttoning his sleeves, and easing his shirt off his shoulders.

Jake's mouth went dry; he sucked in a deep breath, trying not to lose control.

Adding more to the seduction, she ran her fingers over his rock hard pecs, then turned him around and pressed her flimsy negligee against his hot body.

***

Knowing Kimberly wasn't an early riser, Clark had a mug of coffee waiting for her when she pulled herself up to the table for his hastily called seven o'clock meeting.

"Thanks for coming so early," she mumbled; her eyes still half glued.

"You sounded ecstatic on the phone, like you were going to explode." Taking a long sip of coffee, he gave her time to down a couple of short swigs. "So, what's the excitement all about?"

"I found it, Clark. I found it," she babbled. "Twenty-two, I found the connection… you won't believe it!"

"Okay… I promise to believe it." Clark cocked his head in an easy manner, studying her. "Just slow down so I can understand."

She shook her head. "Driving in this morning, I had it all planned out. I knew exactly how I was going to tell you… now I'm a bundle of nerves."

"Okay, now repeat after me." He spoke deliberately. "Twenty-two is a…"

"It's a symbol," she blurted.

Not understanding her thought, Clark stared for the longest moment. "Could you give me another hint?" he asked, patiently. "Maybe step back two or three yards."

A grin broke on Kimberly's face; she sucked in a deep breath and sighed. "Last night I was doing my nightly doodling when suddenly a different image came to mind. I sketched a block-Z on a 45-degree angle and crossed it with another one." She opened her

black notebook, pulled out a sheet of paper and slid it in front of Clark. "There, what do you think?"

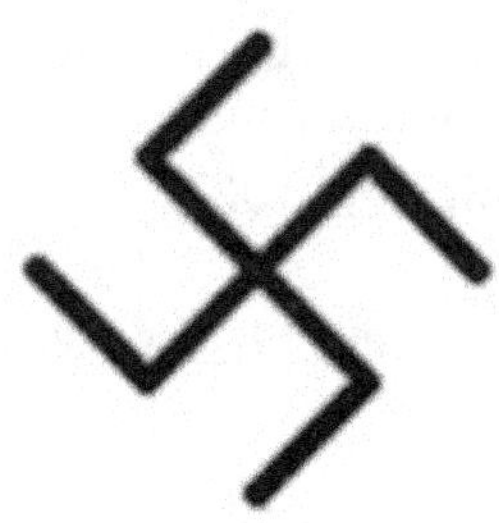

Clark stared, unable to move; slowly he ran his fingers through his crop of sandy brown hair. "Huh… I can't believe it." Picking up the sheet, he gawked — his mind twirled and twisted — his thoughts jumbled, incoherent. "So, what do *you* think?"

"Well… that's the question I pondered all weekend. I went through three bottles of Gallo, and still — I don't know."

Clark rubbed a hand across his jutted jaw. "What's your best theory?"

"I like Veronica's notion that it's some type of communication." Her enthusiasm continued to bubble. "I don't understand how or why… my scenario is something like this… a Nazi group kills a mobster on the twenty-second in a city and they use the newspaper to communicate the murder to other Nazi groups."

"O… okay, where to next?"

"Hmm." Kimberly's eyes darted around. "I suppose someone, somewhere is keeping score, keeping track of what's happening, maybe even directing the next killing, who knows… after that… I'm at my wits end."

"Interesting." Clark paused, his mind on the same track, picking up the pace. "All of those are possibilities… why would they be communicating? People just don't go around knocking off people. There must be a reason."

"I know… don't have a clue where to…"

Clark's brain clicked. "The first one started in 1942… right?"

"Yeah, we need a historian."

"Yes." Clark's mind was already there. "I'm checking with my mom, she taught history for forty years."

***

"Mom, this is the best pecan pie you've ever made."

"Oh, shush…" Fran smiled and turned to the living room. "Don't try to butter me up; I've already given a lot of thought to the question you posed. So, let's get on with it."

Clark smiled to himself. *When she has an assignment, a challenge, or something to do, Katie bar the doors.* "Okay, I'll start with the question I posed on the phone, 'Why would a group of Nazis want to kill mobsters?'"

Placing her hands in the center of the kitchen table, Fran gave him a partial grin. "That's an interesting question. Here's my take… the Nazis persecuted Jews, Gypsies, and others who didn't fit their mold… so there are thousands of people who'd want to *get even.* The Germans killed off Mafiosos? I don't think so. If anything, Hitler would have used the mafia to achieve his goals."

"Maybe someone double-crossed him?"

"Hmm, not likely." Mimicking Hitler, a ruthless sneer crossed her normally gentle face; Fran shook her head, no. "Hitler would have had the SS eliminate whoever it was."

"Just like that?"

"Probably that night. Their network was unbelievable; they were extremely efficient." She ventured a different thought. "Maybe someone is using the swastika as a cover."

Clark cocked his head and sent her a curious glance; he hadn't thought of that possibility. "A cover? You need to expand on that."

"Well, translating a swastika into twenty-two is a very creative communication strategy. So, I would assume… they're also capable of disguising who they are."

Surprise jumped from Clark's eyes glowing with interest. "So we may not be chasing Nazis after all?"

Fran smiled to herself, knowing she'd brought Clark's thinking along, step-by-step. "That's a distinct possibility."

"Wow." Putting on his thinking cap again, Clark ran his fingers through his hair. "So if the Nazis weren't out to get the mafia, who was?"

A smile burst, filling Fran's face. "I thought you'd never ask."

"Thanks, mom."

She slid a pad of paper across the table. "This is pretty complex; you might want to take a few notes."

Caught off guard, Clark pulled out his pen and opened his well-used spiral bound notepad. "Okay, I'm ready."

"Early in Benito Mussolini's career, his ambitions extended far beyond that of being the Prime Minister of Italy. At thirty-nine, as the youngest prime minister ever, he knew he had to neutralize two internal forces — the Catholic Church and the Italian Mafia — both of which stood in his way of becoming the supreme ruler of Italy."

"The Catholic Church? How does that connect?"

"That's another interesting point." Fran raised her hand to her temple. "First, you have to get inside the head of Mussolini. No one, not even Christ on Sunday, could be above him."

"So how did he neutralize the Church?"

"He gave the Catholic Church something it had wanted for centuries."

A bewildered, blank look crossed Clark's face. "I have no idea."

"They wanted to be a free, independent state/country with no allegiance to Italy or any other country."

"And he could do that?"

"Absolutely." Fran's grin broadened into a smile. "In 1929, he pushed through the Italian parliament the Lateran Treaty, which formed the Vatican City as an independent state, free of Italian control."

"Wow, that was quite a coup."

"You got that right, and now… they *owe him*."

"How'd he deal with the Italian Mafia?"

She shook her head. "That wasn't so slick."

He sensed excitement in her tone. "How so?"

"He killed them all, plain and simple."

"Nah, he couldn't kill…"

Fran interrupted, "He killed all of the mid-range capos in Sicily, the hotbed of the mafia. He had a standing reward for anyone known to be associated with the mob. It wasn't long before the few remaining ones went underground until Mussolini was deposed in 1943."

"So, if some of these anti-mafia, Mussolini supporters happened to immigrate to America, we'd have a group of them here."

"It took you a while… but yes, that'd be my conclusion."

***

Clark passed out copies of Kimberly's swastika and repeated the conversation he'd had with his mom. Leaning back in the swivel rocker, he glanced at Kimberly seated at the other end of the conference table. "Anything you want to add?"

Shaking her head, Kimberly smiled; her rosy cheeks aglow. "You've covered it all."

"You cracked it…" Pag jumped up. "Let's hear it for Kimberly."

Applause filled the room.

Clark turned to special invitee Clifford McGill. "How about that?"

"Well, first of all I want to thank Kimberly for her bulldog persistence. Your commitment to finding a solution is truly outstanding. Thanks, from all of us at the FBI."

"Thanks."

Clifford turned to Clark. "This is the biggest revelation we've had in over forty years. The speculation is more than a theory; I think it is the real thing." He stood. "I'm calling Washington right now and have them send it to special agent Grimes, ASAP."

Clark glanced around the table. "Guess we have a real challenge before us. Any thoughts?"

Still surprised by the magnitude of what they'd just heard; responses came slowly.

Mulling over the Church's connection, devoted Catholic, Veronica, didn't hesitate. "I'd like to know more about the Lateran Treaty. I'll do some research on that."

"Good." Clark turned to Pag. "How about you?"

"I've been wondering if you want me to leak this information to the mafia?"

"I talked to Clifford about that before the meeting. He wants to double-check everything with Washington before we move ahead with anything."

"Makes sense." Pag hid his disappointment. "I'll do a little digging on Mussolini. I was always interested in learning more about him, anyway."

Pat Fitzpatrick thought for a moment. "I'll look to see if I can find anything about German defectors. I'm sure there were plenty of Germans who didn't agree with Hitler's plans."

"Yeah, that reminds me." Bennett managed a smile, nodding his head. "I read an article some time ago about the French Resistance smuggling wine and Jews across the border into Italy. "I'll dig into that possibility."

Clark glanced at his watch. "That took longer than I thought. Let's take a short break and we'll let Frank and Pat do their thing on Isiah."

***

"Who wants to go first?"

"I will," Bennett said, eagerly. "I played ball in college and watched hundreds of games in my life time… I can tell you one thing — Isiah Thomas *is* shaving points."

Clark shifted back in his chair, surprised by the firmness of his tone. "That's a pretty bold statement."

"The feds may not be able to prove it, but I can tell by his body language. In the home game last week against the Nets, the Pistons were big favorites. Thomas got twenty-four… but the guy he was guarding scored more — that's never in the stats."

"Anything else?"

"Yes, two things. Last week, Isiah was a world-beater. He shot over 50 percent, led the team in scoring and had four steals and ten assists — they clobbered the Hawks. But, the second item is as Paul Harvey would say, 'the rest of the story,' there was a beautiful woman sitting next to Jake Nicolette."

"He was at the game?"

"Yeah, he didn't move out of his seat the entire game…"

"Shit man, he probably had a hard on most of the game," Pag interrupted.

Clark straightened in his chair. "What do you mean by that?"

"We're on Bennett's nickel. I'll let him tell you."

Clark turned to Frank. "Well, Bennett?"

Bennett rubbed his head, like wiping perspiration from his brow. "She had to be one of the classiest women I've ever seen — long blonde hair, perfect shape — not what you'd expect to see there unless it was a celebrity night."

A vision of the woman he'd met for breakfast after the machine gunning of his car at the Side Street Diner, flashed through Clark's mind. "Tell me more about her."

Bennett rolled his shoulders. "Geez, I don't know, Clark... If you saw her you'd know what I was talking about."

"Pag?"

"I don't know, Clark. I couldn't tell if Isiah was looking at her or Jake... his eyes kept flashing their way."

"We need to come back to that." Clark jotted a note on his pad. "How did Isiah do in the last three games?"

"The Pistons were three-point favorites and lost by seventeen at the Net's place. I listened to the game. Thomas got twenty points, but the announcer wasn't positive about his play."

"And the Pacers?"

"The Pistons were at home and a ten-point favorite. Allen Hilf, the mob's number one gambling man, was there the entire game. They lost to the Pacers by seven... Thomas was four for sixteen, had five turnovers and no steals." Pag shook his head. "He played like a high schooler."

"I saw the Pistons lost to the Cavaliers in overtime last Tuesday. Anything unusual there?"

"I couldn't believe it. Cleveland's record was twelve wins and thirty losses, and they beat us at home. Thomas shot three for seventeen from the field. He made a bunch of free throws... at times, he looked awful."

"So, whataya think so far?"

Pag nodded to Frank. "The *prima facie* evidence is overwhelming, but we'd need a lot more before we could take it to the DA. We'd need player testimony, one or two expert bookie witnesses..." Frank's mouth curled with distaste. "Here's the reality as I see it. Thomas is the biggest star in Detroit since Dave Bing... we'd need a slam-dunk case for any *Detroit jury to convict him*."

CHAPTER TWENTY-TWO

𝔇etroit 𝔉ree 𝔓ress

SPORTS SECTION

February 11, 1984

"HITMAN" HEARNS DEFENDS TITLE TONIGHT

Thomas "The Hitman" Hearns defends his WBC Middleweight Title tonight at Joe Louis Arena. While fighting the European Champion, Hearns at 31-1 is heavily favored to knock out Luigi Minchillo in the scheduled twelve-round match.

"So, is it all you imagined?"

"That and more. The atmosphere is electric. I'm so excited; I've never had front row seats at a world championship event." Amanda pecked Jake on the cheek. "Thank you so much."

"It really isn't a big deal." Jake snuggled closer. "This is part of my life."

"I like it." Gazing at the standing room only crowd, Amanda glanced at the men settling down in the rows immediately behind them, and nudged his shoulder. "Do you know these people?"

Turning from one side to the other, he waved to the guys seated behind her and eased into his chair, facing her. "These are my clients. I purchase the seats in this section every year. They like it and I write it off as a business expense."

"That's a great way to take care of your customers." Her inquisitive thoughts wandered. "Do you buy the tickets just for the boxing events?"

"No, every event in the arena. My clients enjoy all kinds of activities, so it's a nice way to treat them and their families."

Hearns' name was announced.

An earthshaking roar, then cheers and applause filled the venue.

They rose to watch the opening ceremony.

Leaning to Amanda's side, he suggested, "Here, stand close to me. Hearns' entrance into the arena is spectacular, like a king... or maybe, like a gladiator."

She put her arm around Jake and watched the spectacle.

Hearns' gold-threaded silk robe flowed with each step; his gloves waved high over his head, as if signaling a victory, even before the match began.

Her eyes glued on him, Amanda watched every move. Turning toward the steps in the corner of the ring, Hearns nodded to Jake and raised an eyebrow at the sight of her.

Stepping into the ring, the pageantry continued — Hearns paraded around, like on a victory-lap — he opened his robe with a flourish, showing off the gold plated, diamond studded, championship belt.

"The odds in the paper indicated Hearns will knock out Luigi. What do you think?"

Pausing, Jake turned toward her, calculating his words. "Hmm, I'm not sure... he's the European champ. But anything can happen."

The bell rang, starting round one.

"He has a muscular physique."

"In this case you *can* judge the book by its cover."

Amanda stuck her hand in a bag of popcorn as they took their seats to watch the action. *Jake's voice is not his usual tone. That's the second time... I wonder if the fight will go the distance, why not? What's the difference, anyway?*

Hearns added points in every round and was well ahead when the bell ended round ten.

"It's all over..." Amanda announced, "I can tell... Hearns has him set up for the knock out."

Jake didn't turn; his eyes focused on the handler and Hearns.

Amanda thought Jake's head moved slightly, side-to-side. *Maybe it was just me.* She glanced up — the handler said something to Hearns. Everyone in the arena stood for the last two exciting rounds.

Nothing happened in round eleven.

When the bell rang, Amanda peeked at Jake's eyes jumping back and forth with Hearns' handler. *There it is; I know I saw it — a twist of Jake's head indicating "no" — Hearns is not going to knock him out.*

The bell ended round twelve with both fighters in a clench, as they had been most of the round. Hearns touched his gloves with those of Luigi then held his hands high in the air, signifying his victory.

With the crowd still standing, Amanda fell back into her chair.

Jake turned and bent over, leaning close to her ear. "You all right?"

"Oh my, yes… I'm exhausted… I really get into sporting events."

"So, what did you think about the match?"

"I kept thinking Hearns was going to knock Luigi out, but the guy hung in there." She raised her eyebrows. "Hearns is quite a specimen; has muscles bulging all over."

"He's 6' 1" and has an eighty-inch reach, too… that gives him a real advantage in this weight level." Giving her his full attention, Jake paused. "Would you like to meet him?"

"Yes, of course." Her smile broadened like a kid who just walked into a candy store.

He spoke softly with an aura of secrecy. "Next Friday night we're having a little party at his house."

Picking up on the "we're," Amanda eyeballed Jake with a questioning glance. "You have a victory party planned for him?"

"Not quite." Jake's smirk slid into a half smile. "Twice a month the Giacalones run a 'high-rollers' dice game at his place."

"Who are the Giacalones?"

Jake brushed his hand over his lips, wondering if he should have said that. "Friends… they work for us."

Noting a tone of tension in his voice, she dropped her line of questioning. "Can we go?"

His sense of pleasure grew. "Sure."

"What should I wear?"

"Whatever." He rolled his shoulders. "You're always dressed properly… in fact, you're the classiest woman I've ever met."

"Well, thank you…"

Surprised that he'd shared his thought, Jake smiled to himself and finished his point about attire variety. "There'll be a full range of people there — lawyers, judges, politicians, doctors — even a drug kingpin or two. There's no telling how their women will be dressed — some in evening gowns, other something shorter than a mini skirt, still others, business casual — you'll see it all."

***

"And now, I pronounce you husband and wife." Father Dom nodded to Ted.

He raised Laverne's short, white veil, and gently kissed her.

She threw her arm around him and planted a smacker squarely on his lips.

Their friends applauded, and one-by-one congratulated the two.

When the line ended, Ted pointed to the dining room table, loaded with heavy hors d'oeuvres — sliced beef tenderloin, jumbo shrimp, pastas, and sliced lobster — condiments and cheesecake sat prettily on large red hearts, celebrating Valentine's Day. "Help yourself, there's wine and beer on the kitchen counter."

Downing a case of beer and several bottles of wine, a handful of Laverne's closest hospital colleagues mingled with the old gang and Ted's dad and uncle. The party atmosphere continued into late afternoon.

In ones and twos, the hospital friends slipped away, leaving their closest friends, minus Earl.

Laverne raised her glass of wine and jokingly announced, "Let the party begin."

Having heard the phrase many times, the group hooted and hollered.

"Clark, when will we see Earl again?" Father Dom probed.

He hedged, not wanting to suggest it'd be very soon. "Can't really say… we've gotten some help for him… that may speed up the process."

Half snockered, Ted leaned over to Clark, almost falling out of his chair. "Hey… why is it you never tested Uncle Ned when you did the DNA testing?"

"At the time, I thought if you tested one brother you didn't have to test the other one, because it would be the same," Clark admitted, the corners of his mouth turned down. "Since then, I've learned from Sharon that's a common belief, but it's not true."

Overhearing the conversation, a blurry eye Renzo asked, "Why's that?"

Clark glanced around the tipsy group of men. "It's a little complex… let's hold that 'til our next poker night."

"It doesn't matter." Ted spoke up. "Ned is not really my uncle, anyway."

Clark's face went blank. "I don't understand."

Ted slushed his glass toward Ned, spilling some on the floor. Ted quickly hit the deck, his handkerchief in hand, soaking up the white wine. "It's a good thing it wasn't red," he announced and scrambled back to his chair before Laverne noticed.

"Ted."

"Oh, yeah… tell him Ned."

"Fred and I met in 1939; he had a bike shop and I peddled bread in the neighborhood. We became good friend, like brothers. When my wife died, I ended up spending most of the day at their house. One day Ted called me Uncle Ned and it stuck."

Fireworks flashed behind Clark's brow; his brain went bananas. *Damn, the potential connection was right here all the time. It never crossed my mind.* He mulled over his thoughts, buying time. "Did you know that?" he asked Ted, hoping for a clue.

"I guess… I never thought about it… that's the way it's always been." Ted gave Clark a quizzical glance. "Is that a problem?"

Clark shrugged his shoulders. "I'm like you. I never thought about it."

"I-I-I… don't want to get into any kind of trouble," Ned said. "If I need to do something… I-I'd… be glad to cooperate."

Still unsure of what to do, Clark waffled. "I appreciate that… Let me give it some thought… I'll get back to you."

***

Section E

YBI DRUG EMPIRE CONTINUES TO CRUMBLE

The Young Boys, Inc. drug empire took another hit last night when some of Butch Jones' henchmen gunned down Norman "Snead" Johnson, a key associate of Ray Peoples. With both Jones and Peoples serving prison terms, informants say the two men are directing the killings of each other's team members from behind prison bars.

It's the third murder of a high-ranking YBI leader this year. Informants agree there is more bloodshed to come.

"Will it ever end?" Pag asked Woodson, who'd just returned, after completing a three-month assignment with the FBI.

"These guys are crazy… there's no middle ground. It's either Jones' or Peoples' way."

"Funny." Pag chuckled. "The two of them were kings of the mountain and best of friends until they found out they were both screwing the same woman — all hell broke loose!"

"Who was screwing whom?" Clark asked as he strolled into the conference room.

Pag tossed the paper to the head of the table.

"Yeah, I read it." Clark turned, as the rest of the team filed in and took their places.

Eyes fell on Dick Woodson, the FBI agent from Valparaiso, Indiana.

"Hey, welcome back." Kimberly led the parade of sincere salutatory remarks.

Clark picked up on the opportunity. "Dick, as long as you're receiving all of the attention, would you mind giving the team a brief update of your activities with McGill's group?"

"No problem." Woodson stroked a hand over his perfectly level, flattop. "When I was in Chicago, we compiled a list of the Chicago Outfit mobsters with specific assignments or connections to various segments of the community. It served as a good reminder, because it was easy to forget who was connected or who had the responsibility to keep someone in line."

"I like the concept," Bennett spouted. "It's easy to forget who's connected to whom."

"More than people would ever imagine. "Woodson laughed. "By the time we finished, we had close to two hundred and fifty people who had connections to a particular entity or business."

"That's amazing," newcomer Veronica blurted without thought.

"I'll get you the entire list… here's a few names to get you thinking about who's running the city." Clearing his throat, he paused for a moment. "Try these on for size," he jested:

- Tony 'Pal' Palazzola is the new representative to Canada.

- Frank 'Frankie the Boom' Bommarito is in charge of relations with area motorcycle gangs.

- Leonard 'Skippy' Torrice has responsibility for the city's Jewish bookmakers.

- Vincent Meli is the representative to the steel haulers.

- Leonard Schultz is one of many emissaries to local labor unions.

- Anthony D'Anna has very close ties with Ford Motor Company; and there are:

- Representatives for Toledo, Chicago, Cleveland, and every city in Michigan.

Their reach is beyond anyone's imagination… and then, there's their informal network that crisscrosses the country."

Veronica stared, surprised by the scope of the mob's network. "I expected some of the connections, but Ford…"

"They're just an example," He interrupted. "I could have mentioned GM, Chrysler, Delco or any of their suppliers."

***

Archbishop Peter Dooley stepped out of his office and stared at the three men — Father Dom, the Auditor, and the Director of Accounting — and smiled. "I knew when I saw the three of you on my calendar, trouble was brewing. Come in, let's get on with it."

They gathered around a small rectangular coffee table, the Archbishop on one end and Father Dom on the other. The two on the sides turned to Father Dom.

He opened his file. "Archbishop, we have some distressing news to report…"

The Archbishop talked over him. "Let me guess… you found some irregularities in the collection and disbursement of funds at the parish level."

The group was taken off guard. "Ah… yes, we did," Father Dom said, taken aback.

"And you want me to put my stamp of approval on a policy that details specific procedures to be followed in the collection, disbursement, and reporting of all funds collected at the parish level. Right?"

"Ah… yes." Father Dom nodded.

"Done, meeting over." He stood and straightened his robe.

"Thank you so much for your support…"

He smiled. "After our last meeting, I had an inkling of what was ahead."

"Yes… but that's just part of the reason why we're here."

"Ohh…" The Archbishop eased back down into his armchair and motioned for Father Dom to continue.

"We have evidence that at least five and as many as eleven priests at the parish level have received money from parishioners."

"That's not unusual. A small gift to say thanks. We've all received a little cash like that…" He waved his hand in the air. "Not a problem."

"We agree," Father Dom confirmed, on behalf of the group. "Would you classify $25 thousand, $50 thousand, or $100 thousand over an extended period, as a *little* cash?"

"Oh no." The Archbishop fell back against his throne-like chair, and took time to collect his thoughts. "Let me clarify something… the procedures I just approved will control that kind of problem, so it won't happen again, right?"

"Yes, at least we think so," the Director of Accounting spoke up this time.

"Good."

The auditor interjected his thoughts. "We should turn the evidence over to the police, so the priests can be prosecuted — they've broken the law. And how about the crooks that donated the money and turned it around and got money back? We just can't…"

"Now, now," The Archbishop interrupted, raising his hand. "There's no reason to make a hasty decision." He paused for the longest moment. "Anything we do now is like closing the barn door after the horse is out. And further," he stated more forcefully. "We've never questioned the source of funds given to God. We can't make these accusations public."

"Accusations?" the auditor mumbled.

"Hand me the names of those priests accused of wrong doing and I will take care of them. Matter closed."

Looking him straight in the eye, Father Dom handed him the list. "Archbishop, we have a second request. We'd like permission to have the FDIC regional office in Indianapolis review the investments made by the Archdiocesan Financial Committee. We have prima facie evidence of collusion among three members of the committee to, in fact, launder money."

"I don't want any federal agency involved in our internal affairs, plain and simple."

Expecting that response, Father Dom reverted to Plan B. "I know a local banker who's had experience with this kind of issue. Could we hire him as a consultant?"

The Archbishop sucked in a deep breath. "Yes, but I'm not going any further than that."

***

Staten Island

Paul Castellano stood at the head of the long conference table in his spacious ballroom — a fifty-light, crystal chandelier hung elegantly above. Matching sconces lit the wallpapered walls, their beams cascading across the blue-tinted terrazzo floor.

As usual, the Bosses of the other Families of New York and their *consiglieres*, were in attendance; along with the Boss of the Chicago Outfit, Joseph 'Joey Doves' Aiuppa, and his *consigliere*, John "Jackie the Lackey" Cerone. They waited patiently for his opening remarks. Around the perimeter in a half-moon fashion were forty chairs, spaced evenly, for the Bosses and their advisors from the other nineteen mafia strongholds across the country.

Big Paul tugged at his gold-threaded silk robe, straightening the collar and a sleeve. "Men," he stated in a powerful tone and waited until the room was perfectly quiet. "Men, we are confronted with a crisis unmatched in our lifetime… not since Mussolini…" He stopped; his mind full of memories buried long ago. "Who can tell me a story that you or someone in your family experienced fifty years ago, during the reign of Benito Mussolini?"

Hands shot up.

Sensing he'd inadvertently stumbled onto the key to unlocking the mystery behind the mafia killings, he took his time, letting the chatter subside.

He nodded to Joe Bonanno, the senior man at the table. At eighty, his voice was still strong and assertive. "No use to look elsewhere; I was there. The bastards were ruthless." Pausing to collect his composure, Bonanno sucked in a deep breath. "Mussolini's men tortured our tenant farmers, raped their women… And, if that weren't enough, they confiscated our property and publicly slaughtered our livestock…"

"I witnessed the same thing as a boy," Carlo Gambino interrupted. "His army of policemen and militiamen went from town to town rounding up individuals with suspected ties to the mafia."

"They were cruel," Bonanno added. "They extracted confessions from honest men, beat and tortured them, threatened their families… the intimidation and humiliation was unending."

Gambino reflected; his tone heavy. "Where we lived in Palermo, they arrested over 11,000 men — thousands were convicted and sent to prison or internally exiled without trial. Within months they had suppressed the mafia; it hardly existed and those left had a hard life."

Big Paul walked to the end of the table and stood behind the two men. Placing a hand on each of their shoulders, he asked, "How did your families survive?"

Bonanno nodded to Gambino. "They didn't touch our immediate families, nor did they attack any of the wealthy landowners."

"Strange… that's like we've experienced here. They killed capos and murdered lieutenants; interestingly, no one in the upper ranks has been touched." Frowning, Castellano continued his line of questioning. "So, what happened to your parents?"

"My father and many of his mafia friends fled to the United States."

"Huh." Castellano's hand rubbed his jaw; his thoughts zeroing in. "So later, when the tide of the war shifted — when Hitler and Mussolini started losing their grip — it's possible that some of these mafia haters came here, too."

Bonanno straightened in his chair. "I never thought of that… it's more than possible, it's entirely likely. They had connections and the money to do anything they wanted." His fist slammed the table. "The bastards are here… *they're* the ones!

***

Following an extended break, filled with shouting, cursing, and name-calling, as more memories surfaced, Big Paul stood, his hand raised over the angry group. "We need order… a plan; we need to identify and eliminate these malcontents." He flopped down in his chair and nodded to the other end. "First… I'd like to hear the thoughts of those of you around the table. Bonanno, you got us started on this enlightened discussion. Do you have additional thoughts?"

The old man rubbed his knurled hands and cleared his throat. "We must mount an aggressive campaign to search out and eradicate these extremists. There must be a dual effort — finding the culprits in our cities and their supporters in the homeland."

Castellano nodded to Gambino; his hand raised high over his head. "We have to energize our associates…" He paused; his mind retracing history. "I'm afraid we're dealing with some of the radical segments of the European Social Movement. They have to be followers of Rene Binet and Maurice Bardeche. I remember them; they're extremist, neo fascist."

Chicago's Aiuppa asked, "Who are they?"

Binet is a French militant; his group pledged themselves to eliminating the rule of communists and non-whites. The bastard was crazy. Another Frenchman who's trying to rewrite history. His followers are Holocaust deniers. They refer to the Holocaust as a hoax by Jews conspiring to advance their interest… they're nuts. We must determine if any of them are after us."

"I agree wholeheartedly," Castellano announced; his face reddened. "We must also call upon our brothers in Italy. Some of Mussolini's strongest supporters were in his hometown of Predappio. Someone must know who was in his inner circle and continued to employ his strategies. Someone knows who came to the US at the end of WW II. Someone knows who's pushing the buttons. With that information, we'll be able to trace down the culprits residing in our cities."

"All of that is important, but it'll take time." Standing to make his point, Carmine "the Snake" Persico pressed forward. "There are people here, in our cities, who know the guilty ones. We must penetrate their organization and root out the bastards."

Aiuppa pounded the table. "They need to be tortured, just like they killed our men."

Colombo Family Boss Persico stood alongside Aiuppa. "These efforts are well and good, but still… we can't forget the gypsies. There's a possible connection there… and, we can't ignore Bonanno's comment about *their supporters in the homeland*."

CHAPTER TWENTY-THREE

Nursing a second Crown Royal, Tony stared out the window of the Nineteenth Hole at the Country Club. His mind wandered on how he might broach the subject. Jake had maintained high standards his entire life, never deviating, and expected the same from those around him. *I'm not looking forward to telling him that his personal life is out of control, but I don't have a choice. If I don't do it, no one will.*

Spotting Jake bouncing down the hallway like a giddy teenager, Tony knew he was in for a long afternoon.

Entering the bar, Jake called to the bartender. "Would you please bring me a Jack Daniels and a bowl of cashews."

"Right away, Mr. Nicolette."

Jake slapped Tony on the shoulder and slid into the chair across from him. "How are you doing?" he asked in a peppy tone.

Tony faked it, knowing it would take some time to build up to the issue. "I'm fine."

"Good, couldn't be better, thanks for asking," Jake jested. "Hey, how about that Hearns fight? Wasn't that something? We made a bundle on that."

Tony wanted to say something about the blonde who'd been by his side, but knew it wasn't the right time.

Jake continued to blabber; Tony couldn't get a word in edgewise, even if he'd wanted to.

"I see Isiah and Hearns are almost above water," Tony squeezed in.

"Hah, that's only 'til next week. Friday night at Isiah's place and Saturday at Hearns. Their egos are so big; both of them will be down a hundred grand before the nights are over."

"You'd think they'd figure out what's going on."

"Nah… it doesn't matter to them. They think they can beat the odds; besides, they love being the center of attention."

"Giacalone's crew loves it too. For them, Isiah's mansion in Bloomfield Hills is a one-night coup. A celebrity like him will bring in ten big fish. Freddie Salem and Allen Hilf will be there, like sharks in a frenzy over blood in the water."

Tony knew the time was drawing near; Jake seemed more relaxed and feeling good. "Have you talked to Allen lately?"

"No, why?"

"He despises Isiah…"

"Why so?" Jake asked, cutting Tony off.

"They're like oil and water. Hilf would like to put him in the bottom of Lake Erie."

Jake stiffened, fearful Hilf may take matters into his own hands. "Shit, we don't need that. Someone needs to talk to Allen."

"Does that mean me?"

Raising his eyebrows, Jake grinned. "You're the best one we have to let someone know he's off base."

Outwardly oblivious to the suggestion, Tony didn't flinch; his eyes remained focused on Jake.

Knowing the look, Jake stopped cold. "Something on your mind?"

"As a matter of fact, there is." Still hesitant, Tony hemmed and hawed, knowing he had one shot to deal with Jake without him blowing up.

Jake stared at him as Tony stalled for the longest time. "Well?"

Tony knew it was best to deal with Jake straight on.

"You know when I have something to say, I don't pull any punches."

"That's why I've always respected you." Jake flipped his hand, nonchalantly. "Whatever it is, give it to me straight."

Tony took a sip of his Crown Royal. "It has… you have… gotten out of control."

Jake's face turned sour; his voice took on an edge. "Out of control, what the hell are you talking about?"

"You damn well know… Amanda!" Tony slapped his hand solidly on the table. "It's fine to be seen at the Caucus Club or late seating at the London Chop House, but she's been seen every place you've been to this year. *You're too public* with her."

"Big deal." Jake's face reddened to a bright glow. "I'll see her as much as I want. I'm going to ask her to marry me."

"Jake, you can't do that. You have a family, responsibilities…"

"Responsibilities," Jake cut him off. "Crap, I've heard that word since I was a kid. When do *I* count? When do I do what *I* want to do?" He glanced toward the bar. "Bartender, another round," he shouted in a huff.

Tony stared at Jake without a blink or saying a word, unsure how far he should go.

The bartender picked up their empties and placed their drinks in front them with another bowl of cashews in the center of the table.

Jake grabbed his glass and took a slug.

Tony played the waiting game, hoping Jake would come to his senses and talk about it.

Jake's sneer hardened, equaling his attitude.

Tony cupped his hands over his face, his elbows on the table. Slowly, he slid a hand down to the table. "Why do you pay me?"

Jake cocked his head, examining Tony as if to say, 'that's a dumb question.' "To give me advice."

Tony nodded. "Okay… tell me when you're ready to listen to my advice."

Jake stirred around in his chair, like a kid who'd had his favorite toy taken away. Finally, he leaned back and sucked in a deep breath. "Okay, let's get it over with," he said petulantly.

His top adviser threw his napkin on the table and slid his chair back. "I'm not talking to you if you're not going to listen… if you aren't going to take it to heart, I might as well be blowing smoke."

"All right." Jake begrudgingly sat up straight in the chair, drink in hand.

"People are talking."

"Who the hell cares?" Jake cut him off. "Let them talk."

"Damn it Jake, this is my nickel." Tony bristled; the old man felt like throwing in the towel. Instead, he sharpened his tone "Or, do you want to continue acting like an ass."

Surprised by Tony's abrupt sharpness, Jake's cold, piercing eyes shot back. Grabbing his glass, he shook the ice, and downed the remains. Taking out his anger on anything but Tony, he twisted the bottom of the Old Fashioned glass into the table top. "Give us another round," he called out in a blistering tone, then glanced back at Tony. "Go ahead."

"I'll say it again." Tony spoke tersely. "People are talking. You're receiving far too much attention. People are asking questions. Questions... and lack of family values... lead to mistrust. None of that's good!"

Jake sneered, like a teenage boy being lectured to by his father.

"And, you can wipe that sarcasm off your face." Tony glared back then added a positive note. "Until now you've never been in the spotlight... I have to give you credit for that. Your reputation in the community has been exemplary. Yet, I can tell you, it only takes one slip to blow the whole thing — you're too good to let that happen."

Jake's body language shifted; his eyes softened.

"You're not the first man in his fifties to be attracted to a classy thirty-year-old woman." Tony held a palm up to Jake, stopping his attempt to react. "I'm still on my nickel... If this relationship ends up being the real thing and you want to marry her, it's going to take some time — you'll have countless conversations with your wife. Talks with your kids... lot of talks with them — not to mention the frustrating and time-consuming meetings with the attorneys. I'd say it'll take at least two years."

"Okay, I'll work through all of this over the next two years."

"That's your choice, Jake... I'm only here to advise you, right?" Tony tried a more casual approach. "You do want my advice, don't you?"

"Yeah, sure." His tone meant just the opposite.

"Good," he said, ignoring Jake's lack of sincerity. "You need to buy time; let time work this out. And keep the public appearances to a minimum."

Jake glanced up giving him a questioning look.

"I'd suggest you set her up in that place on the street behind yours."

"The one with the tunnel to my place?"

"You got it." Tony nodded; his face more relaxed. "It'd be perfect."

"Shit Tony, it's listed for $500,000 — it's a mansion."

"Does it really matter? You have a real estate portfolio worth millions... that place is a mere drop in the bucket."

"I don't think she'd go for that. She likes to go out — we enjoy going to nice restaurants and doing fun things."

"Fine… take her to Florida, Hawaii, or Aruba… who cares. There's no need to take her to a Pistons game or a fight where thousands of people see you and thousands more watch you on TV."

"What if she doesn't go along with your plan?"

Tony grinned to himself for the first time. "Shit Jake, you know as well as I… it's all about the money. *Everyone has a price.*"

***

Gathering around the poker table, the guys stuffed in one more bite. Renzo flipped the cards in front of each man until the first ace appeared. "Dealer's choice," he declared, sliding the second deck to Ted.

"Want to cut?" Ted slid the cards in front of Carlos.

He flipped his hand, indicating *no*.

Ted called out. "Seven cards, deuces are wild."

And with that, their March marathon was on — five-card stud, straight seven-card, and a myriad of wild card games. With Clark and Ted raking in most of the chips and Father Dom not having a winning pot, he couldn't wait 'til nine o'clock, so he could call, "Break time."

The guys scattered for the head and the table filled with snacks and subs. In random order, each made his stop — either loading or unloading — before returning to their original chairs.

With all of the seats occupied, except that of Ted's, Renzo shouted. "If you don't hurry up we're going to start without you."

"Go ahead. I've got one crossways," came from the bathroom.

"Sounds familiar," Carlos jested.

"Go ahead and deal," Renzo pointed to Clark.

Picking up the deck, Clark paused, and laid the cards back on the table. Glancing at Father Dom, he asked, "Since we have a moment, I was wondering if there was anything new happening with our resident ombudsman."

"Huh." The old man stoked the gray bristles on his chin. "Last month Archbishop Dooley sent out a three-page memo on 'accountability and transparency,' authorizing me to review all financial procedures related to internal spending and external gifting, for each of the parishes in the Archdioceses."

"Wow." Clark's eyes sparkled; he spread his hands, as if to say, 'what more could you ask?' "It sounds like the door is wide open."

"No doubt." Father Dom's smile broadened. "Once I presented my preliminary findings, the writing was on the wall."

Clark's positive attitude turned into a questioning glance. "Preliminary…?"

"I'm looking at the donations made last year by Jake Nicolette, totaling over a million dollars, and his half million dollars this year as reported in *The Michigan Catholic*…"

Carlos waved his arms in the air. "Nicolette has donated $1.5 million to the Church in the last two years?"

A smirk slid across Father Dom's lips as he spoke softly. "$1.5 million in fifteen months."

Renzo raised his eyebrows. "Fifteen months!"

The priest nodded. "And, wait 'til you hear *the rest of the story*."

Eyes around the table zeroed in on him.

"Practically none of those dollars ever reached the Archdioceses' level."

Stroking his long curly hair, Carlos bristled. "Where did it go?"

"Your guess is as good as mine." Father Dom stuck his hands in his pockets, as if someone pocketed the money. "Archbishop Dooley wasn't even aware of Nicolette's donation."

"$1.5 million in donations and the Archbishop was not aware of it?" Unable to imagine such a scenario, Clark was both curious and suspicious.

Father Dom rolled his shoulders. "That's how the Archbishop reacted."

"How can that be?" Carlos queried.

"The Archbishop only saw the financial records submitted by the parish priest. He learned about the last $500,000 when he read about the gift in *The Michigan Catholic.*"

Renzo held his nose. "Smells pretty fishy to me."

"Hah." Father Dom laughed. "Had the news story not been submitted by a newly named assistant priest, no one would have known."

Sitting quietly, afraid to mention the question he'd been dying to ask, Clark couldn't hold back any longer. "Will any of this ever come to light?"

"That'll be up to the Archbishop to determine."

"To determine!" Renzo exclaimed. "Even a novice can see… there's a lot of hanky-panky going on."

"Hanky-panky… there's payoffs and money laundering going on." Clark's words sharpened. "There's criminal activity. We need to…"

Father Dom raised his hand, cutting off the obvious. "The Archbishop will render his decision."

Hearing the toilet flush, heads turned that way.

The door flew open. Ted stepped out and zipped up his pants. "From what I've heard, we've been snookered… none of this *will ever come to public light*."

Father Dom sat quietly, knowing that was likely to be true.

"So, where to now?" Clark asked, hoping the obvious was not correct.

"I'm shifting gears," Father Dom indicated with surprising confidence. "And… if this one pans out there'll be plenty of work for your FBI colleagues."

Feeling better, Clark's interest grew. "Anything you can tell me now?"

"Not especially…" Father Dom downed the last of his Stroh's.

"Here we go again." Ted pouted, like a kid not getting his way. "No one can say anything."

"Not so." Father Dom sounded defensive. "There have been rumors, grumbling, and hearsay… about the happenings going on at the top — big money…"

"With the Archbishop?" Carlos wondered aloud.

Father Dom didn't move; he stared back at him. "Maybe, I don't know. It may be at the level below him without his knowledge."

Clark waved his hands vigorously. "Get on with it."

"Okay, here's the skinny." Father Dom gave it to them straight. "The lay director of finance for the Archdiocese invests millions of dollars annually. He's advised by the Finance Committee, which is composed of five individuals. Two of them are priests — window dressing for the most part — they know nothing about finances."

"And the other three are on the take," Ted spouted.

"Not quite." Father Dom's head wobbled back-and-forth. "The other three are big donors or friends of big donors."

"No need to say more." Clark rose and headed for the bathroom.

***

Waiting at the Top Hat for a luncheon meeting with Rick, Earl couldn't help but watch the extremely attractive black woman strutting his way. *Holy shit.* His eyes unconsciously connected with hers, and moved on to the black leather skirt hugging her shapely hips, and her tight white sweater. He knew by her walk, the seduction was on; she ran her fingers through the soft black ringlets caressing her ears and shot him a profile view, to make sure he noticed the rest of her equipment.

Posing in front of him, she leaned forward and extended her hand. "Hi, I'm Kathy Volson… are you Clarence Tidwell?"

Clarence had read the report on her and nodded. They shook hands. *Kathy Volson—the Queen of the Ghetto—hottest woman in town. Being the favorite niece of Mayor Coleman Young gave her access to any place or office in town, and she played that card often. Known to have slept with every big-name drug dealer in town, she was the eye-catcher at every event.*

"Rick's running a little late… told me you'd be here." She pulled herself into the booth tight against him and eased her hand on his thigh. "I've seen you with Rick several times; he speaks highly of you." She ran her fingers over his firm biceps. "You from around here?"

"Detroit all of my life."

She talked about her uncle and the guys she knew, all the time her eyes worked his muscular body. Placing her hand on top of his growing firmness, she asked, "You have a woman?"

"Yes, a very special person."

She cocked her head back and smirked, her hand easing across his rock-hard tool.

Clarence shifted back, trying to relieve the pressure.

She came on — kissed him on the lips and squeezed his tool firmly. "Doesn't matter… I'm dating Johnny Currie… nothing serious; you want to get together Saturday night?"

Having rehearsed this moment, Clarence *cooled it.* "I really can't… there's…"

Kathy took her hand off his leg and covered his mouth. "I like that." She flashed him a smile and eased out of the booth. "Let's keep our options open, okay?" she said then turned, coming face to face with Rick Maserati. "Good timing." She pecked him on the cheek and strolled out the door.

"How did your introduction go with Kathy?" Rick laughed. "Bet you can't stand up."

Clarence glanced under the table, giving him the response he expected. "Guess you got that right."

Rick slid in across from him. "Let's grab a bite before we deliver the rest of the products."

"Sounds good. I'm hitting the sack early so I can hit the road to Miami in the morning."

"I've increased the order by 50 percent and the mix will be 75 percent cocaine and 25 percent heroin."

"Wow, 75-25, that's quite a change."

"It's only a matter of time before we'll be 100 percent cocaine." Rick shook his head very slowly and chuckled. "The guys in the suburbs are sucking it down."

***

Wearing a tight red sequin dress, Amanda, and Jake paraded into the plush lower level of Tommy Hearns' Southfield home, looked more like a casino than a Detroit suburban home — crap and poker tables, bars aligned in the corners, an ice sculpture of him in the center of a table filled with food. Glancing around, it was obvious the women were more interested in flaunting their wares than protecting their man.

Jake waved to Tommy and the two headed his way. "Tommy, I want you to meet a very special friend of mine… Amanda Howard."

Raising his eyebrows, Tommy extended his hand. "My pleasure, ma'am."

She raised her eyes to his, held his hand tightly. "I've never met a world champion… as a fan, it's something I'll always remember."

Jake stepped forward. "Now you see why she's so special."

"No doubt — brains and beauty — you can't beat that." Tommy winked and took her hand. "Let me introduce you to some of the others." He turned. "Mayor Young, come over here please. There's a special person I'd like you to meet."

Amanda and Jake made the rounds with Hearns, shaking hands and chit-chatting with Detroit's top dogs — judges, doctors, politicians, drug kingpins, Motown stars, and sports celebrities.

Tommy pulled them aside and guided them to the crowded dice table. Tapping a man on the shoulder, Isiah Thomas turned around. "Isiah, I'd like you to meet Amanda Howard, Jake Nicolette's special friend."

Taking his eyes off the table for a rare moment, Isiah gave her the once over. "I see why she's your special friend." He pulled her to the table, beside him. "Wanta try your luck?"

She grabbed Jake's hand and held it tight. "I'd just as soon watch."

CHAPTER TWENTY-FOUR

Waiting nervously at the corner table in the Nineteenth Hole, Jake downed a Jack Daniels. He had begrudgingly accepted Tony's advice — that was one thing, but telling Amanda was something else. *Having her stay in the vacant property with the connecting tunnel would be convenient, but... convincing her. Hmm, I don't know?*

Amanda bent over and kissed him on the cheek, snapping him out of his trance. "What were you thinking about, dear?"

"Oh… hum… ah, nothing."

Glancing at his empty glass, she placed her arms around him and squeezed tight.

He didn't respond.

Backing away with a sense that his mind was elsewhere, she eased onto the chair across from him. "Jake, whatever it is… you can tell me."

Still, he didn't move.

"Jake, I've shared so much with you." She reached across the table and placed her hands on top of his. "Please Jake, tell me. Whatever it is, we can work it out."

Hearing the words, *work it out*, he cracked a partial grin and rolled his shoulders.

She squeezed his hands, gently, and held on tightly to his fingers. "Like you've always pointed out, it's your nickel. I won't say a word, I'll just listen."

He stared at her, like he had lockjaw.

She glanced over at the bartender. "We'll have a Vodka Gimlet and another Jack Daniels, please."

Jake didn't say a word.

Easing back in her chair, Amanda gave him space.

The drinks arrived.

She picked up her Gimlet and waited for him to lift the Old Fashioned glass. "Here's to us." She clinked his glass.

He gave her a half smile. "I'll drink to that."

Taking a sip of her drink, she looked him in the eye, and spoke soft and slowly. "Is this about us?"

His cotton mouth opened slightly. "Kind of…"

Amanda's eyes turned glassy; preparing, she pulled a tissue from her purse.

"No, no, sweetie, it isn't like that."

Sniffling, she wiped her nose. "Jake…"

He cut her off. "Darling, it's not that bad… I just need to make a few changes."

Twisting her hands, she bit her lip, waiting for the first shoe to fall.

"Okay, I'll give it to you straight." He finished his drink, shaking the ice to make sure he got all of it. "I've been advised that my feelings for you have become too public. It has the potential to cause serious problems for me. We must find some alternatives…"

"What kind of alternatives?" she interrupted.

Jake paused, making sure he voiced the words properly. "Our activities can't be so public. We have to…"

"How much less public," She interrupted. "Do I have to watch Tommy Hearns on television?"

"No, it isn't like that." Sounding apologetic, Jake's voice trembled.

"I don't understand." Amanda restlessly shifted in her chair. "You want me to be *the other woman* locked up in a cell?"

"No, I don't want you to be *the other woman*; I want you to be *the* woman."

Catching Amanda's attention, she paused and motioned for him to continue.

"I have a mansion next to my home… there's a tunnel connecting the two. We could be together any time you want, all day if you want."

"And when do we go out — to the theatre, the London Chop House, or to see the Pistons — do I ever leave your mansion?"

"Sweetie, you're making it sound awful… We can travel all over the world. I'll do anything to make you happy."

"You're asking me to change my lifestyle."

"Guess I never thought about it that way."

Amanda spoke firmly. "Can I go freely to L.A. and other places to pursue my career?"

"Yes, of course. You can do anything you want; go anywhere you want."

"Okay," she said, figuring that was the best she could get. "Tell me about *the mansion.*"

"It's first-class, modern… if there is something you don't like, I'll change it."

Placing her hands on top of his, she took her time. "Would you put the deed in my name?"

"Amanda… it's worth a half million…"

"So what? You're not going to sell it." She ran her hand over the top of his. Knowing she had him wrapped around her finger, she took her time. "Okay, I'll be *the other woman,* but I expect to be treated like *the* woman!"

"Oh yes, of course, darling."

Rocking her head up and down, her eyes zeroed in on his. "Here's *the deal…* I want the house placed in my name, I want a $20,000 monthly allowance for incidentals, and I want my lawyer to write it up — with no questions from your lawyer."

Surprised by her bold request, Jake eased back in his chair.

Amanda took charge and drove the deal home. "I'll have my lawyer draw it up. If you're willing… *it's a deal!*"

Recalling Tony's closing remark — *everyone has a price* — Jake stared for the longest moment, picked up his glass, and toasted her. "Deal!"

***

𝔇etroit 𝔉ree 𝔓ress

March 17, 1984

MOBSTERS KILLED IN GANGLAND SHOOTOUT

The parking lot outside the Top Hat Hamburger's, on the corner of Gratiot and McClellan, was the latest site of the ongoing purging of hitmen. Last night, machine-

gun fire riddled two cars parked in the lot. Returning fire, the third car burst into flames.

The murders were one more of a series of "get even" killings. Informants report the five mafia capos killed in the two cars were the same ones who machine-gunned the Sax Club stripper four months ago.

***

Clark sat solemnly, waiting for his team to arrive; the killings at the Top Hat had brought back old memories. *I'll never forget Caroline; she was a wonderful woman. And had a driving commitment to help young girls and pull them out of the gutter, the way her grandmother had done for her.*

Glancing up, he realized the team had assembled in their regular seats. "Who wants to go first?"

Bennett raised his hand. "I'll start."

"Good. Let's hear about Isiah and the Pistons."

"They looked like crap, lost all four games last week."

Woodson shook his head. "Doesn't sound like a playoff team to me."

"Right, and worse yet, they weren't close to the point spread. On the thirteenth, they lost at Milwaukee by twenty-one. They were favored by five. And Isiah shot eight for twenty-one. The next night, they were big favorites to beat Denver. Isiah played well, got twenty-four points, except they lost by four." Turning to Fitzpatrick, he paused. "Tell them the rest of the story."

Pat nodded to Bennett, sitting with his arms folded. "Nah… I'll let Frank carry the ball with the game summaries. I'll fill in at the end."

"Okay." Bennett glanced at his notes. "Another home game, this time against the Nets, we were five-point favorites, ended up losing by nine. Isiah played pretty well, shot seven for sixteen. Three days later, they played at Utah. The game was listed as even; again, we lost this time by eighteen. Isiah shot three for thirteen and sat out most of the second half. The announcer thought he might have twisted his ankle. Whatever happened, it was announced after the game started — someone made big money." Bennett folded his notebook and turned to

Fitzpatrick. "Tell them how you spent your time during most of the game."

Pat couldn't wait to express his finding. "Two weeks ago, Jake Nicolette and a hot blonde were at the two home games. Not only did he hold her hand, he was all over her."

Clark lifted a brow and asked, "Was it that obvious?"

"No, you had to focus on him… it was subtle — a squeeze here, a pat there, and a hand easing up her leg."

"You know anything about her?"

"Not really… but she's one classy woman, not the typical one he might pick up."

"Classy, what are you talking about?"

"She has Neman Marcus clothes on, high heels, and is sharp as hell… you can tell by the way she walked — she has that way about her — seems more like a model rather than someone you'd see at a ball game."

"I'll talk to Clifford and have him put a tail on her, see where it takes us." Clark paused, collecting his thoughts. "Have anything else?"

"Nope, that's it."

"I have just one item today." Clark rolled up his sleeves. "As I mentioned to some of you, we've learned that Ted's Uncle Fred… is an uncle in name only — he's a friend of the family — so Kimberly and I will be observing an FBI interrogation. Both Ted's father and Fred have agreed to the questioning. They're willing to assist us in any way they can."

Kimberly smiled wryly. "I'm really excited… maybe this will be a turning point for us."

"Ha, talking to those old timers…" Pag laughed. "The only thing you'll get is turning back the time."

***

Johnny Curry leaned back in his favorite red leather chair. "Willie Ross, so you're a Philly dude… got any proof of that?"

Not saying a word, Willie tossed an envelope on the table.

Eying him carefully, Johnny took his time opening the envelope and pulling out the introductory letter. "Huh." A sneer passed briefly over his lips; his eyes glared with the strength that could cut steel. "Chuckie Merlino signed it… I thought 'Little Nicky' was in charge?"

"'Little Nicky' Scarfo was doing time when I left."

Johnny nodded, knowing he'd received the correct response. "So why are you in Detroit?"

"I heard it's the place where the action is."

"Action… ha, Detroit is the most dangerous city in the country, and… the eastside is the most dangerous part of the city." He gave Willie an unconscious shrug. "It's a war zone!"

"That's why I'm here," Willie proclaimed, positive he'd sold Johnny a bill of goods.

Johnny's eyes sliced into Willie's thoughts. "I have a basic philosophy — work hard and stick to your plan, never forget where you came from, and you are what you are. How about that?"

Willie smiled, his thoughts flashed back to Philly — growing up on the tough southside — learning the hard way. "You think I'm going to challenge your beliefs?"

Feeling reassured, Johnny's head nodded subconsciously. "Guess you've been around the block a time or two."

"You might say that." Willie took his time, not wanting to seem too eager, before broaching his goal. "Thought you might need a guy like me, you know, to… take care of some of your routine tasks."

Rocking back in his chair, Johnny nodded. "You got balls… I like that."

Willie grabbed his crotch. "I sure hope so."

Catching the humor, "Little Man" as Johnny was known, didn't waste any time. "I have two dozen heroin dens on the eastside, an endless supply of powdery goodness, and am raking in seventy-five million a year, which is likely to grow to two hundred million over the next couple of years." He twirled his fingers around the gold chains hanging from his neck. "I don't drink… do drugs or smoke, so nothing is going out in products; why do I need you?"

Willie drew upon his experience, knowing it was a pivotal question. "It'd be presumptuous for me to respond to that question." He thought it over for a moment, buying time. "You have connections in every nook and cranny in the city and personally know the right politicians… but…" relying on his information about Johnny, "you don't have a reliable man to take care of the little things, that… if not handled properly, can become big issues."

Agreeing with what he heard, Johnny stopped rocking. "Okay, I'll give you a small project and see how well you handle it."

"Fair enough."

"I'd like you to organize a little party for the younger guys, you know, some fun... a way to hook them even more... and for the older guys, a little action."

"That's it?"

"Yeah, let's do one next week and the other a week later."

Knowing the places Johnny frequented, Willie knew where to start. "I'll bring you a plan in a couple of days."

"That soon," Johnny mused, thinking 'no' way. "We'll see."

***

Late the next afternoon, Willie plopped a stack of flyers on Johnny's desk. "What are these," he asked.

Smiling ear to ear, Willie pulled up a chair. "The fliers are for 'Free Night' at Royal Skateland two weeks from Friday. I commandeered the place — on Alter just north of Warren — it's the closest place to Grosse Pointe I could find. Each flier gets a salesman and a new recruit in for the night. It'll be perfect for your expansion into the suburbs."

Johnny stared in amazement. "That's terrific. How'd you come up with those details so fast?"

Willie played it cool. "Never thought about that... it's just the way I work."

"Commandeering, how'd you do... that?"

Willie interrupted, "I told him I was working for you and if we couldn't work out something, you'd be over later... I said I'm positive you don't want that to happen."

Johnny inhaled a deep, calming breath. "I like that."

Willie knew he wasn't home free. "There is one little remaining detail..."

"What's that?" Johnny mused, wondering aloud.

"I need some girls."

"Ha... ha." Johnny's eyes glittered. "At least you need me for one thing. I'll call Kathy. She'll have them there by the carloads."

"Kathy?"

"Kathy Volson, we've gone out a few times. She's the mayor's niece... that way we won't have to worry about the police."

"Pretty smart..."

Johnny grinned, knowing he had a winner and eased out of the chair.

"Wait — there's more."

"More?" Johnny slid back down. "Hell, that's more than I get from five guys around here."

"How about the old-timers?"

"Thought you'd never ask," Willie replied to Johnny's surprise.

"What is it?"

"Next Sunday… *you're hosting* a 'Free Bar' at Stokes. The Pistons will be on all of the TVs and the topless waitresses and strippers will be doing their thing." Willie stopped, waiting for his response.

"Goddamn, you're good." Johnny jumped up and extended his hand. "You're hired, and I want you by my side everywhere I go."

***

The New York Times

March 31, 1984

REPUTED CRIME FAMILY LEADER INDICTED

Paul Castellano, the reputed head of the Gambino organized crime family, and twenty other people were charged in Manhattan yesterday with operating a group that committed over two dozen murders and scores of other crimes.

The charges contained a 51-count Federal indictment, which described the 68-year-old Castellano as the head of a crew that had participated in a "pattern of racketeering activity" since 1973. In addition to the murders, the charges included extortion, theft, prostitution, and drug trafficking.

United States Attorney, Rudolph W. Giuliani, announced this is, "A Very Big Case"; a chance for the citizens of New York to 'get even.'

***

Wearing another sexy outfit, Amanda waited in her bedroom loveseat for Jake's appearance from the tunnel. With the mansion in her personal trust and the $20,000 deposited monthly in her checking account, she had everything she wanted.

Pushing open an eight-by-four-foot panel covered in its entirety with an oil painting, Jake slipped quietly out of the secret passageway and headed upstairs. Seeing Amanda reading a novel in her normal position, he ripped off his tie, loosened his dress shirt, and slipped off his slacks, shoes, and socks.

Sneaking up from behind her, he reached his hands over the back of the loveseat and gently caressed her shoulders.

Slow and easy, he slid his hands under her half-buttoned top and grazed his fingers down her sides.

She sighed, raised her arms — beckoning — for him to join her.

Jake's engine roared. He slid around the loveseat and eased on top of her.

Amanda wrapped her arms around Jake and pulled him tight.

***

Waking up a half hour later, Amanda snuggled with the pillow and walked herself through her game-plan, then tapped him on the shoulder.

Jake stirred from a deep sleep — barely awake.

Kissing him on the forehead, she propped herself up on one elbow. "Honey, can we talk?"

"Of course, dear, say whatever you want."

Amanda took her time. "Hmm, I don't know quite how to say this. You've been so wonderful, but... somehow I just don't feel right."

"Right about..."

Placing her index finger over his lips, she cut him off. "Being the other woman, here, alone... Sometimes I feel like... I don't know... it's just not right."

Jake's mind went blank. *Damn, we just had great sex and it isn't right. What's wrong?* "Would you like to go somewhere?" he asked when nothing else came to mind.

"Yes," she stated, straight out. "I've been thinking about your suggestion. She hedged, "I'd like to propose a quid pro quo."

"A quid pro quo?"

"Yes," she said, hesitantly. "There'd be something in it for both of us."

"O-okay," he interrupted. "Go ahead."

"I'd like to have a ceremony."

Jake leaned to the side, nearly falling off the loveseat. Pulling himself upright, he gave her a subtle smile.

Amanda blew him a sensual kiss. "I know this might seem strange, but I'd like to have a ceremony, like a wedding, with a bridesmaid, flowers and pictures."

"But, I…"

She cut him off. "I know we can't get married… yet… but a ceremony would make me feel closer to you."

Jake stared, trying to comprehend. "I don't understand…"

Amanda charged forward; her voice rose with excitement. "We could go to your place in Boca Raton. Angelo and Catarina could pretend they were standing up for us. Can we Jake, please?"

Slowly Jake rose upright; his head shifting up and down. "Sure, if that'll make you happy… we'll do it."

"Oh, you're so sweet." She pulled him on top. "I want to do it, right now."

"Wait." Pushing back, Jake raised his head again. "What happened to the quid pro quo?"

She kissed him on the cheek, pulled him tight and buried him with a French kiss.

Gasping, out of breath from her deep kiss, Jake turned on his side. "C'mon sweetie, I know you have something up your sleeve… we're not doing it until you tell me."

She hesitated for a long moment. "Okay, here's my plan… I want to throw a celebration party for you, capping off your first five years as the Boss. Whataya think?"

"Hmm, I don't think so… you know me, I'm not much into all that hype and public kind of stuff."

"Before you decide, let me tell you what I have in mind, please."

He took a deep sigh. "Okay, let's hear it."

"First, it won't be a public event. It'll be at the Timberlake Ranch. I know you love the place." Rubbing her hand up and down his back, she kissed him on the cheek. "I want to invite the bosses from across the country."

"All of them…?" He'd never thought of such an idea; Jake's openness grew. "How would we pull off something like that?"

"You've told me, Castellano does it regularly whenever he has everyone to his place."

"Hmm… I don't know… getting all of the guys together, I'd need to get his approval… wouldn't want to get Big Paul's nose out of joint."

"I understand. You won't have to do anything; I'll take care of the details. Will you ask him?" Amanda ran her hand over his hairy chest. Please… sweetie, will you do it?"

"Oh… I don't know… I-I…"

She ripped off his shirt and pulled him tight. "Please, honey, please!"

CHAPTER TWENTY-FIVE

Standing outside the interrogation room in the lower level of the McNamara Building, Clark shook hands with Ned Moomau, Ted's father, and Fred, his uncle. "I'm pleased the two of you agreed to be interviewed today." Clark turned his head to Fred. "Since we didn't take a DNA sample from you this will be a good time to clear you from any wrong doing."

The bald, seventyish man broke into a small grin. "That'd be good." He nodded very slowly, warily eyeballing Clark. "I've been concerned about all of this since Ned told me about the potential problem."

"I can imagine." Clark said sincerely, then turned his attention again to Ned. "Maybe you'll be able to shed some light on the rash of mafia capos killings."

Ned spoke slow and deliberately. "Ted stressed it was important to do everything we can to help... I'm not sure how much I can add, but we're willing to try, isn't that right, Fred?"

The thin man barely looked up, gave Ned a slight nod.

Clark turned for the door. "Come in, I want you to meet Jack Grimes, who spent a lifetime dealing with these killings. He'll ask you a few preliminary questions while I'm processing the paperwork. As soon as he's finished, I'll join the three of you."

The tall, square-shouldered man rose from one of the four chairs stationed at the table in the center of the small, stark room. Glancing at the two men, he extended his hand to Ned and then Fred. "Morning, I'm Jack Grimes, retired FBI agent. I've been following these murders for over forty years. Thanks for coming in."

Fred's eyes lit up in amazement. "Wow, that's hard to believe."

Ned shook his head. "Back in the forties... sounds like you're a real bulldog."

"So I've been called," Jack responded in a light-hearted manner.

Closing the door, Clark gave the group a half-smile. "I'll see the three of you later."

Jack pointed to the two chairs across the table from him. A thick file folder laid on the table across from them. "Have a chair. As Clark mentioned, I have some routine questions we need to get out of the way. You know… name, rank, and serial number." He laughed.

Ned grinned; Fred didn't respond.

Rather than heading for the elevator, Clark turned the other way and walk down the short hallway. Rounding the corner, he winked at Kimberly sitting on one of the folding chairs outside the one-way glass window and speaker box. He slid onto the vacant chair next to her. "This ought to be interesting."

"Interesting!" Kimberly exclaimed, eagerly. "I just hope we can find a clue… if not, it might be the end of the line for my theories."

Clark shook his head rapidly, side to side. "You can't say that — you figured out the swastika — that's the most significant finding we've uncovered so far."

***

Through the window, Clark and Kimberly saw Jack rise and walk out the door. He rounded the corner coming toward them.

She asked, anxiously. "What'd you think about their answers? Any hints from their body language? How about their…?"

Clark raised his hand, cutting her off. "Slow down… give Jack a chance to respond."

Her head bobbed, trying to restrain her excitement, she flipped open the notepad on her lap. "Will do."

Swiping at thin strands of his gray hair, Jack took his time, calculated his words, and spoke softly. "Ned is relaxed, like he's on a Sunday drive… on the other hand, watch Fred, he's really uptight."

A slight frown crossed Kimberly's forehead. "How can you tell?"

"Forty-five years of experience," Jack joshed.

"No, seriously, how can you tell?"

"There's some scientific research out there, but… I watch for three things. Signs of perspiration are the most obvious, usually on the upper lip. Others have the opposite reaction… their mouth is dry, they regularly wet their lips. Fred exhibited a third reaction — rubbing his fingers together, pushing back his cuticle, and clasping his hands.

Watch him when Clark and I go back in — it'll jump right out at you — he's either nervous about being here or he has something to hide."

Clark stood. "Ready to go back in?"

Jack unfolded his hands and gestured. "Not quite." He laughed. "In the old days, I would have smoked a cigarette, playing on their nerves before I went back inside." He winked at Kimberly. "You can tell us when it's time."

Surprised, she pointed to herself. "Me? How?"

"Watch Fred's fingers."

Kimberly peered into the room. Not moving a muscle, she stared. Minutes passed.

"Look, there it is," she said, excitedly. "There, he's rubbing his hands together."

"That's just the first sign, keep watching." Jack turned to Clark. "I'm starting with the killing of Ned's daughter in 1942."

Clark gave him a questioning glance. "Why are you starting there?"

"I-I just have a feeling… if anything is there it may be buried deep in the past."

***

Jack and Clark strolled into the room and took their seats across from the two men.

They looked up at the lawmen expectantly.

Jack opened his yellow pad, ran his finger down a page of scribbled notes, flipped to a blank page, and spoke softly to Ned. "In 1942 your daughter was kidnapped by the Seattle Mafia because you wouldn't pay your protection fee, right?"

The feeble old man nodded, slightly, without looking up.

"She was sold to the Chinese Mafia, who raped, tortured, and eventually killed her, is that right?"

Ned looked like he'd been hit by a truck; his head barely moved. "Yes."

Grimes turned abruptly to Fred and spoke in an elevated tone. "As his best friend, what did you do?"

Caught off guard, Fred hemmed and hawed. "I-I-I didn't do anything."

Taken aback, Grimes thought for a moment. "You didn't talk with him about his loss?"

"Well… yes, of course, we talked a lot… day and night."

"You talked for weeks about it, right?"

"Yeah, he was my best friend."

Grimes pushed on with his strategy. "And, how do best friends react? You don't have to answer… we do whatever we can to make them feel better, don't we?"

Fred's voice sharpened. "You don't understand… you weren't there."

"Oh yes, I was." Grimes pulled a handful of photos from under his pad and spread them on the table, one-by-one — a picture of Ned's daughter posing as a teenage beauty queen, one of her stripping as a pole dancer, another of her being ganged raped by several guys. Grimes paused for a moment, saving the worst one for last. He tossed a photo of her on a kitchen table with a butcher knife plunged into her stomach. Raising the picture to eye-level, he said, sharply, "You think I don't understand," he paused, with an eye on Fred. "Do I need to show Ned more?"

Fred edged closer to the table, his hands shaking. "No, no… don't do that to him."

Knowing he'd touched a tender point, Grimes leaned back in his chair. "What did you do, Fred?"

"I didn't do anything, I-I…"

Raising up, Jack leaned over the table, coming face to face with Fred. "You didn't do anything… for your best friend who was in pain and agony?" He paused, looked Fred in the eye, and shouted, "What did you do?"

"I-I didn't do…" Fred swallowed hard, then spoke slowly, apologetically. "I'm so sorry, Ned. I just couldn't stand to see the torment you were going through. I wanted to strike out, *to get even.*"

Fred broke down in tears.

Consoling him, Ned pulled their shoulders together. "It doesn't matter… I would have done the same thing for you."

"No, no you wouldn't have." Fred pushed him away. *"I made a call."*

"A call?" Ned looked befuddled. "To whom?"

"It's a long story… I had no idea what they'd do…"

Realizing he'd uncovered something, Grimes sported a genuine smile. "Would you like to have a lawyer?"

"Huh." Staring at the blank window, Fred sobered. "What good would that do? I wouldn't have a life." He wiped the glistening from his brow, speaking feverishly. "You don't understand… they're ruthless; they'd kidnap me, too. The day I walk out of the courthouse my life would be over. I can't."

Fred's eyes rolled back, his body began to jerk — uncontrolled, violently.

"Oh no…" Ned jumped up and grabbed him. "He's having an epileptic seizure. Help me lower him to the floor so he doesn't hurt himself."

Clark jumped up, hurried around the table, and grabbed Fred from the back. "Should we call a nurse?"

"No, I can handle it. It usually lasts only a few minutes… we'll have to end the session. He'll be disoriented for some time."

***

Returning to the same location three days later, Fred appeared to be more alert and peppier. He and Ned followed Clark into the room; Fred promptly extended his hand. "Mr. Grimes, how are you?"

"The question is, how are you?"

"I'm fine… ready to tell you everything and get it over with."

Grimes glanced over to the authorized stenographer — a middle-aged woman. "Are you ready?"

"Yes, sir." She nodded from her workstation in the corner.

Grimes pointed to two stacks of paper, each one clipped together. "These are the papers we talked about. The first one grants you immunity for the testimony you're about to give. Do you want to read it, before you sign it?"

"No, if I can't trust you, I don't have a life anyway. Give me a pen."

Placing a pen on the table, Grimes waited for him to sign the document. "Thanks." He picked up the signed document and slid the second one in front of Fred. "The next one authorizes the U.S. Government to place you in a witness protection program, at government costs, for the rest of your life."

"Hand it here." Fred reached. "Where do I sign?"

"Last page, by the X."

He scribbled his name and glanced to Ned. "After all of these years, I'll be free from those bastards."

"Maybe that's a good place to start." Grimes paused, his mood optimistic. "What do you mean when you say *be free from the bastards?*"

Fred sucked in a deep breath. "From the day I reached out to them… they documented everything; stressed that if I ever told anyone, they would know, and I'd be an accomplice to murder. Go to prison for the rest of my life."

The air thickened with tension.

Grimes pulled a chair closer to the table. "Who are they?"

Shaking his head slowly, Fred's hands shook; his voice weakened. "It's a long story… complex, I don't know where…"

Clark interrupted, "Last time we were here you indicated you were born in Budapest, had traveled most of Europe and came here in the '30s from Italy." Clark hesitated; his mind searching for a clue. "Did it have anything to do with Mussolini?"

"Yes." A quizzical expression spread across Fred's face. "How'd you know?"

Clark grinned with pride. "My mother was a history teacher… I had a history lesson at every dinner. What year was it?"

"1938." Fred shook his head. "It seems like an eternity from now. Hitler had gone bananas. I was working in Munich… I knew I had to leave Germany." He paused, a solemn look played over his face. "Hah, we were a motley group — Jews and Gypsies — with one common goal, *get out of Germany* escape the wrath of Himmler and Ritter."

Grimes raised his hand, signaling him to stop. "Sorry, I wasn't a history major; a little background on those two would help."

"Two peas in a pod." Fred wiped the moisture from his cheek. "Dr. Robert Ritter," he declared forcefully, "a racial scientist, whose theories on heredity and criminality were used by the Nazi regime to round up and send nearly a million gypsies to Auschwitz." He choked up and paused.

"Take your time."

"At the same time, working under Hitler, Heinrich Himmler used his belief in an Aryan 'Master Race' and his position as head of the *Schutzstaffel* (SS) to pack Jews on the trains to Auschwitz."

Grimes glanced down; his heart heavy. "Sorry, I didn't mean to dredge up old memories."

"Understood." The old man gave him a polite smile and continued. "As you can appreciate, our goal was to move as far away from Berlin as possible."

Grimes's interest grew. "How'd you do that?"

"It was a long, treacherous trip." Fred stopped, memories of friends dying along the way filled his mind. "It was a long trip," he repeated. "Our fear and agony made it seem like forever. Usually one could travel from Munich through Switzerland to the Italian border in a couple days." He shook his head. "The roads were packed with people seeking to escape. There were German patrols, checkpoints, and military planes flying all over. We travelled mostly at night, hid during the day, and walked the back roads. Farmers along the way fed and housed us — it was a scary time — the trip from Munich to Stuttgart on to Strasbourg, France, took a month. We completed the final leg, through Switzerland to Chamonix-Mont Blanc, in a week. And there, we waited until we were positive the tunnel through the Alps to Entreves, Italy was safe."

"Safe?" Grimes questioned. "You were traveling from France to Italy."

"Mussolini was rattling his saber against France — both sides were nervous, on guard —and criminals and robbers were on the loose."

"How many were in your group?"

"Hmm, to start, maybe twenty… we traveled in small groups of four or five, picked up a few more along the way, some defectors from the German army. They were enthusiastic, like us. We were all avid Fascists. Hitler was a madman; Mussolini wanted to be a king — *nothing wrong with being a king.* We moved to Rome, invested the little we had and got lost in the city."

"What did you do?" Grimes inquired, turning the page on his notepad.

"We started little businesses, like we'd run in the past — tailor, baker, butcher — I sold and repaired bicycles." He cast Ned a broad smile. "That's how Ned and I eventually became friends. After I migrated to the States, we met in Seattle and opened a bicycle shop together."

"A good business it was too," Grimes, the Seattle native indicated, then motioned for Fred to proceed.

Rome was big, hectic, with daily protests. By then, Mussolini had gained power and clamped down on thieves and crooks — an unsettled calm came over the city. He signed a treaty giving *the Catholic Church* the independence and respect it deserved."

Recalling Kimberly's theory, Clark asked, "With all of the turmoil, how did you stay connected with each other?"

"It was hard; we were working different jobs in different parts of the city. We tried to meet once a month at a local bar. By then, there were about thirty-five of us; we met in small groups around the city — we went to different places, so we could maintain a loose network."

Clark pressed further. "How'd you communicate with each other?"

Fred paused, recalling those days. "Funny… one of the fellows, unbeknownst to us, was a German defector. He suggested we meet on the third Friday of every month so we could plan ahead. As you might expect, there were grumblings and questions about keeping track of things. Another defector said, 'Hey, this Friday is the twenty-second… why don't we start meeting on the twenty-second?"

"Is that where the use of the twenty-second came from?"

Fred gave Clark a strange look. "Why… yes."

"Did twenty-two have any other usage or significance?"

"We learned later, it was part of a German code used by the SS."

"To communicate with each other, how so?"

Clark recalled Kimberly's excitement in discovering the swastika.

"We didn't know it at the time, but it was part of a code they had developed for communicating with each other if they were ever captured."

"So now you're meeting on the twenty-second of any given month and all of you are working in Rome," Grimes summarized.

"Yes, but now we're more organized; we start meeting in a single place — usually a local club somewhere in the city — with local fascist leaders. We carried the banner, marched pro-Mussolini, and wrote stories in local papers. We were ready to change the world." Fred took a reflective pause. "You have to remember this was the late thirties, we had grown up under oppressive conditions; we were ready for change — 'Fascism is a breath of life' we used to say."

"So when Mussolini sent Cesare Mori to Sicily to clean up the mafia, we packed our bags and joined the ranks."

"The mafia was oppressive too… how did you rationalize that?" Clark asked, his inquiring mind probing.

The old man smiled in agreement. "Oppression comes in varying forms and varying degrees. The mafia was the face of evil, the bad guys — they were crooks, thieves, extortionists, and thugs — all of us had negative experiences with them. It was the thing to do; we didn't rationalize joining Mussolini; we just did it."

"So where did you go… Palermo?"

"Yes, others went to smaller towns in Sicily. By then we're a tight-knit group — the best of friend, colleagues, compatriots — we met on the twenty-second of every month. We joined in the fight and started killing off mafia capos and lieutenants across the island."

A frown crossed Grimes' forehead. "You only killed lower ranking mafia members, why not the kingpins?"

"I don't know." Fred rolled his shoulders. "It was Mussolini's orders… I guess he wanted to keep the big guys in his corner, I don't know… that's just the way it was, so that's what we did."

Grimes dug deeper. "Was the campaign successful?"

"Yes, over eleven thousand were arrested and hundreds were sent to prison. Crime went down; everything was good until the US came into the war against Germany and its ally, Italy. After that the handwriting was on the wall."

The rich and powerful, mafia families left for America — Carlo Gambino and Joseph Bonanno were among the first to leave, and later became powerful mafia bosses in New York City. We didn't have much money, so we pooled our lifetime savings, and came up with enough to slip out of the country."

"Wow, you must have had a real commitment to get out of there." Clark's interest piqued, fascinated by the insights Fred had shared.

Fred seemed relieved. "Maybe so… at the time it was more of a matter of staying and dying or leaving and surviving. When you look at it that way, it was easy."

"I guess." Grimes ticked off another question on his pad. "How many followers eventually came to the US?"

"Seventy-five, maybe eighty."

"That many?"

"We didn't recruit guys, but we could have had thousands — people were disillusioned, fed up, and wanted to strike back at any symbol of the past. It didn't matter what, we wanted to eliminate it. We weren't bad, we just wanted to start anew — *to have a good life*."

Grimes continued his inquiry. "So what happened?"

"Our German compatriots were relentless; they wanted to *get even* with everyone. By the end of WW II, the mafia was running wild in the urban centers across the US." Fred's eyes opened wide. "They wanted us to focus on mafia capos as a way to hone our network. How could we disagree? The amount of mafia crime here was like we'd never left Europe. So, we committed ourselves to kill capos in the US — the case was made without disagreement."

"How was it determined where representatives of your group would be located?"

A smile crossed Fred's face. "It was decided for us."

Clark's interest grew.

At the time, "The Boss of Bosses," Charlie Luciano, announced that nineteen urban areas, along with the five Families of New York and the Chicago Outfit, would be represented at the next Commission meeting. At our meeting in Philly that year, we agreed to follow the same territorial format."

"Do you still have annual meetings?"

"Nah, that was the last formal one."

"If you don't meet, how do you communicate with each other?"

"Hmm, we don't, directly," Fred said reluctantly, as if he didn't want to say more.

Grimes picked up on his body language with ease. "Well... indirectly?"

"Two ways." Fred spoke, matter-of-factly. "If a mafia-related issue comes to our attention, we send a letter with the news stories and/or other supporting documentation to seven different addresses."

"Seven... does that have a special meaning?"

"I don't think so; it's a smoke screen for the feds..."

Clark cut him off. "Tell us about the other means for communication."

"At first, we used the phone—almost daily. We stopped that when wire taps came into vogue." Fred laughed, seemed prideful. "It's back to twenty-two... whenever there's a killing of a mafia capos it's done on the twenty-second and it's our obligation to send the press clipping to the same seven street addresses."

"Interesting." Grimes paused, making a note. "How long are the same addresses used?"

Fred shrugged his shoulders. "It varies, usually every three to six months, one time it happened in a month. We never know."

Grimes glanced up from his notes. "Any idea how many of your group is still alive?"

"It's not my group. I'm just reporting on things I've heard." Fred ground his teeth. "Many of them have passed away; maybe forty are still active."

"If it's not your group, whose is it?" Grimes asked quickly.

"I don't know…"

Grimes cut him off. "Fred, you've answered our questions and have been quite honest… now I'm going to ask you one more time… who's in charge?"

"Honestly." The old man's lower lip quivered. "I've told you everything I know. If I knew more, I'd tell you. We just got anonymous instructions and followed them."

Grimes' mind probed everything he'd heard. "Tell me about the German defectors; can you describe them?"

"Geez… I…" Fred's eyes indicated he'd never thought about such a question. "There were five of them… like interchangeable parts."

"What's that mean?"

"They're all alike — blonde, between six- and six-foot-three, outstanding physical specimens — they acted the same; they were in charge."

"Any specific characteristics, unique traits or special interests?"

Grimes watched Fred's mind search its cubicles. "Yes," he stated after a moment of thought. "They were all big hockey fans… one liked the Boston Bruins."

"Huh, that's strange." Grimes thought for a moment. "Are any of the addresses from Boston?"

Fred's mind traced his correspondence and grinned. "As a matter of fact, yes, nearly every mailing has a Boston address."

CHAPTER TWENTY-SIX

Nicole waited by the window in an upscale log cabin tucked away on a small lake somewhere in Northern Michigan. It'd been months since they had talked with each other; she had prepared Earl's favorite hors d'oeuvres — boiled shrimp, bacon-wrapped chestnuts, and loaded nachos — a bottle of Champagne on ice topped it all off.

Wearing her most seductive, short, black negligee, she waited anxiously. And then, in the distance she saw the first car in hours, winding its way up the mountain side. In anticipation of his arrival, she placed the snacks in the oven and raced to finish prepping in the bathroom.

Hearing a knock, she stopped fixing her hair and rushed to the door. *Thank God, he's here!* She fell into his arms; the two kissed wildly, their urges firing.

"Oh my God, Earl, the hors d'oeuvres are warming in the oven… I have to turn them off."

She broke away, flipped off the oven, and was all over him again within seconds.

Pushing him down on the sofa, they made love in a hurry because they couldn't wait. Panting and out of control, the two slowed, trying to gain control — neither was interested — they continued.

Exhausted but not yet spent, Nicole wrapped her legs around Earl's firm body, not wanting to let go — it lasted and lasted — Earl melted in her grip and the two collapsed in ecstasy.

***

By the time Earl cracked an eye, an hour later, Nicole had set the table fit for a king. Slipping off the sofa, he walked up behind her and kissed the side of her neck.

She shivered. "Earl, you know that gives me goosebumps when you do that."

"Of course. And you know you love it." He laughed, turned her around, and planted a smacker firmly on her lips.

"Earl, if you don't stop you'll have to eat a warmed-over dinner."

"Well, the first part sounds interesting, but warmed over… I don't think so. I haven't had a home cooked meal in months." Releasing her, he pulled open the fridge. "I'm having a beer to tide me over, want one?

"Nah… I'm having wine with dinner."

Earl popped the cap and eased onto a bar stool at the kitchen counter. "Anything new with the crime and drug-free areas around your stores?"

A smile rose on Nicole's face. "The drug problem has intensified, crime is on the rise across the city. But we've doubled our efforts and refined our reporting processes. Police respond within minutes and most of the crooks have been apprehended."

"Good for you… too bad we don't have more thorn birds like you."

Earl's comment about thorn birds triggered a thought about an incident that happened two weeks ago at her convenience store on East Warren. She wrinkled her nose in a quirky way. "There is one thing, Earl… there's this kid who keeps stopping by, acting like some hot-shit dude; he's a menace."

"A menace? How so?"

"He struts around, grabs himself in the crotch like he has a big one and pushes up against me. I told him to go away or I'd call the police."

"Huh… tell me about him."

"He's been in the store four or five times. Last time, he pushed himself close, almost touching my breasts, and slapped me on the butt. "Ready for a little action?" he touted.

"I shoved him away, and said, 'I'll give you a little action, okay. I'll send you to the principal's office at the middle school down the street.' Unshaken, he stepped back and eyed me. 'Look, I'll give you more than you ever imagined, a marathon all night.'"

"Get out of the way, I don't have time for your trash mouth."

"Trash mouth… nothing wrong with saying I'll take you higher than you've ever been."

"I laughed, and pointed out, 'You don't have a clue what it'd be like.' He cocked his head to the side. 'Well then, if you're so experienced, I'll let you bang me all night.'"

"'No, I'm not talking about you.' I pushed him away. 'Get out of here before I call the police.'"

"Shit, they won't do a thing. I own them too."

Earl pecked her on the cheek. "He sounds arrogant as hell. What else can you tell me about him?"

"Let me think… he's maybe five-foot-four, a blonde white kid, twelve maybe thirteen at the most."

"Twelve or thirteen? Do you know anything else about him?"

"Apparently he's the local drug dealer and runs the entire area around the store."

"At twelve? He must be older. I'll check him out. Do you know his name?"

"Rick Wershe. All of his buddies are black; they call him 'White Boy Rick'." Nicole pointed to the freezer. "It's going to be a while before dinner. Let's open the champagne; you can update me on your activities."

"Sounds good." Earl pulled out the bottle, worked for a minute to loosen the cork, popped it, and slowly filled their glasses. "Here's to the most beautiful woman in the world."

"Earl, I told you before, any more talk like that and I'll turn off the stove."

"Okay, I won't say a word." He zipped his lip.

She smiled, clinked his glass and took a sip.

Earl stood and stepped to the loveseat.

"Good thing." Easing onto the loveseat beside him, she placed her hand on his leg, and asked, "How are things going with you?"

He pointed to his lips.

She laughed. "Earl, you haven't changed a bit… I mean, Clarence. Okay, you can answer my questions."

"Clarence has been extremely busy, moving up the ladder."

He emptied his glass.

Nicole refilled it.

"Maserati Rick is sometimes referred to as the kilo man — he delivers 2.2 pounds of cocaine or heroin every time he makes a drop. The amount of money he's taking in is unbelievable. He told me his net worth is over twenty million. Can you believe that?"

"No way..." Contemplating the thought, Nicole brushed back her long black hair. "He can't spend that amount... what does he do with it?"

Feeling fatigue setting in, Earl responded slowly. "He's invested millions in local businesses — car washes and hair salons — which also double as drop off and pick-up points for his runners. Ha..." Earl laughed to himself. "Wait till you hear this... last week Rick told me to take his car down to the car wash..."

"How's that a big deal?" Nicole interrupted.

"Normally it isn't... in the middle of the car wash, the system stopped. The back doors and trunk flew open. Guys zipped in from both sides; before I knew it trash bags were stuffed into every corner of the car."

"Trash bags...?"

"Yeah, they were filled with fifties and one-hundred-dollar bills. There must have been a million dollars in cash; it was unreal."

Nicole shook her head. "Guess I'm in love with the wrong guy?" She laughed.

"Well, if you want to change, you better hurry." Knowing he had her attention, he thought he'd give her a dose of reality. "This July, Rick will be twenty-five..." Earl ran his hand over his shiny head. "I'll bet you... he won't see thirty."

"Thirty?" Nicole was surprised. "Why do you say that?"

"Word got back to Rick that a DEA officer indicated he'd made enough enemies to fill Tiger Stadium. Besides, I've heard there's a guy who bought marijuana from him some time ago, named Edward Hanserd. He's still steaming about how he was treated in one of his purchases."

She winked at him. "Guess I'll keep the guy I have."

***

Clark closed the door to the room, grabbed a mug of coffee, and laid his folder on the conference table. Easing into the vacant chair, he smiled at his team members. "Looks like we have a bunch of eager beavers here today." He slurped his steaming mug. "I have two brief points to cover before we move on to your reports."

Staff members leaned back for the moment.

Opening his file, a smirk crossed Clark's face. "Good news about Earl. Agents following Maserati Rick spotted Earl driving him in a Cadillac convertible around Belle Isle… and hear this… there were two blonde bombshells all over Rick in the back and another one hanging on Earl."

"Tough duty," Pag said, with an odd little smile.

"Yeah, wait until Nicole hears about this."

"All in the line of duty," Clark said, protecting his old friend, then changed the subject. "Remember when Pag and Frank reported seeing the knockout blonde with Jake at the Pistons' game?" he asked rhetorically. "The FBI followed up on the tip and found she was living in a mansion on the next block, behind his place. Several surveillance teams reported seeing him in the place, but no one saw him go in."

Frowns and scowls peppered team member faces.

Pag raised his hand. "I've heard rumors for years there are tunnels between several of the houses in that area. I assumed it was nothing, more likely part of the aura about the mob."

"You never know… I'll pass it on to the FBI anyway." Clark continued his original line of thought. "Regardless, the FBI decided to bug the place. The advanced team reported there were two German shepherds roaming inside the six-foot wrought-iron fence."

"What did they do?" Kimberly asked.

"Perfect question… you'd make a great straight person," Clark jested. "One night they tranquilized them and replaced them with lookalike dogs. Two nights later, the team went in and bugged the place. When they were finished, the original dogs were returned — no one knew the difference."

Kimberly's expression revealed her excitement. "Ingenious, I say."

"I'm not surprised." Woodson interjected. "The FBI has been fortunate over the years to have strong leadership and attract top-notch people. Whenever we call Washington, it's good to know the most talented people available will be by our side the next day."

"Huh." Pag grunted and shook his head. "Sounds like night and day between you folks and the Detroit Police Department."

Woodson nodded. "That's why we have over two hundred agents here."

***

"Bennett, want to go first?" Clark asked, after a short break.

"Sure." He opened his folder, pulled out a stack of one-pagers, and distributed them in each direction. "Here's the one-pager Clark requested. If you are interested in knowing more on any point, let me know."

"'Protecting the Wine,'" Fitzpatrick read aloud. "Sounds like fun. When writing this, how many bottles did you go through?"

"My secret," the normally quiet New York agent replied. "Uncle Fred's testimony was right on target. French winemakers hid and smuggled Jewish refugees, along with their wine, across the Italian border. Hitler was not interested in collaboration; he was interested in the *bounty* — in milking France for everything he could. He said in one of his speeches, 'We will give back nothing and will take everything we can make use of. And if the others protest, I don't give a damn.'"

"Was he a wine connoisseur?" Kimberly probed.

"Not at all." Bennett wrinkled his nose. "But, some of his top brass were — Field Marshal Goring and Propaganda Minister Goebbels prided themselves in their knowledge of wine and extensive collections." Bennett paused. The Fuhrer was not; he once called French wine 'nothing but vulgar vinegar.'" Bennett laughed. "Guess that's enough for now."

"Excellent." Clark turned to Pag. "Anything you want to add on Mussolini?"

"Volumes have been written about him." He hesitated, decided not to go into detail. "In terms of Uncle Fred's testimony, it fits. Mussolini sent Mori as he described, to eradicate the mafia in Sicily."

"Was he successful?" Kimberly asked.

"Hmm, yes and no." Pag's jaw jutted out. "Like Fred mentioned, thousands were arrested, many were convicted in mass, and hundreds were sent to prison without a trial. Crime rates went down; people felt safer — Mussolini claimed victory. Mori killed off lieutenants and lower ranking mafia capos. Interestingly, wealthy landowners were not touched. In his memo to Mori, Mussolini made it clear, 'Eradicate crooks, criminals, and others feeding off the people; do not approach the wealthy; they're important for our future.'"

"Huh." Clark thought that to be interesting. "I wonder if that's why all of our murders have been at the capos level."

"That is certainly possible," Pag agreed. "It fits perfectly with Fred's comments."

"The rest is in my report," Bennett concluded.

Clark turned to Veronica. "How about you?"

"As a devoted Catholic, I was interested in learning more about the Lateran Treaty." She started by saying, "I didn't find anything related to the case, but there were two points I found personally interesting."

"What were they?" Kimberly interjected.

"The first was the Treaty itself. It was composed of three distinct sections. One defined the territory and gave sovereignty to the Vatican City-State. Another specified the financial conditions. And the third concordat established relationships between the Catholic Church and the Italian State. Over the years, the Catholic Church conveniently dropped any reference to the last point."

A frown on Pag's face faded to a look of surprise. "Why is that?"

Veronica's eyes brightened; her lips turned down. "It violates a basic Church principle—the separation of church and state. The Fascist government was the enemy; the treaty recognized them, which is contrary to Church doctrine."

"Right, so they pretended it didn't happen." Not being surprised, Pag shook his head. "What's the other issue?"

"It's some of the actions taken and comments made by Pope Pius XI." She opened the folder in front of her. "Here, listen to these:

- The Pope cooperated closely with Mussolini for more than a decade, lending his regime organizational strength and moral legitimacy.

- He once stated, 'The true totalitarian organization is not the Fascist State or the Fascist Party, it is the Roman Catholic Church.'

- The Pope began to see the possibility that Mussolini might be the person sent by God who would be able to prevent the socialist takeover of Italy.

There are more… I think you get the message."

"That's a good history lesson. I'm going to share some of your thoughts with my mother; I'm sure she'll be interested in your observations." Clark nodded to her then pointed to Fitzpatrick.

Pat turned his head toward Clark. "I couldn't find anything about German defectors in the late '30s... there's a lot of material on defectors in the '40s when some of Hitler's tactics became clearer and the tide of the war began to turn sour for them. Sorry I don't have more..."

"No problem; guess that's the way it was." Clark turned to Kimberly. "Do you have anything to add?"

"Not really." She straightened and eased closer to the table. "It sounds like Uncle Fred's analysis of the situation was right on target. With Mussolini's pressure to destroy the mafia in Sicily, several members of the mafia fled to the US. I found it interesting, too, that several of Don Vito's followers came here."

"Who is he?" Woodson asked.

"He was accused of committing sixty-nine serious crimes, including twenty murders. The sources I reviewed called them 'students of crime.' Sounds like most anyone could immigrate to the US. If I had a record like that, I'd be glad to start over here, too."

"Interesting... anyone else have something to add?" Clark glanced around the room, not a hand or nod appeared. "Sounds like everything we've found is consistent with Uncle Fred's testimony.

***

Puffing on a Corona, Lewis leaned back in his wicker chair. Clark closed the slider door, handed him a bottle of beer and plopped down in his chair on the other side of the porch. "We sent the report of our investigation on Isiah Thomas to the NBA; we have him dead to rights."

"Can you tell me about it?"

"Sure, it'll be public in no time." Clark raised his bottle as if to salute his dad. "Hats off to you. Even with all the evidence we had, the staff agreed with you that we'd never get a conviction in Detroit, so we've sent the entire packet to Commissioner Larry O'Brien, in hopes of getting a fair hearing."

Lewis returned the bottle salute and downed a slug. "Don't be surprised if the NBA deep-sixes it!"

"Dad, I don't see how they can; listen to this." He straightened and leaned forward. "The FBI has surveillance tapes of "Tony Jack" Giacalone and "The Capital Crew," headed by Freddie Salem and Allen Hilf, going into Thomas's red brick mansion, just off Lone Pine in Bloomfield Hills, to host bi-monthly dice and card games."

"So… do you have evidence of his winnings?"

"Yes, the FBI has copies of the checks Thomas and the Giacalone brothers cashed at his friend's supermarket. He's going to jail too. In total, they laundered millions at the grocery store."

"Sorry, I don't get it," Dad interrupted.

"Wait, there's more." Clark took a short sip. "Isiah was the mark. They wanted him at the events, like a big fish, to lure others — judges, lawyers, and doctors — big spenders. The gangsters were like sharks smelling blood in the water." Clark shook his head. "Crazy, Isiah is so arrogant he thought he could beat them — wrong! They leveraged him… and he played along, shaving points to pay back his debt. The mob made millions."

"Do you have anything from his teammates?"

"Sure do. Mark Aquirre, a teammate and friend since grade school, contacted the FBI. He was really concerned about Isiah's gambling habit and worried about his safety — they have direct testimony — he's dead in the water."

"Humph." Lewis's head seemed to nod automatically. "Here's my thinking… O'Brien has a plate full of public relations issues; he can't afford having the media lay out a case on one of the league's superstars. I hope not, but don't be surprised if the NBA buries it."

"Buries it! The NFL didn't bury the report on Alex Karras. Why would the NBA do it?"

"Karras and Hornung were different — that was driven by the Commissioner — it was in his best interest." Dad took a drag on his Corona. "Son, you're talking about one of the biggest stars in the game. Times are different now. The NBA doesn't want any bad publicity; everything is running smoothly… I don't know… I'm just saying it's a strong possibility." He took a couple puffs on his Corona and released a perfect smoke ring. "Anything significant come out of your interrogation the other day?"

"Yeah, Ted's uncle walked us through how he got here, indicated some German defectors may be behind the murders of the mafia capos."

"Can you tell me about it?"

"Yes, there are some interesting historical connections."

"Maybe your mother would be interested too."

"Good idea. Put out your cigar and I'll invite her to join us."

***

Pad and pencil in hand, Fran opened the sliding door and used the pad to push the smoke away. "Turn on the fan, Lewis."

"Sorry, dear." He rose and pulled the chain.

Easing onto the side-chair by the television, Fran assumed her position — pencil and paper in hand — as she did whenever someone mentioned the word history.

Clark watched her straighten her blouse and waited until she finished her settling into routine. "Mom, I had two interesting historical experiences during the past ten days."

"Oh?"

"Last Friday, I was part of the FBI interrogation of Ted's uncle, Fred. You may…"

"Yes, I recall," she interrupted. "You didn't do a DNA test on him because you thought he was Ted's *real* uncle."

"Right." Clark paused, knowing her mind was as keen as ever. "I'll come back to that… the second event was a series of staff reports on the times around Mussolini's rise to power."

"Sounds interesting."

"It was." Clark wore his excitement on his sleeve. "I heard reports on the French Resistance efforts to smuggle Jews, Gypsies, and wine into Italy; Mussolini and the Lateran Treaty, and how German military defectors made it out of Germany and piggybacked with other immigrants to the US."

Fran gave him a questioning eye. "I'll be interested to hear more about that… I haven't heard anything about German defectors immigrating to the US that early in the war. Can you give me more details about that?"

Nodding, Clark had an outline in his mind. "I'll come back to that. First, I want to walk you through how Fred made it from Germany to the US."

"Good." Fran crossed her legs, propped her pad on her knee, and winked at Clark. "Let's hear it."

Clark walked her through Fred's trip from Munich to Strasburg, through Switzerland, and with the help of the French Resistance, on to Italy.

Nodding throughout, she smiled without taking a note.

He described Fred's experiences in Rome, meetings with his colleagues, and how they'd connected with the Fascists.

"There's not much written about those times. I bet Rome was a hotbed of political reaction and interaction."

"That's the way he described it. Apparently, the revolution was well underway. Mussolini was gaining power with every step."

His mother nodded. "Like Hitler, most people don't understand the conditions. People had been oppressed for years — Mussolini and Hitler were considered a *breath of fresh air* — they had a vision for change and presented a ray of hope."

"That's how Fred portrayed it — they were young radicals willing to fight for the cause."

Fran relaxed and leaned back in the wicker chair. "I certainly understand that."

"So when Mussolini sent Caesar Mori to Sicily to eradicate the mafia, Uncle Fred's group jumped onboard. They left their jobs, joined the military force, and headed to Sicily to help wipe out the mafia."

Jotting down a note, Fran wrinkled her brow, but remained silent.

Clark continued, describing Fred's portrayal of his escape to the US and how the group had communicated with each other. Fran followed each word, scribbling in her notebook. At the end, Clark smiled, feeling good about the history lesson he had shared with his mother. "So, what do you think?"

Fran hesitated for a moment, as if not wanting to burst her son's bubble. "Tell me again, when did Fred come to the US?"

Clark tossed her a questioning look. "1938... why?"

"Because..." She paused, collecting her thoughts. "Fred's tale connects the dots, but the dates don't fit."

"*The dates don't fit,* what do you mean by that?"

"The Lateran Treaty was signed in 1929... that's a big leap to 1938..."

Clark cut her off. "It was a treaty... so what... anyone could mess up on the date."

"You're right," she said. "I let that one slide, but when he said he joined Mori's police force in Sicily that's… just not possible."

Clark couldn't believe what he'd heard. "How can that be?"

"Mori was sent to Sicily in 1925 and recalled by Mussolini in 1929… that's nine years before 1938… I don't think so; something is *not right*."

CHAPTER TWENTY-SEVEN

FBI Agent-in Charge, McGill, leaned back in his swivel rocker and turned toward Grimes, sitting in a side chair to the right. "Well Jack, any thoughts about the disconnect of the dates suggested by Clark's mother?"

Jack took his time before glancing up. "I'm not big on espionage, counter intelligence, and all of that kind of stuff, but I do know it only takes one slip-up or a false statement to trip someone up."

The tall Texan leaned forward on his desk. "My exact feeling… I called the research people in Washington for that very reason."

Sitting on pins and needles to the left, Clark couldn't wait for his response. "Well, what'd you find out?"

Squeezing his clasped hands tightly, McGill gave him a wry grin that turned into a broad smile. "Your mother was right. For him to do the things he talked about, he'd have had to be there in the early '30s."

"Wait 'til she hears this," Clark expressed joyfully. "Have any idea why he would have made up such a story?"

"Could be because it sounded good… and he hoped we wouldn't notice the dates."

McGill cut off Grimes. "My first thought, too… I wanted to give him the benefit of the doubt, but having second thoughts, I asked the same question to experts in Washington."

"And…" Grimes' interest heightened.

"They weren't so generous." Knowing he was in the driver seat, McGill rocked slowly, took his time. "An old-timer in the Research Division recalled some undocumented rumors that Hitler had a grand master plan to conquer the world."

One of his mother's comments flitted across Clark's brain. "Yeah, now that you mention it, I recall hearing the same thing."

"He knew at some point he'd have to neutralize the United States."

A nodding Grimes jotted down a note. "Makes sense."

"Patching together our intel, the best we could come up with suggests Hitler could have had a small band of SS soldiers infiltrate Italy and then immigrate to the US."

"Why…?" Grimes face went blank. "I don't understand."

A smirk crossed McGill's face. "To act as spies and saboteurs."

"You're right." Grimes agreed. "Hitler knew there was a large sympathetic base of Germans here. He also knew that Americans are fickle and grow weary of wars that linger on."

"So he rolls the dice." Clark speculated. "Creates a network to be ready when the time comes to disrupt communication systems and wreak havoc throughout the country."

"Right." McGill explained with hand gestures. "He handpicks a few of his top SS officers to lead the operation."

Grimes gave him a curious look. "How would the Führer be able to dig deep into the ranks of the SS?"

"My thought, too." McGill nodded. "I asked the people in Washington the same question."

"And?" Clark spouted unable to wait for a response.

"He goes to the head of the SS…"

"Erich Von Richter," Clark quipped.

McGill winked. "Excellent, your mother taught you well."

Leaning back smugly in his rocker, Clark basked in his glory.

McGill eased closer to the table. "Erich Von Richter is still at large. He's the highest-ranking German officer still unaccounted for."

"Huh." Grimes glanced across the way at Clark. "So, if you had an extremely important assignment to make… who would you give it to?'

Clark shrugged his shoulders. "Someone I knew and had confidence in."

"Or, maybe a brother," McGill offered.

Blank looks raced across their faces.

Grimes fell back in his chair.

Clark stared at McGill.

"Turns out the file on Erich's brother Frederick, a young lieutenant in the SS ended in 1937, not a single entry after that."

Clark squinted, a frown crossed his forehead. "So Fred's entire story may be a fabrication."

"Right." Grimes agreed. "Do you think Fred is really Frederick Von Richter?"

276

McGill rolled his shoulders. "That's the question the research team in Washington is trying to determine. If they think it's possible; it'll be our task to figure it out."

Thinking reflectively, Clark summarized, "So Frederick was sent to the US as part of an advanced guard to build a subversive network that would mess up our infrastructure and soften us up for a German invasion."

"That's the theory." McGill smiled broadly. "I couldn't have said it better."

"So what's next?" Grimes asked.

"Hmm…" McGill pressed his lips together, deep in thought. "I have an old friend… I need to give him a call."

***

In the lower level of the McNamara Building a large, barrel-chested, bearded man sat in a second interrogation room, at the end of a six foot rectangular table. Stroking his eight inches of chin growth, he thought about the countless times he'd been in this position. Starting his career as a young staffer in 1944 at the Nuremberg Trials, he'd been a prosecutor, a judge, and a panel member. He'd retired five times, only to come out of retirement to hear "one more case."

McGill ushered Uncle Fred into *the room*, pointed to the chair at the other end of the table, turned, and closed the door behind him.

The old frail man, half the size of the man he faced, tried a half smile that barely cracked his lips. "Morning," he uttered softly.

The man's beady eyes sharpened their focus, penetrating Uncle Fred's soul.

Fred shifted uncomfortably and looked down.

"Look at me," the bearded man demanded. "Where were you born… when did you come to the United States?"

"I was born in Munich…"

"Speak up, I can't hear you," *the man* said sharply.

Fred raised his head, spoke slightly louder. "I was born in Munich. I ran a bicycle shop there. We were gypsies and we traveled a lot."

"How did you make your way to Italy?"

"We traveled at night on the back roads to Stuttgart and walked on to Strasburg. We finally made it over the Alps through Switzerland to Chamonix-Mont Blanc, France." He took a deep breath. "We stayed in the basement of an inn there until it was safe to cross through the tunnel to Italy."

"Safe?"

"Yes, the inn owner paid off the German guards with a case of expensive wine. There was a twenty-minute gap when there were no guards, so we hurriedly traveled into Italy."

"When was that?"

"1937."

"And what did you do there?"

"I opened a bicycle shop in Rome… after a while I moved to Sicily to fight for Mori against the mafia."

"When was that?"

"Ah… early in 1938."

"You fought for Mori in 1938?"

"Yes sir."

A sneer crossed the interrogator's face — *he knew he'd caught his prey* — he pounded the table. "You didn't fight for Mori in 1938. Mori was called back to Rome by Mussolini in 1929. You're lying."

Freezing in place, a blank look shrouded Uncle Fred's features.

"Stand up Frederick," the barrel-chested man shouted, with a strong German accent.

Pressing his hands against the table, the slight man stood as told.

"Turn to the right."

The door flew open.

A three-star general with an MP on each side, marched in, coming face-to-face with him. "Frederick Von Richter, you are accused of war crimes during World War II. Our records show you personally led SS squads that herded thousands of Jews onto trains bound for Auschwitz. You tortured men, raped women, and molested little boys."

Raising his head, Uncle Fred's eyes glared. "I didn't touch one boy."

"Huh," the general grunted, hearing the slip of the tongue. He spoke sternly, "Frederick Von Richter… you're a prisoner of war. I command you to come to attention — give your name, rank, and serial number."

Fred didn't react.

The general shouted, "Frederick Von Richter, come to attention, and give your name, rank, and serial number."

Still, he didn't move.

The general repeated the same command again, again, and again.

Uncle Fred stared straight ahead without flinching.

The General stepped within inches of him; his voice thundered, "Frederick Von Richter speak up."

The old man continued staring, and then, seemingly, for no reason, his blank facial expression became dynamic — alive with vigor; his eyes piercing. He abruptly clicked his heels and came to attention. Raising his right hand over his head, he gave a German salute, and shouted. "Hail Hitler!"

A sneer crossed the general's face; he commanded once again, "Give me your name, rank, and serial number."

The rejuvenated man's eyes came face-to-face with the general, and saluting, he stated, powerfully, "My name is Frederick Von Richter. I'm a captain in the SS, my serial number is SS439."

"Describe your mission in the United States."

"My name is Frederick Von Richter. I'm a captain in…"

"At ease, soldier… you may be seated." The bearded man interrupted and nodded to the general. "That'll be all for now. You can wait outside the door."

***

Standing behind the glass window, Clifford and Clark eyeballed each other, both dumbfounded.

The bearded man appeared around the hallway corner and extended his hand. "Need anything more from me?"

"Guess not." Clifford glanced at Clark and received a shrug. "No… thanks, for a great performance."

"Glad to be of service." He winked and walked away.

Clifford nodded to Clark. "Guess we're ready to put Plan A into operation."

Clark still felt the shock of Fred's revelation. "Lead the way."

The two walked back into the room and assumed their positions — Clifford at the head of the table and Clark to his left.

With his identity revealed, the invigorated man sat comfortably at the other end of the table.

As agreed upon, Clifford took the lead. "Frederick." He waited for the man's eyes to reach him. "Frederick, life is full of choices… you've made some very bad ones and I'm sure the remorse is gnawing at you. I'm willing to give you another choice."

Frederick's head elevated, defiant.

"You can continue to be Frederick Von Richter, walk out the front door, and the general will escort you to a military tribunal where you'll be found guilty and sentenced to death." He paused, letting the consequences set in. "Or, you can describe your mission and agree to work with us in getting to the bottom of these mafia capos killings. In that case, I will escort Uncle Fred out the side door and you'll be a free man… it's your choice."

Taking his time, the old man glanced down at his slender body and slowly straightened in the chair. Thank you, sir… I choose to be Uncle Fred."

"Good, would you like to take a break before we start?"

"No, I'm fine… ah… yes, I do have a question."

McGill nodded. "Go ahead."

"Is the witness protection form I signed still in effect?"

"Yes."

"Fine… ask your questions."

"I have several…" McGill turned to Clark. "You can go first."

"Sure." Clark opened his notepad. "Let's start at the beginning, when you arrived. Why did you decide to focus on killing members of the mafia in the US?"

"Two reasons…" Fred seemed more relaxed. "First, several of our men had fought with Mori in the twenties — they told many stories about the atrocities committed by the mafia — it was gruesome." He wiped his mouth. "Secondly, when we arrived in New York City, we saw the same thing happening. It made sense and was a good way to hone our organization."

Clark continued. "How did you decide on where your teammates would locate?"

"Huh." Tired and drawn, with dark circles under his eyes, Fred spoke openly, as he had before. "The mafia did that for us. When The Commission was formed back in 1933, Big Boss Charlie Luciano decided there would be twenty-four seats in the room. It was a no-brainer; all we had to do was to have at least one member of our team live in each area."

Clifford slid up to the table. "You mentioned twenty-two was part of the SS code. How did that work?"

"There were several nuances," Fred said in a tranquil tone. "The event…"

"You mean the killing," Clifford interrupted.

"Yes, it was a game. It didn't matter where something occurred, by having it happen on the twenty-second, we knew it was one of ours."

"You mentioned there were several nuances…"

"Yes," Frederick cut him off. "We also put notices in the 'want ad' section of the newspaper. We coded items for sale, things we were looking for turned into something to buy or a person we were searching for — it was a game — a challenge." He chuckled.

"Who did the killing?"

"I don't know… I'm only a scout."

"A scout, what does that mean?"

"There was at least one scout in each area. It was our job to identify atrocities that had been committed by a member of the mafia. We would make copies of the newspaper story, rate the event, and forward it up the ladder."

Clark leaned forward. "How did you rate the event?"

"On a scale of one to five, five being the most brutal."

Clark continued. "And who decided the next step?"

"I don't know. I think there were five enforcement squads that took care of business."

"How do you know that?"

"Each group had its own signature… like the one who used the gypsy calling card in Detroit."

"How did gypsies come into play?"

"They were a decoy — phony as hell — we knew everything about gypsies. It was easy to take their identity and disappear." He sucked in a deep breath and sighed. "German researchers did extensive studies, trying to prove there was a connection between their heritage and criminality."

"How'd this keep going on for so long? And when does it stop?"

Fred scrunched his shoulders and shook his head. "I don't know… the orders kept coming down and we carried them out… it is our mission."

"There must be some overall goal?" McGill interjected.

Fred sat still, without moving a muscle. "I guess it never stops — we are soldiers fighting for our cause."

"And just what *is* your cause?"

Fred spoke exactly, like he was reading from a script, "We are fascist soldiers building momentum, sponsoring protests and marches, building networks and alliances to take aggressive action, and, when the time comes, to disable US infrastructure and cripple its military capability."

"You have been here for forty years." Clark stated; his voice calm. "When the time comes? How will you know?"

"When we're told."

"C'mon Fred, you must know more than that." Clifford's tone elevated, he stood and confronted him. "So who is the brains behind this… is it your brother Erich?"

"I don't know."

"Fred… you must have a sense of who it might be."

He shook his head emphatically.

"You know Fred, it's Erich, isn't it?"

"I can't say for sure… really, I can't… I don't know."

"Describe the person in charge. How does he act?"

Fred took his time, collecting his thoughts. "The person has a 'steel-trap' mind; he thinks out every detail, and leaves nothing to chance." He paused, reflecting. "Huh, the more I say it aloud, the more it sounds like Erich… still, I can't say for sure."

McGill pulled a sheet of paper from his folder and read each point.

- "He joined the *military* because of his devotion to his country rather than for the Nazi Party; he's known to defy orders from the German High Command.

- He's an independent, scheming and detail-oriented person, who takes every variable into account, then uses the *Blitzkrieg* tactic.

- He sees the battlefield as a chessboard where he can express his intellectual supremacy."

McGill stopped. "Do you know who I'm reading about?"

"No… it sounds like…"

"Sounds like!" McGill tossed the sheet on the table, in front of Fred. "Here, read this. What is the title?"

Fred picked up the sheet and read aloud. "General Field Marshall **Erich Von Richter**."

"If you had to make *one* statement about your brother Erich, what would be *the defining characteristic*?"

Fred thought for a moment. "He sees everything as if *it's a game; his motto is Schachmatt (Checkmate)*. He's always planning, scheming, conniving, staying three, four, five steps ahead of everyone; and I'll never forget, he *always has one more trick up his sleeve*."

CHAPTER TWENTY-EIGHT

Walking down an upper hallway in the Detroit Archdiocese's office building, with the auditor and a tall, slender black man, Father Dom chatted with his invited guest. Reaching the door of the Accounting Office, Father Dom led the way in.

The Director of Accounting was waiting.

Father Dom gave him a subtle wave.

"Right this way." The director pointed. "There's coffee and sweet rolls in my conference room."

"Sounds good," Father Dom replied appreciatively. "I could use another coffee."

The three followed the Director into the conference room. Each grabbed a sweet, filled a cup, and took a seat.

The Director pulled out a chair at the head of the table, with the auditor to his right, and Father Dom and the black man on the left.

Nodding to Father Dom, the Director asked, "Would you like to introduce our guest?"

"Yes, of course." Father Dom turned to the black man. "As both of you know, the Archbishop indicated he'd rather have a local investment professional guide us rather than a federal outsider from the FDIC." He turned to his guest. "It's my pleasure to introduce Lawrence Brown, the Senior Vice President at American Savings and Loan."

Mr. Brown picked up after the father's comments and continued by sharing his many accomplishments.

Hearing his title and extended resume, the auditor smiled to the Director of Accounting. His colleague sent an agreeable nod back his way.

Father Dom added, "After our recent meeting, I met with Lawrence to outline our concerns with the Archdiocese's Stewardship and Development Committee. Having dealt with other situations like ours, he indicated he'd work gratis."

"I like him already," the Director of Accounting announced.

The auditor grinned accordingly.

Settling in comfortably, the expert opened his notebook and glanced up. "Father Dom gave me a brief overview; I'd like to hear how the two of you perceive the issue."

"I'll start." The Director of Accounting raised his hand. "Acceptable accounting practices are followed in recording the funds. I have no concern in that regard. The problem I have is a judgment matter. They consistently show excessively high rates of return — quarter after quarter, in the 25 to 30 percent range — that's hard to imagine."

"And, millions keep flowing down the stream," the auditor added. "It's nice to see higher returns, but the meeting's minutes suggest the committee is controlled by a few."

Father Dom started to raise his hand, then pulled it down.

The auditor raised his, stopping the anticipated question. "In checking the minutes, I've found there are three individuals leading the discussions and making the motions."

"Is that unusual?" Father Dom posed.

"Yes, typically I see a couple of committee members push an item, then another person chimes in on another item. By the end of the meeting, I'd expect to see a balance between the ones making the motions…" He paused. "That is, except for the priests… they're pretty much window-dressing — they fall in line with the majority."

"Is that well-known throughout the leadership team?"

Receiving a nod from the Director of Accounting, the auditor continued. "Yes, particularly on the committees dealing with financial matters. It's simply not an area of interest or expertise for most priests."

"And so," the Director of Accounting interjected. "They follow the same basic tenets of *faith management* practiced throughout *the Church.*"

Lawrence's large, black eyes flashed on alert. "I can tell you without hesitation, *money has a way of corrupting.* I've seen people with the highest ethical standards and those with moral values beyond reproach, succumb to *the almighty dollar* — it's like nothing else matters." He smiled at the two financial professionals. "That's why every organization has people like you… keeping an eye on *everyone.*"

A smile filled the face of the auditor. "Interesting you say that." He took a slug of coffee, washing down the last piece of a double-chocolate donut. "And the amount doesn't seem to matter. I've seen an individual fudge $20 on a travel expense report… a mid-level manager cheat by adding a hundred miles to his monthly travel allowance… it's crazy to risk your job for literally nothing." He shook his head. "Yet… people do it all the time."

Lawrence glanced to one side, then the other side of the table. "So… is there anything else that leads you to suspect foul play or the possibility of money laundering?"

Father Dom tapped on the table. "Yes, I have another observation… I checked on the key players… the Chief Finance Officer just bought a new home in an upscale community. He makes a nice salary, but from my observation, it is well beyond his pay grade."

The auditor spoke up, "Yeah… we had coffee the other morning, and all he talked about was his trip to Mexico and his latest cruise. He's living pretty high on the hog, if you ask me."

Lawrence turned back to Father Dom. "Have you picked up anything on the citizen board members who've been making the motions?"

"No… they're all prominent men from different parts of our community—Grosse Pointe, Redford Township, and Northville."

Nodding, Lawrence hesitated. "I'm reluctant to ask, but… do they have a similar ethnic heritage?"

"Yes, now that you ask, they're all Italian Americans."

Lawrence's confidence grew. "Can I see a list of where the funds have been invested?"

"Yes, I have it right here." The auditor pulled a folder from the stack in front of him and handed it to the banker.

Lawrence ran his fingers down the spreadsheet and stopped. A smile lifted the corners of his mouth. "Here's what I was looking for. Atlantic Offshore Drilling; it's supposedly located in Bermuda. I saw the same listing three, maybe four years ago. It's a *paper organization, part of a money laundering scheme used by the mafia.*"

"Are you positive?" Father Dom asked.

"Absolutely." Lawrence eased away from the table. "I'll be glad to review the rest of the investment portfolio, but I can tell you right now… this is the first of several illegitimate entries."

A clearly upset auditor sucked in a deep breath. "Where to now?"

Lawrence paused for a reflective moment. "If you'll provide a list of the committee membership, I'll be glad to ask a friend of mine to see if they have any crime-related ties."

"Sure, I have the committee membership right here."

***

Willie shouted to the boy walking ahead of him. "Hey kid, wait up."

The white boy didn't turn or slow down; instead, he picked up the pace.

"Hey kid, slow down or I'll shoot you in the ass."

The kid stopped immediately, and slowly turned around, facing Willie. "What do you want, man?"

"I want to talk with you."

"I don't have time to talk." He turned around and renewed his pace.

"You have time, or you'll be doing time, I have a warrant for your arrest."

The kid froze in his tracks and glanced over his shoulder. "For what, jaywalking?" He laughed and started off again.

Willie shouted, "Thirteen counts of drug trafficking and resisting arrest if you don't stop."

Stopping without taking another step, the kid turned around — *a white kid, twelve or thirteen at the most* — a lanky, baby-faced kid with a mop-top.

"Who am I talking to?"

"You're talking to me," Willie announced. "And if you're not careful, you'll be talking to the Feds."

The kid sneered; his distaste for any directive clear. "Sounds like you think you're some kind of a big shot."

A smirk crossed Willie's face — he'd been there, when he was about the same age — that didn't matter now — he had an assignment. "See that park bench over there?" He pointed. "Sit your ass on it... we're going to talk."

Buckling to Willie's aggressive manner, the kid walked over and eased onto the bench.

Willie slid onto the opposite end. "You're Rick Wershe, aren't you?"

"Yeah, what's it to you?"

Willie bit his tongue. "It's about your life and whether you want to live it here or in a correctional facility."

"You some hotshot undercover agent?"

Sliding closer on the bench, Willie leaned over and whispered. "As a matter of fact, I am."

Rick bent away in surprise. "You are?"

"Yes, and you're going to listen to me."

The punk wrinkled his nose.

Willie grabbed him by the collar and pulled it tight. "We have enough on your dad for selling weapons to drug dealers to put him away for a long, long time."

"I've heard that before… he'll pay someone off and that'll be the end of that."

"And just how many FBI agents has he paid off?"

The kid swallowed hard.

"If you'd rather do time, that's fine with me — it doesn't matter — the FBI has enough evidence to lock you up so long you won't see a pussy until you're an old man." Willie laughed. "The guys in the juvenile correction facility always like a piece of fresh, white meat — they'll have a feast on your little white ass — when they're done, you'll be promoted to the real pros in the state house. Your ass will be so red you won't be able to wipe… you hear me now?"

Such prospects hit home; Rick gulped air and replied, "Okay… so what's the deal?"

"The deal is your ass will be sitting on this park bench tomorrow, at the same time, with your dad. You're too young to be an informant, so I'll have a copy of everything I've mentioned today in an agreement for your dad to sign. Got it?"

"Yeah, I guess."

"There's no, I guess… asshole." Willie exclaimed. "You'll be here… your dad will sign the agreement to keep himself out of jail and you'll go to work for the FBI. It's either that or the two of you will be serving long prison terms. You got that?"

Nodding, the kid sneered. "I'll tell him."

Willie jumped him and leaned over Rick, coming nose to nose with him. "You'll do more than that... the two of you will be sitting here, waiting for me!"

***

Parked in his Bronco at the north end of Clark Park, near the corner of Scotten and Verner, Willie watched as the two approached from different directions — the kid crossed the park from the east near Western High School, and the older man from the other side of the park.

Taking his time, Willie walked down the sidewalk, turned to the right, and headed through the grass to the park bench. Standing in front of the two, he asked the kid, "Did you explain the arrangements to your dad?"

"Yes."

Willie sat down between the two and stared the old man in the eye. "Do you understand the agreement I have in my hand?"

"Yeah," he snarled.

"Want to read it?"

"Nah, give it here. I'll sign it." He grabbed for the stapled sheets.

"Just a minute." Willie pulled them back. "So there's no question, tell me the essence of the agreement you're about to sign."

The older Wershe balked. "Give it here."

Willie stared at him, without saying a word.

"Okay, it says if I agree to Rick working as an FBI informant, the feds won't press drug or gun charges against me."

"Fine, here's a pen and the papers."

The old man scribbled his name at the bottom of the last sheet. "Anything else?"

"No, you can leave. Rick and I have some business to take care of."

The old man stood and headed west across Clark Park.

Willie rose and motioned for Rick to follow him.

"Where are we going?" the kid asked.

Willie pointed to his wheels at the end of the Park. "When we get in my Bronco I'll tell you more on the way."

Several blocks later, Rick asked, "We're going to Royal Skateland, over on Alter, aren't we?"

"Yeah, I'm glad to see you know your way around the eastside."

"Why are we going there?"

"We're going to pick up a couple chicks, take them back to my place, and bang the hell out of them."

"Sounds good to me," Rick replied, playing along. "Do we have a game plan?"

Willie glanced his way. "Guess you know how to play the game. No, we're not picking up chicks… I'm going to introduce you to the right people and you're going to work your way up the chain of command of the Curry Brothers."

"Curry Brothers, man you don't mess around."

"From my knowledge, being on top is the only place to be."

"Huh, think you're pretty cool, don't you?"

Willie thought for a moment. "I thought you were the cool one?"

Holding back a partial grin, Rick nodded his head. "I think we're going to be a good team."

"We'll see how well you perform tonight." Willie turned off the ignition and led the way into the skating rink.

That was just the beginning.

Rick Wershe followed Willie's directions to perfection, meeting with him weekly to report in and receive new instructions. Within no time, the novelty of a young white kid hanging round a black drug kingpin was gone — he was Johnny Curry's shadow.

Willie taught him the ways of the *black inner-city culture*. Rick learned quickly. To those around him there was no difference — black or white — in the way he acted, the girls he dated, the people he hung around with, and the things he did.

It wasn't long before he became Johnny's ace protégé — "White Boy" Rick.

***

Waiting for Rick Carter to come out of his modest bungalow on Birwood Avenue, Clarence rubbed his hand over the top-grade leather interior of Rick's Mercedes Benz, wondering about the plan for the day. *One day we're on our way to Miami and the next day I'm delivering crack to a fancy place in Grosse Pointe. Before I know it, we're at a lavish party with women draped all over us at his riverfront condo. He's one amazing guy. Next day, we're in the projects, helping people, paying the rent for someone he'd never met before. We change into sporty suits and we're back on the glitz trail.*

"Clarence," Rick called. "Got a tank of gas? We're going on a road trip."

"I just filled it up. Where are we going?"

"I'll tell you on the way." Dressed in a new suit and tie, Rick slid into the car and pointed to the east. "Let's go."

Passing Woodward, Clarence turned toward Rick. "Can you give me a hint?"

Several blocks went by.

"Turn right at the next light."

Clarence kept his eyes on the road.

"Slow down." Maserati pointed at an old, run-down two-story, woodframe house. "That's where I was born, lived there until I dropped out of school. Stop, right here… I want you to take a picture of me standing in front of the old place so I can give it to my mother."

The two got out of the car.

Rick handed Clarence a camera then posed for three or four photos. Sliding back into the car, Maserati pulled out a handkerchief and wiped the tears away. "We had nothing and now…" He brushed his face and pointed. "Drive down the next block. I want to show you Demetrius Holloway's place; his mother was a mail carrier for the post office. He was a meticulous dresser in high school — he wore suits, looked like a million dollars."

"Funny, how things work out."

"Yeah, now we got money and… the kids in the projects have nothing. Worse yet, no one cares."

***

THE DETROIT NEWS

May 17, 1984

ARCHDIOCESES UNCOVERS INVESTMENT FRAUD

Finance Officer Fired

Today Archbishop Dooley of the Archdiocese of Detroit turned over all Church financial investment records to the SEC and FBI for the last seven years. In a rare move, Archbishop Dooley stressed, "No entity is above the law..."

His words were praised by church and local officials.

Financial Officer Harold Dugan was removed from office and indictments were issued for three Finance Council members.

Chewing on a cigar, Renzo fired away at Father Dom as he walked in for poker night. "Hey Father, I didn't see your name in the paper today, why not?"

"Just as well." The ombudsman laughed. "No need to be in the news for the good stuff, sooner or later you'll be in there for the bad stuff."

"Good point." Carlos stared up anxiously. "So, what's going on downtown?"

"Clark knows. The three men mentioned in the paper were all associated with the mafia, in one way or another. The finance officer was on the take too, so they had four votes out of seven. They were using the same scam Clark uncovered in the Nash case five years ago."

"Yeah, I remember that... his wife was forging her husband's name."

"And the number two guy in the mafia, Angelo Travaglini, was banging her," Ted reminded the group. "Huston Nash lost on both ends."

"Poor guy... he just got out of jail last month," Father Dom noted.

"Well Father, since you have the spotlight, anything else you can tell us about your saintly colleagues?" Ted asked, tongue in cheek.

"Yes, as a matter of fact, there is." He raised his hand in surprise to the group. "I scored another point with the Archbishop... well, maybe not a point, but at least we cleaned up another area that bothered me." He paused, taking a short sip of Stroh's. "The Archbishop approved the new policies and procedures I developed on how the priests at the parish level handle their funds."

"Good for you," someone stated.

"Does that mean we won't see any major gifts from guys like Jack Nicolette?"

"Well, if you do, you can rest assured the money will be used to do good things in the church… and not go into his back pocket."

Clark's interest grew; his thoughts shifted back to business. "How about Nicolette and the others who have laundered money in the past?"

"Whose deal is it?" With a wink of the eye, Father Dom ignored the question.

CHAPTER TWENTY-NINE

Sitting beneath a large, lime-green umbrella, Clark gazed at the wrought-iron fence surrounding the Side Street Diner's patio on Clair Street, a block south of Kercheval. The garden-like area outside the crowded Grosse Pointe eatery had not changed since the first time he'd met her here, nearly two years ago.

As before, the other four tables were packed. Filled with church goers, women dressed to the hilt and men in suit and ties, and younger couples savoring stuffed French toast and three-egg omelets loaded with mushrooms and spices — the restaurant's popular breakfasts.

A warm May morning sun beat down on the umbrella, calling for iced tea rather than the coffee they'd had last time.

Hearing the creak from the courtyard gate, Clark laid the May 20th issue of the *Detroit Free Press* aside and glanced that way. Dressed in a stylish beige pantsuit, she flicked her wrist, sending him that familiar wave.

He gave her a thumbs-up and shifted his eyes away from her trim body, knowing he'd gawk as he had the first time.

Sashaying in, her tan heels clicked sharply on the brick pavers. Stopping in front of him, she extended her hand; her eyes admired his clean-cut appearance. "Nice to see you again, Clark."

He stood and shook her hand. "Always a pleasure."

"Well, enough of that… have you ordered?"

"No, I was waiting for you."

"How nice. I'll have an iced tea."

"Sounds good." Clark motioned to the waitress then ordered. "Two iced teas, unsweetened," he said, catching her pleasant nod.

She glanced at the menu. "I'm starved… think I'll have a Farmer's omelet, how about you?"

"The stuffed French toast was great last time. I'm doing a repeat."

"My old standby too."

Clark cocked his head, sending her an enthusiastic glance. "You seem to be in a groove today, anything happening with you?"

"Oh my, I'm so excited." She took a deep breath, let out a deep sigh, and shifted the conversation to him. "You've had another tremendous year."

Rocking back in his wire chair, Clark shrugged his shoulders. "It's kind of hard to tell. When you're in the trenches, it isn't always easy to see the light."

"I understand that… I've had my ups and downs too."

The iced tea arrived. It was quiet until the server placed them on the table.

She picked up her glass and took a long swig.

Clark unwrapped his straw and took a short sip.

She eyed him. "How are your parents?"

"Just like always," Clark indicated, nonchalantly. "Seems like things don't change much with them."

"I guess." Her eyes drifted around the garden area. "I really like it here — it's so relaxing — I haven't had much time to do that in the past year."

Clark wanted to ask her how the year had gone; felt it better for her to carry the ball. Instead, he picked up the menu and pretended to study it, trying to buy time.

She seemed hesitant too, finally asked, "Ready to order?"

"Yes."

Clark motioned to the waitress.

She hustled over. "May I take your order?"

He nodded across the table. "Go ahead."

"Thank you. I'll have the Farmers omelet and a large orange juice."

"The stuffed French toast with double syrup." Clark eased back, hoping she'd take charge.

"Could I refill your iced teas?" Nothing was said while the waitress attended to them.

"Yes." She gave the petite blonde a pleasant smile. "And keep the refills coming, please; I'm as thirsty as a horse." Staring over the wrought-iron fence, she laughed. "Bet you've been wondering about me since I was last here."

"As a matter of fact, I've wondered numerous times." He grinned. "I hoped you'd call again, but figured… sooner or later you'd tell me whatever I needed to know."

She smiled politely. "That's nice of you to say it that way."

He leaned back — giving her full range.

Continuing to stare off into space, she took a long sip of tea. "I have so much to tell you, but first… I want to provide the background, so you have a better appreciation of why I had such a burning desire to do…" She stopped abruptly.

"Yes, I'd like that." He swirled his glass of tea. "I've thought about the *why question… I don't know how many times.*"

The breakfast plates were served.

She glanced up from her heaping plate. "Mind if we talk over breakfast?"

Clark smiled; *always ready to eat, and in this case, most interested in what she had to share.* "Yes, of course, I can handle both," his knife carved into the stuffed French toast.

"I'm Amanda Nash."

Startled, Clark shook his head, trying to recall… to make the connection.

"You remember… when my daddy Huston Nash was at the podium after his grandson's death, I was on the left side of the stage. You were in the center of the gallery section, fourth row."

"You're his *daughter?*" He expressed louder than he'd thought — covered his mouth and glanced around — no one noticed.

"Yes… the years have gone by so fast."

"I would have never imagined…"

"Over the next couple of years, I struggled with all of the crap. First, I learned Nicolette had ordered the kidnapping of my sister from the prep school in Massachusetts; and worse yet, had put her to work in a whorehouse. She had never before even smiled at a guy, let alone *do it.* Being drugged and raped by men had to be worse than dying a hundred deaths." Amanda pulled a tissue from her handbag and wiped her nose. "Samantha — she was so innocent and fragile — she committed suicide for her own sanity, and to save my brother who was in debt big-time to the mob."

"More tea?" the waitress asked.

"Yes." Amanda emptied her glass and slid it across the table.

Clark paused, shaking his head.

"Next thing I know, my brother is in prison." She sniffled, wiped her nose, and sniffled again. "Then, I learned my mother had forged my dad's name on bank documents for years, sending him to jail. And... can you imagine... all of this time, Angelo Travaglini had been banging her. Talk about trauma, I had it!"

Clark sat dumbfounded, not knowing what to say.

Amanda blew her nose, gently.

Composing herself, a look of resolve came over her face. "All I could think about was how I could *get even.* Over and over at night — *get even* — day after day — *get even!* It became an obsession — I couldn't think of anything else."

"So that's why you're here."

Nodding, she wiped her soft lips. "That was the best breakfast I've had in months. Thank you so much for listening."

"Hey, no problem." He winked, trying to convey his sincerity. "Seriously, I welcome your sharing... there was no way I could have managed the issues you had to deal with. It must have been extremely traumatic."

"I guess... maybe I should have told you sooner, but..."

"Hey, no need to second guess."

"Thanks." She sucked in a deep breath and leaned back. "I feel like a ton of bricks has been lifted from my shoulders."

"Guess that means you're close to accomplishing your goal."

"Almost." Her pleasant smile broadened across her face. "Just a few more details to cover, and tennis star Jack Nicolette and playboy Angelo Travaglini will be devils of the past."

"You're not going to...?"

"No, no... nothing like that..." She stopped. "I'm getting ahead of my story."

"Sorry." Leaning back in his wire-back chair, Clark flicked his hand. "It's your nickel."

She curled her mouth with distaste. "I studied every possible way to *get even* with them, and finally concluded there was only one way."

Clark's interest piqued; he leaned forward in his chair.

Hesitatingly, she spoke of her planned ordeal. "There were so many layers of lackeys, bodyguards, and security systems. I knew there was only one way; I had *to use my body.*" She swallowed hard. "At first I thought '*no way.*' Weeks passed. I thought about it more and more. Then, piece by piece I came to accept. I realized — I didn't have a choice." Amanda raised her eyes to look at Clark. "I talked to my adopted sister about my feelings. Interestingly, although she doesn't hold the same ambivalence toward Nicolette, she detests Angelo Travaglini, and wanted to *get even* with him just as bad."

"Why's that?"

"Turns out when she was adopted, my mother was the most prominent woman in town—she was the queen of the ball; *the queen of every ball*!"

I was off to college, so Catrina watched mom go downhill. At first, she didn't notice anything… she heard rumors and finally figured it out — Angelo Travaglini was doing our mother. As bad as that was, he sapped mom's energy; her commitment to dad, her excitement about our community — all of that was gone. Everything had to be about him — our family was nothing."

"Catrina?"

"Yes, your agents have seen her — everywhere in town — she's on the same mission, has been sleeping with Angelo since last summer."

Clark's eyes bulged. "The one with the big…" His hands rounded the shape of a woman's breast.

"That's the one."

Clark's mind raced with questions. "How does she fit into all of this?"

"It's a long story… I'll try to make it brief." She counted on her fingers. "Some twenty-five years ago, Angelo spent the summer in Sicily. He got a woman pregnant." Amanda sneered; her voice quivered. "Some time later my mother — Barbara Nash — saw the little girl at a Catholic church in Sicily and wanted to adopt her. Dad was opposed, but finally caved. They raised her like the rest of us, and when she was old enough, they sent her off to boarding school, just like me."

"That's why she wasn't at that press conference for your nephew?"

"Right… anyway, she has the same feelings toward Angelo as I do against Jake. She wants to confront him face to face."

"What's she going to do?"

"I don't know… maybe kick him in the balls."

"So all of this is a scam to *get even* with the two of them."

"Yes, we both agreed that was the only way. I know it sounds strange, but it was the only way the two of us could *get even.* They had destroyed the lives of my sister and brother. They turned my mother into a slut and left my dad to rot in prison; we decided to take care of them."

"Take care… you said you're not going to kill them…"

"I wanted to a thousand times, but decided it was better to make him suffer. I'm going to make sure Mr. Jacob "Jake" Nicolette never plays tennis again," she stressed in a cool, calm voice. "Any questions?"

Overwhelmed with what he'd heard, Clark raised his eyebrows. "Wow, I don't know where to start."

She smirked. "I'll wait."

"I have a perspective of your vindictive feelings, but I can't imagine how you could have gone through all those events."

"Events, like what?"

"You're the woman spotted at the Pistons' games, aren't you?"

"Yes, and all of the restaurants and at his mansion… whoops, I should say *my* mansion."

Clark picked up on the subtlety. "*Your* mansion?"

"Yes, that was part of the deal. I told him I wasn't going to play second fiddle and…"

Clark cut her off. "He gave you the mansion, just like that?"

"No, not quite… it was a business deal — *I was on a mission* — I knew what I wanted. I knew what he wanted. Well, I wasn't going to spread my legs for nothing," she stated, cold heartedly. "My lawyer prepared the agreement; the mansion was placed in a blind trust and later sold. He'll never figure out where the money went," she spoke matter-of-factly. "He'll never find out where it is or who I am."

"And, the information we gathered about L.A. and Stanford?"

"I went to Stanford… after that, everything else is part of a scam."

"I don't understand… our agents called Stanford and verified everything. How did you…?"

She cut him off. "My friends ran a phone bank that followed the same protocols as the Stanford switchboard."

"And the other contacts, you did the same thing?"

"You got it." She laughed. "Your agents and the mobsters fell hook, line, and sinker for the phony phone numbers I placed on my country club application. Everyone took the bait!"

Clark shifted in his chair; surprise written all over his face. "Well... I have to give you credit, you thought through every possible angle."

"I didn't have a choice... I knew our game plan had to be flawless; if not, the mafia would sniff us out. I had to cross every 't' and dot every 'i' if I was going to stay alive." She reached down to pick up her purse and pulled out a small wrapped package.

Easing up to the table again, she slid it in front of Clark. She looked at it with a hateful sneer. "Here's my diary for each day since I met Jake, plus tapes for every time I was alone with him in *my mansion.*"

"Every moment?"

"Yes, if you want to listen to *it* you may... either way... there is lots of evidence in the pillow talk." She laughed, a hearty laugh. "It's amazing the things guys say when their pants are down."

Clark measured his words. "I've had a similar experience in the locker room — I always thought the same thing."

"Really, maybe we should write a book," she jested.

Clark's eyes bugged. "I-I-I... don't think so."

"You're probably right." She took her time, downing the last of her tea. "I have the grand finale planned — it must go flawlessly — there's no margin for error, otherwise all of this will be for naught."

"From the way you've handled the details thus far, I doubt if there'll be any foul-ups."

"I hope not." She shook her head. "It just takes one slip."

"I don't think you need to worry," Clark said, wondering about her *grand finale...* his mind wanted to push for details, but he thought better of it, and decided to wait for her to open up.

Letting out a deep sigh, signaling the moment, it didn't take long. "On Saturday, June 11th, I'm throwing a huge celebration party for Jake Nicolette at the Timberland Game Ranch in Dexter — *its purpose is to celebrate his five years as Boss* of the Detroit Mafia."

"Great idea."

"Thanks, but you haven't heard the clincher." She paused, taking her time — she strung Clark out and then hit a home run. "I've invited

The Commission members from all over the country." She hesitated. "You know who they are, right?"

"Yes, we have their names and pictures on a large map in our conference room."

Smiling, she rocked her head up and down. "I thought you might."

Clark gulped down the last of his iced tea.

"With their bodyguards and a few *consiglieres*, I expect there'll be somewhere around seventy-five to eighty men in attendance. And there'll be plenty of Jake's favorite food dishes and his best wine. The guys will start arriving around six-thirty and dinner will be served a little after eight."

"Sounds like you've taken care of every detail."

"I've tried to." She flipped her hair aside. "By nine o'clock most of the guys will be tipsy and bragging about their successes — the killings they've done and scams they've managed."

Amanda rubbed her forehead. "By the time the night is over, they will have bragged enough to provide enough evidence to put all of them in jail for a very long time. So, here's where you come in." Eyeing him, she raised an eyebrow and placed a sheet of paper in front of him. "This is a list of the vendors who will be working there that day — food services, electrical company, sound systems — get the point?"

"Those are the ones we'll use as our cover."

"You got it. Your men will have all day to bug the place. Each table will be numbered and have name cards for the Bosses to be seated there." She unfolded a large sheet with the table seating arrangements and handed it to Clark.

"Guess you've thought of every detail."

"I've tried to." She paused. "After dinner, everyone will be half snockered by nine o'clock. That's when your team will raid the place."

"Where will you be?"

"In the bathroom… and listen… this is extremely important. On the left side of the banquet room, there's a hallway leading to the bathrooms, at the end there's a large bookcase. Just below the fourth shelf on the right, is a small button. Push it and the bookcase will rotate halfway around. Inside is a secret room with a door to the hidden parking lot out back. Jake and Angelo will be waiting for you there."

302

"And, what about the two of you?"
She smiled. "Gone."
"Gone, what does that mean?"
"Gone, to start our lives anew."

CHAPTER THIRTY

Black limousines took turns pulling in front of the Timberland Game Ranch in Dexter, north of Ann Arbor, and less than an hour from Metro Detroit. The remote hunting camp run by the mafia served as the location where Jack Nicolette had been named Boss of the Detroit Mafia, nearly five years ago to the day.

Watching the men strut in, Amanda thought about the stories Jake had shared about that afternoon. *Everything had been arranged in a secretive manner in 1979 when Jake squeezed out Anthony Zerilli and took over as the Boss.* She smiled to herself. *Interestingly, Jake's inauguration was the last time a large congregation of Detroit mobsters had met in one location, other than for weddings and funerals of family members. The Timberland Game Ranch was a perfect place to meet. An upscale hunting lodge owned by family members Antonia "T.R." Ruggirello and his brother "Louie the Bulldog," made it an easy place to set up without anyone knowing.*

Standing next to Amanda in the front entrance, Jake welcomed his counterparts from around the country — Russel Bufalino from Buffalo and Anthony Giordano from St. Louis—next in line, Santo Trafficant Jr., from Tampa stepped up and bear hugged Jake. "My old friend, how have you been?"

Jake nodded to Amanda. "Whataya think?"

Trafficant's eyes lit up. "Yes, guess it couldn't be better."

"You got that right." Jake motioned them inside. "Join the group. We'll talk later."

Stepping into the rustic lodge, he was taken aback by the festive atmosphere, like the other Bosses had been. On the small stage, Motown's greatest were taking turns, belting out their top hits:

The *Queen of Motown,* Mary Wells, performed her top hits — "Two Lovers," "You Beat Me to the Punch," and "My Guy."

Smoky Robinson followed with "Tears of a Clown," "I Second that Emotion," and his most recent hit, "Ebony Eyes."

Local star, Aretha, paraded onto the stage, as only she can do, and brought the rafters down with "Chain of Fools," "Who's Zoomin' Who," and "Amazing Grace."

Settling in at the guest of honor's table near the stage in the center of the banquet room, Jake leaned over and kissed Amanda on the cheek. "I don't know how you pulled this off."

"I learned it all from you." She blew him a kiss. "I met Smokey Robinson at Tommy Hearns' home that night, remember?"

"Yes, I thought he was hitting on you."

"To the contrary, he was extremely nice… I was planning the events for tonight."

He winked, in a most caring manner. "Tricky, aren't you?"

She gave him a fake frown. "You haven't seen the last of it," she said, only half jesting.

"Hey Jake," the boisterous Nicodemo "Little Nicky" Scarfo from Philadelphia, slapped him on the back. "How the hell are you?"

Glancing at Amanda, Jake gave her a soft glance. "Couldn't be any better."

Giving her the eye, Little Nicky waved. "I should say so."

Jake stood, threw his arm around him and walked to a nearby unoccupied corner. "Anything new with you?"

"We've gotten into narcotics trafficking, big time."

"The black gangs were cleaning our clock. I had to put a bunch of them out of commission."

"Yeah, so I heard… guess you're dealing with a lot of crap."

Little Nicky wrinkled his nose in distaste. "Not any more… there were a lot of turf battles going on. I had to wipe out a bunch of punks; they thought they knew more than I did." He glanced at the five tables of hors d'oeuvres lining the front of the banquet room. "Great idea… numerical ice-carvings — 1-2-3-4-5 — for each year commemorating the years you've been the boss. Good for you."

"Best to follow the numerical order… that way you won't lose track.

"That'd be easy to do, after all of the bottles of wine I see at the tables."

"Save room for dinner — New York strip, lobster, pasta, and twice-baked — and a dessert tray that won't stop," Jake boasted.

Corks popped and the wine flowed.

The various entourages sampled freely from a wide selection of Italian favorites: prosciutto, mortadella, bresaola, cheeses and breads, small sandwiches of panino, bruschetta and crostino, and cold salmon, and prawns.

The men gathered around the tables — laughing — in one-on-one conversations, and in groups trading jokes. Slowly the Bosses and their *consiglieres* moved to the assigned tables. The bodyguards made their way to the tables near the front of the room:

TABLE #1	**TABLE #2**	**TABLE #3**
Anthony "Fat Tony" Salerno Genovese Family, NY	Tony Acdardo Chicago	Carlos Marcello New Orleans
James Licavoli Cleveland	Nicodemo "Little Nicky" Scarfo Philadelphia	Philip "Rusty" Rastel Bonanno Family, NY

TABLE #4	**TABLE #5**	**TABLE #6**
Carmine "Junior" Persico Colombo Family, NY	Anthony "Tony Ducks" Corallo Lucchese Family, NY	Peter Milano Los Angeles
John La Rocca Pittsburgh	Santo Trafficante, Jr. Tampa	Joseph Todaro Buffalo

TABLE #7	**TABLE #8**	**TABLE #9**
Joseph Campisi Dallas	Peter Balistreri Milwaukee	Raymond Patriara Providence
Nicolas Civella Kansas City	Russel Bufalino Scranton	Anthony Giordano St. Louis

TABLE #10	**TABLE #11**	**TABLE #12**
Body Guards	Jake Nicolette Detroit	Body Guards
	Angelo Travaglini Detroit	
	Paul Castellano (absent) Gambino Family, NY	

Jake stood and welcomed the group, gave regrets from the Boss of the Bosses, Paul Castellano — banned by court order from leaving New York, and, offered grace.

Dinner was served and conversation flowed.

Corks popped and wine poured.

Placing his knife and fork on the table, Jake nudged closer to Amanda. "This is the nicest night of my life; it's just perfect!"

"Thank you, darling." She ran her hand up his leg. "I can't wait till later…"

Jake raised his eyebrows. "Sounds like the best is yet to come."

"You're right about that." She pecked him on the cheek. "I'm going to make a quick stop before the program starts."

"Fine with me."

Amanda turned to Catrina. "Need to powder your nose?"

"Thought you'd never ask." She laid a smacker on Angelo and stood. "I won't be long."

"Hurry back, I can't wait."

***

"POW… POW…" Shots fired into the ceiling. "POW… POW!"

FBI agents streamed in from the front and two side entrances, shouting, "Hands up… this is a raid. You're under arrest!"

"Let's sneak out the back way." Jake grabbed Angelo's arm and hurried down the hallway past the bathrooms. Pushing the secret button, the bookcase turned ninety degrees. Jake squeezed through the opening and waited for Angelo to slip through before hitting the button. Making sure the door closed tightly, the two turned, coming face-to-face with Amanda and Catrina.

"Glad you made it out of there." Jake waved to the two women. "C'mon, let's go… the feds are all over the place," Jake called to Amanda.

She didn't move.

"Amanda, we have to get out of here, we don't have much time."

She pulled a pearl-handled .380 ACP CPX-3 and leveled it at his head. "*We're not going anywhere,* we're going to talk."

"Amanda, we can talk later. Right now, we have to leave."

Jamming a Berretta into Angelo's gut, Catrina motioned him aside.

"Sweetie, we have to run… hurry lets go."

"*We're not going anywhere.*" She waved the Berretta wildly, side-to-side.

"Okay… okay, relax."

"You can relax… sit your ass on that chair, over there." She pointed to the corner.

Jake stepped in front of Amanda, an arm's length away. "Amanda, have you gone crazy?" He laughed. "You're not going to shoot me… after all of those nights… C'mon, let's go."

"After all of those nights… shit, each night was another reason to shoot you."

"How can you say that?"

"It's easy… you think sex is all about you."

"It doesn't matter, sweetie… right now, we need to hustle our asses out of here."

"We're not going anywhere."

"How can you say that?" He frantically waved his hands in the air. "The feds will be here in no time. We can do whatever you want later. Right now, we have to leave. There's no time to waste!"

Amanda stood her ground and squinted, growing more and more irritated all the time. "You don't seem to get it… how many times do I have to say, *we're not going anywhere.*"

"Okay… I got it." Jake raised his hands in a sign of surrender. "I give up… tell me what you want."

"I want you to drop your pants."

"Are you out of your mind?"

"No, but you will be if you don't drop your pants."

"I don't think so."

Amanda pushed her .38 in his gut. "I don't think I'll miss from here."

Jake stood frozen, like a statue.

"Look, I'm serious, unbuckle your pants." She waved the gun Angelo's way. "You too, asshole."

Watching Jack drop his pants, Angelo stood and followed suit.

The two stood in their boxer shorts, exposing their hairy legs down to the pants bunched around their ankles.

"Two sets of scrawny legs — aren't they pitiful." Catrina cringed.

"C'mon Amanda, the feds will be in here before we know it."

Having calculated every move, she took her time. "I've thought about this moment for years." Her eyes narrowed in an unmerciful glare.

"Do it!" Catrina shouted. "No reason to let the bastard off now."

"I know… I just want to watch him sweat."

"He never sweats — when he put our sister in the whorehouse or when he put our brother in prison — he never broke a sweat, 'cause he has no feelings."

"You're right about that."

"Who?" Jake pleaded, as if knowing nothing. "I don't have a clue about any of this."

"We're talking about you being an asshole, a conniving creep…" Amanda stopped. "Don't get me started or… I'll shoot you right now."

"Please, Amanda, I had nothing to do with whatever you're talking about."

"Oh yeah." She shook her head in disgust. "You're the Boss and you know nothing… that's bullshit!"

"Do it!" Catrina waved her Berretta. "Do you want me to shoot him?"

"No way… after five years, this is my satisfaction."

"After all of those nights, sweetie." He took a step closer. "How can you say that?"

"Stop right there. I have a thousand reasons why I should kill you."

"Fine…" Trying a different angle, he tossed his hands in the air, in resignation. "Okay, do it."

"I never did like it when you used that tone." Her resolve obvious, *the time had come*. "I'm going to blow out your knees, one at a time, so no one will ever have to listen to how great a tennis player you are."

"You're doing…" He lunged toward her.

Amanda stepped back and pulled the trigger of her pearl-handled .38.

"POW!"

The bullet shattered his right knee.

"Oh my God." Grabbing his knee, he stumbled.

"POW!"

His left knee splintered into pieces.

Crumpling down in a heap, Jake's eyes flashed a sense of disbelief.

Gushing blood formed pools around the strands of tissue where his knees once were. He lay helpless, unable to move.

Seeing Angelo lunge out of the corner of her eye, Catrina whacked him across the forehead with the barrel of the Berretta.

Catching him full force, Angelo staggered backward.

The back door flew open.

Barbara Nash raced in.

A startled Amanda, shouted, "Mom, who invited you to the party?"

"Amanda?" Barbara questioned, not positive because she still wore the persona of her hidden identity.

"Yes, it's me… why are you here?"

"I heard via the grapevine about the celebration for Jake, and figured Angelo might have forgotten to tell me, so I thought I'd slip in the back way and surprise everyone."

Amanda reordered her thoughts. "Well then, welcome to the party — an unexpected visit — at least this saves me additional work later on." She waved the .38 toward Jake, moaning on the floor. "There's the asshole who destroyed our family… look at him. Without his lackeys around him… he's nothing… a lying sack of shit."

Unable to deal with the sight of the gore, Barbara glanced the other way. "Catrina, why are *you* here?"

"To pay homage to your lover boy… the co-conspirator in the demise of our family. When you adopted me, you were the *Queen of the Ball.* It didn't take long for him to drain every ounce of your energy… making you think your life revolved around him."

"That's not fair for you to say…"

"Don't tell me what's fair or not," she cut her off. "Now you can see, first hand, what we think about asshole Jake Nicolette and your lover boy, Angelo.

"You're sick." Barbara eased closer to Angelo.

"Me, sick? Look at the two of you… aren't you a lovey, dovey pair?" Catrina sneered at the thought of seeing the two of them together. "And, here's to your lover boy, Angelo," Catrina shouted. "Look at him… pathetic… bowlegged, knobby knees."

She aimed the Berretta at his crotch.

He took a step toward her.

"One more step and it'll be your last one."

"Well… just how are you going to do that?" he questioned in a wise-ass tone.

Catrina recalled fond memories of boating with her brother and sister on the Detroit River, and tightened her grip on the Berretta. "I'm not going to kill you… that'd be too good for you." She pointed the gun at his crotch. "It's time for you to join your partner in crime."

"No, no, you can't." Barbara lunged in front of him. "He's…"

"POW… POW!"

Stumbling backward, Angelo grabbed his shattered right hip. But he only took one bullet.

Barbara staggered toward Amanda, her arms reaching for her daughter, and fell to the floor — blood spewing from her chest.

His hip giving out, Angelo fell, wounded, on top of her.

"Hurry up, we have to get out of here," Amanda said. "Wipe down the Berretta and shove it in Jake's hand."

"Will do."

Amanda wiped her prints from the.38 and clasped Barbara's hand around it.

Catrina cleaned off her fingerprints and squeezed Jake's hand around the Beretta; she headed for the back door leading to a small parking lot, surrounded by pines and undergrowth, it provided cover for their old '68 Ford get-a-way car.

Glancing around the room to make sure there was no evidence of their appearance, Amanda hustled toward the back door, then paused thinking she'd heard something. Stepping back inside the door frame next to Catrina, she stared across the room.

"Help me," Jake mumbled. Slightly louder, "Call a doctor."

Half propped up against the wall, he waved the Beretta wildly — his eyes blurred, his body running on the last drop of adrenaline — he pointed the gun in their direction, and eked out, "Help me."

Turning toward their getaway car, Amanda shouted over her shoulder. "Help yourself, you bastard!"

He fired at them.

"POW… POW… POW!"

FOR HIRE

CHAPTER ONE

Detroit Free Press
August 10, 1984

RALPH PROCTOR MURDERED

At approximately one o'clock this morning, 61-year-old Ralph Proctor, former Teamsters leader, was found shot to death in the front seat of his 1981 Cadillac Seville. Parked in the lot of the Livonia shopping mall, at Six Mile and Newburgh, the engine was running and the headlights were on.

A woman living next to the mall, indicated she'd heard a series of "popping" noises about 10:15. The county medical examiner's report was incomplete, but preliminary findings indicate Proctor was shot in the cheek with a large-caliber weapon by someone in the passenger seat, and eight times in the back of the head with a .22 caliber gun by someone in the back seat. The examiner described the killing as a professional execution-style murder.

A staunch Jimmy Hoffa loyalist, Proctor was a truck driver in Hoffa's Local 299. When tensions between Hoffa and the mob peaked in 1975, Proctor was physically assaulted when leaving a bar in Melvindale, fracturing his jaw and two ribs. Following Hoffa's disappearance in July, 1975, the impeccably dressed Proctor, also known as "The Silver Fox," quickly ascended up the ranks to become president of Teamsters Local 124 in 1979.

It's reported Proctor had long-standing feuds with the mafia representative to the steel haulers and Pete Karagozian, president of Teamsters Local 299.

***

THE DETROIT NEWS
September 10, 1984
Section A

JEFFERYS DISCOVERS DNA

LEICESTER, ENGLAND. At a press conference at the University of Leicester, Professor Alec John Jeffreys reported he had a "Eureka Moment," in his research laboratory. By analyzing X-Ray film images in an ongoing DNA experiment, he found similarities and differences between the DNA of the members of his experimental group.

Professor Jeffreys pointed out the scope of DNA fingerprinting is unlimited. It will become an essential ingredient for forensic scientists, and assist police detective work, legal persons to resolve paternity cases and immigration disputes.

A spokesman for the Detroit Chief of Police's office indicated the use of DNA will change the way we do business, and will certainly impact future criminal

activity. "Individuals will no longer have to fear intimidation by gangsters and other persons in positions of power. DNA findings are indisputable."

***

Downing the last slug of beer, in a dimly-lit blind pig somewhere on the eastside, Clarence Tidwell slid a bowl of pretzels across the table. Willie Ross, the other black undercover agent from Clark's task force, met with him monthly to compare notes. A Detroit basketball star on Clark's high school team, Clarence's real name was Earl Walker. Willie had recently joined the group after being reassigned as a DEA agent from Philadelphia. Physically the two were as different as could be. Still working out on a regular basis, Clarence was slim and trim — a real specimen. Willie, a scrawny five-foot-eight, boyish face guy, appeared as if he'd struggle to lift fifty pounds.

Rubbing his shiny, shaved head, Clarence gave his counterpart a subtle glance. "Hear any rumblings about Proctor?"

"Only second-hand stuff, apparently Mafia Boss Jake Nicolette is interested in wrapping up their efforts to eliminate anyone who might have any knowledge of Hoffa's disappearance."

"Hell, that was nine, ten years ago."

"Yeah, but the FBI files are still open." An excited laugh expressed Willie's mood. "Guess they want to be certain no one is left to have second thoughts and spill the beans."

"Wouldn't that be something?" Clarence cocked his head, sending Willie a curious glance. "The discovery of DNA would make it easier to identify the guilty person."

"You think the two are connected?"

"Who knows? The mafia certainly had to know that it was coming."

"How are things going with you?"

Clarence paused, giving Willie a reflective moment, and continued, "Hmm... I'm not positive... sometimes I think it's really good and then I-I-I wonder."

"Wonder...? You trying to tell me something?"

"I know too much. I'm aware of organizational details — names, places, and phone numbers — I know everything about Rick Maserati's network. There's no way he'll let me out."

"Hell, he might be gone next week."

Clarence gave him a you gotta be shittin' me look. "Hmm, I don't think so, but..." A hint of nervousness caused a little tremor in his voice. "That might make it even worse... Being in the two-slot, even the lowest salesman would expect me to take over."

"Jesus Christ, Clarence, back out, groom someone else."

"I've suggested that... I've told him we need to build a top-level organizational team."

"How'd he react?"

"Shit man, he blew me off. His ego is so big, he doesn't' believe anything will ever happen to him."

"That's the way it is with every local big shot." Willie shook his head side to side. "Everyone is *for hire.*"

"Why do you say that?"

"You got time for another beer?"

Clarence glanced at his watch — 2:45. "Yeah, sure, I have an hour... need to be home by four so I can get five or six hours of sleep."

Willie waved his hand in the air, two fingers extended. "Bartender, give us another round," he called out. "I've counted six, maybe seven power struggle killings in the last month."

"The last month... no way, I can't believe that."

"It's true... some never appear anywhere on paper; they're not even reported in the news." He held up his left hand and pointed to his index finger. "On August 15th it was Herman Brunson." He raised a finger with each name. "With the Jeffries Boys it was Tiger Brown; Georgie Elliott took over and before the end of the week, he was knocked off."

Clarence shook his head in disbelief.

"A week later, the head of the 8 Mile Sconys gang was blown away. He was replaced the following week. Last week Brownie Wilson, from the Dexter Boys got hit." Willie flipped his other hand up. "Shit, that must be six or seven... hell, if I knew of every drug dealer killing in the city, there was probably a dozen or more."

"Why? Do you know the cause?"

"It's all about the money; there's no loyalty."

"My God, it can't be that bad."

"You're locked up with Maserati; I'm on the streets every day, working for the Curry brothers. They keep track of every detail;

they're a family organization, like the mafia." Willie wrinkled his nose. "The rest of the gangs are made up of guys right off the streets — neighborhood buddies — they don't give a shit about anyone else."

"Why so?"

"The SOB underlings see the amount of money coming in... Imagine you're nineteen or twenty years old in a small drug operation, making ten, fifteen grand a week. Your best friend is twenty-three and he's raking in a million dollars a month. It doesn't take long before you turn on him." Willie shook his head in disbelief. "I'm telling you everyone is *for hire*!

***

DETROIT POLICE BLOTTER
September 1984

Chester Wheeler Campbell Released

JACKSON, MI—Chester Wheeler Campbell, 54, has been released from the Michigan State Prison. He's a convicted murderer and reputed hit man, serving a 1975 sentence for possession of drugs and weapons.

Known as "The Black Hand" and "The Angel of Death," Campbell is expected to return to his familiar stomping grounds in urban Detroit. Rumored to have murdered over two hundred individuals, Campbell takes no prisoners. His alleged list of killings covers the gamut of blacks and whites alike—drug addicts, lawyers, police officers, prosecutors, Italian mobsters, and black drug lords—only the money matters.

A product of an underprivileged Detroit black family, Campbell's early life was filled with one defeat after another, giving some to describe him as a "money hungry, emotionless, relentless killer." For whatever reason, he sees his role in life much like the run-of-the-mill worker—do a good job and take care of business. Allegedly, he believes he was placed on earth for the

sole purpose of killing people, so he does it and he does it without remorse. By his definition, that means it's okay to kill someone who is seen as an undesirable by the person picking up the tab.

Campbell owns a two-story brick home on Ivanhoe Avenue, a four-block-long street on Detroit's west side, midway between east/west arteries Joy Road/Tireman Avenue and north/south Livernois/Grand River.

Campbell is armed and known to carry multiple weapons. He's EXTREMELY DANGEROUS!

DO NOT APPROACH CAMPBELL WITHOUT FBI AUTHORIZATION!!

***

Laughing and joking with an attractive blonde hanging on his arm, Freddie "Cool Freddie" opened the door of his shiny, yellow Corvette. She stumbled, fell into the passenger seat, and slammed the door. Smiling to himself about the all-nighter about to occur, Cool Freddie fired the engine, checked both ways, jammed the car into gear, and peeled down Eight Mile Road.

A black Dodge Diplomat slowly pulled out from a side street and followed at a discreet distance.

Reaching a major street, Cool Freddie turned to the right and sped down Gratiot, zipping through one intersection after another — Seven Mile, State Fair, and McNichols. Slowing at Flanders, he turned left, zipped past a couple of side streets, and turned into the driveway of a large two-story home. Slamming on the brakes, he barely waited for the garage door to open and quickly pulled in.

The Dodge Diplomat crawled passed the driveway and stopped a half-block away.

Lights flashed on and off, as the couple passed through the kitchen, living room, hallway, and up the stairs. He pulled down the shade. Its dim light framed the front window.

Cool Freddie slipped Diana Ross's 1979 tape "The Boss" into the console and stepped up to the portable bar. He flirted with the blonde as he fixed them a couple of Manhattans on the rocks. The two made touchy-feely love, teased each other, then got into it—hot and heavy—Cool Freddie's engine cranked up. He tossed his empty glass against the brick wall, flipped off his shirt and shoes, stripped down to the gold chains around his neck, leaving only his black Speedo shorts to disappear against his dark skin.

Walking over to the bed, he folded back the blanket, puffed up the red silk pillow cases, and slipped onto the matching silk sheets. With Lionel Richie's and Ross's "Endless Love," playing in the background, Cool Freddie flipped his hand, motioning for the blonde woman to strip naked to the sensual sounds.

Accommodating his command, she flipped off her high heels and moved slowly toward him — her blouse, slacks, bra, and panties falling by the wayside. He pulled her on top and within moments the two were engaged — their bodies pumping to the beat.

The door opened, revealing the unnoticed silhouette of a tall man. Stepping softly to the bedside, the man eased the barrel of a sawed-off shotgun onto Cool Freddie's belly button and pushed the end of its cold steel barrel into his gut.

"Jesus Christ," Cool Freddie shouted, "Who the hell are you?"

The barrel pushed harder against his stomach. "Don't make a move." The man flashed a light into Cool Freddie's eyes and then took his time running the beam up the blonde's shapely body to her shocked face. "Seems like the two of you are doing okay."

"Who invited you?" Freddie shouted. "How did you get in?"

The man spoke slowly. "That's a lot to answer in one breath. "How about asking me one question at a time?"

"Can I put a top on?" the woman nervously asked.

"No... I like you the way you are; besides, I've never killed a man while he was getting laid."

"Killed a man! Wait, who are you? What do you want?"

"There you go again, spouting off like a nervous kid..." The tall black man's voice sharpened. "I told you one question at a time."

Cool Freddie didn't say a word.

"I heard you were a big shot and thought you could skim drug money off the top. Blackie doesn't like that!"

"I never did that... I..."

"Shut up." Moving the barrel of the gun up under his rib cage, he eased it up to Cool Freddie's throat. "I haven't had a chance to answer your questions." The man loosened his black suit coat. "I'm Chester

Wheeler Campbell. Your security system sucks; it was simple to neuter. I didn't break a sweat." He laughed. "And, plain and simple, I have a contract on you."

"Wait, I'll double, triple…"

"Shut up… break a contract for a scum-bum like you. You think I have no ethics?"

"Yes, I'm sure you have ethics, but wait… there must be something I can do."

"Hah." Campbell chuckled. "You can put your hands over your ears so you don't hear me blow off your head."

Sneering at the order, Cool Freddie slowly lifted his arms.

"POW! POW!"

The woman grasped her mouth, holding it tightly with both hands, sensing she shouldn't scream.

Campbell turned to her. In shock, the breathless woman, still straddled the headless drug dealer.

Sliding the barrel of the shotgun slowly up her abdomen, he lodged it under her right breast. "You didn't see anything, did you?"

"No, no," she gasped.

"Good. Get your ass out of here, before I change my mind."

***

A short, bald headed Latino man lingered under the street light, lit a cigarette and took a couple of drags, before tugging the leash. Upon command, his reddish-brown cocker spaniel sprinted; instinctively turning down the dimly lit sidewalk of the west side neighborhood park. The cocker pulled the man to the first fire hydrant, did his duty, as he had most of the nights of his life, and then meandered along the edge of the grass-line, sniffing each bush as he passed by.

Behind a clump of trees midway into the park, a tall man stood behind a large oak calculating each move, as he had for the last week. He had studied sketches of the floor plan of the Latino's home, knew when his wife went shopping, when she had her hair done, when he took the trash out, and when he walked the dog.

Sniffing at a bush in front of the tree, the dog stopped and growled.

The short man tugged on the leash. "C'mon Spanks lets go."

Failing to respond to his master, Spanks leaped between two bushes and barked at the base of the tree. The Latino pulled back on the leash. "Spanks, there are no rabbits tonight, I want to see the second half of the football game."

"No Monday Night Football tonight," a voice rumbled out of the darkness.

Startled, the old man took a step back and pulled Spanks to his side.

A black man, dressed in black slacks and a matching sports coat, leaped over the undergrowth onto the center of the sidewalk. "Are you Luis Martinez?"

Nodding, the trembling man stared down the barrel of a sawed-off shotgun. Having heard stories about Chester Wheeler Campbell and how he had killed other informants, Luis feared for his life. *I guess being a T-3 — the highest level and most trusted FBI informant doesn't mean much — I'll be another feather in his hat.*

"Do you know who I am?"

"Mr. Campbell, I presume."

"Good, you got that right… and why do you think you won't see the end of tonight's game?"

"Ah… I don't know, sir."

"Let me give you a hint." Stepping back with a smirk, he motioned the old-timer to a park bench on the other side of the sidewalk. "Have a seat."

Following directions, Luis eased onto the bench and patted his lap.

Spanks jumped up.

"You're Clark Phillip's top informant, aren't you?"

"Ah… yes."

"And you worked on his behalf to find the culprits who killed his old girlfriend."

"No, not true."

Contorting his face, Campbell snarled, "Okay… put it in your own words."

"Yes, I located the mafia capos who murdered her, but Clark didn't want to know… he saw it as an ethical violation; it didn't matter how bad he wanted to *get even*, he just couldn't do it."

"An ethical violation… has he no balls?"

"Yes, he has balls…" Luis paused, reflecting on his admiration for Clark. "He has principles too."

"Principles… huh, who has principles around here?"

"He's a police officer… he knows he must honor the code he's sworn to follow."

"That's bullshit. I don't know any cops around here who follow an honor code — they're all crooked as hell."

"Maybe most, but Clark Phillips is a straight arrow."

"Huh." Taken back by the revelation, Campbell rubbed his fingers across his small mustache and goatee. "So who killed the capos?"

Luis sucked in a deep breath. "I had them killed."

"You… that doesn't make sense. You're an informant, why would you do that?"

Luis cleared his throat. "Well, Mr. Campell, it may not make sense to you, but it seemed like the right thing for me to do…

"The right thing," Campbell cut him off. "I don't understand."

"Clark Phillips has always been fair-by-me. He's an ethical man… I respect and admire him."

"So you did something you knew he couldn't do, is that right? You saying that?"

"Yes, sir… he's a good friend, I helped him out."

Campbell waved his shotgun back and forth across Luis's body. Breaking the stock, he pulled two shells from the double–barrel, and tossed them — one at a time — to Luis. "Here, you can have these as souvenirs. Any man who'd do that for a friend doesn't deserve to die for a mere $10,000."

***

Sitting in a black Dodge Diplomat, Chester Wheeler Campbell waited outside Ruby's whorehouse, a rundown tenement on East Warren. Having been out of Michigan State Prison for less than a month, he had already finalized three contracts — tonight, Joseph Pagnozzi would be the fourth. *I have to clean up the backlog. I must have a dozen contracts to take care of before the end of the year. Dirty cops are the worst; they got no ethics! Better yet, being a member of Clark Phillip's special task force, he brought a higher bounty than most — $15,000.*

Like always he'd done his due diligence — he'd sketched the floor plan of Pagnozzi's home, double-checked his daily patterns at home, and decided Pagnozzi's wife didn't deserve to find his body.

Seeing his target open the front door of the whorehouse and head down the alley, Campbell slid out of his car and double-timed it across the street.

Taking long strides, he narrowed the gap between the two men. "Hey, Pagnozzi," he called.

Startled by hearing his name, Pagnozzi stopped and slowly turned, his hand sliding inside his coat.

"Don't even think it." Flicking on his flashlight, Campbell leveled his sawed-off shotgun at Pagnozzi.

Instinctively, Pagnozzi raised his left hand, covering his face from the blinding light.

"Drop your gun or I'll blow your head off." Campbell stepped closer, his shotgun in his right hand, flashlight in the other.

Pagnozzi eased his Berretta out of his shoulder holster and tossed it to the ground.

"Do you know who I am?"

"No… I only have a couple twenties."

"I wouldn't give you twenty cents for your life."

Thoughts of the police blotter on Campbell crossed his mind; Pagnozzi's skin crawled. "What do you want with me?"

"There's a contract out on you… have anything to say?"

"You must be mistaken. I'm a Detroit police officer."

"Yes… I got that."

"I don't understand… why me?"

"You owe Blackie big time."

"Blackie Giardini? He's my buddy. We played on the same little league baseball team."

"So he mentioned." Campbell raised his shotgun, pointing it at Pagnozzi. "Friends are friends, as long as they pay their tab."

"I did… I delivered the information, just like he asked."

"You delivered shit… you told him what everyone else knew."

"No, I told him details no one knew."

"That's bullshit… you made it sound like a big deal; you double-crossed him. No one double-crosses Blackie Giardini." Campbell pointed his shotgun at Pagnozzi's chest.

"No… wait, I'll do whatever it…"
"POW… POW!"

MAFIA WORKS BY LES COCHRAN

The Detroit Thorn Birds historical crime fiction series follows extraordinarily brave inner-city citizens fighting an uphill battle, against all odds, trying to save their homes and way of life. These are real-to-life individuals taking on the mafia and street gangs. They are committed, willing to die for their cause, much like the characters in *The Thorn Birds* published in 1977. Because of these similarities, the driving characters are called the Detroit Thorn Birds.

The series begins in the late 1970s with each book taking a two-year snippet out of the history of the Detroit mafia. It brings to life real crime scenes never before released.

MAFIA WORKS #1

SAX CLUB portrays the efforts of Detective Clark Phillips, his friends, and colleagues, to combat crime. Detroit is hemorrhaging; corrupt politicians offer no help. Yet, people in small neighborhood enclaves are unwilling to succumb to evil forces; they're clawing for survival, to save their homes, their dignity, and way of life. They won't be slaves to the mob bosses and won't yield to the street gangs.

MAFIA WORKS #2

MAFIA WORKS #4

BLIND PIG, the second in the "Detroit Thorn Birds" series, continues as Detective Clark Phillips ups the ante, with his team of police officers and FBI agents. Tired of paying monthly taxes to the mob, Clark's buddies unite around the wife of a fallen friend. She's unwilling to be bullied. They embark on an operation to undercut mafia run "blind pigs" and unmask mafia ties with the Catholic Church.

FOR HIRE, in progress.

OTHER NOVELS BY LES COCHRAN

A reviewer characterized this trilogy as "an excellent portrayal of the double life of a sex addict — his trials and tribulations, and struggles against all odds."

A highly successful university president, Steve Schilling, weaves his way through the politics and backroom machinations of academic life. He turns around two universities and is recruited by the first female president of the United States to help reform our public schools. There's both mystery and espionage. Steve's leadership abilities are equaled only by his lovemaking skills—he treats each woman as if she is the only one—OMG!

Go To: **http://amzn.to/2baf4La**